The Book of Loss

JULITH JEDAMUS

St. Martin's Press ❧ New York

To Stryker, who made it possible

www.stmartins.com

Library of Congress Cataloging-in-Publication Data

Jedamus, Julith.
     The book of loss / Julith Jedamus.—1st ed.
          p. cm.
     ISBN-13: 978-0-312-34907-3
     ISBN-10: 0-312-34907-6
     1. Women—Japan—Social conditions—Fiction. 2. Japan—History—
Heian period, 794–1185—Fiction. I. Title.

PR6110.E33B66 2006
823'.92—dc22

                                                                2006040114

First published in Great Britain by Weidenfeld & Nicolson

First Edition: June 2006

10 9 8 7 6 5 4 3 2 1

Watching through door cracks is of advantage to women. Nevertheless it is also shameful.

I CHING

The Setting

The events described here take place in the last decade of the tenth century, in and around Heian-Kyō (now known as Kyoto), the capital of imperial Japan. Readers who would like to learn more about the Heian world may refer to the Glossary.

The Characters

THE NARRATOR Age: 29
Daughter of a provincial governor. In service to the Empress;
a writer of stories and romances. Lives in the Umetsubo (Plum
Courtyard) of the Imperial Palace. In love with the exile, as is
her rival. She has a young son living with relatives on the
island of Kyūshū.

THE RIVAL, IZUMI NO JIJŪ Age: 27
Also the daughter of a provincial governor. Lives in the Imperial Palace in the Nashitsubo (Pear Courtyard). An accomplished poet. Had been friends with the narrator when she
came into service with the Empress, but they have fallen out,
in part because of their love for the exile.

THE EXILE, TACHIBANA NO KANESUKE Age: 30
A nobleman from the Tachibana clan, and an ally of the
powerful Fujiwara family. Has a house in the Third Ward in
the capital and estates near Nara. Appointed Imperial Envoy
by the Emperor. Beloved by both the narrator and the rival.
Banished for seducing the Vestal of Ise, the Emperor's favourite daughter. Lives in Akashi, a coastal region southwest of
the capital.

EMPEROR JOTŌ Age: 36
Second son of the former Emperor Suzaku, he wields less
power than his office implies. Vain and prone to fits of temper,
he is less interested in governing than in indulging his epi-
curean tastes.

EMPRESS AKIKO Age: 34

A member of the Fujiwara family and sometime ally of the exiled Kanesuke. Although she has no official powers except as an arbiter of taste, her influence in the political sphere is considerable. Divides her time between her apartments in the Imperial Palace and a house, the Ichijō Mansion, in the First Ward.

PRINCESS YUKIKO, THE VESTAL OF ISE Age: 17

Daughter of the Emperor and Empress Akiko, and her father's favourite. Chosen to serve the Great Shrine at Ise, which is dedicated to the sun goddess Amaterasu. Seduced by Kanesuke, and about to be brought back to the capital in disgrace.

PRINCESS SADAKO Age: 19

Half-sister to the Vestal, she is of lesser rank because her mother was a commoner. A friend of Izumi's. Potential successor to her sister as Vestal of Ise.

PRINCE REIZEI Age: 11

First-born son of the Emperor and Empress Akiko, and the heir apparent.

THE MINISTER OF THE LEFT Age: 35

Brother to the Empress and the most powerful man in government. Potential regent should the Emperor be deposed.

DAINAGON Age: 36

Widow of a former major counsellor, she is a lady-in-waiting to the Empress. The narrator's chief friend and confidante.

MASATO Age: 23

Of aristocratic background, he works in the Bureau of Divination in a post well beneath his rank. Studied the I Ching and various methods of divination during his trips to China. Lives with his parents in a mansion in the Fourth Ward. He is known only by the pseudonym given to him by the narrator.

RYŪEN Age: 22
The narrator's younger brother and a novice at Enryakuji, one of the many Buddhist temples on Mount Hiei northeast of the capital. A calligrapher and sometime secretary to the Abbot. Ryūen is his Buddhist name; he is also known by his childhood name, Tadahira.

AN UNNAMED BOY Age: 8
The narrator's son, by an aristocrat of the Taira clan who has since left the capital.

TAKUMI Age: 34
The narrator's cousin and guardian of her son. She lives on the island of Kyūshū.

BUZEN Age: 25
A lady-in-waiting who lives in apartments adjacent to the narrator's in the Umetsubo.

UKON Age: 23
One of the narrator's maids. She lives, along with various attendants, in rooms adjoining the narrator's.

Prologue

You may think that the sheaf of paper you hold in your hands is a book. It is not. You may presume that the fine black lines that fill its pages describe a world that exists, but you are mistaken. Do not be deceived. What you are about to read is as empty as a locust shell, and as immaterial as smoke. It is a house of lies.

Lies, lies, a house of lies: such is the place you are about to enter. It is a flimsy construction, made of ink and white paper, as ephemeral as the shrines dedicated to our native gods, which are built every generation only to be torn down and built again. Do you choose to pass through the red gate that leads to its fictitious precincts? Be careful. It may collapse at any time. The garden through which you will walk, verdant as it is with moss and camellias, may wither in a moment. Do not stray from the stony path. Leave your possessions by the door. Prepare yourself for all you had not expected.

Why, you may ask, should you listen to my warnings? Is my word any better than the author's? Trust me, for I knew her well. She served my mother once, and I spent long hours in her company. I listened as she declaimed her poems and read her romances.

There were those who said she was the finest writer since Ono no Komachi, though as far as I am concerned their only commonality was the looseness of their morals. Izumi, her great rival, was to my mind a far better poet. Her rhythm was more delicate, her allusions subtler, her images wholly original. How sad it makes me that we shall not hear her voice again. She will not lead the winning side in our poetry contests; we will not search for her verses in the new imperial anthology.

Yet perhaps my grieving is selfish, for Izumi has transcended not only speech but time itself. She has abandoned the illusions of this world, just as I myself shall soon renounce them. Yet her sacrifice was complete. She gave up her life, whereas I shall relinquish only the little freedom that has been granted me since my reputation was irreparably damaged by rumour and false accusation.

The source of those rumours will become clear during the course of this narrative. My readers will discover that Izumi suffered from slander as much as I. If the author of these pages chose to depict Izumi as no less capable of deceit than she, perhaps we should consider her judgement as slanted as her handwriting.

I find it inconceivable that the two of them were friends. That epoch is unfamiliar to me, for I was only six when they came to court. By some coincidence – a fatal astral conjunction? – they were both sent to the capital in the second year of my father's reign. They were daughters of provincial governors, though Izumi's family was of higher standing. Both had been educated privately and excelled in the classics; both wrote superlatively from an early age. My mother, always eager for new talent, was glad to take them into her service.

How naïve they must have been, those two provincial girls. I wonder what they felt when they first entered the Ninefold Enclosure. Before them stood the Great Hall of State, with its green gabled roof and vermilion pillars. It must have seemed as vast as a city. What did they think when beyond it they discovered buildings of every size and description, and vast pine groves, and gardens so rare and precious that each ancient tree and clump of bamboo possessed its own name?

And when they were taken to the rooms where they would lead their sequestered lives, were they seduced by the beauty they found there? Were they impressed by the damask screens, the Chinese scrolls, the lattice windows? Did they delight in the graceful trees in the courtyards: the pears and plums and violet-flowered paulownias?

Did their new companions seem equally rich and rare? Those women with their long trailing hair, clothed in robes the colour of wisteria and chrysanthemum – how faultless they must have seemed. That great array of consorts, havens, concubines, dowagers and princesses must have appeared as irreproachable as Kannon in all her incarnations.

Just how long was it, I wonder, before those two girls came to see their new surroundings not as a shelter but a prison? When did they begin to perceive the duplicity behind the powdered faces, the mendacious gestures, the plots and intrigues?

They found that deceit within themselves. Most of you are familiar with the story of their rivalry, for by the time my mother was made Empress it had become all too clear. At first it seemed a matter of professional pride. How fiercely they competed for my mother's favour. No one strove as hard as they to compose finer verse or wittier letters. Their writing circulated throughout the court, until each of us was familiar with their conceits.

When their rivalry extended to the object of their love it grew vicious indeed. And when they both fell under the sway of the same unprincipled man (even now his name makes me so bitter that I shall not mention it) their friendship disintegrated.

At first the tension between them was subtle, but soon it escalated into public affronts and retaliations. The author of this manuscript was inevitably the perpetrator, and Izumi strove to take higher ground.

Yet Izumi had her faults. I myself suffered from her

silences. Some less charitable than I attributed them to her secretiveness. But to suspect her of the crimes described in this narrative is to place her on the same level as her rival, and I for one refuse to believe she would have been capable of such treachery.

As to Izumi's disgrace and the tales that surrounded it, you must recall that at the time I was removed from the palace for reasons beyond my control. My knowledge of that scandal is scant and second-hand, and I have never reached a satisfactory conclusion as to what happened.

You will see that the cause of my exile was the sole responsibility of the same woman who slandered Izumi. As these pages make clear, her jealousy so corrupted her character that she sought to harm Izumi by circulating lies about me. She accused me of the same mendacity in which she excelled. I have paid the penalty for her lies these three long years. And Izumi, though she soon came to recognise the falsity of her rival's claims, paid for them more dearly than I, for fate was cruel to her indeed.

Perhaps the greatest cruelty of all was her tie to the man who brought such misfortune on my family. For it was he who destroyed my sister's reputation, and sent her back from the shrines of Ise in shame. It was he who made our father disown us, and caused the lasting rift between our parents.

As for the writer of this manuscript, the story of her disappearance is well known. It happened in the Sixth Month, at the height of the plague. The events of that time are still so painful to me that I cannot describe them. I shall confine myself to relating the circumstances of her departure.

You have heard how her maids came into her room to find it in disarray: silks and fans littering the floor, half-burnt papers in the brazier, brushes stiff with ink scattered across

4

her writing desk. She left no notes or instructions; she sent no letters of farewell.

You will have heard, too, the conjecture regarding her motives. She had run off with a lover, or was escaping a scandal (for there were always several, some publicised by her enemies; others, with her tacit approval, by her friends). She had gone to search for a son whom she had left in the care of a cousin years earlier. She had fled to a convent in the mountains (though those who knew her had trouble imagining her with her long hair shorn and dressed in the drab gowns of a nun). She had drowned herself in the Kamo River – or had feigned her death and surfaced in another guise, to tempt her lovers once again.

Each surmise was justified by a scrap of evidence, much of it no doubt spurious: a half-burnt letter from a woman on the island of Kyūshū, describing a boy in her charge; a sodden jacket embroidered with lilacs discovered by a fisherman on the Kamo River; a white fan found in an inn near the Otowa Falls, inscribed with her name and the phrase 'to my dear Lady Han'.

It was the name given to her by a lover, and she hated it. Why she would have chosen to keep such a talisman is unclear. Perhaps she had crossed the line between reason and madness, as the legendary Lady Han had done. And indeed there were times when one of us caught her off guard and wondered if she were more than a little unbalanced.

Once a maid found her gouging her mirror with a sharp stone, which cut so deeply into the bronze that the polishers were unable to restore its lustre. And one summer day I walked past her rooms and saw her pounding a slab of ice with a wooden mallet, like the jealous wife who drove her husband to distraction by beating on a block of wood. Slivers of ice flew across the room; I watched, riveted, as they melted.

One spring when several of us had gone on retreat to

5

Ishiyama we came across her standing in the middle of a stream, throwing paper figures in the water. Her robes were soaked well past her knees, and when she bent to cast the pieces of paper her long hair trailed in the current. She started like a deer when we called to her, and fled to the opposite bank. I was tempted to ask her later whom the figures represented, but I doubt she would have given me a truthful answer.

It is the Fifth Month now, almost three years since she disappeared. The purple irises, her favourite flower, are blooming, and the long rains have arrived. Her rooms in the Umetsubo are empty, for no one wants to occupy them, defiled as they may be by a spirit tormented by violent death or the sin of suicide.

Some say there are men still anxious for her return. A few have donated holy images and books to the temples she loved best. One is said to have offered a bowl filled with silver ingots to the priests at Hasedera. Her brother, who will soon take his final vows at Enryakuji, is said to be disconsolate. Knowing the degree of their estrangement, I find this unlikely.

During the months since this manuscript came into my possession I have read it often and pondered what to do with it. Izumi herself gave no instructions when she handed it to me. At the time she was so weak from loss of blood that she had barely the strength to speak. What an irony that she should die hours after her greatest happiness! Her husband had so wanted a son. I find it impossible not to blame him. Weren't his improprieties the cause of his double banishment? Had he not been sent to the northern frontier perhaps Izumi would have received better care.

How Izumi acquired these pages I cannot say. She never told me; I doubt she told anyone. I cannot believe that her rival would have given them to her, incriminating as they are. Perhaps in her haste to flee the palace she left them behind.

When I read this manuscript, certain passages so infuriated me that I was tempted to burn them. Yet if I am honest (for it is my misfortune to be incapable of duplicity) I must admit that some of her stories moved me to tears. What was the source of such grief and longing? It is as if they had been written by another hand.

I hope you will understand that my decision to circulate this diary was not impetuous but the result of long reflection. I decided that I could not be like the Mute Prince in the Buddhist parable, who so feared the perils of speech that he chose to remain withdrawn and silent. As fate has delivered me this story, so it has vested me with responsibilities. Like the soothsayers who read the future in the creased and mottled pages of our faces, I am obliged to instruct those who knew this evil woman about the dangers of her company. For what if she should reappear in our midst, like the gaudy phoenix who dies in the flames of his own house only to return to flaunt his colours once again? What if she renounces the world not once but twice, only to reappear as a vengeful ghost?

I wonder if I would recognise her. I trust my sight no more than the silent prince trusted words. In this era of decline our very senses are corrupt, and even the signs sent by the gods are dubious. Portents are as ambiguous as speech, and omens harbour ill as well as favour.

I shall soon renounce this world and follow my father to the cloister. I only hope that my vows are more sincere than his.

Thus I release these fair copies, which have been made by the finest calligraphers at my considerable expense. I expect neither reward nor remuneration for this heavy labour, either in this world or the next. I only hope that those of you

7

who knew the author will read these pages and judge her cruelty for yourselves.

Slide back the door, and behold the architecture of a devious mind.

Seventh Month

He is gone. Dainagon told me; I did not see him. She says he left at dawn, riding out of the gate of his house in the Third Ward, on his favourite horse, the white roan that he rode in the archery contest for the Iris Festival. He didn't dare leave in a carriage, not even a plain one. An exile must affect humility, even if he feels none. But how like him to leave riding the finest horse in the city.

I was searching for my comb when she ran in to tell me. The maids had just raised the blinds; a cold breeze was blowing, scattering the last red leaves of the plum trees in the courtyard. She had heard the news from one of the Royal Guards who had just come on duty. He had five or six of his men with him, she said, and several servants and packhorses, and they rode south past the leafless willows on Suzaku Avenue, toward the Rashō Gate.

I dropped my comb. Dainagon picked it up and ran it through my hair. I turned towards the curtain and bent my head. Don't worry, Dainagon said. How lovely your hair is, she told me. It is as thick as a girl's; look how it trails along the floor. How it glints in this light, she said; it has the same sheen as a kingfisher's wing. She talked on and on, but I sent her away and lay face down on my mat all morning, wrapped in his old green robe and crying like a child.

People tell me he spent his last night in the Nashitsubo, with Izumi. I heard it from Buzen, who heard it from one of Izumi's maids. They said he rose early, at the Hour of the

Tiger, and returned to his house in the Third Ward, where his men were waiting.

I heard he sent her a letter on thin green paper, knotted around a sprig of five-needled pine, to show his constancy. It was hardly original, but perhaps he thought his message in keeping with Izumi's character – she of the derivative verse, the false compliment, the devious smile. And I had no more than a note on thick white paper, folded like a business letter, and delivered the day before his departure by a sullen boy in a tan hunting jacket – and all because I told him I was angry. He said he was sorry; he quoted the verse about tangled seaweed on the Suma shore; the writing was hasty and ragged, not like a love letter at all. I threw it in the brazier, and regretted it as soon as I saw the edges darken and curl, like the anise leaves one lays on the altar in supplication to the compassionate gods.

I do not believe in compassion. I do not expect it; I do not confer it. It belongs to another realm.

Buzen says that Izumi has not eaten for two days. She refuses everything, even fruit and rice gruel. She lies all day in her room, the curtains pulled tight around her bed, speaking to no one.

So we compete in grief, as we competed in love. But I shall win.

Six days now since he left. The palace echoes with rumour. Now that the man who caused the scandal has been banished, thoughts turn to the guilty woman. Hardly a woman, for she is twelve years younger than I. And a Vestal, nonetheless, the pure protectress of the realm! No wonder people speak of ill omens and unlucky conjunctions of stars and planets. The gods are planning their revenge.

It is his fault. He has a weakness for sequestered women. And who could be more of a challenge than she, the Vestal of Ise, the Emperor's favourite daughter? How tempting to seduce her, a slender child in white gauze robes living in her lonely house near the sea.

He had a pretext. For isn't he, as Imperial Envoy, expected to visit the shrines of Ise twice a year? Isn't he charged with conveying messages from their Majesties, and seeing to her needs and comforts? Does she need gowns, fans, incense, lamp oil, salt? Are her priests conscientious, her servants efficient, her lodgings secure?

How courteous he must have been, how solicitous his manner. I can picture every gesture. And she so wary at first, and then so deliciously yielding . . . How we fought about it, once the news got out. For it seems that some of the Vestal's attendants were less than discreet, and word eventually reached the capital.

The Emperor is furious. The Council of State meets late into the night, trying to decide what should be done. Should the Vestal be recalled? There are no precedents. Must she be replaced? The talk is inescapable. Every gallery and aisle is filled with whispers, and even the maids and guards are ready with an opinion, if anyone cares to listen.

All this has given me a headache. I will have Buzen comb my hair, and then I am going straight to bed.

Eighth Month

Twenty-two days and still no word from him. As far as Dainagon can learn he has sent no messages at all. Perhaps he ran into difficulties on the journey – perhaps his boat capsized in the Suma Bay. It has been so windy lately; the sea must have been high when they made the crossing. Yet surely we would have had some news if something had happened.

Dainagon says that the doctors have been twice with their needles to relieve Izumi's fever, but it has done no good. Her condition is winning her a great deal of sympathy; Dainagon says she looks as wan as the dying Murasaki in The Tale of Genji. I find her suffering wilful and vain. How like her to go to such extremes.

Word is out that the Emperor has received a letter from Kanesuke. Buzen says it was brief and contrite, and done in his most elegant hand. Apparently he made the journey without mishap, though as I suspected the seas were high on Suma Bay, and they had to delay their crossing. Whether he sent other letters I am not sure. I have received nothing. I write to him nearly every day, but throw half my letters into the fire. When the messenger returns to Akashi I shall give him those I have kept. Perhaps I should rewrite them, for they are all very angry, and he will never respond if I am so unforgiving.

★

Twenty-six days now. My headaches persist. I rose in the evening to dress for the moon viewing. Buzen helped me with my clothes: a green chemise; five aster robes shaded from pale to dark; a train embroidered with silver thread; an emerald Chinese jacket set with mirrors. Buzen said I looked as if I had been caught in a snowstorm, for the mirrors flashed like ice.

How cold it is this autumn, and such a bitter east wind! I shared a carriage with Dainagon and two other women to the Imperial Gardens; and we shivered and wished we had a brazier of hot coals between us. Everyone was there, eighty of us or more, though I did not see Izumi. The wind was so strong that we dared not board the boats moored by the lake, and they clashed fiercely and made me think of the high seas in Suma Bay.

We gathered near a grove of oaks, whose scarlet canopy had been depleted by the wind; I could scarcely make out the colour of the leaves that remained as the moon rose through the branches.

The Emperor, resplendent in his forbidden purples, seemed to increase in substance as the moon reached its height, and I was pleased to be close enough to see his noble profile. Reizei stood nearby, his face as impassive as his father's. The Emperor's women were hidden by gauzy screens, but the wind was so impertinently strong that their attendants had a difficult time keeping the enclosures erect. More than once I caught a glimpse of the Empress and the Haven, and I could feel their chagrin.

For a moment when the crowd shifted I saw Sadako. I felt such a stab of jealousy I could hardly stand. How like the Vestal she looks, though they are only half-sisters. Just two years ago they stood here together, before the Vestal was sent to Ise. And I remember thinking even then, before I had cause for my ill feeling, how one was the mirror of the other, and both were faultless.

13

The music of the flutes and zithers seemed altered by the wind, and I took no pleasure in it. The moon, once high, lost all its mystery, and became the object of stale poems and sentimental feelings. I was cold, and my hands were numb; they are so even now, though the fire burns beside me. My women are asleep; I hear them breathing. As soon as the trite moon sets I will set my brush aside and try to rest.

Midnight. The rattle of dice. Clatter of *go* stones in a wooden box. Some of the women are playing backgammon for stakes, and distract me with their clever talk. Yet I am glad of their voices. They dull the edge of my loneliness, which never leaves me, even in the banality of midday.

I will write Kanesuke a letter about the game of *go*. It was a secret language for us once. 'You are very greedy,' he would say if he saw me flirting with another. 'You have a reckless disregard for strategy. All you think about is capturing territory. You must take care when you launch several campaigns at once.'

And I would counter that women are allowed certain liberties, and that the boldest players strike out on several fronts. Nothing is to be gained by holding back, I told him. Then he would say I was yielding my hand too easily, and that no man enjoyed playing with a woman who strove to fill up her spaces too quickly. I must make sure, he warned, that in the final stages of the game when it came to parting the pieces the counting did not get too tedious – for even the most avid player might walk away.

And so we would bait each other, and in time our language broadened to include observations of those whose ranks were so high that we dared not describe their dalliances directly. So we would speak of a consort in the northeast quarter who ceded her ground too quickly, or a princess who distracted an unwanted suitor with false eyes, or a government minister who kept his hand too close and missed an opportunity, or a Haven whose vantage was more assailable than His Majesty might suspect.

What good will such talk do now? He is too far away.

I feel the *go* stone in my hand. It could be black or white; it could be enemy or friend; it could tilt the game in his favour or mine.

Yet once my palm is stretched flat the stone becomes what it is and shuns what it is not. It has a colour. Black, white. It has an allegiance, his or mine. It can aid in his victory or my own. It can be surrounded, captured, discarded, counted in the final tally.

I do not know if the letters I write will win or lose him. I do not know if they will strengthen my hand or force his against me. I hold the words in my mind, not knowing whether to disclose them. For once they are set down, black on white, the viscous ink contending with the bright expanse of the paper, they become part of the game. They can be understood or misinterpreted; they can be scorned, burned, thrown away. If I am not careful they will serve the purposes of my rival, whose words may prove more persuasive than my own.

How difficult it is to send them. How tempting to shut them in a box like the *go* stones. I will not write my letter tonight; I shall wait until tomorrow, when I am stronger.

Slept not at all last night. The storm was so fierce that several of us sat up late, huddled around a few coals. We dared not light the lamps, for fear of fire. The wind whipped around the eaves, tearing loose great swaths of shingle from the roof. They fell into the courtyard with a crash, each one as loud as the last. Rain pelted against the blinds, and the wind whistled through every chink and cranny. We could hear the men from the Office of the Grounds rushing about in the dark, battening the shutters and securing the double doors. We felt as if we were on a ship at sea, and we knew that if a fire did break out we would be lost, for the boards that kept the storm away would make our escape all the more difficult.

By morning the winds had died down. We rolled up one of the blinds and peered through the broken lattice into the courtyard. The white gravel was littered with debris, as if a great wave had crashed over the palace walls and left a flotsam in its wake. Two of the plum trees were damaged by falling shingles, and drifts of coloured leaves pressed against the inner walls of the veranda, as if they, too, had tried to escape the typhoon.

As the day wore on news reached us of the storm's destruction. A fire, as we feared, had broken out in the Imperial Stables, and five horses and an equerry were killed. (The smell of smoke hung in the air all day, reminding us of life's impermanence.) The orange tree by the steps of the Shishinden, which was planted long ago in the times of Nara, split in two. In the Imperial Gardens, oaks and laurels lie uprooted across the gravel paths, and the fishing pavilion is in ruins.

Rumours have spread of strange clouds in the northeast and unnatural flights of birds. The Emperor has summoned his diviners to assess the auguries and signs. There is talk of sequestering the royal family until the dangers have passed. Courtiers and ministers hurry down the halls and aisles, and everyone speaks of Kanesuke and the Vestal of Ise, and how it is their fault.

I pity her a little, that white-robed child in her house near the sea, but I have no pity for him at all.

By dusk it was so calm that some of the page girls hitched up their skirts and went out to see the destruction for themselves. They brought us back the broken stalks of asters and valerians, and wind-torn pinks and gentians, and drowned crickets in their battered wicker cages.

I am so tired I cannot sleep. I think of the singed horses, and the boy face down in the straw.

Received a letter. The messenger was brusque, his clothes spattered with mud. The journey from Akashi took eleven days.

I waited until everyone was asleep to open it. It was brief, written on thick white paper in his beautiful running hand. The paper was creased and smudged from the journey; there was no discernible fragrance, save that of damp and leather; he left no signature, but that I expected, for we were always careful that way. What did he say? Very little. That the journey was difficult; that the house is rustic but suits him well; that the local dialect is unintelligible; that the people are courteous and strange. He hunts, reads, practises his calligraphy. Sometimes when the wind blows from the east he smells the smoke from the salt kilns.

I read the words over and over and smelled the paper and smoothed it with my hands. Then I looked at the spaces between the characters – their vast white emptiness – and thought about all the things he hadn't said.

For his pains I gave the messenger two lengths of blue brocade and a packet of four letters, for all the rest I have burned or hidden away. Compared with his, he will find mine importunate and sad.

Three weeks at least before I receive a reply.

I saw Izumi. She was sitting with the Empress and reading something aloud to her, one of those illustrated romances she fancies, the sort filled with feuds and jealousies.

I had gone to deliver a message to Her Majesty from the Empress Dowager, and did not see Izumi straightaway, for she was hidden by the curtain of state. Her voice reached me first, but by then it was too late to leave the room.

I waited until the proper moment, got through my bows and explanations, handed over the letter and went away.

She is thin, more so than I expected, and the rouge on her cheeks only heightened the pallor of her face. She wore a lespedeza layering in shades I found unbecoming, and her wrists, which protruded from her sleeves as she held up the scroll, were as bony as an old woman's. Yet her hair was as lustrous as ever, and there was just enough of her former beauty about her to make me feel thoroughly distressed.

She bent her head as I spoke, feigning indifference, but just as I asked my leave she looked up and caught my eye. And I knew from that single glance, that small look of triumph – something about the curve of her lip or the tilt of her head – that she had received a letter, too, and that it had not been a cool, brief, straight-folded letter on thick white paper, as mine had been.

Slept fitfully and dreamed of Kanesuke. In the morning when the blinds were opened I knelt and held up my mirror to look at my face.

It is not beautiful, like Izumi's. It never was, even when I was young and sleep was not the rarity that it is now.

How could he love such a face? We talked about it once, one morning in spring. Wakefulness was a pleasure then, when I was with him, though I complained sometimes of what it cost me. Those shadows under my eyes, and all those wrinkles!

'Wait,' he said, and he went out into the courtyard and picked up a sharp stone. I watched him through the blinds. His robe slipped off his shoulder as he bent down, and I caught my breath and hoped no one was watching.

He came in and knelt behind me and took the mirror from my hands. 'Here,' he said, 'This will make you happy.' Then before I could stop him he took the stone and scratched two Chinese characters into the bronze.

Was he teasing me? It was the word for beauty.

'You've ruined it!' I cried, pushing him away. 'I'll have to send it to the polishers, and heaven knows if they can fix it.'

He laughed and lifted my hair and kissed my neck. 'Come now,' he said. 'You can't be all that cross with me.'

Some time that summer the mirror was sent back from the polishers. The scratches were gone, but the face that looked back at me was even more worn than it had been before, for by that time I knew he was seeing Izumi.

This morning when I picked up the mirror its unblemished surface seemed to rebuke me. I slipped into the courtyard and found a stone to suit my purpose.

I etched the same characters into the metal. Just as I had finished I heard a cough. I looked up and saw Chūjō, Izumi's maid. She hovered there in her pink and yellow gowns, her brows lifted, her hand poised on the sliding door.

'Excuse me, my lady,' she said. 'I was looking for Buzen.'

Then she darted away, like a dragonfly bent on its own trajectory, and I knew she had seen everything, and that she would tell Izumi.

Ninth Month

How long it seems since the last Chrysanthemum Festival, when I looked forward to putting on my gold and russet robes and walking with the women through the Emperor's gardens, admiring the frost-withered flowers.

Why should the chrysanthemum be the sign of longevity? Why not the camellia, whose flowers stay fresh just as long but are not tainted by the smell of mortality?

I hate chrysanthemums. Their colours are as drab as widow's gowns. Left to stand in a vase too long, their slimy stems stink like corpses.

I prefer flowers that have the grace not to endure: the campanula, the hollyhock, and the morning glory that opens at dawn and withers by the end of the day. They are true because they are fleeting; they are honest because they do not last.

So I stayed in my room and read while the other women strolled through the Shinsen-en. The effects of the recent storm can still be seen. The wattled fences have tumbled down, they tell me; the fallen trees have yet to be chopped into firewood; the broken reeds rattle at the borders of the Dragon Pond.

Now it is dusk, and the lamps are being lit. Soon the women of the Office of the Grounds will take their skeins of floss and spread them over the chrysanthemum beds. All night long the flowers will lie smothered beneath the silk, as if a storm had buried them in specious drifts of snow. And in the morning, when the dew has imparted the scent of the leaves to the floss, Ukon will come running into my room with a bit of the drenched cloth, saying, 'Quick, my lady! Rub it on your face, and see how young your skin will look!' and I will refuse her, because I do not believe in permanence.

Since I am tired of composing letters to a man who never writes, I distract myself with calligraphy practice. I grind my ink and set out my brushes with care, like an acupuncturist arraying his needles before a patient. Try as I might, my characters are too bold. How bored I am with these strictures, which say that a woman's strokes must be as delicate as her feelings are strong.

I copy out a poem from the Manyōshū, the one written by a border guard who has been sent to the eastern frontier. The guard speaks, and his lover answers.

> If I leave you behind
> I shall miss you
> Oh that you were
> The grip of the birchwood bow
> That I am taking with me.
>
> If I stay behind
> I must suffer
> The pains of longing.
> I would rather be the bow
> You carry on your morning hunts.

*

The Hour of the Boar. Cool and damp. The palace guards twang their bowstrings to ward off evil spirits.

We held our incense competition on a night like this, Kanesuke and I. It was late last summer when I was almost sure of him – though I was less so when the contest ended than when it began.

It started with an argument. We were lying under his robes and he was stroking my back. Somehow the conversation came round to scent. He insisted that women make better incense than men. I told him he was wrong: the Buddha was the consummate perfumer. Didn't the scriptures say that he rewarded the virtuous with breath as sweet as blue lotus flowers, and skin that smelled of sandalwood?

'Then you must have no virtue at all,' Kanesuke told me, 'for you reek of garlic,' and he kissed me in spite of it.

We agreed to hold a competition. For days I was busy with my mortar and pestle. Some of my friends – and a few of my rivals – entered the contest. Whether Kanesuke was the one who persuaded Izumi I was never sure.

My pages brought us intelligence. It seemed that Kanesuke had laid his hands on some recipes from the time of Emperor Nimmyō. He opened his storehouses and searched for resins and spices, and stayed up half the night perfecting his blends.

I decided to make a Hundred Steps incense and give it to him afterwards. He would no doubt discern my double motive. Not only would it announce his presence from the distance of a hundred paces, but it would betray him should he stray to rooms other than my own.

After much grinding and pounding the blend was satisfactory. But how to make it distinct? There is no artistry in slavish copying of recipes; one must improve and extend. I sent my servants into the fields west of the palace to hunt for wildflowers. They protested that their forays were unsafe. Thieves might spring out from abandoned buildings and attack them, or they would be trampled by cattle. I was forced to hire two guards to protect them.

Their venture was successful. They brought me carnations, borage, burnet, and drifts of gardenias. The burnet had faded to shades of rose and madder. I crushed it and added it to my potion. Would my competitor remember, I wondered, when we lay in a meadow thick with burnet and the scent stole up through the sunburnt grass? Perhaps my incense would remind him.

I sealed it in a jar and sent my pages to bury it on the banks of the Kamo River. For three weeks I left it to ferment. During that time I often saw Kanesuke. Never, during our games of *go* and backgammon, our talks and late-night love-making, did we mention our perfumes.

Nor did Izumi. Yet I heard – for Sadako told Buzen, and Buzen told me – that she had hidden in her room for days, fussing over her blend. I heard it was sweetly vernal, and reeked of violets. Had she slept with Kanesuke on a carpet of spring wildflowers, as I had lain with him on a meadow strewn with burnet? I forced myself not to think of it.

On a breezy morning near the end of the Seventh Month I sent my boys to dig up my treasure. I put it in an inlaid box and set it aside for the contest.

We held it on the last day of summer, at Kanesuke's mansion in the Third Ward. I recall little of that evening now – for it was too painful – except for a single conversation when the contest had ended.

We were in the great room in the south wing. The women were hidden behind their standing curtains, and the men paced back and forth; I could recognise them by their voices. The room was thick with fumes. Dainagon fanned me; and I folded and unfolded the note I held in my lap. A page had delivered it and a little red box with a firefly trapped inside. The note was from Kanesuke; he said he looked forward to my contribution. I had thought he was encouraging me; perhaps he was.

The musicians played their lutes on the veranda.

Soon the scents we made had all been burned. Cutting things were said, insinuations made; the men laughed, and the women fanned their flushed faces and plotted their revenge. Kanesuke observed that my blend was just a shade too strident, and Sadako concurred. Izumi's incense was praised by the Minister of the Left, and there was a murmur of approval. Was I the only one who detested that mawkish odour of violets?

New flares were lit in the garden. We drank rice wine and ate peaches and smoked trout. Then Sadako proposed another game.

We had been speaking, as satiated people often do, about renunciation. 'Let's assume,' Sadako said, 'that each of us had to renounce all colour and fragrance, as monks do when they take their vows. Which would be the most difficult to give up? For me it would be the scent of lilac.'

So we confessed. Izumi expressed a partiality for aloes; I, for the twice-dyed colour of *futaai*, that violet shade favoured by vain and handsome men.

And Kanesuke? How well I recall his voice when he told us. 'And you?' Sadako had asked him. 'What would be hardest to renounce, if you were to shave your head and give yourself up to the Five Precepts?'

'It may seem strange,' replied Kanesuke, "but I have a weakness for the scent of violets.'

No need to describe how I felt. Dainagon gave me a pitying look. I told her I had a headache, and slipped out of a side door into the garden.

Why do I recall the hours I spent there so well? I suppose it is because I was cold, and I had no reason to be there.

The flares had died down, so I found it easy to hide. I was glad of the dark colours of my dress, and of Dainagon's discretion. No one would miss me unless she chose to raise the alarm; they would think I was sulking behind my curtain. They wouldn't notice my absence for an hour or two, until Kanesuke escorted them to their carriages.

Of course he might invite someone to stay. There was always that possibility.

I passed the bridge over the pond and made my way up a little slope to a grove of maples. My slippers were soaked, and so were the hems of my robes. I leaned against the smooth trunk of a tree. In the half-light I could just make out the red veins of the maple leaves. I tore off a leaf and crushed it in my palm. It had no scent. I could hear music and the murmur of voices. Kanesuke was saying something clever, and people were laughing.

An owl called, and I turned my head to look for it. I could just make out the roof of the chapel in the grove of cypresses. So that was where he went to do his penances. Had he a conscience? He said he did, and sometimes I thought he might. He loved religion; its aesthetics pleased him.

Was he sincere? Even now I'm not sure. For a man so skilful at deceit he had a hatred of falsity. He hated flattery – yet he would condescend to me. He despised arrogance but he was proud. And if he loved me as he said he did, how could I be sure he didn't lavish the same words on others?

I crushed the leaf in my hand and remembered one dawn in early spring when we had lain in my room and listened to the waking birds. As he held me close he sang the refrain that runs, 'The cherry blossoms that I thought to deck myself with are gone.' And I knew he meant me to think of the verse about the Chinese girl who, torn between two men, went to the woods and hanged herself from a tree.

'Don't worry,' I told him teasingly. 'I have no other lover.'

'I know,' he said. 'You prefer your men one at a time.'

And then we bantered about the flowering cherries and which ones we favoured: the single-petalled ones, or the showy kind that flaunt their colours twice over.

Two months later I discovered that he was seeing Izumi.

And I wondered then, as I do now, if it was she he was alluding to in that refrain.

I looked down the slope. A heron stood in the stillness of the pond. He turned his head and fixed his cold eyes on me. I stared back with equal coldness until he flicked his head and dipped his beak into the water.

I heard wheels rattle in the courtyard, and watched the coaches drive through the gate. I was shivering, but I couldn't leave the shelter of the trees. How humiliating it would be to be seen! What if one of the gardeners discovered me and called to the others? I regretted leaving the safety of my curtain, and wondered what excuse Dainagon had made for me.

I knelt on the mossy ground to make myself less visible, and cried as the damp seeped through my robes.

If there were footsteps I didn't hear them; I must have been distracted by my sobs. Someone bent and picked me up. His robes were nearly as wet as mine, and thick with incense. As he carried me back to the house he told me he had looked everywhere for me, and that he was sorry for what he had said.

Later that morning, as we were reading side by side in his bed, Kanesuke asked me if he should light a lamp. The room was dim, for it was raining. I told him I would rather be like the poor scholar in the Chinese tale who read by the light of the fireflies he had trapped in a silk bag.

'Ah, yes,' he said. 'The fireflies.' And I knew he was thinking of the note he had sent me. Then he slipped his hand inside my robe, and told me he preferred the other poor scholar, the one who read by the light reflected off the snow outside his window.

So we matched each other word for word, like two rivals in a poetry contest. It was like that when we got on. We had a history, a secret store of knowledge, and we guarded it jealously, as if it were a recipe for happiness.

But I have forgotten Kanesuke's incense. It won the competition, and not just because of his name or what his guests thought they owed him. I can find no words to describe it, perhaps because it made me so sad. For it was the scent of loss, of the rendering of the self, and it foretold everything that would come between us.

I missed him all day today. The worst so far.

The bright days are hardest. The bright days of autumn hardest of all.

I woke and forgot he wasn't there. How long did I lie on my bed before I remembered? I lay listening to the voice inside my dream. That voice, thick as incense: how it stung my throat. And when I realised where it came from I hated them both: Kanesuke for his absence, and the dream for revoking it.

How long before I grow accustomed to the idea of never? It grows by the hour. It fills the silence of my rooms; it sits beside me like a traitorous friend. It taps against the walls of my veins, the very pulse of loneliness.

Why am I so sure I won't see him again? Is it my fear that makes me certain? Is it my mind, my most intimate and loquacious enemy? Should I trust my premonition?

I see it floating like driftwood, the idea of never. Every evening I think it will be carried away, and every morning it comes back to me.

Does Izumi have the same presentiment? Does she wake to the same voice? I hope she does not. I do not wish to share his absence any more than I did his body, for I am as selfish in my lack as I was in my completeness.

Tenth Month

Fourth day of the Tenth Month, when the gods are absent.

Since the gods are away, I chose to profit from their lack of vigilance. I stole a letter – or rather, someone stole it for me. I will not name the thief, for she is a friend, and I do not want her to come to any harm. Enough to say that it was easy. The letter was by Izumi's bed, slipped part way beneath a cushion. Within the space of a few minutes my accomplice had hidden it in her sleeve and delivered it to my room.

I waited until Buzen had left and then I opened it, my hands trembling. It was written quickly, in his lovely running hand, on blue Chinese paper that had been twisted at the ends. There was no signature or date, but I gathered that it had been written some time during the previous month, for he asked her about the typhoon, which ravaged his gardens as it did our own.

Why did I read it? It has only caused me pain. I see that they are laying plans for her to visit Akashi, possibly in spring, under the pretext of her annual pilgrimage to Sumi-yoshi, where she goes to pray for her dead parents. For Sumiyoshi is near the place where the boats leave to cross the Suma Bay, and it would be easy for her to slip across for a few days . . . or so he proposes. Come for a little while, he says. Come in the Third Month, when the sea is calm and the wisteria is blooming.

I folded it quickly, before the words burned too clearly into my mind. Before I read it I had intended to keep it, folded inside out and propped on my writing box, where no one would think to look for it, its place being so plain. But the paper was too distinctive to be disguised, and the contents too distressing to be read again. No, I will have my friend put it back at the first opportunity. Then I shall decide how to spoil their plan.

Evening of the same day.

I hear that the letter has been safely lodged beneath its cushion. The return was more difficult than the theft, and required some ingenuity; I will not describe the details, for they are best left unexplained. Sufficient to say I spent two anxious hours waiting for my friend to accomplish her task. I am lucky, for she is steadier than I, and less apt to betray her feelings.

As the sleet fell all day long I pondered what to do with the knowledge that is so painful to me. And it occurred to me that, rather than concealing their plan, it was better to bring it out into plain sight. If I hid it, I would be colluding with their secret. If I revealed it, the damage would be greater.

I didn't need silence. I needed rumour.

For rumour is the spurned woman's friend. It is like a handful of dye cast into a vat. It doesn't matter which particle of water is coloured first, for soon every drop is seized with the same hue – the hue of conjecture, false or true; it makes no difference.

And I will fix my dye well. My rival knows not the mordancy of my tongue. The colour of revenge is fast.

I waited for an auspicious day and cast my dye. By the following evening the story had found its way back to me – altered somewhat, but the same story nonetheless.

Did I know, asked Komoku, the First Consort's lady-in-waiting, that Izumi was planning a secret trip to Akashi? We were sewing a bombasine gown for the Gosechi Dances, and she poised her needle in the air as she leaned forward to whisper her question.

'No – you don't say!' My eyebrows lifted in mock incredulity, and my needle flashed back and forth through the blue silk, like a wasp darting amongst a bed of delphiniums. 'And for what reason?'

'Why, to visit her man in exile,' she replied, drawing the thread between her reddened lips to moisten it. 'They say she is going by way of Sumiyoshi, some time in the spring.'

I plied my needle as deftly as I could. 'You must be mistaken,' I said. 'Banished men aren't allowed to see their lovers.'

Dainagon, who was sitting on a cushion nearby, sewing beads on a brocade train, fixed her black eyes on me. I had not brought her into my conspiracy, but I could tell she suspected it. 'I hear Izumi has already received a letter from Her Majesty,' she said. 'Apparently the Empress was very put out, and demanded that Izumi explain herself so she can put an end to this tale.'

So we gossiped as our needles flew. Komoku said it surprised her very little, given how impetuous Izumi was. So I defended her, saying surely she would never do such a risky thing. She could be dismissed from service if word got out of her plans.

'I can hardly imagine,' said Dainagon drily, 'that she would have been so foolish as to let anyone in on her scheme.'

'Indeed,' I said. As everyone knew, I observed, she had few friends, apart from Sadako. I told them I felt so sorry for her I had a mind to visit her myself, or at least send her a letter.

'How very kind of you,' said Dainagon. 'Perhaps we should all take out our inkstones and compose our letters of sympathy.'

Komoku reached over and picked up the sleeve I had been

sewing. 'But look!' she cried. 'You've sewn it back to front!'

So I had. I spent the next hour picking out my stitches, while the talk shifted to the best kind of face powder to wear in damp weather, and the young priest who had come to read the Emperor his devotions during his days of abstinence.

I knew I had done my work well when that evening, as the maids were bringing in the chamber pots, I heard them discussing the punishments sure to be in store for a certain lady who was planning to visit a disgraced man somewhere outside the city.

I saw Izumi. I had avoided the Nashitsubo, skirting around it as if it were an unlucky destination. But this morning the Empress summoned me early, to her sister's quarters in the Kiritsubo, and I had no choice but to pass nearby.

She was kneeling on the veranda and looking into her mirror, the one decorated with cranes that she has had since she was a girl. She was wearing red trousers and a violet nightdress, over which she had thrown a blue robe of Korean brocade. The wind was blowing, carrying the scent of rotted leaves and damp, and it lifted her hair and fanned it about her. And I thought as I watched her – for it was as if I were standing outside myself, seeing her with a stranger's eyes – that she was like a diver who holds her breath to hunt for treasure, and plunges headlong into the dark.

She looked up and drew a sharp breath. Perhaps she had glimpsed me in her mirror. Then she gave me a look I will never forget. It was a look of surprise, a little icy shock, as if she had been plunged into cold water. Then, as I gathered my skirts about me and prepared to hurry past her, it changed into a look of such black hatred that it seemed no light could reach it, as if she had dragged us both to a great depth and had cut the ropes that could pull us back to the surface.

31

Received a letter from Kyūshū, the first since spring. Takumi says the boy is fine. He is tall, his head level with her chest; and his hair is short, for they have cut it already, though I asked them not to. Takumi says it was too much trouble for them to keep it long, and it is not the custom in the country.

Someone – the gardener, perhaps, or Takumi's husband – made him a ball of deerskin, and he kicks it all day long. Sometimes he disappears into the woods and they can't find him until after dark. He made a bow and some arrows and goes off to hunt partridges. He spends hours in a little house he has made in a hollow tree, and claims to have been visited by bears. Takumi must have been reading him romances, to give him such ideas.

The priest comes twice a week to give him lessons, but with all the storms this autumn – for they have been even fiercer on Kyūshū than they were in the capital – he has missed several. So I am paying him for nothing! All those parcels of silk twill and incense gone to waste ... They have to keep after the boy to do his writing practice. Takumi sent me a page from his copybook so I can see his progress. How thick and square the letters are, but I suppose that is to be expected. 'Ah, the flower that blooms in the port of Naniwa!' he writes, as if he were accustomed to such sights.

The paper on which he wrote is blotted and smudged. I can see his ink-stained fingers, thin, like mine, and in the down strokes of certain characters I see traces of his father's hand – but perhaps that is just my imagination.

My last parcel of books and scrolls has still not arrived, and I fear it may have been stolen. No doubt some ship captain's child is fingering them even now, and gaping at the illustrations, which depict a world as far from his experience as the sevenfold clouds of heaven. It makes me cross, but I suppose given how corrupt things are it is to be expected.

I think about the story of the Leech Child. My mother told it to me when I was a girl. She said I would ask to hear it again and again, as if something about his misfortunes struck my fancy.

He was the first child of Izanagi and Izanami, the incestuous brother and sister who created our world. Their other children were strong, and became the sun and moon and all the islands of our homeland and its trees, waterfalls, rocks and storms. But the Leech Child had no bones. He was white and formless, and he couldn't stand or walk.

When he was three his parents put him in a boat and set him adrift on the sea. No one rescued him, nor was he transformed through luck or magic into a mythical creature – a phoenix, perhaps, or a dragon. He simply died.

How did he die? I would ask my mother, but she couldn't tell me. I imagined him parched by the sun or cast into the water by a wave.

And did his mother miss him?

No, my mother would say, she was busy having other children. But her last child, the god of fire, scorched her when she was giving birth, and she died. Her husband Izanagi sought her in the underworld and begged her to return. She replied that she could not, but promised that she would appeal to the gods, and warned him not to look at her until she did so. But he broke his vow, and saw her corpse riddled with maggots.

Izanagi was so repelled that he fled the underworld and found a river and bathed himself over and over to rid himself of the taint of his wife's body.

There are no sins in this story, nor any sense of guilt. The

Leech Child is born and is left to die; the mother dies also. No one can bring them back.

The Vestal has returned. People speak of nothing else. She arrived late last night, having travelled in secrecy from Ise, escorted by twenty guards armed with bows and swords and seven outriders. Her carriage was drawn up near her quarters in the Tōkaden, and she covered her head with a robe so that no one could see her face. The Empress has been with her all morning, scolding and admonishing, and Buzen says that the girl's sobs can be heard up and down the galleries.

No one knows what to do, for not since records began has a Vestal been recalled. A company of priests have come to recite the sutras in her name. They hurry up and down the corridors, their purple stoles wafting behind them.

There is talk of sending Sadako to Ise, for there are no other princesses or daughters of princes of sufficient age, and to choose a girl from outside the royal family would be out of the question. Yet her rank is low, for her mother was a commoner, and even if the Emperor were to overlook this it would be months before she were ready to go to Ise. She must be purified and taught the native rites and incantations; she must live in the sacred grove of Nonomiya.

And in the meantime, who will preside over the shrines of Ise? The priests remain, but they are men, and not kin to the goddess whom they serve. And should a Vestal not appear to guard the sacred mirror, who knows what sights it will reflect? Fires, wars, disease and tempests: all await us, unless a girl is sent to Ise.

Eleventh Month

How slowly the hours pass when it is snowing! It is as if time itself were trapped within the drifts. I peer through a gap in the blinds into the courtyard. Everything is veiled, like a bride concealed beneath the dazzling burden of her robes. The world seems empty of colour, just as the cold has drained the blood from my fingers, leaving them as pale and stiff as elder wands.

I warm my hands over my stove and watch the ice melt at the edge of the blinds.

My thoughts drift like the snow. How wonderful it is, that moment when ice yields to the heat and is transformed into something quick and supple.

I love a man who yields as ice does when it melts. It is not a weakness, that yielding, but a kind of strength.

Of all the men I have known only two possessed that quality. Once they yielded to me; perhaps now they do so to others.

I spent two winters once lying under the robes of a man who gave himself up in that way. Sometimes I made him cry. That is not a weakness, but he saw it differently. Perhaps that is why he left – because he felt ashamed.

Sometimes late at night he would talk about his home in Michinoku and about the horses his father raised there, the blue roans the colour of metal and the white ones that have no colour at all.

I cannot write about him now. He hurts me still.

And Kanesuke? He yielded to me, too, but in a different way.

I miss his eyes, his voice, his limbs as pale as peeled willow, the pith and marrow of his singular self. But he is gone from me, banished like the summer, and I am left with the snow and my scattered thoughts.

I caught a thief in my rooms – or I almost caught her, as she was too quick for me. When I came in (it was dark, and very late, as we were returning from the dances at the Kamo Shrine) she scurried like a rat through the sliding doors, and by the time I reached the corridor I saw nothing more than the pink streak of her robes and the glint of her hair.

I don't know who it was – no doubt some servant hired for the purpose. The night was advantageous, as we were all away.

Why hadn't I planned for this possibility? Izumi has no scruples, and I should have known she would stoop to thievery.

I returned to my room. It was a wanton scene. Papers and scrolls littered the floor; my copy of The Tales of Ise, given to me by my brother on my twentieth birthday, was in tatters. Boxes of gowns and sashes were upended, and the brazier was tipped over, the white ash scattered everywhere. How lucky she hadn't started a fire!

I sent my women to another room, and cleared things up myself, for I didn't know what might be strewn about, and I was sure that they would find the opportunities for gossip all too tempting.

My gowns are ruined. In my hurry to collect the papers strewn on my desk I upset my inkstand, and the black drops flew everywhere. My very skin is stained. Even now, after several washings, my hands are marked as if I were infected with smallpox. My celadon water jar rolled off the desk and smashed into pieces. The tortoise on the spout was split in half – hardly a good omen.

My letters were rifled, though none was missing, as far as I could tell. Fortunately those that mean most to me were well hidden. These pages, likewise, were cleverly concealed, but my heart pounded as I felt for them in their hiding place.

Still, there was plenty of harm done. That very day I had been writing to Kanesuke. Dissatisfied, I tore the letter to pieces and threw them into a basket, being too rushed to dress for the dances to take the time to burn them. I knelt to retrieve them, and found that most of the pieces were missing.

Why didn't she take them all? Why not hide the basket in her robes and relay its incriminating contents to her mistress? I can picture Izumi piecing the scraps together and smiling as she read my reproaches and entreaties . . . Clearly the servant was poorly instructed, but I expect she will be more thorough when she returns.

Now it is morning and I haven't slept at all. I sent away my breakfast and spent two hours tidying my room. I cannot find my copy of the Kaifūsō. Did she take it on a whim? It had a beautiful cover of blue watered silk . . . How I hate this naked feeling! I feel like a caged bird in the marketplace that is prodded by dirty fingers.

Ukon and the others hover in the anteroom, not daring to disturb me. I know the story will spread through the palace, just as the ink blackened my desk. I must pull myself together and deprive my enemies the pleasure of my distress.

It makes sense now, the look Izumi gave me at the Kamo Shrine on the night the thief crept into my rooms.

I was standing under a grove of cedars near the first bridge at the Upper Shrine. It was late and a light snow was falling; I could see the flakes swirl in the light of the torches carried by the men. I was shaking with cold, despite the thickness of my robes, and so were the other women who stood nearby. We crowded together like penned animals trying to keep warm, and our breath rose with the smoke from the torches and caught the boughs of the cedars high above our heads.

The dancers stamped across the bridge, and soon the leaders came into view. Why did they frighten me so? The sheaths of their swords flashed in the torchlight, and their faces were as stern as flint.

The musicians followed, the sound of their flutes mingling with the rush of the stream.

How cold the sound of a flute is on a winter night! It pierces to the bone. I remembered a story Kanesuke had told me about a captain of the Inner Palace Guards who once led the dances at Kamo. He fell from a horse and broke his neck, and it was said that his ghost haunted the waters under the bridge by the Upper Shrine. I shuddered, and wondered if Kanesuke had invented the tale just to frighten me.

Flakes of snow brushed my cheek, and I lifted my sleeve to wipe them away. I must have turned my head, for I noticed Izumi standing nearby. She was watching me. When our eyes met she lifted her chin and smiled. It was a secretive smile, lit with hidden knowledge, and it left me flushed and disconcerted. I turned away and watched the envoys pass. How proud and vain they seemed, dressed in their vernal robes of willow green, the paper wisterias crowning their hair as false as Izumi's smile – and Kanesuke's story.

It is a curious thing, is it not, to call a woman a haven? 'The Emperor's Haven has gone to the shrine at Uzumasa,' we say, or 'The Haven is indisposed, and hasn't left her rooms for three days.' The word slides off the tongue as an old robe slips from the shoulders, and we do not think about its provenance, or the texture of its meanings.

Few women are havens, of course, though many aspire to be. Even a consort is deprived of that title until she bears the Emperor a child. Only then is she acknowledged as his place of refuge: his haven, mooring, citadel. There are many metaphors to describe her, should one be inclined to do so.

A woman of lesser rank who bears her husband a child is not given that name. An unmarried woman is even less worthy of it. Granted, her lover may tell her how much he desires her, and praise her with metaphors of every description. But she is not a haven.

And a woman who gives birth to a child unknown to its father – how could she possibly expect such a name? Though she bleeds the same blood and suffers the same pangs as those who have been granted that honourable title, she is always denied it. Even if she loves the father of her child past all understanding she will never be his haven, port or fastness – or any other thing of that kind.

Buzen tells me that the Vestal is distraught. Her shame has made her thin; she eats little or not at all, and will not leave her rooms in the Tōkaden. The Empress visits her daily but her father still refuses to see her, for he is too angry.

Her maids have hidden the scissors from her, for she has threatened to cut off her hair.

Poor girl, that she should find the cropped hair of a nun so attractive! Does she think that by parting with her locks she can sever her bond to Kanesuke? No, she is wedded to him for life; their names will be linked until she is dead and burned to ashes. She may not be his wife, but her fate is bound to his, just as an ox is bound to its burden by its traces.

If it were as easy to renounce a man as it is to discard one's finery! If I thought I could give up those I should not have loved by cutting off my hair and putting on a grey gown I would have done so long ago.

39

I hear there is talk of sending the girl away, to the Empress's mansion in the First Ward. Dainagon says they are refurbishing the west wing; the men are being paid twice the usual wage so that it can be finished by the New Year. How strange to think that the Vestal might spend the rest of her life there.

Once she had a name and the semblance of a future, though the choices of princesses are narrow, and bound by custom and expectation. Now she has neither name nor prospects, thanks to the whim of a man whose weaknesses are as well known to me as the veins in my hands. I hope for her sake that she does not love him.

News reaches us daily of disturbances in the capital. Violence is so common that courtiers of high rank fear to leave the imperial precincts, and venture forth only when accompanied by armed escorts.

Scarcely eight days ago the Biwa Mansion was robbed, the thieves so bold as to attack just after dusk. Two guards were badly injured, one with stab wounds to the chest; and many valuables taken, including a collection of Chinese jade and various scrolls and scripture cases.

Fires, many set deliberately, have broken out in several wards. Taking advantage of the general confusion, thieves made off with luxuries of every description. Mansions in the districts of Sanjō, Gojō, and Rokujō have been damaged, and a house near the Taiken Gate was burned to the ground.

And the municipal police? Their incompetence is appalling. Yet what can one expect, when they are led by a seventeen-year-old boy who acquired his post because of his rank and good looks? Those whom he commands are no better, for they devote more attention to their dress than to keeping order. All of us suffer, from the fish vendors in the marketplace to the Emperor himself, whose lack of judgement is no small part of our difficulties.

Kanesuke's enemies – and they are many, the Emperor among them – blame him for the unrest, which they see as retribution for the Vestal's wanton ways. Yet his supporters, including the Empress and various ministers, are calling for his banishment to be lifted, for only then, they say, will the calamities subside.

There is talk that the Emperor plans to hold a service of intercession to try to quell the violence. Priests will come from Enryakuji and Mount Kōya to recite the sutras, and all of us will be expected to attend.

And Kanesuke? Will the Emperor extend his exile, or will his allies prevail and see that he is restored to favour? I fear both prospects, for if he returns, his enemies will be all the more inclined to do him harm.

Received a letter from my brother, who tells me he will be coming down from Enryakuji for the service of intercession. The Abbot has called for more than a hundred monks from the temples on Mount Hiei to assist with the ceremony. Ryūen has been chosen as secretary – an honour for one so young. It is true he has a fine hand; I can almost forgive his faults when I see his writing.

Yet he never fails to slip in a barb. 'I am sure,' he wrote, 'that you know the purpose of our coming, and that you are familiar with the history of the man thought to be the cause of these misfortunes.' So he knows of my relations with Kanesuke, though we have never spoken of him directly.

They will leave on the eighth day of the Twelfth Month, the oracles having deemed it safe for travel. Ryūen says they will be escorted by armed guards – yet he insists that the Abbot is merely taking precautions, and would never inflict violence except in self-defence.

He closed quickly, saying that he would not dilate on matters that would not interest me. Monks must have a good reason to conduct a profane correspondence, he reminded me, and even though we are brother and sister our bond must not be too strong. For I am a woman with many secrets and few scruples, whereas he, though as secretive as I, saves his love for his sutras.

Dreamed of Ryūen last night, and could not forget his face throughout the whole long sleeting day.

He was a boy – just eight or nine, the same age as my own – and his name was not yet Ryūen, for he knew nothing of religion and cared only for games and his friends. We lived more freely then, in our house in the uncouth provinces, and our relations were less constrained.

'Tadahira!' I called, and he came running across the length of the garden and caught the silver fish that I dangled in one hand. I had trapped it in the pond, and held it, bright and struggling, by its bony fin. 'Don't!' I shouted, for he made as if to fling it at my dress, but then he turned and threw it high, and it landed in the reeds by the edge of the pond.

We ran to find it. It was flopping from side to side, its tail beating against the mud, its pink eye staring. Tadahira ran to fetch a pole. 'Stop! You'll hurt it!' I cried as he prodded its belly. He flicked the fish into the water, grazing its side, and it darted off, trailing a thin plume of blood.

Later that summer I left our house in Mino and came to live in the capital, behind my curtains and screens. And still, fourteen years later, I dream of Ryūen as he was then, swift and defiant, his legs spattered with mud and his hair unshorn and tangled, like a woman's.

*

Returned late from a concert in the Empress's chambers and found a letter propped against my pillow.

It was wrapped in plain Michinokuni paper and had no adornment of any kind. I broke the seal and found a single sheet of paper inside. It was mauve, of a shade used for letters of condolence. On it were pasted, in rearranged order, scraps of my letter to Kanesuke, the one that was stolen from my room.

There was no salutation, no signature – nothing in any hand save my own. They were my characters, all of them, but distorted to a malevolent purpose:

> you are . . . nothing
> your silence . . . is necessary
> lies . . . vanity . . . unspeakable
> you damage me constantly
> why do you not . . . drown
> no reason to live on
> your exile . . . interminable
> you are . . . despicable
> love is . . . beyond your power

No words to describe how I feel. She has stolen them all.

Still no news from Akashi.

Buzen tells me I should travel – visit a shrine or temple, or arrange a tryst at a country inn. What good would that do? I am bad company. There is nothing worse than idleness when one is unhappy, and travel is nothing but idleness compounded by expectation. One waits for the carriage to arrive, for one's room to be ready, for one's things to be unpacked. One waits for a meal, a bell, a chance encounter with a stranger, a view to surpass all others, a revelation.

The worst thing about travel is that one always brings oneself. Yet we never cease to expect that it will change us – that we will be not just transported but transformed.

If I am unhappy I prefer to stay at home. I would rather be in my rooms watching the rime form at the edge of the blinds than admiring the view of Mount Fuji or the Otowa Falls.

What are the thoughts of an exiled man?

How I envy his freedom. His prison is more spacious than my own. He walks along the beach and sees the hills obscured by brushfires. He sees the divers returning with their trove of shells, and the salt makers gathering kelp.

How strange those women are! I have read of them in poems. But an exiled man can see them.

Perhaps he will fall in love with one. He might even love two at once, as Yukihira did. No doubt Kanesuke will remember his story. For there is no better companion to a banished man than a fellow exile, even one who has been dead these hundred years.

For wasn't Yukihira sent to Akashi, the favoured place of disgraced men? Didn't he see the same pale hills, and hear the geese cry in autumn? It is always autumn in Akashi; the exiles write of no other season. It suits their melancholy.

They were sisters, the two women Yukihira loved. He saw the girls for the first time as he walked along the beach in the early morning. They were pouring water over a heap of kelp. Their sleeves were tied back and he could see their forearms, as white and supple as the necks of swans.

For five days Yukihira watched them. On the sixth he brought them a gift. He laid two lengths of yellow silk upon a rock some distance up the slope. Still they did not look at him. But when he returned the next day the silk was gone.

This ritual continued until his stores were almost

depleted. He resorted to gifts more easily replenished: apples, partridges, dried fish. His servants, who were well trained in discretion, asked no questions when he ordered his delicacies.

One day he found the women bent over a pyre of ashes. For the first time he approached and asked what they were doing. To his surprise the taller one explained (though she would not look at him) that they were sifting the ashes of the kelp, which they had burned in the kiln the night before. They would place the ashes in a pot, she said, and stir them until they settled. When the brine rose to the top they would skim it off and boil it down until it turned to salt.

Why, Yukiriha asked, did they not simply boil the seawater until they obtained the same result? 'Because that is not what we were taught,' the girl replied, and she smiled as she stirred the ashes.

They began to meet in a house roofed with felt in a pine grove near the sea. The girls would build a fire, and they would eat strips of blackened fish with their fingers. Sometimes they would sing. Yet they repelled him even as they drew him in. Their guttural speech unsettled him. From their bodies arose a marine odour, a rusty scent of both fecundity and decay. Still he found himself imagining them as they would look in the dark, their bodies lit with phosphorescence, their limbs twined about him.

Some time later they began to meet Yukihira singly, as if by unspoken agreement. The pattern of their comings and goings was not clear to him, and he never knew which one to expect. And in this way he learned of their differences: their fears and hesitations, their needs and predilections, and his own changed with them.

And then – who can tell why it happened? – they began to visit him together. There were times when he was so blinded by his pleasure that he couldn't distinguish one from the other. Later he would watch their faces. The expressions that flickered across them were so subtle that he was taken aback. He did not expect such women to be capable of nuances of emotion, any more than he expected them to play the *kin* or dance the Gosechi Dances.

Why were they not jealous? It was incomprehensible to him. He was accustomed to rivalry. In his letters from the capital (for there was a lover who still wrote to him) he detected evidence of old wounds and recriminations. The sisters were not the same. Yet their lack of guile only deepened his suspicion. Perhaps they were witches, or ghosts who had returned to relive old desires and sufferings. He couldn't trust them. He resented their simplicity as much as he resented their hold on him.

So when Yukihira received word the following year that his banishment was lifted he was relieved. His life would resume its old patterns of patronage and obligation. All the pleasures of the capital would be open to him. And if the woman he had loved hesitated to accept him, not knowing the reason for his long silences, it would make his second conquest of her all the more beguiling.

There was no question of his remaining in Akashi. He had no livelihood there; no friends or family; no future. Even so his choice was more painful than he had anticipated, and he put off telling the sisters.

When at last he broke the news to them they made no protest. Their faces, once so expressive in the darkness, were as glazed as the surface of the sea. He set his guilt aside and pressed ahead with his plans. For several days he didn't go to the house where he had met them. He was not witness to their grief. Still he wondered how they might have implored him, and if they would have made him change his mind.

One windy morning in the Ninth Month the boat that was to take him back landed in the bay. Before he left Yukihira and his men knelt in the sand and prayed to the God of Sumiyoshi for safe passage.

46

The following day the sisters walked down to the beach. They stood in the gashes left by the boat and wept.

I suspect that the presents Yukihira left were no comfort to them. The damask robes were too precious to put on; the jewelled pins too fine for their hair. The sticky balls of incense confused them; they didn't know what they were for.

How did they mourn him? I have tried to imagine it but I cannot. Nor, I am sure, could Yukihira. Granted, he may have thought of them now and then, for exiles, once they have returned, are prone to melancholy and introspection. They find to their distress that they have not left behind the autumn of their banishment. They have brought it with them.

If he did recall those girls he must have done so not with longing but with fear. Their love threatened him. They would love him until they died, with the feral intensity of their kind. Even after he was burned to ashes they would still love him.

Would he return to visit them? He knew he would not. Would he write? What need is there to write to those who cannot read? Perhaps he would send a messenger and have a letter read out to them. No, he must have thought, it was better not to. It would only increase their suffering. He would write a poem about them, and remember them in his prayers.

So I think of those two sisters, whose lives are closed to me. I bleed as they did. I feel the temptation of their manner of grief. It is there in the distance, always.

Twelfth Month

Received a letter from Kanesuke, who had clearly heard from Izumi about my campaign against their rendezvous in the spring.

What he wrote can hardly be called a letter. It was a declaration of war.

He said, 'Do you think that rumour is a weapon? Then remember this.' And he quoted the Tao to me: 'Fine weapons are nonetheless ill-omened things. For to think them lovely is to delight in them, and to delight in them means to delight in the slaughter of men.'

Does he think that he can threaten me with this talk? It is a game like any other. I would rather fight than have him retreat even further. Angry words are preferable to silence.

A clear cold night. If it were autumn the gardens would be lit with flares, but tonight there are only stars and a thin crescent moon.

I think of Lao Tzu: 'The world is full of people who shine. I alone am dark.'

I am dark also. Are there virtues in obscurity? Not virtues, perhaps, but possibilities.

I was white once, and shone like the rest. I powdered my face; I wore brocades that dazzled the eye; I was brave and guileless.

But then in time I became appalled by whiteness, which is the colour of death and deceit. For powder cannot conceal an ageing face, just as a guileless manner does not disguise a liar.

I do not trust things that are white any more than I trust men who say they are honest, or virgins who believe they are pure. For white is the colour of snow and ashes, and belongs to the realm of priests and sorcerers. Still I envy the certainty of those who despise its opposite. The dark is full of doubt.

If doubt is a virtue, it can also be a weapon.

As Izumi doubts her enemies, so I shall make her doubt her friends.

An ally of mine, who shall go unnamed, has hinted to Izumi that it was Sadako, not I, who circulated the rumour about her journey to Akashi. Why would the Princess do such a thing? Because Sadako herself was in love with Kanesuke. Had Izumi not heard how they had been seen alone several times, long before Kanesuke's affair with the Vestal of Ise?

My ally reported to me that Izumi rose to the bait quite easily, and pressed him for specifics. Where had they been seen, and by whom, and how often? My ally, who takes no pleasure in cruelty, was loath to give details. Nonetheless he provided sufficient evidence to make Izumi weep in vexation. My friend, generally the model of restraint, was so moved that he reached under the curtain to grasp her sleeve.

'So it must have been Sadako who saw the letter in my room,' Izumi told him – and she came out with the whole story. Yes, she recalled that on the same day she had received Kanesuke's letter she and Sadako had been chatting in her apartments. She had gone out briefly – why she could not recall – and had left Sadako alone. The Princess would have had ample time to search through her letters, if she had wanted to.

So I had been doubly lucky! Not only had Izumi failed to realise that the letter had been stolen from her chambers, but Sadako had been there on the very day when her presence was most incriminating.

As soon as my friend took his leave Izumi shut herself in her room. Late in the afternoon, my spies tell me, she called for a messenger. Her letter was brief and unadorned. I can only assume that it was addressed to Sadako, for later that evening the Princess went to Izumi's apartments, and they argued.

Why weren't they more restrained? They must have known that half the women in the courtyard were listening.

Who won the contest? That is hard to say, though I heard that Sadako was as adamant in her denials as Izumi was in her accusations. Who, the Princess wanted to know, had suggested such a tale? But Izumi saw no need to name my ally, whose ties with me are so tenuous as to remove me from her suspicion.

It was a proper shouting match, by all accounts. Judging from the words that were exchanged the damage seemed irreparable.

I thought I would relish this victory. Why, then, does the whole episode fill me with unease? I suppose because my ruse came too late to protect me from Kanesuke's anger. Will he suspect that I fabricated this rumour? Izumi is bound to accuse him of this new infidelity. My only consolation is that when she hears his denials she will trust him less.

I hired, at great expense, a young man to take my letters to Akashi. Shall I name him? No. He is the brother of one of my accomplices; I like his face, and he rides well. He came early this morning, when most of the women were still sleeping. When I handed him my packet he gave me a quick intent look. Beneath his deference I detected a mixture of

50

curiosity and contempt. How could a woman well past her prime be so desperate? I saw him glance at my uncombed hair and ink-stained fingers. Then he was gone, leaving nothing but a pool of melted snow to betray his visit.

Ten days or more before my letters reach Kanesuke. How much will I pay for this boy to convey my parcel? Bolts of linen and damask, a dark blue dress cloak lined with violet, some grey laced trousers ... But it doesn't matter. I hope the trails aren't blocked with snow, for if they are the price will be even higher.

And now, lest I forget, an inventory of my arsenal. They were not as beautiful as I would have liked, my four long letters, since I could not adorn them with leaves or flowers (for they would suffer from the journey, and might be seen in their withered state as a symbol of love's loss, rather than its constancy).

The first: calm and restrained, on thin green paper, written in strokes half light, half dark in my most elegant hand. In it I alluded to the rumour of his affair with Sadako – for I know he will hear of it from Izumi. If I bring it up first, perhaps he will be less likely to suspect that I am its perpetrator. I know the rumour is false, I told him (as indeed it is, as I made it out of whole cloth). To have seduced not only the Vestal but her half-sister – it is unthinkable. I am well aware of his weaknesses, but he is not capable of this double treachery, I am sure of it.

For has he not always told me that he finds Sadako a little too vain, a little too common – too frivolous and flirtatious for his taste? (And indeed he had told me all these things, though in such a way that made me suspect that in time he might succumb to her charms, though I never found proof of it, nor did I reveal my suspicions.) No, I told him, I knew he wouldn't stoop to her level.

I closed with a poem about my fidelity, and left the letter unsigned, as is our custom.

Let Izumi do the accusing. Hadn't she believed the rumour about Sadako as soon as I introduced it? Well, then, she may play the part of the jealous lover, while I, in a rare show of magnanimity, will tell him that this time I do not doubt him.

The second: playful and combative, written in bold strokes on stiff Chinese paper, the running script as fine as I could contrive it. I told him I was glad to be his opponent. Were my weapons not as well tempered as his? Did I not have judgement, boldness, finesse? Wasn't I seldom discouraged and downcast? And, once a battle had been won, didn't I show mercy for the vanquished?

Yet I fear my tactic was wrong. Will he see that my bravado is just a screen to hide my desperation? He knows that when our fights become battles of will I am rarely his equal. I am more vulnerable to stratagems; I am prone to tears; I resort to taunts and invective.

Perhaps I should have tried to win him by confessing my weaknesses rather than flaunting my strength. By admitting my faults I would have underscored my advantages, just as woman's modesty enhances her perfections.

The third: written in delicate *kana* script on fine-grained tan paper, some strokes so light as to be barely seen. I told him a parable about the nature of our love. I said that it was like the Imperial Jewel, which lies concealed within its casket, its shape and colour indeterminate, yet its power all the greater because of its vagueness. No one is allowed to see it, for doing so would rob it of its beauty. Closed and concealed, it is pearl, jade, ruby; revealed, it is only one of these. Even the legends one hears about it are imprecise; no words or metaphors suffice, for each is its own limitation.

So our love is known only to itself. It exists in the dark, and even we who make it know it incompletely. We call it one thing and it becomes another. It eludes our sight and touch. Yet it persists.

What will he think of this little tale? Will he find it false and sentimental? All I know is that I cried as I wrote it.

The fourth: I recall neither the paper nor its colour. The writing, done in the half-dark after several hours of weeping, was no doubt poor. I sealed it straight away, having no desire to reread it.

It began, as far as I can recall, with a high-minded screed on expedient means. I reminded him of the chapter in the Lotus Sutra that describes how the Buddha dissembled to his disciples to make them see the truth.

Did he lie to me about Izumi for the same reason? I didn't care about the Vestal, and I knew that the rumours about Sadako were untrue – but Izumi was another matter. Hadn't he told me that he didn't love her? Hadn't he said that he preferred my company to hers? Didn't he swear that though she was lovelier – and how it hurt to hear him say it, though I knew as well as he did that it was true – I was more passionate?

Then why did he spend his last night in the city with Izumi? Why send loving letters to her and be so cold and taciturn with me? Why conspire to bring her to Akashi (for the rumours were everywhere; how careless she had been to let out their secret) but not invite me?

There was only one explanation. He had lied to make me see the truth. He loved her more. He didn't care that I had known him longer or understood him better. All our years and secret histories were dross to him. He had melted me down, as an assayer does his ingots, and he had cast me with all my impurities into a contemptible form.

Would he not melt me once again and cast me in a shape more to his liking? If he loved me best, I would be as he asked. I wouldn't be jealous. I wouldn't scold or plead.

I believed every word I said when I wrote that letter, but I dared not copy it over lest I change my mind.

*

My dye is spreading further than I had anticipated.

Rumours of Sadako's liaison with Kanesuke have reached the Empress, who, according to Buzen, called the Princess to her rooms. How dare she have taken up with such a man? the Empress asked. (She did not shout, as Izumi had done, but the exchange was heated enough to be overheard by several ladies-in-waiting.) The very one who, because of his relations with the Vestal, had already threatened the safety of the realm! Wasn't she aware of the disturbances in the capital? Didn't she know to whom they were attributed? Hadn't she betrayed not only the Vestal but her stepmother? How could she presume that the Emperor would ever consider sending her to Ise? How sorry she was, the Empress said, that she had ever supported Kanesuke. She had not agreed to his exile – that was the Emperor's doing – but now, to have two princesses with ruined reputations! It was too much. Couldn't Sadako see how selfish she had been?

Sadako's replies were not conveyed to me, but it is easy enough to imagine them.

It is only a matter of time before the story reaches the Emperor, who is sure to be equally incensed by his daughter's indiscretions.

I spoke with Ryūen, who has come down from Mount Hiei for the service of intercession. He came to my anteroom late in the afternoon and sat on the other side of the standing curtain. Through the gap near the floor I glimpsed the grey folds of his robes. I don't think that he saw me, for I was careful for his sake to keep my distance.

'I trust you are well,' he said – and already I was on my guard. Something in his voice – its sarcastic edge, its superciliousness – never fails to set me against him even before he makes his insinuations.

Insinuate he did. 'I am sure you have heard the same gossip that we have,' he said. Rumour seems to travel quickly to Mount Hiei; the porters convey it as readily as they do the Abbot's wines and Chinese sweets.

'I don't know what you mean,' I said. If I let him tell me the story about the Vestal and Kanesuke it would give me time to think.

Yet the gossip he relayed was indeed new to me, and it gave me more of a shock than I cared to reveal. I must have heard, he said, that the Vestal was to be sent to the Empress's mansion in the First Ward as punishment for her tryst with the Imperial Envoy. And I must know that Sadako was to be banished also, to her mother's house in the western hinterlands, near the Katsura River. He assumed I knew of her affair with Kanesuke.

So my false rumour had spread to Mount Hiei! I admit I was more appalled than pleased. And Sadako was to pay a price for my story. I hid my face behind my fan, as if the curtain weren't sufficient to conceal my guilt.

'And how did you come by this intelligence?' I asked. He said he had heard it from the prelate who was serving as the Emperor's night chaplain at the time the story about Sadako was making its rounds. The prelate had returned to Enryakuji the previous week and had relayed the news to the Abbot; Ryūen had overheard them speaking about it as they sat at dinner.

'How efficient of Kanesuke,' my brother observed, 'to have dispatched two princesses in a matter of months.'

And I replied that I had heard he was a charming man indeed. His efficiency, as Ryūen put it, did not surprise me.

'No,' said Ryūen drily, 'I can hardly imagine that it would.' For he had heard, he said, that Kanesuke was wonderful with words, and he was sure that he had many other fine qualities.

'He has a better hand than you,' I replied, a little too hotly.

'Does he? Then perhaps when his banishment is lifted he can offer his services as amanuensis to the Abbot. No doubt after these long months in exile his thoughts will turn toward a religious life.'

'But he could never fill that role as well as you. And of course he wouldn't be as discreet.'

'I do not make a habit of indiscretion,' my brother said mildly. 'And when I do you are the first to profit from it.'

'Tell, me, then, if you are so keen to increase my knowledge: how did the Emperor take this news about Sadako and Kanesuke?'

'Badly, as you might expect,' Ryūen said. The prelate had told him that His Majesty had stayed up all night in his rooms in the Seiryōden when he heard the news, ranting to various ministers. At one point he had even threatened to have Kanesuke killed.

Killed! My blood ran cold at the prospect. But I said nothing, and was grateful for the damask that hid my emotion.

At that point, Ryūen continued, the Minister of the Left had stepped in and tried to persuade the Emperor that it was more dangerous to condemn Kanesuke to death than to leave him in Akashi. He reminded him of the story of Sugawara no Michizane, who died in exile and returned as an angry ghost. What vengeance Sugawara had exacted! He struck the Great Hall with lightning; there were fires and floods and earthquakes.

Then the prelate himself stepped in to calm the sovereign, reminding him that it had been sixteen years or more since a nobleman had died by imperial decree. Certainly the Emperor did not wish to imperil the future of his soul by ordering Kanesuke's execution.

And so, Ryūen told me, they brought His Majesty to reason – or as much reason as could be expected of a drunken man in a fit of temper. Some time past dawn his attendants coaxed him to lie down; the prelate heard him snoring within his curtained bed.

I had grown so cold during the course of this story that I was shaking, and I strove to keep the tremor from my voice. 'I hope you will forgive me,' I said, 'but I'm very tired. There is a concert this evening, and I must rest before I dress.'

'Of course,' Ryūen said with uncharacteristic gentleness, and I wondered if he thought that my unease had any source apart from my fears for Kanesuke. 'I will look for you at the service of intercession.'

He left me then. How glad he must have been to be released from the precincts of jealous women! His sense of relief was palpable – or did I imagine it in my heightened state? – and hung in the air like the incense burned into his clothes.

The eleventh day of the Twelfth Month, morning. A clear sky the colour of lapis lazuli. Sunlight glances off the snow and hurts my eyes; the icicles glitter like crystal rosaries. I kneel at my desk, looking out at the snow, and think about the service of intercession. Was it only last night? It seems as if it were days ago.

We stood in the Great Hall of State, hundreds upon hundreds of us, pressed so close that our robes were half-crushed. I saw Ryūen pass, though he did not see me. He is tall now, and slight; his face has an angular cut, and his skull, its shape made clear by the tonsurer's blade, has a blue sheen. His red robes mocked me with their sanguine purity. When the chants began I thought I heard his voice, though I might have been mistaken.

But the face I sought above all others was Sadako's. At

last the crowd shifted, and I saw her. She was standing near
the royal dais, next to her half sister. She wore white – was
it a night for mockery? – with layerings of plum. The Vestal's
eyes were downcast, her face half hidden by her fan, but
Sadako looked straight ahead, her eyes glinting.

I watched her throughout the chants and supplications.
Her stare was as implacable as the gilded Buddha's.

My body ached under its panoply of silk. Throughout the
night a single verse ran through my mind. 'The world is full
of people that shine. I alone am dark.'

It wasn't until I left and returned to my room that I
realised I had forgotten to look for Izumi.

I was awakened before dawn by the sounds of shouts and
stamping feet. For a moment I feared there was a fire, and I
leaped up and looked outside. It was snowing hard, and I
could see neither flames nor smoke. Then I remembered: it
was the morning of the Emperor's hawking party. The men
were getting ready, for it was a three-hour journey to the
Serikawa River, and they hoped to arrive just as it was getting
light.

I went back to my bed and curled up under my robes,
glad that I had no need to go out on such a cold morning.
But by then I was thoroughly awake, so I lay in the dark and
thought while the snow piled up in the courtyard.

Was it just this spring that Kanesuke had gone hawking
with the Emperor? It must have been in the Second Month,
just after the Kasuga Festival. He was still in favour then,
though his relations with the Emperor were strained. And
this was not because of the Vestal – for no one knew of their
liaison – but because Kanesuke and the Emperor were rivals,
and had been so for a long time.

They were not rivals in romance, for Kanesuke had always
been careful not to stray onto the Emperor's territory. They

were rivals as cousins are rivals, in blood and sport and accomplishment – and in subtler ways as well. For Kanesuke was younger than the Emperor, and less constrained by duty and rank. And he was a Tachibana, and a favourite of the Empress and all the Fujiwara.

So I was not surprised when Kanesuke was exiled. But the Emperor may discover that he is more easily banished from his sight than from his mind.

I thought of that spring morning when Kanesuke had gone out hunting. I had woken early to watch him dress. How eager he was, like a soldier strapping on his quilted armour – and all for the sake of a few birds! He put on his boots and leggings and heavy robes of figured silk; his russet cloak was embroidered with cranes. He had written in ink on the sleeve, 'Let none find fault . . .' And I wondered, for I knew the verse and its provenance, if it were a veiled message to the Emperor, for he and Kanesuke had quarrelled a few days earlier.

I looked through the blinds that day and watched them leave. It was well before dawn, the sky blue-black and clear. The Emperor was seated in his litter, and around him milled a cacophony of dogs, pages, horses and courtiers. The hooded falcons brooded in their wicker cages. Then there was a shout, and they all passed through the gate in a blaze of noise and torchlight, and I went back to my bed and slept all morning.

They returned late that night; I was in my room writing a poem when Kanesuke tapped on the blinds. He was covered with mud and his hair was damp. I sat him in the anteroom, next to the brazier, and we talked for a while but he wouldn't stay. He smelled of sweat and saké, and there was blood under his nails.

'So,' I teased, 'was it a success?'

'Not quite.' So he and the Emperor had argued; I could see it in his face. He pushed back his sleeves and warmed his hands over the coals. His arms were scratched, the dried blood the same colour as his cloak.

'Was he so very cruel?' I asked, and was sorry as soon as the words came out.

He stood up. 'No,' he said. 'Yes and no. You wouldn't understand.'

I realised after he had left that he was right. I had never ridden a horse, never balanced a falcon on my wrist, never watched a crane tumble out of the sky. I had never seen the Serikawa River or crossed the Saga Plain. That whole male world – the drinking, the noisy jocularity, the cousinly rivalry – was outside my experience.

Today it snowed all the time the men were gone. Buzen combed my hair, and we chatted with the maids. Everything I did seemed trivial and small, as if I were a doll inside a paper house, moved about by childish hands. I thought of the hunting parties, the one in the spring and the one going on as I warmed my hands by the fire. How was it possible to hunt birds in a snowstorm? I laughed, picturing the arrows piercing empty clouds.

Reizei had gone in the palanquin with his father, Buzen said. It was the boy's first hunt. Would he be allowed to ride and handle a bow, I wondered, or would decorum confine him to a view bound by brocade curtains?

I imagined the expedition that whole long afternoon. I saw it as if it were painted on a folding screen, just as the Emperor, disposed on his furs and cushions, watched it from his palanquin. For kings are even more confined than falcons, who are granted a few hours of freedom before they are returned to their cages.

I thought of Kanesuke, and wondered if he were hunting in Akashi, his white roan concealed by the snow. And perhaps for that reason – because I missed him – I went out in my carriage late that night and watched the men ride back through the Suzaku Gate.

The snow had stopped and the air was very still. There was no moon, and the stars shone with unrivalled brilliance.

The men shouted and laughed as the dogs leaped at their feet. Frost clung to the manes of the horses and the bright cloaks of the riders. From the saddles hung, limp and dusted with white, the slaughtered birds.

What a mockery they were. Cranes, their fabled lives cut short, as inert as bags of rice. Pairs of mandarin ducks, faithful even in their death. And the geese dangling from their girlish necks, making not a sound of protest.

A shout startled me. I looked towards the gate; the men were bringing in the palanquin, its roof heavy with snow. How exhausted they were! I saw one whose face was as blanched as the ground. Then the Emperor stepped down, his eyes glistening, his cheeks flushed from drink and the warmth of his mantles.

Reizei was asleep. A servant lifted him down to the Emperor, who insisted on carrying him the few steps to the litter that would convey them to the Seiryōden.

I felt a pang so sharp that it hurt to breathe. My own son will never be held in his father's arms. He will never know, even in his dreams, that kind of tenderness.

Word is about that the former governor of Iyo is leading an uprising in the south. His men have commandeered hundreds of boats, and are raiding up and down the coast. Even settlements in northern Kyūshū have been plundered, and buildings set afire. We do not know which towns have been attacked, and I can only hope that my boy is safe. I have received no letters from Takumi since autumn, but I had attributed the lapse to stormy weather and high seas rather than the depredations of rebels.

How hard it is to have so little news! One never knows whether to believe tales of this kind. The Emperor has many enemies, even within his own family, and some would think nothing of spreading false rumours if they thought they would damage his reputation. His influence over the provinces is (dare I say it?) tenuous at best, and news such as this only helps to undermine his authority.

So I must wait – as I wait for letters from Akashi. Luckily, it seems that the brigands have not extended their reach as far north as Suma Bay. If they do I must also fear for Kanesuke.

Evening of the twenty-second. Rain and heavy winds.

All the Buddhas – past, present and future – have been named, and I am exhausted. What hardships one must endure to atone for the sins one has committed throughout the year! So many Sanskrit words: they jangle in my mind like the metal rings on the priests' staves.

In the afternoon I waited on the Empress in her chambers. She was tired from the three nights of prayers and wanted me to read her some poems from the Kokinshū.

She had asked that the screens depicting scenes of the horrors of Hell be moved from the Seiryōden to her apartments, so she could study them at leisure.

'Just look at the quality of the brushwork!' she said, lifting her elegant hand to point out a particularly fine scene. It showed a man suffering the torture of eternal falling. He stretched out his arms as if to fend off the black wind rushing towards him. His mouth was open, and I imagined his scream trailing behind him like the white plume of a comet.

Yes, the brushwork was surpassingly fine. The tortured man's robes were executed with grace; the horror in his face conveyed with economy. Just a few strokes, rightly placed – that was all.

I felt ill. Would the Empress mind if I lay down for a while? No, of course not, she said, a look of concern crossing her lovely painted face. She led me to an alcove behind the screens. Once my vertigo passed I fell asleep, and dreamed of nothing.

The last night of the year.

Dainagon and I were talking in her room late this evening when we heard a commotion in the courtyard. It was the Devil Chaser. We slid the door open a crack to see if we could glimpse him. By the light of the half-moon we could just make out his vermilion colours. His gold mask glowered.

His men were shouting, and shooting wooden arrows left and right; one of them hit a pillar just in front of us and clattered down the steps. The Devil Chaser leaped onto the porch, waving his spear and holding his shield high, as if to parry a thrust from an unseen enemy. He was so close I could hear his breathing.

Arrows hailed down, and one of them hit him in the arm. He cried out in mock pain, and all the women laughed to hear him suffer.

A few hours later, when the year was well over, I returned to my rooms. From far away in another part of the palace came the sound of shouts and twanging bowstrings as the actors made their rounds.

When I stooped to arrange the bedclothes I saw a small white parcel leaning against my pillow. I picked it up and unfolded the paper. Something heavy slid out and fell onto the floor. I felt its shape in the dark: it was the blade of an arrow.

My breath came fast. I leaned over and picked up a coal with the tongs and peered at the paper. Something was written on it. The strokes were clumsy and thick, but it was a woman's writing – I was sure of it – disguised to look like a child's.

There were just two lines:

Because your heart is wrapped in darkness
The Devil's shape must be clear to you.

First Month

The first day of the First Month. We are a year older, Kane-suke and I.

Will he look at the sky tonight and search in the constellation of the Great Bear for the new guardian star? Will he bow to the four directions and scan the west for a sign of Paradise?

He is west of me, in a paradise I cannot seek. He has put on his vernal robes of red and green, but I cannot feel their softness.

Perhaps others can. But I mustn't begin the year with jealous thoughts. They are inauspicious.

Shall I write to him and say, 'It is the New Year today. Send me a letter – no, two – and fill them in with news, for it is spring now and the days are lengthening.'

Shall I plead with him not to bruise me with imperatives? Shall I say, 'It is the New Year, and ill-omened speech is forbidden. Do not wound me with angry words.'

Shall I suggest that nothing is worse than his silence? It is tempting. I believe I will.

The First Day of the Rat. A thin snow, then blue sky. I rose early for the progress to the country to pick spring herbs. We were sixteen carriages in all; the green gabled roof of the Empress's coach swayed before us like a quaking mountain. The air was cold and sharp, and the snow crunched pleasantly beneath the carriage wheels.

Buzen and I were sitting next to each other, and at one

65

point the wheels caught in a rut so deep that we were knocked together, and the combs fell from our hair.

We stopped near the bank of the Katsura River, on a slope of elms whose limbs bore their freight of white as easily as the sky held its drifts of cloud. Everything was still, even the river, whose currents had been seized by the cold.

Buzen and I stepped onto the frozen ground, and the cold crept through our court shoes and stung our feet. I held my fan close to my face – for even in the wilderness one must be modest – and my breath steamed against it and left little droplets on the rosy silk.

We scattered across the hillside, the bright colours of our robes blossoming in the drifts like a sudden spring.

We knelt by an uprooted tree and scraped the snow. Pale shoots of bracken poked through the black earth. I snapped them off and put them in our basket.

I looked down the slope towards the frozen river and saw Izumi standing with the Empress; they looked like sisters in their plum-coloured gowns. Their outlines stood out sharply against the snow, like pictures cut from a scroll and pasted onto white paper. Izumi's face was half-turned, and I strained to hear her words . . . but then Buzen came running up, her cheeks red with cold, and showed me the sprigs of parsley she had found.

On the way back we stopped by a grove of white pines, and everyone rushed out to dig up the seedlings that grew through the snow like tufts of grass.

Once I believed in those green talismans. I thought that spring herbs would make me strong; I thought that the seedlings would make my life last as long as the pines. But now I am more cynical – or perhaps I was just tired. I sat in the carriage, blowing on my stiff fingers, and watched two women trying to pull up a little sapling. It clung to the ground, and after a while they laughed and gave up and strolled off into the woods.

I closed my eyes and thought about Akashi, and whether the sky was as clear there as it was here, and whether he was off in the woods or in his house, reading. I saw his hands as they held the book, and I watched him turn the pages.

The Empress's voice startled me from my reverie. She was walking with Izumi; their shadows, as long and blue-black as their hair, followed them discreetly along the snowy path.

I must have moved, for the Empress saw me and gestured with her fan.

'Ah!' she said, smiling, her teeth as dark as her shadow. 'So you don't care to pluck your seedlings! You must be certain that you shall live a long life.'

I searched my mind for a clever allusion, but I was so distracted by Izumi's loveliness that I simply laughed. In the cold air my voice sounded thin and false.

Something flickered across Izumi's face – a wintry derision, half-disguised by her fan and her need for composure in the Empress's presence. 'Yes,' she said to the Empress, 'she is as certain of her longevity as she is of her beauty.'

Her cruel words stayed with me all the way back to the palace, and spoiled my pleasure in the scenery.

I was rummaging in a cupboard this afternoon and discovered my magnolia-wood fan. It was wedged behind a stack of scrolls. The purple paper had faded and was sticky with cobwebs.

Three summers since he gave it to me.

I was staying then in a temporary house outside the palace, to be closer to the Empress, who was ill. The building was old and roofed with green tiles, and there were no lattices on the side facing the garden, just bamboo blinds. It was very warm that summer, and the tiles stored the heat from the sun. At night it was stifling.

We would lie near the porch, Kanesuke and I, waiting for a breeze. We burned incense to drive away the mosquitoes, and once in the evening a swarm of hornets flew in through a gap in the sliding door, and one stung Kanesuke on the shoulder. Sometimes before a storm the blinds would lift and we could smell the roses and the yellow day lilies in the garden. When the rain came down we would lie on our backs and let the sound wash over us, our bodies still as trout poised in a current.

We were happy then. He told me he had never loved anyone as he did me, and I believed him.

One morning I had been crying because he was leaving for two months on a tour of the southern provinces. (How dangerous it is to fall in love with an envoy who wakes each morning to a different view, while we must be content with the same green blinds and smoke-stained ceilings.)

'Surely those aren't real tears,' he teased me.

It was a joke between us. When he cried I would tell him he was just like Heichū, the deceitful man who tried to win his lover's sympathy by wetting his cheeks with a bottle of water that he hid in his sleeve. Once, when Heichū's lover discovered just how monstrously deceptive he had been, she was so furious that she filled the bottle with ink. When he dabbed some drops on his face she held up a mirror and said, 'You have shown me before that you are a liar, but how can I tolerate this: your face stained with ink, and you married to another?'

And so the story – the false tears, the lies, the ink-stained face – became a symbol of our tempestuousness.

I made him promise that he would write. I kept his letters in a yellow brocade bag, and when he was away I would spread them out on the floor and study them as a geomancer does his signs and symbols.

'I shall write even now,' he said, and he fetched my ink-stone and a brush. 'Give me your arm.' He knelt and pushed back the orange sleeve of my shift and rested my arm on his leg. 'Stay still,' he told me, and I tried, though I was shaking with laughter.

He wrote three lines of a poem; I need not say which one. The ink was warm. A drop ran down my wrist and fell onto the mat. He lifted my arm, holding back the sleeve so it wouldn't be stained, and blew on my skin.

'There,' he said, and when the ink was dry he kissed me.

'So you wish me to be Heichū's messenger,' I told him later, as we lay cooling ourselves on my mat. 'Is this verse intended for me or someone else?' For Heichū had asked his lover's son to carry his messages, and the boy had done so, pushing up his sleeve to show his mother the characters painted on his arm.

'No, it's for you and no one else,' he said, 'because I love you best.'

Perhaps what he told me was true. No one else knows his mind as I do. No one else can read his moods.

Yet I do not love his deviousness. I have tried to explain it by blaming my own. But I cannot manage it.

For the sake of those three lines on my arm I shunned my bath for days.

The Seventh Day of the First Month. Cloudy and cold.

Dainagon and I went to see the Procession of Blue Horses. We arrived early, so we would have a good view; our carriage was positioned near the Office of the Quiver Bearers, and several of the guards, resplendent in their red hunting robes, hurried back and forth shouting orders.

All the noble families from the city came; we watched their carriages drive through the Taiken Gate, the wheels jolting over the great crossbeam fixed in the ground. When the courtyard was nearly filled the Emperor's palanquin arrived, borne by twenty men, their faces flushed and straining.

I saw the Empress on the viewing stand, and Reizei, looking older than his years in his leaf-green robes – but I did not see the Vestal or Sadako.

When I remarked on this to Dainagon she told me that they had been confined to their rooms, under the orders of the Emperor, and would likely not be seen in the company of their father again.

'He has disowned them,' Dainagon said. Had I not heard? She had seen the Empress weeping with rage about it. They were to be sent off, soon – the Vestal to the Ichijō Mansion, Sadako to her mother's house near the Katsura River.

So it was just as Ryūen had told me.

Dainagon must have noticed something in my expression, for she gave me a keen look. 'Well,' she said. 'Perhaps it is their fate. There is cause and there is effect.'

Perhaps. Yet was I not the cause, as was Kanesuke?

'How I pity them,' I said sincerely.

Dainagon gave me another sharp glance, and then she peered through the blinds and lifted her hand.

'Look!' she said. 'They are coming.'

When the horses were led in a hush fell over the crowd. There were twenty-one, all white roans with proud wary faces. They stepped so high and pranced with such avidity that it seemed as if the ground were covered not with ice but with burning coals.

Kanesuke rode such a horse when he left the city.

Why do we call them blue, these auspicious horses? When my father was young they were steel grey – I still remember the stories he told Ryūen and me – but now blue roans are rare, and white ones are in fashion.

Will the sight of them bring me luck? Will they bring me

70

health and happiness? Will the Vestal and Sadako, deprived of their benevolent influence, have neither?

No matter. I suspect that the powers of blue horses are as counterfeit as their name. Still, they were lovely to look upon, and for a few moments while they passed I forgot about everything else – about Kanesuke, and the absent girls, and my seditious rumours.

Received a letter from Kanesuke. The messenger arrived just as I was leaving to attend the Empress, so I had to wait all day to read it, wondering all the while if it contained good news or bad.

He loves me still. I had to read between the lines, but I can tell.

He didn't intend to fall in love with Izumi, he told me. It was beyond his control. There was a bond – something foreordained – he couldn't explain it. But I would understand, would I not, for hadn't the same thing happened to us?

So he went on with his talk of destiny, which explains all mysteries and excuses all faults and improprieties ... but I did so want to believe him.

And his lies? He went on and on about my rants against his falsity, and quoted the Tao to me: 'It is by not believing people that you turn them into liars.'

He said he didn't choose to set Izumi against me. That was my doing, he said; I had made her my rival. His tie to her was something apart; it had no bearing on his love for me.

Yes, I thought. He argues well that he may share himself. But he was never very glad to share me.

Still, I pondered what he said about Izumi. Had I been too eager to set myself against her? Did I assume too much and understand too little? Was it not my very need of her (for I had loved her once, too, when we were younger) that made me turn against her when she had no need of me?

Only when she began to be cruel did I feel that we were equals.

But I am forgetting Kanesuke. He told me of his nightmares, which oppress him throughout the day. Perhaps it is nothing, he said. Just too much time – the exile's only surfeit – and too much reading.

So he is lonely, and he misses me a little. I shall write again and see if I can make him miss me more.

The water clock drips. The plum tree blooms. I am mocked by the coming of spring.

If spring were perpetual I wouldn't fear its arrival. How I dread the sight of the faint green haze upon a slope of birch trees! The leaves rustle, and within that sound I hear their impending fall. I see it all, implicit in that green haze – the transit of days both innumerable and uncounted.

I find no comfort in the change of seasons.

Once I lived in a different kind of spring. It was a spring outside of time, filled with phoenixes and udumbara flowers. The phoenixes spread their wings, fanning the flames of their own destruction. The flowers fell from the sky. I didn't see the phoenix's bright feathers; I never knew the colour of the udumbara flowers, though I felt their petals brush my face. My eyes were closed. I was blind – and so was Kanesuke. And yet it was blazing. We were consumed within that time, consumed and made again, like the phoenix.

You might ask: wasn't it confining? Was the bed of aromatic twigs too narrow? Was the day too long?

No. It wasn't confining at all. We had no need to change, no desire to go elsewhere. We were each other's destination.

Who can say how long that season lasted or when it might come again? Will it return every six centuries, like the phoenix? Will it bloom every three thousand years, like the udumbara flowers? Will love persist past aeons, like the reign of emperors, whose bodies decay yet whose office exists in perpetuity?

They are false, those symbols of longevity. They endure because we wish to think them lasting. They are as far from our grasp as the red petals of the mandārava, which blooms only in Paradise. Yet if I close my eyes I can see them. I can see them.

I must say a prayer to Kannon. My boy is fine.

Takumi's letter arrived late this morning. The writing was clumsy; she has lost her refinement after living so many years in the country. But I musn't be churlish. As the news was good, I shouldn't fault the style of its delivery.

The village where they live was spared by the brigands, who concentrated their attacks on the coast. But travel is dangerous and supplies are short. Few boats bringing goods from the mainland have landed, and even rice and barley are scarce.

I was lucky to receive the letter at all. Takumi sent it with two monks who were returning to their monastery near Lake Biwa. Their faith makes them impervious to the threats of pirates, and they have nothing worth stealing, apart from their rosaries. One of them must have held the letter close to his skin, for it retained the double scent of sweat and incense.

My parcel of stories never arrived. I will send another soon, though I have little faith that Takumi will receive them. I can only hope that should they be stolen they fall into the hands of someone who can read them. More likely they will be sold for a few handfuls of rice. Then they will be lost, their pages scattered like the pirates' boats, their intricate plots to no purpose.

Second Month

I decided to go on retreat to Hase Temple. Kanesuke and I
went there often, and I wanted to see it again, though I knew
it would cause me pain.

I left at dawn, in a basketwork carriage, with no one
to accompany me but the driver and three escorts. Buzen
handed up my bundles and boxes. I could tell she was upset
that I hadn't offered to take her, but a servant's prattle is
always tedious, and I cannot trust her to be discreet. Should
I have brought a friend? Perhaps. It would have been pleasant
to have a companion to share the long journey. We could
have draped our sleeves outside the windows and hoped that
someone would ride by and admire them; we could have
speculated about the guests and our prospects. But I am
poor company now, and have much to read and write.

When Kanesuke and I went on retreat we always travelled
separately, and would arrive a few days apart. And this was
not for the sake of propriety – for by then we cared little
what people thought – but to prolong our anticipation. How
pleasant it was, jolting up some forsaken track and knowing
that he would take the same road a few days later. He would
see the same cedar with the double trunk, and would smile
as I did at this timeworn symbol of conjugal happiness; he
would breathe in the scent of the camphor trees, whose
twisted branches recall love's entanglements.

Sometimes as we lay together in the evenings, our arms
entwined and our breath mingling, he would recite the
poem that begins: 'One thousand branches grow upon the
camphor tree in Izumi's wood.' And I wondered later if

74

that poem foreshadowed his new attachment, or if he was referring to a bond that had already grown between them.

But I am digressing. I broke my journey south of Uji, and reached Hasedera on the evening of the third day. The torches on the gate had been lit, and the stones in the courtyard were white with frost. Lamps flanked the steps to the temple, and light shone through the open door. I heard a conch being blown, and the ringing of bells.

My room was not yet ready, and there was some confusion about the woman who was to wait on me; it seemed that her husband had suffered an accident – the priest said something about a fall from a horse – and she was not expected for some time. I strove to repress my annoyance, reminding myself that this was a place for calm . . . but how noisy it was! A party of elderly women bustled past me, their threadbare clothes turned inside out. I saw them glance at the embroidery on my Chinese jacket and my long train. Two servants hurried past, one carrying a roll of straw mats, the other a brazier. One jostled my shoulder, and I could barely hear his apology over the clatter of his wooden shoes.

I stepped outside for a moment's quiet. I performed my ablutions, and then I walked towards the temple and began to climb the log steps. A group of priests passed me, as nimble as deer despite their high clogs, and one of them turned back and glanced at me, as if he recognised something in my manner and dress.

I was struck by his face, as sharp and clever as a fox's, and then I remembered: Kanesuke had spoken with him once. They had stayed up half the night, discussing the parables of expedient means. I had passed Kanesuke's room near dawn, and caught a glimpse of him through the door. His hands sketched the Phantom City in the air until I could see its very towers and pavilions.

I approached the top of the steps. The light from the temple grew brighter, and I heard the sound of chanting. I slipped on the last step, and caught the wooden railing to steady myself. I was trembling from the cold and the sudden fear of falling, and I held tight to the rail and closed my eyes.

'Forgive me, but are you all right?' I turned and looked into a man's face level with my own, for he was standing one step down.

A man or a boy? It is hard to say. I could see both in that open face – the boy he had been, and the man he had become, and later, when I knew him better, I could see glimpses of the man he would be when I no longer knew him. It was not just his openness that I liked – for I liked him immediately, in a way that surprised me – but his seriousness, and his careful way of looking at things. He read my face as an oracle reads his bones.

Did I think of that image then? I can't recall. Perhaps it seemed right only in retrospect.

I told him I was quite well; I had just stumbled a little.

'Well, then,' he said, 'Shall we go in?' Casually, as if we were a couple.

The temple was brilliant with tapers; the gilded Buddha seemed to flicker in the glare, like a phoenix illuminated by its pyre. I was escorted to an empty enclosure and knelt within the screen to pray. Would he kneel nearby? No – he had walked away. I closed my eyes and told myself not to worry. Perhaps he was just being discreet. The chants were so loud and the crowd so thick that I couldn't concentrate.

Later, as I was about to leave, I heard his voice. 'Here. This is for you.' He was standing so close that his scarlet robes brushed my hand. He held out a branch of anise, its withered leaves soft and brown, like a monk's habit.

That faint sanctified fragrance ... I didn't want to be reminded of it. Whenever we went on retreat Kanesuke and I would write poems to each other on anise leaves. They were our secret petitions, allusive and profane, and we laid them not on the altar but on our outstretched palms.

Tears filled my eyes, and I brushed them away with my sleeve and thanked him. Did he think me sentimental, or just a little unbalanced? Perhaps he was used to the excessive gratitude of older women. Yet I could tell from his glance that he was more worried than flattered, and he bowed his head and walked away.

When the service ended I didn't see him. I walked down the steps, caught in a current of silks and voices, and managed to find someone to take me to the women's quarters. My room was small, but the mat on the floor was thick, the water in the basin still lukewarm. I was overcome with exhaustion. Through the thin partition I heard the sound of two women arguing. One wanted to leave the next day, for she was bored and had spent all she could afford on prayers and petitions, but the other wanted to stay.

My maid came in, profuse with apologies, and offered me some chestnuts and fruit. Her eyes were swollen from crying and her gown was rumpled, as if she had slept in it for days. I offered her my sympathies – for hadn't the priest said something about an accident? – and she took them graciously enough. But she said nothing more about her troubles, and I didn't press her, though I was curious to hear the story.

In the morning I was awakened by the sound of bells, and took my gruel as the woman combed my hair. It had snowed a little in the night, she told me, but the sky was clear, and the sun was already melting the icicles along the eastern porch. I was anxious to see the gardens, and asked her to bring me some overshoes. As I stepped into the hall a door slid open, and I saw two women come out from the adjoining room. They were dressed in their travelling clothes: so the bored woman had won. I fancied her to be the tall one in the sable cloak.

'Be careful of fire,' she said to me as they passed. Yes, she was the bored one; I recognised her voice. 'The rooms are very dangerous.'

Was it a warning, or had she hoped to frighten me? I decided to take it as a friendly gesture, and bowed without a trace of swagger as they shuffled past.

It was freezing in the garden; even the shadows under the cedars were blue with cold. I warmed my hands in my sleeves and breathed out great clouds of steam, like a dragon. I could hear the sound of the river, and the chatter of a group of priests crossing from the refectory to the temple. I would find the tree I was looking for and then I would go back to my room and lie under my robes. It was too cold to linger, and for all I knew the man I had met had already left. I found myself wondering what his carriage looked like, whether it was plain or grand, and which road he might have taken.

The tree I sought was not as I remembered; it was not as tall, and the bark was less smooth. Perhaps I was confusing it with the wild cherry Kanesuke and I had lain under in the woods, near the bank of the river. I looked up into the dazzling sky. Snow had settled on the branches of the tree and on the little twigs, all red with buds. We had stood under this tree two years ago, Kanesuke and I. It was twilight, and very cold, and far away someone was playing a flute.

What is it about the sound of a flute on a winter night that stirs one so deeply? We tried to describe the quality of that sound. Then we recalled the names of famous flutes, the ones handed down from father to son in one illustrious lineage or another, until we came to the Inakaeji, whose name means 'I would not exchange'.

'That would make a good name for you,' said Kanesuke, and I was flattered. Yet I wondered long afterwards if he had been referring to his possessiveness or mine.

Tears again. Had I come on retreat simply to cry? It was infuriating. I walked back to the inn, my feet frozen past

78

feeling. As I bent in the vestibule to remove my overshoes I heard that boyish voice.

'Out so early?' I knew he was teasing me, for it was well past noon. He was dressed in willow robes and wide laced trousers, and his face seemed even younger than it had the night before.

I looked down, not wanting him to see my red-rimmed eyes. 'I thought you had left,' I said, before I had time to regret it.

'Not for two days,' he said. 'It's an unlucky time to travel northwest.'

So he would be taking the road to Nara – or perhaps he was travelling further, to Uji, or the capital. There was nothing to do but ask.

So ask I did, because time was short. As we walked up and down the galleries – for he offered to accompany me, and I saw no reason to refuse – I learned that he lived in the Fifth Ward with his parents, and held a post in the Ministry of Central Affairs, in the Bureau of Divination. He had just returned from China, where he had been studying.

'So you have had adventures,' I said. 'How I envy your freedom!'

He looked at me with curiosity, as if freedom were a commodity possessed only by men.

'Not many,' he said. 'I'm too busy with my books and my divining sticks.'

'So you can foretell the future?'

'No. I have no such power,' he said, with a high seriousness that amused me. 'But I do predict' – this with a smile – 'that you are going to be very cold and hungry in a little while. Perhaps we should meet after you have had a rest.'

He escorted me to the women's quarters, and I lay down and shivered under my robes for a while, and then I got up and washed my face, and ate some hot watered rice and salt plums. I had the girl fetch some paper and an inkstone, and

79

I wrote out my petitions – for Kanesuke, and my son, and his father. How I wished I could afford a thousand prayers for each of them! But my estates hardly yield the means for such extravagances.

I will not squander my meagre earnings on prayers for my own safety. Perhaps if I wilfully neglect her Kannon will avert her gaze, and I can savour some slight taste of danger.

I had arranged to meet my acquaintance after the evening recitations, and I looked for him after I handed my petitions to the priests, and again when I was escorted to my enclosure. But the temple was even more crowded than it had been the previous night, and I didn't see him until I had nearly reached the bottom of the steps.

He greeted me courteously, but there was a distance in his expression that I had not yet seen. Perhaps it was because he was leaving.

Still he walked with me across the courtyard, and inquired if I had been successful in delivering my petitions. So he had noticed me speaking with the priests – that was encouraging.

'Yes,' I said. 'I paid them well, so I hope they will enunciate clearly. I can't imagine that the bodhisattvas pay much heed to prayers that are mumbled.'

'True,' he said. 'Supplications must be clear.' We paused to look at the crescent moon. 'So may I walk with you? Or is my request too vague?'

So he was capable of innuendo – that was encouraging, too. I had thought he was too forthright to have a talent for stratagems.

'Surely,' I said as we walked down the gallery, 'your studies must have acquainted you with the nature of ambiguity. I imagine that an interpreter of omens and signs must be an expert in double meanings.'

'But women are the experts in that regard, are they not?'

'In what – interpreting double meanings, or implying them?'

'Both, I would imagine.'

'I've known men who far surpassed me in their talent for duplicity,' I said as lightly as I could, but the bitterness crept into my voice. 'So – let's speak of something else. Tell me about your adventures.'

'You must mean my travels. But ocean voyages are very dull. The same view, the same food, the same tedious company . . .'

'Rather like being on retreat,' I teased.

'No, but on retreat you can get away – take a walk, see a waterfall. On a boat there is no escape.'

'Still,' I said. 'Something must have happened. Storms, brigands – the sorts of things one reads about in romances.'

So I coaxed the whole tale out of him. There had been storms, but no brigands; heavy winds blew them off course; and only after a long overland journey did they reach Wu-t'ai. What had he seen? Rivers as broad as oceans; great hunger and unexpected courtesies; women with unblackened teeth and bound feet, their necks heavy with jade; monks drinking thick green tea; priests who spoke more animatedly of cuisine than religion. But there was one sight that impressed him more than any other. It was the statue of the Bodhisattva of Manjushrī riding a lion. Yet it was not the saint that moved him, but the lion, which seemed to breathe steam from his mouth, and walk like a living creature.

I asked him about his studies. He had gone to learn geomancy, but had abandoned it for the I Ching, for he found in its sixty-four hexagrams a key to life's mysteries. (They were like living pictures, he told me; they moved as the lion moved.) I watched him as he spoke, and his face reminded me of Kanesuke's when he was describing the Phantom City. I envied his conviction, though it amused me. How like a man, to be animated by the statue of a lion and the patterns of hexagrams!

'And do you go on retreat often?' I asked him.

'No, very seldom.'

'So you do find temples as dull as ships.'

'Hardly. I've just been very busy. Surely you have heard how taxed we've been, with all the storms and fires and ill omens, and now this scandal with the Vestal of Ise.'

So I couldn't escape my troubles even here. He would have heard of Kanesuke, and even the rumours about Sadako might have reached him.

He must have seen a change in my expression, for he stopped and looked at me. I hadn't noticed the flecks of brown in his eyes, and how high his forehead was.

'But I should leave you now. You must be tired.'

Why did his dismissal wound me? He was only being kind. Yet as I lay in my room in the half-dark, the light from the lamp casting long shadows, I began to cry. Perhaps it was that banter about supplications and double meanings, or his talk about the Vestal. Mindful of the thin walls, I tried to suppress my sobs, and my chest ached with the effort.

Some while later I heard a tapping on the door. I held my breath and waited. There it was again – I was not mistaken. Had I disturbed someone, and they had come to complain? There was no more privacy here than there was at the palace.

I got up and stood by the door.

'I'm sorry,' he said, 'but I was walking by, and I thought I heard you crying.'

I let him in. How could I not? But then the tears came again, and my shoulders were shaking. He put his hand on my cheek, and gave me such a grave troubled look – what had I done to deserve such tenderness?

I must have cried in his arms for an hour.

Later, when I was calm, I asked him if he would read my fortune. Not now, I said, some other time, when we were back in the capital.

'Oh, I don't know,' he said, stroking my hair from my forehead. 'You might not like what I say.'

'Why. Will the answer be ambiguous?'

'That depends. If you are direct and honourable in your intentions, the answer may be clear – though it is always subject to interpretation. But if you are devious, and your purpose is uncertain, the answer will be as dubious as your question.'

'I feared as much,' I said. 'For you know I am as unreliable as The Tales of Ise.'

'Yes, I thought perhaps you were,' he said, and kissed me.

Did I please him? I so feared that I would not. But I must have pleased him a little, for he returned the following night, and we didn't sleep until morning.

'Now,' he said as the light grew stronger, 'You must put your head to the north, and turn on your right side, for that is how the Buddha lay when he gave up his body and passed into oblivion.'

'Show me,' I said, and he turned me on my side and held me tight, his chest pressed against my back.

'I don't want to give up my body,' I said.

'Then you will be reborn again and again. If you are devout you must strive for annihilation.'

'If I wanted annihilation I would jump into a river and drown.'

'That is a heavy sin. You would be reborn into a life of suffering, and your children would have to do penance for you their whole lives long.'

Did my spine stiffen? How our bodies betray us, reluctant as we are to leave them!

'I have no children,' I said.

'That's a lie.'

'What?' I asked. 'Do you think you are as clever at reading my past as you are my future?'

83

'No,' he said. 'I can tell by the width of your hips.' And he turned me on my back to show me.

How could he know me so well? How could a man as young as he have such experience? He frightened me.

Still I was glad, for innocence implies a certain responsibility. Perhaps he was less vulnerable than I had thought. Some day I might find out. But there was no time now for inquests and experiments. He was leaving.

Two more hours until he returned to the capital. He was riding back alone; he had no friends or retainers to accompany him. His horse was a chestnut, not a roan like Kanesuke's; he would take the track by the river because it was quicker. He would ride back to his family's house in the Fifth Ward, and I would stay for three more days, as I had planned, for it seemed rash to change my mind, and I didn't want to seem as if I were pursuing him.

I couldn't depend on this boy. I barely knew him.

We spent our two hours without speaking. Only as he knelt to take his leave did he say with the same teasing gravity, 'You must have been virtuous in a previous life.'

So he was telling me he thought me lovely, for the Perceiver of the World's Sounds rewards virtue with beauty. And I recalled the characters that Kanesuke had engraved on my mirror, as if to mock me for what I no longer possessed.

'Ah,' I said, as lightly as I could, 'but I am not virtuous now.'

'Are you so devious?' he asked, stroking my cheek. 'Or do you like to exaggerate your vices?'

'I never exaggerate. It's my sole virtue.'

'I thought as much.' And he kissed me again.

'Will you come and see me now and then?' I asked as he put on his cloak. That neediness; it was so unseemly.

I was wrong to press him. His expression changed, and in it I saw the same guardedness I had noticed two nights earlier, when I had met him on the temple steps.

'Perhaps,' he said. 'I don't trust you very much. You know that, don't you?'

I said nothing.

'Close your eyes.' I did as he said. He traced a pattern of lines on my forehead.

'What is it?' I asked. 'Is that for luck?'

'No.' He smiled at me. 'The opposite: Kuei Mei, the Hexagram of the Marriageable Maiden. Advance brings misfortune. No goal is favourable. To achieve one's aims one must be aware of one's mistakes at the beginning.'

'I am highly aware of my errors,' I said.

'And so am I.' He kissed the hem of my sleeve and left, sliding the door behind him.

How did I spend those three last days? I hardly remember. I heard bells, gongs, the gossip of strangers; I knelt in the smoky stalls, and wrote poems on anise leaves; I walked in the garden and watched the snow melt from the red-budded twigs of the cherry trees. But I didn't search in the woods for the place where I had lain with Kanesuke – for I had done that once, and had never quite recovered – and I tried not to think of that serious boy riding a chestnut mare back to the city, and of his unlucky hexagrams and strange courtesies.

Two letters were waiting for me when I returned.

The first was from Ryūen, who said he was busy day and night, taking down letters for the Abbot. He feared for his sight, working as he did so late by the dim glow of the lamps. There were disputes over reclaimed land, and difficulties with tithes and taxes, and quarrels with other sects. How he longed for the days when he spent his time calmly copying the sutras!

And he had heard rumours. The Emperor wrote to the Abbot often, and while Ryūen was not privy to their correspondence he had gathered from snatches of conversation (for monks are no more discreet than ladies-in-waiting) that His Majesty feared he would be forced to abdicate. For what reason? That he had no daughters worthy of the shrine at Ise, and was therefore a danger to the realm.

Who was behind such a scheme? The Empress's family, including the Minister of the Left. For the minister wrote to the Abbot as well – Ryūen recognised his official seal. No doubt he was pleading the case for the Fujiwara.

And what would become of the Vestal, should the Emperor step down? The heir apparent, being only eleven, could not be expected to produce a suitable daughter any time soon. Ryūen presumed they would break with precedent and choose a girl from outside the royal line. Had I seen, he wondered, the eldest daughter of the Minister of the Left? She was sixteen and perhaps a virgin, and by all accounts a lovely girl.

Yes, I had seen her. She danced at the Gosechi Dances, and Dainagon had praised her. I had been so caught up with my poisonous plans that I had barely noticed.

Look what those plans might set in train! A royal daughter disgraced, an Emperor deposed, a new Fujiwara in the ascendant (for surely the Minister of the Left would be chosen as regent). Should I be flattered that my manipulations might have such effect, or should I be frightened?

I am frightened. What will Ryūen think if he finds out that I was the agent of such a scheme? I couldn't have foreseen the consequences of my plan, but did that make me blameless? And what of Sadako, who has been banished because of my insinuations?

I must conceal these papers well. How fortunate that I had told Buzen to hide any letters I might receive while I was away! If Ryūen's had fallen into the wrong hands, and rumours of the Emperor's abdication had been spread about . . .

The second letter was no less dangerous. It was from the

man I met at Hasedera. (I shall call him Masato, for his real name doesn't suit him, and even if it did I wouldn't disclose it, lest it be tainted by association with my own.)

My hands shook as I unfolded the yellow paper. It is the wrong season for such a colour; why did he choose it? Coming from a man so fond of signs and symbols, there must have been a reason.

When I read his poem it became clear. He had written in Chinese,

> Although it is not autumn, I long for a woman.
> I hear her voice, a lute in the *richi* mode.

So he knew the Book of Songs, even to its commentaries. I called for Buzen to fetch some lavender paper from the palace workshops, and as soon as she returned I wrote back:

> Because it is spring, I long for a man.
> I hear his voice, a flute in the *sō* mode.

So he had missed me. I was more pleased than I ought to have been, given his warnings and prognostications. But I must wait, for that is a woman's lot. He will bolt if I pursue him.

The Empress, who has been indisposed, decided to remove for some days to her mansion in the First Ward. She asked me and a few others to accompany her. I expected that she would ask Izumi, but it seems she is in the country, visiting her sister. I hadn't been to Ichijō Mansion for some time, and the thought of returning caused me some anxiety, for I didn't want to see the Vestal.

I knew the chances were slight. No doubt her mother

kept her confined to her rooms in the western quarter, for I had heard that they barely spoke. Still, I might come across her in the garden, or hear her voice through the blinds . . . I couldn't eat the day we left, and when I was shown to my room I felt so light-headed that I had to lie down. I lay gazing at the ceiling while the other women were unpacking, and I listened to them comparing their new spring gowns.

I spent the first night in no small distress. I lay on my mat thinking of Kanesuke, and wondering if the girl in the southeast quarter was thinking of him, too. Does she hate him? Had he forced himself upon her? I doubt it; that is not his style. He would have tried very hard to elicit some strong feeling from her, if only to hear what she would say.

Can a girl of seventeen speak passionately? Yes. Who can't recall that desperation? At seventeen everything is black and white, and there is nothing that is not worth risking.

There are times now when I feel just as I did when I was her age. Perhaps for that reason I often think of the Vestal with something approaching sympathy. Yet I do not flatter myself into believing that I am kind.

I awoke after that first night with an aching back and a bitter taste in my throat. The day rebuked me with its beauty. The sky was as clear as a virgin's conscience; the light as dazzling as her smile. I dressed carefully and walked out onto the veranda. A cherry tree, nearly as tall and lovely as the one in the gardens of Hasedera, spread its boughs beneath the azure sky. Why had it bloomed so early? Its double flowers, tinged with pink, clustered as thickly as clouds.

I heard a whistle and saw a boy running down the garden path. His purple robes streamed behind him, and his unkempt hair reminded me of Ryūen's when he was young. He must have seen me, for he slowed his pace to a walk and straightened his sleeves. It was Reizei, looking much younger than his eleven years – Reizei, who, if rumours were to be believed, might soon replace his father on the throne.

I bowed, knowing that he would attach to this gesture no great significance, and he smiled back. His teeth are dark (an imperfection he has had since birth) and his smile is as winsome as a woman's. I hid my feelings behind my fan, and we exchanged pleasantries.

'How lovely the cherry is!' I said, gesturing with my hand. 'The ones at the palace haven't even begun to bloom!'

He looked at me and laughed.

'But the flowers aren't real!' he said. 'Look – can't you see the threads?'

Of course. The blossoms had been tied on. But how skilfully they were made, and how subtle the colours of the paper! It was a wonder. I almost didn't mind that they had no scent.

'My mother had them put up,' Reizei said. 'They're for my sister.'

So the Empress was trying to reach her daughter, though they didn't speak. Kanesuke and I had done that sometimes – tried to heal an irreparable breach with gestures.

'And how is your sister?' I asked, as artlessly as I could.

'I don't know,' he said simply. 'I never see her.'

It was hardly surprising, for he was old enough to be sequestered from her. Yet I found his answer disconcerting.

I spent the morning with the Empress, who was feeling poorly despite the change of scene. We sat by the double doors that open onto the garden and looked at coloured pictures from The Tales of Ise. 'As unreliable as The Tales of Ise' – the phrase ran through my mind as I held the scroll in my hands. I had said those words at Hasedera, and then that grave young man had kissed me. I felt such a longing for him that I couldn't speak, and I had to turn my head and look out at the trees so as not to show my feelings.

We came to the picture of the boy teaching his sister how to play the *kin*; he leans over her shoulder and adjusts her wrist as she plucks the strings. I wondered if it would remind the Empress of Reizei and the Vestal, and half-hoped that she would speak of them. But she only sighed and leaned back against her cushions. I thought she looked sad, but perhaps it was her illness that made her face seem so drawn.

She looked out into the garden.

'Have you any daughters?' she asked, and I confined my answer to a simple 'No.' I had never told her about my son, and was not inclined to now.

'How lucky you are,' she said bitterly.

I decided to venture a question about the Vestal. 'Is the Princess unwell? I haven't seen her.'

'If she were I would be the last person she would tell,' said the Empress. 'She doesn't speak to me.' I recalled the arguments they had before the Vestal left the palace, and the Empress's threats and remonstrations. I was glad I had never had a daughter. It was too painful.

I could think of nothing comforting to say, so I offered to read to her. She declined, saying she was too tired. She drew her magenta cloak about her. Did I not feel the chill? she asked. Perhaps I would ring for someone to put more charcoal on the fire.

Then I left her. Later in the afternoon I walked with some of the women in the garden. We admired the pond and its artificial beach of crushed white stone, and the hills festooned with groves of budding trees: birches, cherries, willows, elms, and wild saplings transplanted from the mountains whose names I didn't know. The red blossoms of the plums overhanging the stream were nearly gone, but the wisteria was just beginning to unfurl its silken buds.

'Come in the Third Month, when the wisteria is blooming,' Kanesuke had told Izumi in the letter I had stolen.

Why did every sticky new leaf, every blossom's slow unfolding, remind me of all I had lost? I couldn't see the trees for what they were, for they reminded me of others I had lain under; even the names of the flowers brought back the scent of those that had been given to me. I wished a sudden snow would fall and smother every sign of spring.

On our way back to the house we passed the Vestal's rooms, but the shades were drawn and I could see nothing.

In the evening before the light became dim – for it was growing cloudy, and looked like rain – I sat with some of the women as they were doing their embroidery. Bright skeins of silk were scattered about the floor, and the Empress's cats were playing with them.

A few of the matrons who lived at the house had joined us, and before long they were gossiping.

'It's such a pity,' said the older one, whose name was Taifu. She was a slight woman, as frail as paper, and her hair was silky and grey like the buds of the wisteria. 'She was such a lively girl, and now she hardly leaves her room.' They were speaking of the Vestal, whom they called Yukiko, for they had known her long before she went to Ise.

'We had to hide the scissors from her,' said the younger woman – I think her name was Sagami. 'She kept threatening to cut off her hair. Imagine: wanting to be a nun at seventeen!' There was something coarse about this woman, with her fuchsia dress and unplucked brows. She was the sort of person who attracts scandal.

I recalled hearing the story Buzen had told me soon after the Vestal had returned to the palace. So the Princess was as desperate now as she was then.

'We even took away her dagger,' said Taifu, 'for we were afraid of what she might do. Poor girl – how many times I've heard her say she didn't want to live!'

'But you know how she is,' replied Sagami. 'Always acting out her tales and romances. She's very dramatic – and stubborn, too. She refuses to eat, and if you ask her a question she won't answer.'

'Does she speak to anyone, then?' I asked.

'Barely,' said Taifu. She smoothed the satin jacket on her lap. 'I try to talk to her, but she'll have no more to do with me than she will with her mother. She'll write her a note now and then – if she wants something. And of course the Emperor will have nothing to do with her. But she says she doesn't care.'

'Surely she is allowed to send letters,' I said.

'No,' Taifu replied. 'The Empress has seen to that. She caught her trying to bribe a courier with one of her hair combs – the very one her father gave her when she was sent to Ise – and now she is forbidden correspondence of any sort.'

'Do you mean she can't even receive letters?' I asked. Sagami gave me a sharp look, as if she found my interest in the matter excessive. 'I tried to send her one myself,' I lied, 'but it was returned. The messenger said it was a day of abstinence.'

'Every day is a day of abstinence for her,' Sagami said. 'The Empress intercepted a letter for her soon after she came here, at the beginning of the year. Her Highness kept the messenger waiting by the gate and steamed the letter open so as not to damage the seal and read it. She was furious – you should have seen her face. Then she sealed it up again and gave it back to the man, saying that her daughter couldn't accept it.'

'Who was the letter from?' inquired one of the women. I was grateful that someone else had asked the question.

'I expect it was from Kanesuke,' said Sagami. 'The messenger looked as if he had come a long way.'

How I hated hearing his name said by such a woman – in such an offhand tone, as if she knew him well. I thought that some of the others glanced at me, though I had no reason to suspect that they knew my history, unless the gossip about my private life had spread further than I had anticipated.

So Kanesuke had written to the Vestal, knowing full well

that the letter might fall into the wrong hands. I wondered if it had been sent in the same packet with the letter I had received from him soon after the New Year. He had said he was lonely, and I thought he implied that he loved me.

We heard the bells ring at Shakuzen for the evening service.

'But I must go to Yukiko,' said Taifu. 'I hadn't realised it was so late.' She dropped the jacket she had been embroidering and hurried down the hall, her lacquered shoes tapping on the floor.

'One would think she was minding a child, not a grown woman,' I observed.

'It's just that we must never leave her alone – Yukiko, I mean,' said Sagami. 'We take turns.' She explained that one evening in the First Month Taifu had left the Vestal's room to fetch a lamp, and when she came back the girl was gone. They searched the house and the gardens, and found her hiding in a grove of willows not far from the pond.

'That's hardly a crime,' I said. 'Perhaps she just wanted to be alone.' What a prison it was for her here; she had had more freedom amongst her priests at Ise.

I left the women then and went back to my room, and stayed up late reading the Manyōshū. When the moon was high I got up and looked into the courtyard. I could see a light behind the lattices in the western quarter. Was she awake, or was some woman watching over her? How she must resent their constant presence.

I put on a padded jacket and slipped out into the gallery. I crossed the bridge over the stream that ran between the house and the west wing. The air was cold, and the sound of the running water seemed very loud. I felt for the door and slid it open. The glow of the lamp drew me. I slipped into the anteroom and looked through a gap in the standing curtain. A woman was standing with her back to me. All I could see was the black river of her hair, which flowed past her gowns onto the floor.

I must have made a sound, for she turned towards me. For an instant I saw her as Kanesuke must have once: her brilliant eyes, her thin red lips, her white forehead as smooth as polished stone. Then her face contracted in fury, and she snapped her fingers as if to banish a ghost.

'Be gone!' she hissed, and pulled the curtain across. I stood there trembling. Had she known who I was, or had she simply taken me for a servant who had come to spy on her? That look she had given me – how poisonous it was!

I woke in the morning to the sound of rain. Some time later I heard a noise in the courtyard. I got up and pulled back the blinds and looked out. Two men were busy tearing down the sodden flowers from the cherry tree. Heaps of crumpled paper lay upon the ground.

We spoke of the incident later that morning, as I sat with the women as they were doing their embroidery. Taifu wasn't there, for she had been up late with the Vestal, who was suffering from a headache. The lamps had been lit, for it was too dark to thread a needle, and rain drummed on the roof.

'The Empress was furious,' Sagami told us. 'She had told the men to take the flowers down before dawn, before anyone could see them.' Her Highness had docked them a month's wages for their carelessness. Then all the women agreed that she had a right to be angry, for there is nothing less appealing than the look of paper flowers after they have been drenched.

Found a copy of the I Ching, and studied the second hexagram. K'un, the Passive One. Six broken lines to depict a woman.

K'un, the Passive One. Sublime success! She is a shining

vessel, both empty and full. She is a haven, both dark and soft. She is a mare wandering unfettered through her confines. She loses her way but then finds her bearings. She makes friends in the south and west, but loses those in the east and north – yet both are cause for rejoicing.

I read the commentaries on the lines, each its own poem.

The first line: Hoarfrost underfoot betokens the coming of solid ice. Winter is approaching and we must proceed with caution.

The second: The way is straight and broad. Though we do nothing, all our affairs prosper.

The third: Beauty is finest when hidden. Deference is more fruitful than contention.

The fourth: Taciturnity: no blame, no praise. When we are watchful we escape trouble.

The fifth: A yellow jacket. Sublime good fortune! Virtue is the finest raiment.

The sixth: Dragons fighting in the wilderness spill black and yellow blood. When a woman strives to be like a man, her merit is exhausted.

Do these six broken lines describe my life? I do not shine; I am not a haven; my confines are too cramped to permit unfettered wandering. I have no sense of direction, and my friends become my enemies all too often. I am not cautious, modest or taciturn, and my virtues have been stained irreparably by my vices.

Yet I have striven to be like a man. Of all the wisdom in those lines, that is the truest.

The nineteenth of the Second Month.

I learned this morning that Izumi has contrived her own fiction, and has spread it wide so as to damage me.

She wrote a story and copied it out and gave it to her friends. Even the Empress has read it, Dainagon says, and was much amused. It is only a matter of time before it spreads to the Emperor and the senior courtiers. I suppose that then it will filter down, just as silt settles to the bottom of a pond, until the very guards and chambermaids will laugh as I walk past.

How did I learn of this little tale? I had gone to Buzen's room to borrow a mirror. She was sorting her gowns with her friends in preparation for tomorrow's festival.

They all looked up as I walked in, and I thought I had surprised them in some secret conversation, for Buzen coughed and looked down at the green dress that she held in her lap.

'I'm sorry,' I said hastily. 'I didn't mean to intrude.'

'It's nothing,' she replied – but she wouldn't look at me as she spoke.

I retrieved the mirror, went back to my room and rummaged in the box where I keep my sashes, for I worried that the one I planned to wear the following day was the wrong shade. I turned and noticed the pages on my writing desk. Was it a letter? It wasn't folded. Perhaps someone had opened it in my absence.

It was Izumi's story. Someone had left it for me while I was out, though I had been gone only a short time.

When I found Dainagon in her rooms a while later (for I had to wash the tears from my face and fortify my looks with rouge and powders) she had already read it.

She was sitting in the anteroom, playing the *biwa*. Her back was very straight, and her hair fell in clean lines all around her. I looked at her long fingers as they held the plectrum and I heard the notes fall one by one. It was a tune I didn't know, a Chinese song in the *ōshiki* mode.

I stood and watched her, envying her graceful rectitude. She looked up, and her eyes filled with tears.

'I'm sorry,' she said, laying down her instrument. 'I would have come to you, but I didn't know what to say.'

She stood and looked at me closely and then she leaned and touched my cheek. I had not been touched like that since I was a girl. I closed my eyes and thought of my mother, and of Masato, who had traced the lines of the unlucky hexagram on my forehead. The Marriageable Maiden. Advance brings misfortune. No goal is now favourable.

Would he read Izumi's story, too? Would someone whisper the plot in his ear, saying, 'Listen to this tale of an unbalanced woman.' Perhaps he would laugh, recalling my tears and pleadings.

Dainagon walked to the sliding door, glanced up and down the hall, and closed it. We would have a few minutes alone. Her maids were gone, sent off to the Imperial Wardrobes to find a beaded train for the next day's festivities. How I dreaded them now, those sentimental ceremonies in praise of blossoming cherries: the songs, the poems, the Emperor's smiles and dispensations, and that sea of pale curious faces.

We sat on cushions in the anteroom. The winter light was thin. I pressed my lips together and tried to control my feelings.

'So,' said Dainagon, as gently as she could, 'Is it true?' And I knew she was referring to the rumours.

So even she suspected that I was capable of such treachery. I recalled the look she had given me at the procession of blue horses, when she told me that the Vestal and Sadako had been disowned. 'There is cause and there is effect,' she had said. Then she had given me that cool admonitory look, as if to say that if I had been an agent in this plot I must be prepared to suffer the consequences.

For plots, as any writer knows, must be played out; they must twist and ramify until they reach their inevitable conclusion. The good must be rewarded, the cruel vilified and punished. If they are not, one's readers will be disappointed. And how realistic should such a cautionary tale be?

97

Should its author take her characters from life and base them on her own experience? Should she draw the blood straight from the vein, dark in its implication? Or should she write an allegory or fable, set in some place far removed in distance and time? Should she create another past, and thus evade her own? Or will her readers accuse her of invention, of false and imperfect depictions of people whose language and customs are so unlike our own as to be incomprehensible?

Should she write, say, of the loves of Yang Kuei-fei, and in so doing cast some light on our own unfortunate passions? Should she write of the ancient Han, or the blue-eyed barbarians who make love in the snow? Or should she confine her talent to close observations of her own world?

Either way she cannot win. She will be accused either of falsity or lack of imagination.

And how did Izumi choose to cast her little tale? Oh, it was very real, and she was scrupulous in her observations – though many of her sources were second-hand and not to be trusted.

She wrote about a woman (the name had been changed) who was so unbalanced that she scratched words on her favourite mirror, and hired messengers at exorbitant prices to carry her letters far and wide. It was said she had them sent as far as Akashi, but the letters were returned unopened, and she kept them in a yellow brocade bag. Her hair was unkempt, her fingers stained with ink, her nails bitten to the quick. At night she wore the same lavender shift regardless of the season. Lately she had taken to reading the I Ching, and she had been seen on more than one occasion painting its hexagrams on her arms.

She never slept. She sang to herself. On various public occasions – parties, progresses, moon viewings, confessions – she could be seen standing alone, her black eyes staring.

How did this proud mad woman spend her time? She

recited poems, and bantered in the halls with men; she told stories, and coaxed tales out of her friends, and even from the guards and maids. No secret was safe with her. She broadcast everything she heard.

And she was adept with rumour. It was her speciality, just as other women excel in dyeing cloth or playing the zither. Her sources were variable, her methods unrestrained. She stole letters and bribed accomplices; she invented tales.

She had been known to spread stories about envoys and princesses. Some of her rumours had abetted their banishment.

Was the heroine of Izumi's tale punished for her manipulations? Did she suffer a fever or fall from a flight of steps? Were her rooms struck by lightning or wrecked in a typhoon?

No. She suffered no such thing. In this regard Izumi showed an appalling lack of imagination.

And if she spared her heroine bodily harm, did she blight her with guilt and remorse? Did she suffer nightmares? Did she find no comfort in the sutras?

No. She was not punished at all. Those who have no conscience cannot suffer its effects.

That, of course, is my own interpretation, for Izumi was too clever to resort to such heavy-handedness. She merely described, and let her readers draw their own conclusions.

Dainagon had drawn hers. 'So is it true?' she asked me again.

'Do you think I would be capable of all that?' I said, hoping my tone would mask my guilt.

'Well,' she said lightly, 'One does all sorts of things for love.'

She picked up her plectrum and turned it in her hands. I waited for another question. I had almost hoped for an interrogation so that I could defend myself.

'And Kanesuke?' she asked. 'What does he know of all this?'

'He'll know everything soon enough,' I said. Someone would send him a copy of the story, or it would be described to him in a letter.

'What a pair you are,' Dainagon said, picking up her instrument. 'One liar deserves another.' She had always disliked him – that was plain. Now she would dislike me.

I sat and bit my lip, but I couldn't stop the tears from running down my cheeks.

Then she played that song again, the Chinese one in the *ōshiki* mode. She watched the strings as she plucked them, but I could tell that she knew I was crying.

'The difference is,' she said as she played, 'that you lie for love, and he lies for pleasure.'

'That's not true. Why do you hate him so?'

She glanced up. 'Look what he's done to you.'

I left her then. The clear strain of her song followed me down the hall.

Ukon had spread out my clothes for the following day. She was lacquering my shoes; the odour made me feel faint. She wouldn't look me in the eye. So she had gossiped about the lavender shift and Kanesuke's letters!.I wore the shift because Kanesuke gave it to me; he had bought the silk in Kyūshū when he was on one of his journeys. He didn't return my letters unopened. That was a lie. And who had told Izumi about the hexagrams and the I Ching?

'May I get you anything, my lady?' she asked, and I told her coldly that I wanted nothing. She crept away, no doubt to report my mood to her friends.

I read Izumi's story one more time – for I couldn't resist that last twist of pain – and then I burned it in the fire. I looked at the clothes splayed on the rack: the rose-coloured trousers, the pale green gowns, the red jacket embroidered with five patterns of mauve and purple thread, the damask train. Would their beauty make me strong? Would they shield me from tomorrow's furtive smiles and glances?

No, they would not. I would trade them all for a demon's straw cloak, for only it has the power to make me invisible.

The twentieth of the Second Month, evening.

I am shut in my room. The dances go on. The blinds are closed but the music seeps in like the moonlight.

The others are gone, and I am glad of my prison. My festive clothes hang on their frame, the arms outstretched in welcome. Outside the dancers toss their sleeves, and the petals of the cherry trees fall to the ground like motes of dust, like ashes.

It is untrue that cherry blossoms look like snow. The poets have sworn it so many times that we believe them.

Are the petals falling from the Cherry of the Left? We stood in the Great Courtyard and bowed to it, and addressed it as if it were a living person. The courtiers declaimed their poems in its honour. The Emperor extolled its modest virtues. The dancers spread their arms to mime its arching boughs.

But the Orange of the Right is split. The typhoon damaged it, and despite its props and trusses it will never thrive as it did in the times of Nara.

Whom did I see at this splendid ceremony? I saw Izumi, though she wouldn't look at me. Her colour was so heightened that she seemed to blush, and her lips were trembling. I saw her friends, and heard one say as she passed by me, 'Look! She's not wearing lavender today.' I saw two nobles from the Ministry of Central Affairs, and they smiled at me, and one whispered to the other, 'It's Kanesuke's mad lover.'

How I needed him then. But he is too far away.

I didn't see Masato. Perhaps he had heard Izumi's story and decided not to come.

I saw the Emperor, who stood on the dais near the steps of the Shishinden, his face the image of beneficence. I couldn't see Reizei or the Empress, who stood on either side, enclosed within their screens. I thought of Sadako and the Vestal, as invisible as demons, and wondered if they were shut up in their rooms.

How I envied them! I wished I were hidden in a house far from the palace, or shielded by screens and curtains, like the Empress. Instead I stood, bare and affronted, my shame as vivid as the clouds at sunset.

Dainagon found me when the crowd broke up for the dances. She looked at my face and saw everything I had tried to conceal.

'Has it been so very hard?' she asked me, and I nodded my head.

We stood side by side in the twilight, watching the dancers. The flutes and drums echoed in the frost-bound air. We watched the men mime the Spring Warbler and the Garden of Flowers and Willows, and then I left her and returned to my rooms.

I wrote to Masato. The letter contained not a single word, just a pattern of six straight and broken lines. Ming I: The Hexagram of Injury.

Would he come, hoping to find how I had been wounded? Or would he stay away, fearing that my hurt would injure him as well?

Four days of waiting. Nightmares in the dark, a dizzying clarity in the day. Outlines too sharp, noises too loud, whispers as portentous as shadows.

He came, and was so appalled by what he saw that he took me away. 'What have you done?' he asked, leaning over me as I lay on my bed. He brushed my hair from my face, and didn't seem to mind my wrinkled dress or my eyes encrusted with tears or my thinness. He pressed his hand to my forehead, as a mother does to assay a fever, and said he was sorry he couldn't come sooner. His mother was ill, and he couldn't travel, or even send a letter. It was only by chance that he had received mine, for it had arrived on the very day she had taken to her bed.

I looked at him and marvelled at how much I had forgotten. The high forehead, the wide eyes flecked with brown, the flared cheekbones, the faint blue shadow above his lip. If I had misremembered him so thoroughly, how could I possibly rely on my recollections of Kanesuke, whom I haven't seen since the first days of autumn?

He lifted my hair, which spread in tangles across the bedclothes, and lay by my side. 'You must rest,' he said, 'and get away from all of this.' Did he know, then, the cause of my affliction? I wasn't brave enough to ask, so I closed my eyes and listened to his plan.

He told me that his mother had a house east of the city, in the foothills near Mizunomi Pass, not far from the Otowa River. We could go there; it was not very far. It was empty at this time of year, for it was barely spring in the mountains. We could stay for a few days until I was better. He would send a carriage for me in the morning, to the Kenshun Gate, and he would follow me as soon as he could, after he had seen to his mother. The caretakers would look after me until he arrived; I was to show them a letter, which he would entrust to my driver.

I pondered the ease with which he proposed these arrangements, and wondered how often he had made them before, and for whom.

Was I to be jealous so soon? I had sworn I wouldn't open that door again, knowing full well that my resolve would weaken. Hadn't I been glad he was not too innocent? I was not glad now.

'Why are you so kind to me?' I asked, and half-hoped

he wouldn't answer. I didn't want his pity, and his manner worried me. Was I as ravaged as his look implied?

'I'm not kind. I'm very selfish,' he said, and kissed me.

'You may take your maid with you if you like,' he added. 'Though I'm very good at combing hair.'

Yes, I was sure he was – and not his mother's.

I shook my head and told him I preferred to make the trip alone. 'You must leave now,' I said. Ukon was sure to be back soon, and there was no telling who else might have heard us. It was risky for him to come; I shouldn't have asked him.

'Can you be ready early? It won't be too much of a strain?'

'No,' I said, and smiled at him, though his solicitude provoked me. I wasn't infirm like his mother.

I rose early and packed my things. When Ukon asked where I was going I told her I was visiting a distant cousin.

'Ah, a cousin,' she said, and I fled from her sceptical look.

I recall little of the drive, for I was tired and slept most of the way. The day was overcast and cold. A fox ran across the road, and I saw three sparrows sitting on the branch of a chestnut tree.

I thought of Kanesuke. How many times had I driven up a mountain road in anticipation of our meeting? I would look at the view spread out like a scroll and see it with his eyes, not my own. I lived inside his mind; the twisted track would unwind from his vantage.

Why, then, this new betrayal? Was this boy merely filling an absence? Did I find him less complicated? More worthy of my trust?

Yet he did not trust me at all. His reserve was palpable. The Marriageable Maiden. (I was not.) Advance brings misfortune. (It always would.) No goal is now favourable. (Nor would it be, ever, and he knew it as well as I; it was the foundation of our understanding.)

Can love be made of negation? Could he say 'I trust you not' and make me think he might trust me yet? Can trust be made of mistrust? Can love be made from want of love? My thoughts went round and round like the wheels of the carriage; they meandered like the bends in the road. Yet as I looked out and saw the budding laurels, and the glades of elms and oaks, and the sky half-cleared of cloud and filled with the light of early spring, I wished that love could be made of negation – and almost thought it possible. And I felt guilty for wanting it, because of Kanesuke.

We arrived near dusk; I saw two swallows dip under the eaves of the house and flicker off into the twilight. The villa stood on a rise, the wooded slopes of Mount Hiei to the east and the valley of the Otowa River spreading beneath it. I saw cedars, dark against the twilit sky, and groves of bamboo. A woven fence enclosed the house, whose upswept curves and shadowed foldings reminded me of a bird as it alights and settles its wings. Its deep porches were hidden behind tall rhododendrons and camellias, whose white buds shone within the mass of glossy leaves.

I stepped down and smelled wood smoke and the clean resin of the cedars. Dogs barked, light spilled through an open door, and a girl in blue twill, her hair pinned up and her apron blotted, reached up and handed me a branch of pink camellias.

'The first ones. The others haven't opened,' she said, as if she had known I was coming and had waited for me the whole afternoon.

Why should that simple gesture by a girl in a dirty apron bring tears to my eyes? The dogs ran up, barking and wagging their tails, and the girl and her brother – I assumed it was her brother, for they had the same foxlike faces – were so busy holding them back that I managed to wipe my eyes with my sleeve and behave as if nothing had happened.

I handed my letter to a slight and civil woman in a green patterned robe who seemed too old to be the mother of the children – but then I am hardly experienced in country ways.

She bowed and took the letter inside, pausing to leave her hemp sandals on the porch – and only then did it occur to me that she couldn't read it. I heard a man's voice and a brief exchange of words, and then they both appeared (the man lean, quick, deferent, younger than the woman – her son, perhaps?) and helped me with my bags and boxes.

And I wondered as they led me through the house (which was dark but clean, the cypress floors scrubbed and the pillars gleaming) at the ease with which they took me in. Were they accustomed to sheltering injured women? No, surely not; the others would have been gayer, and younger than I . . . but I mustn't think of it.

The wing where I was to be installed gave to the east, as far as I could tell, for it was nearly dark. Far down the slope I could hear the sound of the stream. The room was wide and cold, and I waited impatiently as the woman unrolled the mats and fanned the coals in the square iron brazier. There was a chest against one wall, and a cupboard full of scrolls and scripture cases, and a deep alcove for a picture, but it was empty.

I drank a bowl of soup flavoured with miso and thin shavings of lotus root. The lacquered bowl, deep brown with reddish flecks, was light in my hands. I stood, my legs stiff from tiredness and the ride in the cramped carriage, and walked about the room. The standing curtain by the bed was hung with stained yellow brocade figured with vines and chrysanthemums. I opened the chest, which smelled of incense, and smoothed the silks and damasks. They were women's clothes: gauzy summer shifts and robes patterned with hail and clouds, and layerings of rue and maidenflower. Who had worn them?

I studied the scrolls and picked up the scripture cases, though I dared not open them. There was a black one inlaid with shells and whorls of mother-of-pearl. Had he held this case when he was a child? Did he trace its filigrees, as I did?

I laid the branch of camellias in the empty alcove, and thought of the boughs of anise that Masato had given me at the temple of Hase. Their leathery softness. Their sanctified fragrance, which reminded me of Kanesuke. I thought of the statue that Masato had seen at the temple in Wu-t'ai of the Bodhisattva of Manjushrī riding a lion, and how the flanks of the lion rippled as if it were a living creature.

It came to me then that the only thing that is holy about a temple is its emptiness. Everything else is superfluous.

I lay on the mat and grew tired of waiting. In the dark – for the wicks had burned down – all the fears that I had managed to push to the boundaries of my mind crowded in, like weeds in an unkempt garden. He wouldn't come. He had changed his mind. His mother was worse, and had asked him to stay by her side; he would send word tomorrow with a messenger. He had been attacked by bandits (for Ryūen had told me stories about the empty tracks near Mount Hiei) and was lying by the side of the road, bleeding.

How luxuriantly one's fears grow in the dark! Exposed to the sun they wither and recede, but at night they are rampant.

I must have fallen asleep, for when he touched my cheek I started. He had lit a lamp, and I saw his face, drawn with concern and tiredness.

'I'm sorry I'm so late.' No explanations. 'Are you warm enough? The fire must have burned out.'

'No,' I said, and he slid under the robes and lay by my side.

'Your hands are cold,' I told him, and I took them and slid them under my robe and held them to my dress. He kissed me, and I reached up to hold his face. I touched his cheeks and felt their smoothness, and stroked his hair, which was still cool from the journey.

'Lie on me,' I said, and he obeyed (was he always so docile?), balancing himself so as not to crush me.

'No, with all your weight,' I told him, and he did as I said – and I was glad to have him heavy on my chest, though I could barely breathe.

He kissed me again, and turned me on my side so we were facing each other in the half-dark, with no one nearby to overhear us, and not a sound except the noise of the stream.

'So,' he said, stroking my hair from my forehead, 'What is your injury?'

I told him everything: about my lies, and Izumi's story, though I left out the part about the lavender shift and Kane-suke's letters. Why? Perhaps because I didn't want him to know how fraught I was – and because I didn't want to make him jealous.

When I had finished he lay on his back and looked at the ceiling, from which came an indeterminate rustling – of birds or squirrels or some such creature.

'What are you thinking?' I asked.

He said nothing.

'I've made you angry.'

'No,' he said after a while. 'I was just thinking how easy it is to ruin a life.' And I knew he meant the Vestal and Sadako.

'And will I ruin yours?' I asked, with no small measure of bitterness.

'No, I don't think so,' he said. 'But you might try.'

The wick burned down and we lay in the dark for a while without speaking.

'I don't believe in confessions,' I said.

He laughed. 'Don't you?'

'People confess because they want to be absolved. They expect a reward.'

'Absolution isn't a reward. It's a gift.'

'But you won't absolve me, will you?'

'That's beyond my power.'

'Like telling the future,' I teased him, remembering our conversation at Hasedera.

'Exactly.'

'And you won't forgive me, either?'

'Probably not,' he said.

'But you understand why I did what I did – spread the rumours, I mean?'

'I expect you thought you did it for love,' he said, 'or fear of losing it. But I imagine that pride had something to do with it.'

'Did it?' I asked, trying to keep the defensiveness from my voice.

'You could still take it back – your insinuation.'

'How?'

'You could go to the Empress and say that the rumour about Kanesuke and Sadako was false.'

'But Izumi implied that in her story. And she said that I was the one who spread the rumours about the Vestal, which isn't true.'

'So you would use her as a screen to hide your guilt.'

'But I couldn't possibly go to the Empress and tell her. It would make me look cruel.'

'Indeed.'

'But people are already gossiping about me!' I began to cry. 'You should see how they look at me – as if I were mad.'

'Like Lady Han,' he said quietly, and stroked my cheek.

I sat up. 'Don't ever, ever call me that,' I said. I still remembered the day Kanesuke sent a white fan to me, inscribed with the words "To my dear Lady Han.'

'I'm sorry,' he said, and I think he meant it, for he kissed me even as I cried. His mouth tasted like salt, and his hands were gentle as they held me.

Later he reached over and brought the lamp close and raised the wick. Then he said in that high serious tone of his, 'Let me look at you. Just for a little while.' And he took the shift that was bunched around my waist and drew it over my head.

I turned over, cold and humiliated, and lay with my face to the mat. How dreadful it is to be seen without clothes! I felt like a caterpillar torn from its silken shroud.

'But I have so many flaws,' I protested, my voice muffled by the bedclothes.

'Have you?' he asked, stroking my back.

'Yes.'

'Let's see, then.' And he turned me gently until I lay on my back, and I closed my eyes and trembled with embarrassment.

'No, I don't think so,' he said. 'Not that I can tell.'

'But I have other flaws,' I said, my eyes still closed.

'Perhaps.' He caressed my breasts.

'And you mustn't trust me.'

'I don't.'.

'And it would be very wrong for you to love me, because I love someone else.'

'I know.' He slid his hands down to the small of my back, and tilted me up, and kissed every curve and hollow.

Later I lay on his chest, my head resting on his shoulder. I looked at the yellow curtain as he stroked my hair.

'You won't ever say you love me, will you?'

No answer – but he still stroked my hair.

'Even if you did, you would never say it, would you?'

Still no answer.

'I won't tell you I love you, either,' I said to the yellow curtain.

'Ah,' he said. 'So then we're even.'

How that hurt me. It had been a game until then; I held the stone in my hand, not knowing if it were black or white or if I had a chance of winning.

I drew a breath. 'So,' I said, 'tell me something philosophical.'

He laughed. 'What do you mean?'

'If you won't say you love me, tell me something else.'

'I was thinking I wished I could be the one to carry you across the Mountain of Death.'

So he was saying, in his calm elided way, that he wished he had been my first lover.

'And would I be as light as my sins?'

'Much lighter.'

'But you've had more lovers than I,' I said, not wishing for an answer.

'It's best not to speak of that, isn't it?'

'And if you carried me to the River of Three Fords,' I said, 'which one would we have to cross?'

'The very deepest,' he replied. 'Without a doubt.'

'Why did you bring me here?' I asked. 'It wasn't to make me better, was it?'

'I don't know.'

'And are you sorry, now that you've seen all my flaws?'

'Yes and no.'

'And what does your book of divination say about us? You must have asked.'

'It says it is all your fault.' And he turned my head and kissed me again, and I pressed against him as hard as I could so that I might crush the breath out of him.

'It is your fault,' he said, in rhythm with our lovemaking. It is your fault. It is your fault. It is your fault.

How did we spend the rest of those three days? Already I am forgetting. I see him in the bath, his body wan as a ghost, and I think it was the second day and not the first. I see his face as we lay under the plum tree in the garden, his closed eyelids translucent like the fallen petals; and I can't recall if it was then that he said that I reminded him of his sister who died when she was nine, or if it was the following morning.

I wish I had a scroll so long I could write down everything: the words we said and the others we implied, and the silences in between. And I would read it even when I could no longer see him, when he had changed in ways that were unknown to me.

On the last afternoon we took a walk through the woods at the edge of the garden to an outcrop of rocks where a stream ran down to the valley. Where the path was rough he picked me up and carried me. We rested by the stream, on a smooth stone overhung with maples. The trees were just coming into bud, and the mossy rocks of the stream were bordered with arching sprays of kerria roses.

I leaned my head against his chest.

'Do you remember?' I asked. '"On the rock we write verses and brush away green moss."'

'Yes, but that poem is about autumn,' he said. 'I was thinking of the one that says, "Late at night I lie down alone. For whom shall I dust off the bed?"'

'That is very sad,' I said, and I turned and kissed him.

'There was a frost last night,' he said, brushing his lips against my cheek. 'So did you dream of home?'

'No.' I looked at the stream. 'Tell me what you looked like when you were a boy.'

He smiled. 'I was thin.'

'And were you mischievous?'

'Very.'

'But not cruel.'

'Sometimes. You know how boys can be.'

'And were you philosophical?'

He smiled again.

'No. All I cared about was kickball.'

'Just like my son.'

'I knew you had children.'

'Only one.'

'And is he philosophical?'

'I wouldn't know.'

I turned and threw a pebble in the stream, and he asked,

sensing my aversion, 'So what did you look like when you were a girl?'

'I hardly remember, it was so long ago. I had very long hair.'

'And was it as thick as it is now?' He ran his hand through it to show me.

'Thicker.'

'You'll never cut it, will you?'

'Perhaps when I'm thirty-seven.'

'That's a dangerous year for a woman.'

'Yes, it's very unfair. You won't be in danger until you're forty-two.'

'That's not so very long from now.'

'You're being philosophical again,' I said, pulling his sleeve. 'But it does mean we have quite a long time, doesn't it? I have eight years, and you have nineteen.'

'Yes,' he said, and he loosened the cord at my waist.

The next morning he left when it was still dark, riding his chestnut mare. I left a little later in my carriage, which no longer seemed cramped, but wide and empty.

'Late at night I lie down alone. For whom shall I dust off the bed?' The words ran through in my mind as we pitched down the rutted road, and then I realised I was saying them in his voice and not my own.

So I lived in his voice now, not Kanesuke's. The thought frightened me. We were not alike, this boy and I. I remembered what Dainagon had said about Kanesuke on the morning I discovered Izumi's story. 'What a pair you are,' she had told me. 'One liar deserves another.' It is true: we are bound by our cruelties and our faults. I don't deserve this boy with his gentle hands and grave pronouncements. I will harm him just as surely as I have the others, whether I want to or not. He said so himself. And I felt the burden of his prediction more keenly than I had felt the weight of his body.

We crossed the moat with its stench of rubbish and rode through the Yōmei Gate into the city. The air was thick with crows, and a cold wind blew through the bare branches of the trees. Courtiers hurried by, holding their black caps to their heads. When I stepped down my gowns blew about me, and the white stones of the courtyard hurt my feet. I called a guard to take my things, and I went back to my blinds and screens and thin-walled rooms.

Last day of the Second Month. Abstinence.

I have been barricaded in my rooms since I returned and have seen no one but the servants and Dainagon. She brought me a copy of The Tales of Ise, and I wondered if she did so to remind me of the dangers of loving Kanesuke.

She didn't ask me where I had gone, but I could tell she was curious. If Ukon had told her the tale about my cousin I'm sure she didn't believe it.

I kept my composure as we spoke, and only as she stood to take her leave did my eyes fill with tears.

'You must be proud,' she told me. 'Hiding in your rooms will only make people talk.' She looked me up and down, noting the shadows under my eyes and my bitten nails. 'Come to me if you need me.' Then she slipped past the screen, her brocade robes trailing behind her on the floor, and I wished that for just one day I could inhabit that faultless body.

I kneel at my desk and try to write, but Masato's letter distracts me. He sent it yesterday; I keep it in my sleeve. It is blue and says little, for he is as circumspect in his correspondence as he is in his speech. But if I read it very closely I am sure that I see, hidden within the expanse between each line, evidence that he loves me.

Third Month

First day. The Hour of the Snake.

I was surprised late last night by the voice of a privy page announcing that I was wanted by the Empress in her chambers.

I shivered as I dressed. Surely she wanted to speak to me about Sadako. She would accuse me of spreading false rumours, and I would be dismissed ... I shouted at Ukon for snagging the comb in my hair, and spilled powder on the floor, and scolded myself for having been too lazy to take a bath or blacken my teeth. It took me the better part of an hour to put myself together. I tied the cords to my trousers tightly, to give myself some semblance of rectitude, and as a result I could barely breathe.

The corridor was empty. I walked as decorously as I could, holding my fan before my face and hoping I wouldn't be seen. Two palace guards sauntered past but took no notice of me, and I confess that even in my consternation I felt a pang that they had no regard for my finery.

When I reached the doors of the Kokiden I could sense that something was wrong. Pages and courtiers idled in the halls, trying to look inconspicuous, and I could see the robes of various ladies-in-waiting flowing from behind the screens where they had tried to hide themselves.

I heard voices, and then I understood. The Emperor and the Empress were arguing. The words were indistinct, but it was clear enough that the exchange was not pleasant.

So the Emperor had gone to her apartments; that in itself was something to remark on, for as a rule she goes to him.

I stood in the hall, wavering. Surely the Empress would have no use for me, and I could retreat to my rooms. But then I heard her mention Sadako's name, and I decided to stay.

I crept along the hall, hoping that the eavesdroppers wouldn't notice me, until I came to a vestibule where the chambermaids wait until they are called to duty. Luckily it was empty. I slipped inside and knelt on the floor, too shaken to stand.

'She is my daughter, not yours,' the Emperor was saying. So they were still speaking of Sadako.

'That may be,' said the Empress with her usual calmness, 'But you have no right to punish her if she is innocent.'

'I will do with her as I like.'

'So you think rumour stronger than truth.'

'A rumour is nothing – but it is everything if people choose to make it so.'

'So you would be governed by falsity?'

'I am governed by what I believe to be true: that my daughters have deceived me.'

'Our daughter was seduced.'

'And she seduced me into believing in her purity.'

'She never lied to you.'

'She never told me the truth. If I choose not to speak to her it is my right. She is nothing to me!' He was shouting. She doesn't exist, and I will not have you speak of her.'

'Nor of Sadako.'

'No.'

'Though she is your daughter, and may well be innocent.'

'She is not my daughter, and she is not innocent.'

'My Lord,' said the Empress, 'You don't deserve your throne.'

'And you don't deserve your tongue. If I had my sword I would cut it out.'

'Your sword!' she mocked him. 'Your sword that keeps you company when you visit your havens and consorts! Your sword that rests by your pillow as you sleep! Can your sword put out fires? Can it banish disease? I hope that it can, for if you do not forgive your daughters these things will happen.

'My Lord' – her tone softened – 'at least forgive Sadako. For if there is no girl to send to Ise – and you know this as well as I – may Kannon in all her guises save us.'

'There is no disaster worse than the ingratitude of a child.'

He left her then. The Empress was weeping. Her women abandoned their hiding places and gathered round her, and I fled down the corridor.

As I turned the corner to make my way back to the Umetsubo I heard the Emperor ranting as he returned to the Seiryōden. I looked down the gallery and saw his privy gentlemen clustered round him, supporting him as he walked.

Ukon was gone – eavesdropping with the rest of them, no doubt. With shaking hands I removed my gowns, and then I lay down in the dark. Despite my distress I felt relieved.

There is no need to confess my guilt to the Empress. Let her draw what inferences she will from Izumi's story. Let her decide if I am the liar or if Izumi falsely accused me. If she threatens to dismiss me I will plead my innocence. Either way it will make no difference. The Emperor will not pardon his daughters, whether they are guilty or not. That much is clear.

Cold and bleak. Wind blowing from the north; the sky so thick with cloud that it seems as if the day has turned to night.

Ukon is away, visiting her mother. The servants shun me, fearful of my eccentricities, and I am not sorry for it.

I spread Kanesuke's letters on the floor. Paper the colour of grass, pollen, dust. Paper vivid as love. Paper white as anger: the sheets thick and unbending, the words harsh.

117

The brocade bag scarcely large enough to contain them. The yellow silk stained by my own fingers, the drawstring unravelling.

Masato's letters I keep elsewhere, as if one man might pollute the other.

In a third place (which must remain undisclosed, and is the most capacious), are the letters never sent, and those that were returned. I never read them. They are abhorrent to me the moment I am done with them – but I keep them all the same.

I pick up a letter from the floor. It is thin, vermilion; the cursive breathtaking in its beauty. He wrote it on a day as dark as this one – the day of the eclipse.

He had come to me that morning, despite the prognostications. It is dangerous to travel on the day of an eclipse, the diviners say. One must stay indoors and close the shutters. One must await the coming of ill fortune, then hold still until the shadow passes and all is safe.

He came in full light, at the Hour of the Horse, when the sun was still whole and the leaves in the courtyard glowed red as blood. My women laughed to see him – so bold and proud and opulent in his dress – for they tolerated my flights of madness then, and did not fear them. I had dared him to come, and he had. He walked in laughing, holding an armful of asters and valerians, as if he hoped that their auspicious colour would ward off the disaster that awaited us.

'Be gone!' He dismissed Ukon and the others with a wave of his hand. 'It is unlucky to be seen in the company of a man on the day of an eclipse.' So they fled, and left us to ourselves.

How did we pass the time? We resumed our game of *go*, his pieces advancing on my own and mine on his. He sang. I read him a story I had written about a diver and her son. (I never told him about my own son, but sometimes the secret crept into the stories, and I wondered if he guessed.)

But the best we saved for last, when the light had faded. For half of love is savouring its prospect, and so we waited.

We had canted the blinds so that the light fell in bars upon the floor. Throughout the morning the bars crept across the room. Then – and this happened very slowly, so that at first we were not aware of it – they disappeared. Perhaps it was a cloud depriving the moon of its foreordained duty . . . but we looked out, and the sky was clear.

A quiet fell over the palace. All morning we had heard footsteps, voices, gongs, the brush of brooms. Now the sound faded with the light, and there grew in its place a heavy expectancy and a brooding quiet, as if everything, even the spiders in their webs, were waiting for the moon's advance.

Advance it did – but slowly. And we advanced like the moon, according to our own predestined plan, for we had made a wager that we could devour each other as quickly as the shadow did the sun.

And did we succeed? I'm not sure, but by the time we restored our world to some kind of order the bars had returned to mark the floor – and might have been there for hours, for all we knew.

A two-day reprieve, and then the Empress summoned me. I wore lavender, hoping it would convey my loyalty – for I do love this woman who controls my fate. She is my equal in daring and wit, though it is treasonous to suggest it, for her prestige so exceeds my own that I dare not touch the hem of her dress.

It was a brilliant morning, the sky swept clean by a strong east wind and every leaf and bud trembling with the prospect of its own fullness. Why is it easier to be devious on such a day? Perhaps its radiance gave me strength.

I planned my stratagems as I walked. The Emperor's

intransigence gave me hope. I would wear it like armour. His rigour would give suppleness to my lies. What a strange thing, to use lies to create a semblance of innocence. It is like trying to turn ink into water. A futile endeavour, but one must try.

Perhaps for that very reason I was calm. I felt a strange elation, as if I had become a witness to my own fate. And it occurred to me as I walked down the galleries that this is how men feel before a battle. They fight for this moment of heightened calm, this poise before the plunge, when the dagger in the hand is still clean and no one knows the outcome.

Of all the times I have striven to be like a man – in my writing, and in my struggles with myself and others – this is the first time I felt I had succeeded.

So I walked into the Empress's chambers, where I had cowered two nights earlier, and I felt brave. She was seated on her curtained dais; I saw the richness of her silks falling onto the floor from behind the green brocade. The Chamberlain escorted me up the steps, and I made ready with my bows.

But there were two women behind the curtain.

'Come and sit with us,' said the Empress, gesturing with her hand. 'We are choosing silks.' She inclined her head toward an empty cushion, and I had no choice but to kneel next to Dainagon.

Dainagon, so calm in her lilac gowns, her pale face floating like the moon in all its spectral beauty.

I felt as if every scrap of light had fled the room. My courage left me. If it had only been someone else, even Izumi! Then I could have lied with all the pleasure of a man confronting his enemies. But I couldn't lie in front of Dainagon.

I sank onto my cushion. The floor was piled high with bolts of silk: damasks and bombasines, brocades and twills.

Their colours spread across the floor, and the two women sat quietly in their midst.

The Empress turned to speak to the Chamberlain, and I ventured a look at Dainagon.

How mysterious it is, the wordless telepathy of friends! She gave me a single look: a glance that was cool but not cold, and contained both a warning and a promise. She was telling me to be silent. K'un: The Passive One. Taciturnity: no blame, no praise. I knew that she was advising me not to confess my guilt. She and the Empress had spoken before I arrived, and she had done all the lying for me.

How did I know that she had told the Empress I was innocent? Even now I can't explain it. Yet I sensed also that the Empress hadn't believed her, and that she would test us both. And I trembled when I recalled her voice as she scorned the Emperor for his weakness.

'Now,' said the Empress, 'you must help us. Dainagon and I have been choosing silks for the Kamo Festival. She has given me her opinion, and I would like to see if you concur.'

'But it is not my place to make such a suggestion,' I protested.

'You will make it if I ask. Tell me: which colours are your favourites?'

I surveyed the array of silks. 'I suppose I would choose lavender,' I said. 'Lavender or mauve.'

The Empress laughed. 'How timid you are! Wouldn't you prefer something bolder?' She reached for a length of violet cloth. 'What about this? Do you care for *futaai*? Or do you dislike double dyes?'

'But it is a summer colour,' I said.

'True. Still, it is lovely, isn't it?' She turned to the Chamberlain. 'Show the ladies and me all the shades of *futaai*.' And he spread the silks before us, in shades veering from violet to dark blue with barely a tint of scarlet.

The Empress turned to me. 'Tell me, which shades of *futaai* do you prefer for a man?'

'That depends on his age and complexion.'

'And what complexion do you think most becomes a man?'

I glanced at Dainagon. Her lips were pressed tightly together, as if to encourage my reticence.

'Pale, your Majesty.'

'You surprise me. Pale, but not pallid?'

'Pale but not pallid.'

'Yes,' said the Empress with a smile, 'A pallid man is dull indeed. So tell me, what shade of *futaai* should a pale man wear?'

'That depends on his age, does it not?

'Well, then, let us say a man of thirty.'

Kanesuke's age, of course. My heart beat fast.

'I suppose,' I said as neutrally as I could, 'He would be just on the cusp between blue shades and violet.'

'So he would be on the cusp.'

'Yes, I suppose the colour would be his choice,' I said, not daring to catch Dainagon's eye, for the conversation was taking a dangerous turn. 'Within a certain realm of possibility, of course, and within the boundaries of taste.'

'Ah, yes,' said the Empress. 'The boundaries of taste. And what exactly are those?'

Before I could answer Dainagon interjected in her calm voice, 'Why of course, Your Majesty, they are set by you and the Emperor. Only those with the highest standards of elegance may presume to be the arbiters of taste.'

'The Emperor is the arbiter of nothing but his own misfortune,' said the Empress bitterly. 'I thank you for your opinion, Dainagon, though I didn't ask for it.' She turned again to me. 'Now tell me, what are the boundaries of taste?'

'I would agree with Dainagon,' I said. My hands were so

cold that my fingers had gone white, and I hid them within the folds of my sleeves.

'Yes, I thought that perhaps you would,' she replied. 'And what of the forbidden colours?' She reached over and fingered the bolts of deep red and purple. 'Are they becoming to a man of such a complexion?'

'Only a very high-born man may aspire to them,' I said.

'And does he aspire to them openly, or in secret?'

Dainagon coughed, and I took care not to look her in the face, for fear I would lose my nerve.

'Why, openly, Your Majesty.'

'And may he wear more than one forbidden colour at a time?' I knew that she meant Kanesuke and the two princesses.

'No,' I said, feigning impartiality. 'That would be the height of ill breeding.'

'Indeed,' ventured Dainagon. 'One mustn't wear colours that will clash.'

'So tell me, then,' said the Empress, fixing me with a pointed look. 'What shall the princesses wear to the festival? Of course they will probably not attend, but in the event that they are pardoned we must be prepared. Shall they both wear the forbidden colours?'

'That is not for me to say, Your Majesty.'

'Or should they wear grey-violet, like wives mourning their husband?'

'I couldn't say.'

'Or perhaps you think that Sadako, being the eldest, can take more liberties with her dress?'

'I don't think she can take liberties at all,' I replied. 'She is a princess.'

'She *was* a princess,' corrected the Empress. 'So you think, then, that if she does take liberties she must have been persuaded to do so?'

'I don't think anyone would have that licence, Your Highness.'

'So if she were to wear ten scarlet gowns to the Kamo Festival that would be her choice and hers alone. It is a sumptuous colour, isn't it? And as you know at times forbidden.'

'She would be scorned by everyone if she wore such a colour in such a season.'

'To be sure,' replied the Empress. 'It must be humiliating to be mocked in such a way.'

I said nothing, nor did Dainagon, but the memory of the day of my shame at the blossom viewing hung in the air. So the Empress must have heard the slander about me even then. It was even worse than I had expected.

'Come, then,' said the Empress, shaking me out of my consternation. 'Let us choose a proper colour for Sadako.'

Dainagon reached for a figured silk. 'Perhaps we should choose pale green for her. She looks beautiful in green, and it is fitting for the season.'

'Green it is, then,' said the Empress. 'Though I didn't ask your opinion. And you?' She turned to me and arched her brows. 'What shade would you wear to the Kamo Festival?'

'Whatever suits you, Your Majesty. It is not mine to choose.'

'That doesn't sound like you at all,' replied the Empress with a smile. 'Is this a new humility you are affecting?'

'I will affect whatever you like.'

'And if I choose a genuine shade of humility for you to wear, and not an affected one?'

'If it pleases you I shall wear it gladly.'

'Well, then,' she continued, 'Perhaps we will choose a mauve for you. A calm, decorous mauve. What do you think, Dainagon? Does mauve suit her?'

'It suits her perfectly, Your Highness.'

'Mauve it shall be, then,' said the Empress, and I saw a

glint of warning in her eyes. 'For you are reaching the age, you know, when bold colours don't suit you. You must learn to be discreet.'

Tears stung my eyes. 'Yes, Your Majesty.'

'So it is decided,' said the Empress. 'One last thing. What sort of shading shall we have for you?'

'Even, if it pleases you,' I said, not knowing where her gambit was leading.

'Even?' asked the Empress. 'No – a mottled shade becomes you more. What do you think, Dainagon? Shall we give her a mottled colour?'

'Forgive me, Your Highness,' said Dainagon. 'But I think it suits her not.'

'Oh?'

'An even shade becomes her,' insisted Dainagon.

'Are you so certain?' asked the Empress. 'For when it comes to matters of taste I prefer women who never waver.'

'I do not waver, Your Highness,' Dainagon said.

'Well, then,' the Empress replied. 'An even shade for an even temper. Let us hope one will match the other.' She reached for a bolt of plain unfigured twill of mauve-grey. 'Chamberlain?' He stood by her side. 'Please wrap this up and have it delivered to the lady in her rooms.'

'Yes, Your Majesty.'

'Take it to the Office of the Wardrobe,' the Empress told me, 'and tell the Mistress that I said to make it up for you. You should get six gowns from it. See that you wear them to the festival.'

'Yes, Your Majesty.' I bowed and took my leave as quickly as I could, so she would not see my tears.

Six robes of plain mauve twill! Six robes of the same penitential hue, without shading or modulation! How everyone at the festival would mock me! She was punishing me severely – yet I knew it could have been worse. She could have accused me directly of spreading my rumour; she could have held me responsible for Sadako's disgrace. I could have been dismissed and sent to live out in the provinces.

I thought it over as I sat in my room warming my hands over the fire. The day was still clear and fine, but I didn't feel brave at all, and I felt that the warmth would never return to my fingers.

It was Dainagon who had made the difference. She had argued in favour of my innocence. And she had done so at the risk of her own reputation. Now she was dyed with the same double shade, and I knew that one day she would pay the price for it.

Then before I had time to realise it she was there. She stood by my side, pale and shaken, and handed me a parcel.

'Open it,' she said.

I unwrapped the paper. It was a heavy rose damask with arabesques of vines and flowers.

'Make it into a jacket,' she said, 'and wear it when you are unhappy.'

'Then I shall wear it all the time.'

'Don't cry. You must be proud.'

'Why did you do it, Dainagon?'

She bent and kissed me on the forehead. 'One liar deserves another,' she said. Then she left, and I had only her perfume to remind me of her presence.

Seventh day of the Third Month.

A strange tale reached my ears this morning, and I wonder whether it is false or true.

Buzen came in soon after I had finished my gruel and told me that she had heard from one of the Outer Palace Guards that a woman was attacked last night in the pine groves west of the Naizenshi. It seems that she was set upon by thieves. Finding nothing of value on her except her robes, they took those, and left her stripped to her shift and trousers. A guard heard her cries, but by the time he reached her the intruders had fled.

All this took place, Buzen said, in the early hours of the morning, just before first light. What a woman was doing wandering at that hour in her finery, unescorted and with no clear purpose, no one can tell.

I hear that she is being seen by doctors from the Bureau of Medicine, who are examining her to make sure she has come to no harm. In any case there are bound to be rumours. Some will say that the men overwhelmed her; others will speculate that she was attacked by ghosts.

After Buzen left I tried to read, but the story she had told me seemed more vivid than anything on the scroll. How dangerous the palace precincts are now at night! Only one gate guarded, and the rest open to the depredations of strangers. And the western expanses near the pine groves the most treacherous place of all.

What would tempt a woman to go there? Was she meeting a lover, or delivering a letter to a courier? Surely there are less risky means to accomplish both. Was she fleeing someone, or escaping the palace itself? Or was she simply distraught?

I should like to know her story. I must press Buzen to learn what she can. I must resist the temptation to make my own inquiries, for I do not want it spread about that I, the object of scorn and injury, might entertain an excessive interest in a woman more damaged than myself.

The same day. Evening.

Dainagon came to me as I was rinsing my brushes. The news she brought shocked me as much as if she had pushed me into a bank of snow. Yet at the very moment she told me I knew that I had known already, and that the news she delivered was not a surprise but a confirmation.

The woman attacked by thieves, the woman wandering in the middle of the night in all her tempting finery – I know her. It was Izumi.

Did my emotion leave me as quickly as the colour fled my face? Did my sympathy for the woman more damaged than I vanish with the knowledge that she is my enemy?

No. But I felt less pity than wonder. Why was Izumi drawn to such extremes?

Received a letter from Ryūen. He will be coming down from Enryakuji next month for the Washing of the Buddha. The Abbot himself will be attending the ceremony, though Ryūen believes there are other reasons for his visit. He will meet, Ryūen suspects, in secret conclave with the Emperor, to discuss the pressures that may force His Majesty's abdication. He can speak more fully when he sees me, Ryūen said. He asked that I destroy his letter, which I have done; the pages are blackening on the coals even as I write.

Why am I compelled to record each detail of this tale as it unfolds, knowing all too well the risk that this involves? Perhaps I do so because its plot contains my own. If I have a purpose it is concealed within this larger tapestry. Within its warp and weft I am a single thread.

And if the Emperor should abdicate – for the pressures on him are strong, both from the Empress and the Minister of the Left, as Dainagon herself has told me – shall my hue stand out more clearly? I can't stop myself from brooding about it, guilty as I am for the role I played in forcing these events.

Yet perhaps my guilt shall be eased should the Emperor step down. Surely then the Vestal and Sadako will be free to return from their domestic exile. Even so they will be tainted by their past, and it may affect their prospects. They may not be princesses, unless the Emperor chooses to restore their titles, and they will never be Vestals. But they will be freer than they are now.

And what of Kanesuke? Will the Empress, angry though she is, find it in her favour to pressure the regent for his pardon?

Dare I consider such a possibility? Dare I picture that white roan cantering through the Suzaku Gate? I mustn't count on it – not yet. It is too soon, and too many obstacles still stand in his way.

Yet do I wish for them? Do I hope for those very impediments?

I must be honest, if only with myself. Why does the possibility of his return so unsettle me? Do I truly want him here, or is it easier to love him from a distance?

Or is it his wounds I fear? I wonder how he has changed during these months in Akashi. Perhaps he will be angry. Perhaps he will scorn and hurt me. Or – and this frightens me most – he will repay distance with distance, and treat me with indifference.

I worry that his deviousness will increase my own. If he is the reflector of my darker self, what will I become when he returns? For his sake I ruined my own mirror. (I keep it in a box, where I cannot see those scrawls that make a mockery of beauty.) Will I corrupt myself to match his image of me?

So I ponder Ryūen's burnt letter, and all the questions that it raises. But there is one I dwell on more than any other: Why, after all these months of waiting, after all this anguish and expectation, do I not wish for Kanesuke's return?

Ninth day of the Third Month, morning.

Dainagon sent me a note, asking me to accompany her on her visit to Sadako. She is going at the behest of the

129

Empress, who is concerned about her stepdaughter's state of mind. There are rumours that the Princess says almost nothing, and that her body is as slender as her speech.

Dainagon will leave tomorrow, near midday, and will return late in the afternoon. Shall I go with her? Every bone in my body is set against it, but my mind yields. Not that I wish to speak to her. I would go only on the condition that my presence be concealed. I want to see the house where she lives, and find if it conforms to the picture in my mind. I would stay in the carriage and peer through the blinds, and Sadako would never know I was there.

Would Dainagon lie and say she had gone alone? Dare I ask her to deepen our conspiracy?

It is tempting – and for yet another reason. We could speak freely, Dainagon and I. The rattle of the carriage would conceal our conversation from the driver, and we could talk as openly as if we were in the middle of the Saga Plain. I can ask her about Izumi, and the pressures on the Emperor to resign.

Yes, I shall go – but only if I can be as invisible as a demon in his straw cloak.

Tenth day, evening.

I sent a note last night to Dainagon, and she agreed to my condition. Why does she love me so, that she is willing to comply with my deviousness? I don't deserve her goodness.

We drove in a wickerwork carriage, whose bamboo blinds shut out all but our mutual regard. From time to time I peered through the gaps to catch a glimpse of that western hinterland so foreign to our eyes.

How near it is, that wasteland west of the palace! And how enticing in its rank luxuriousness! I saw trees choked with mistletoe and ivy, and barren ground overgrown with artemisia. I saw houses destroyed by earthquakes and fires, and left in ruins like the fortunes of their luckless owners. I saw women bent over plots of parsley and onions, and flooded fields that held the image of the dark grey sky. And I wondered what it would be like to live in such desolation, where thieves consort with tree spirits, and silver foxes share their lairs with demons, and owls call from the pines.

The carriage rattled, and we talked under its clamour.

'Is she better?' I asked.

'Izumi? I haven't seen her,' Dainagon replied, folding her fan. 'But I heard she has spent the past two days in bed, and does nothing but write letters.'

Letters to whom? The question hung in the air like the clouds over the rice fields, but there was no sense in asking.

'What was she doing out in the pine grove in the middle of the night?' I asked, knowing well enough that this question was as pointless as my unspoken one.

'Who can say?' Dainagon replied. 'Yet I hear that she told her maid to send her summer gowns to the fuller's, and to have her packing cases ready.'

'So she was planning a journey.'

'Perhaps. And five or six days ago she had a parcel of letter paper delivered. Her maid said she argued with the man who brought it, because it was the wrong colour.'

'What colour was it, do you know?'

'It was blue Korean paper. But she wanted a different shade.'

'Blue-grey. Kanesuke loved that colour.' How many letters of that hue did I have in my yellow brocade bag? Six or seven, possibly; he chose that shade when he was melancholy, and it suited him. Blue-grey, the colour of the sea in Akashi, the colour of clouds when it is about to rain . . .

'Don't,' said Dainagon, for she read the look on my face. 'You must forget him, you know.'

'How can he still hurt me so?' I was crying. How could

131

he damage me even when I didn't hope for his return? How could I let myself feel this jealousy again? So he wanted her back; she must have been out that night to meet the man who would arrange her trip to Akashi. Perhaps he was late, and she was waiting for him when the thieves caught sight of her. What had they done? I wondered if she would postpone her flight because of the harm they had inflicted, or if she would hasten it, desperate to flee the rumours of her violation. And what would she tell Kanesuke? Would she avoid the story altogether, hoping that it would not reach him by other means, or would she confess and run the risk of his repugnance? I didn't envy her predicament.

'He hurts you,' said Dainagon in her even tone, 'because you allow him to.'

I knew that as well as she, but I chose not to reply. We sat for a while in silence, and then I asked, 'Do you think the regent will pardon him?' For we had spoken about the Emperor's imminent abdication (though I was careful not to attribute my intelligence to Ryūen) and we both knew the consequences it might have.

'Let us hope for your sake that he does not,' said Dainagon. 'You mustn't wish for it.'

'I don't.'

'You may think that, but you are just as good at lying to yourself as you are to others.'

How could I explain that she was wrong? How could I tell her that I feared his return as much as I feared Izumi's departure?

'Perhaps you should talk to her,' Dainagon said. 'No one knows how much she may have suffered.' I looked through the blinds at the shimmering fields. It had begun to rain. 'You more than anyone else should be able to understand how she feels.'

'Why?' I asked bitterly. 'Because we love the same liar of a man?'

132

'Because you are passionate, and you both love words.'

'And why should Izumi trust me, just because we love words?'

'She doesn't trust you. But perhaps she will listen in spite of that. She has a hunger for stories, just as you do.'

Yes, I knew about her hunger for stories. She had written one about me. 'And what story shall I tell her?'

'That is not for me to say. Perhaps you should see if she might tell you hers.'

Did I want to know what had happened to her that night? Did I wish to hear her plans, and how she had conspired with Kanesuke? I did, very badly, but the last person I would ask about it was Izumi.

'I will never ask,' I said, 'and she will never tell me.'

'Then we won't speak of it.'

Rain pelted the roof. The ruts in the road filled with water, and the grass on the verge bent under its weight. We passed some cattle grazing in a field and the crumbling walls of an abandoned villa. Then we turned onto a muddy track and climbed a low hill bordered by stands of oaks and beeches. I heard the driver shouting to the ox, and then we pulled into a grassy yard. I saw a gate with the courtyard beyond, and the thatched roof of the house overgrown with ferns.

The driver rang the bell by the gate, and we waited. Dainagon had sent word ahead with a rider, so we knew we were expected. The gate was tall and must have been imposing once. Swallows nested under its eaves, and its tiled roof was pitted and scarred. The wooden doors sagged on their hinges.

'Will you go in?' asked Dainagon, and I could tell from her expression that she knew my answer. 'All right, then. Hide yourself. I won't be long.'

I slid into a corner of the carriage and covered my gowns with a quilt brought for the purpose.

A man appeared, dressed in faded blue, his hair tousled

as if he had been roused from sleep. He spoke to the driver and disappeared through a side door. A little later the doors to the gate swung open and we drove into the courtyard.

The driver unhitched the ox and handed Dainagon down. I heard a woman's voice – a servant, judging from her accent. I risked a glimpse through the blinds, and saw a girl in a linen gown holding an orange umbrella over Dainagon's head.

They walked up to the porch and the door closed behind them. I let out my breath. The driver was speaking to the ox. He brought it a bucket of water and it drank noisily and shook its harnesses.

We had stopped near an archway giving onto the garden. The rain slackened and the light grew stronger. I heard birds singing and wondered what kind they were. How I wished I could step outside and walk through the drenched grass and see the trees and flowers! I shifted my position to ease the cramp in my legs, and looked through the archway into the wilderness on the other side of the wall.

I saw a magnolia and several willows, their silvery buds still enclosed like silkworms in their cocoons. Wisteria hung in heavy clusters from vines trained along an ochre wall. White flowered trees – pears, perhaps? – stood in the tall grass, as prim as girls. Several paths cut through the grass, and I wondered what had made them, for they seemed too narrow to allow for the sweep of a woman's robes.

Did Sadako walk there, I wondered? Did she recall how her beaded trains had swept down the galleries of the Kokiden? Did she miss the dances, the poetry contests, the late-night banquets, the gossip and flirtations?

I had taken all that from her. I had silenced her orchestras and stopped her dances. I had torn up her gowns and burned her letters. I had sent away her suitors, and deprived her of her father's affection. And I had left her nothing but this garden and a rundown house thatched with ferns and no one but her mother to speak to – if she spoke at all.

Her mother. I had never thought of her. She had never once returned to the palace after she fell out of favour with the Emperor – it was a history that preceded my entry into the Empress's service, and I didn't know its details. She was banished to a life of rural obscurity, as her daughter was after her. To me she had never been anything but a name. And yet she lived and breathed only a few paces from where I now sat – and I had no image of her at all. I knew she had been lovely, but her beauty had no specificity; she existed in a blank expanse like an empty scroll.

How she would hate me. It seemed a miracle that she couldn't sense my presence. The words she would fling at me if she knew I was the cause of her daughter's disgrace! I shrank back in the carriage and pulled the quilt over my skirts.

I was hungry but I couldn't eat the rice cakes that Dainagon had left me, so I managed with a sip of water. How long had Dainagon been? I wished for the palace gongs that mark the time. I closed my eyes and leaned against the back of the carriage. Then there came into my mind – suddenly, without prompting – a memory of my own garden, and Ryūen.

I was fourteen; Ryūen was seven. It was the summer before I left Mino and moved to the capital. It was hot; I was sitting on the moss under a birch tree, reading a scroll, and Ryūen was kicking a ball.

He kicked too hard, and the ball landed inside the fence that enclosed the tangerine tree that our father had planted before we were born. He had fenced it to keep away the deer in the early years when the tree was young, but though it was tall now he had never bothered to take down the palings. The branches arched over them, and in summer the orange fruit hung like lanterns amidst the glossy leaves.

'Come and help!' Ryūen shouted, for he wasn't strong

enough to undo the twine that bound the poles together. I struggled with the knots, and then he slipped inside.

'Look!' he cried. 'See what I've found!' He made me peer through the gap at a dark shape in the grass.

It was a fox, and it must have been dead for a short time, for there was no odour about it, aside from its own feral smell, and its body was still intact, though scores of ants swarmed around its open eyes.

'It must have got trapped,' I said.

'Look how soft it is.' Ryūen stroked the reddish pelt.

'Don't touch it!' I scolded. Then, before we knew it, our father was there. He made us wash our hands in a bucket by the porch, and for three days we stayed indoors, as if a relative had died and we had been tainted by the body. Ryūen cried, for he couldn't understand our father's anger, and when the gardener burned the fox on a pile of sticks Ryūen buried his face in his bedclothes and refused to look at us.

From then on Ryūen avoided that corner of the garden, and refused to eat the tangerines that the servants peeled for him. And I was changed too. During the first years when I moved to the palace, when Izumi and I were friends and I was still homesick for the provinces, I dreamed often of that tree. Then over time I forgot about its cloistered beauty, and I dreamed of other things.

A bird sang. I thought it was a nightingale, but it couldn't have been; it was too early in spring, though perhaps it is different in the country.

Would I live in a house like this? I knew I would, as clearly as if Masato's hexagrams had spelled it out. I would be exiled to a place like this one; it was only a matter of time before it happened. It might be soon, if the Empress decided she still mistrusted me, or it might be later. I knew it the moment I recalled the image of the tangerine tree. No one would hide me there within that fragile enclosure; I would hide myself. And would I thrive in that prison of my own making? Who could tell?

How fortunate it is that the walls we build around ourselves conceal us from the long view of our lives. If our sight were clear we couldn't bear it.

Is Sadako content within her garden? If she forgoes the world of words, if she renounces love as nuns renounce colour and fragrance, who is to say that she isn't wise? If the Vestal shuns her mother, if Ryūen shuts himself up with his scrolls and rosaries, who can tell if they are right?

Did I choose to abandon my son? Did I want his father to leave me? Did I seek the exile of Kanesuke? Did I wish for Masato to meet me at Hasedera, when he handed me the branch of anise leaves and I felt I had known him all my life?

What desire had I now? I threw off my quilt and smoothed my gowns. I would go and speak to her. I would lay down my lies like the leaves of the anise tree, and I would ask her to forgive me.

I put my hand on the door, but something stopped me. K'un, The Passive One. Concealment constitutes the right course. Confessions are selfish, because those who make them expect reward.

She wouldn't want my explanation. It would make things worse. She didn't know who had spread the rumours; it wouldn't help to put a face to them.

Then I heard voices, and the decision was taken out of my hands. I retreated to the back of the carriage, and in a moment Dainagon had climbed in next to me.

We drove through the battered gate. Dainagon didn't speak. Had she become mute like the prince in the story, like Sadako herself? I watched her for signs.

Her forehead was clear, the lines barely perceptible in the dim light of the carriage; her brow was not furrowed, yet it conveyed a vague unease. Her lips were not pressed tight as they had been when she urged me to taciturnity, but there was a strain at the corners of her mouth, as if she were forcing herself to hold back some emotion she didn't wish to reveal. Her eyes were dark, and fixed on nothing visible; her shoulders drooped, as if she had been released from a heavy weight. As I watched her I found myself wondering if she had ever wanted children, for I sensed in her the preoccupation of a mother whose child is ill.

'How is she?' I asked, unable to wait any longer.

'How is she?' repeated Dainagon, looking at me for the first time, her brows arched with scorn. 'You would know as well as I.'

'Did she speak to you?'

'No. I spoke to her mother.'

'And did Sadako look well?'

'Did she look well?' repeated Dainagon. I felt her emotion rising with her inflection. 'She is so thin you can see through her fingers. She is so thin she cannot stand.' Her lips trembled, and I said the first thing that came into my head – not because I wanted an answer, but because I thought if I provoked her I could stop her from crying.

'And what does she do all day?'

My ploy was successful, for her eyes flashed, and she looked at me incredulously. 'She looks out of the window. She listens to her mother play the zither. Sometimes she reads.'

'And her mother?' I asked. 'Is she still lovely?'

She laughed – but it was not a laugh, really, just a sharp release of breath. 'She is as lovely as you can expect of a woman who lives at the sufferance of others.'

And so we left it. The carriage turned east onto the muddy road; we passed two men on horseback, their panniers laden with fresh green herbs. The sky had almost cleared, and the flooded fields looked as bright and hard as ice.

'Dainagon.' I watched her averted face as she looked out

at the road. 'Dainagon.' I touched the hem of her sleeve. 'Should I have gone in?'

She turned and looked at me, her face restored to its austere beauty, though her eyes seemed tired. 'No,' she said quietly. 'It wouldn't have made any difference.'

We sat in silence until we drove through the Sōheki Gate.

'I don't want to see Izumi,' I said. 'And I'm sure she doesn't want to see me. But I'll go to her if you ask me.'

Dainagon looked out of the window. 'That is your choice,' she said.

Evening of the same day. I wrote to Masato and told him that I missed him. I tried not to plead, but I hope he will realise how badly I need his company. I kept my tone bright, and varied my strokes between light and dark, in the playful flirtatious way of women.

I thought of the fields as hard as glass, and studied the I Ching. Each time new obscurities, new revelations.

'Hoarfrost underfoot betokens the coming of solid ice. An urgent need for caution. The assassination of a ruler by his minister does not result from the events of a single day and night. The causes have gradually accumulated, and, though they should have been observed long before, were not noticed and put right in time.'

Can this book help us put things right? Can it stay our hand before the damage is done?

Kanesuke would understand it. His mind is subtler than mine. Perhaps it would warn him against Izumi. Perhaps it might force him to confront the cruelty that makes him wound me.

I will send it to him – no, I shall ask Izumi to take it with her when she goes to Akashi. The irony pleases me. She may refuse, but no matter. I will gather up all my courage, and I will place it in her hands.

★

I bought a copy of the I Ching from a dealer of Chinese books in the Eastern Marketplace – but something happened there that I dread to relate.

What a strange world it is, that great place of commerce, where men buy and sell with such noisy ferocity that they sound like a flock of ravens perched on the ridgepole of a house. I think of it even now in my distress.

I had hired a modest coach, in the interest of inconspicuousness, and left early, at the Hour of the Dragon. I took a single escort, wanting as few people as possible to observe my errand. We followed his horse through the Suzaku Gate, the willows along the avenue just leafing out, the mansions as grand as palaces.

As we travelled south the city changed. I had never been on the side streets past the Sixth Ward; it was all new and strange to me. The houses were crowded close together, like spectators at a parade, and the streets were crammed with people and vehicles of all kinds. Men staggered carrying burdens of every description, their bodies disguised by their loads. Seen from a distance they resembled fantastic animals: I saw a lumbering bundle of thatch, and a pair of thin legs surmounted by seaweed, and heads that sprouted antlers made of kindling and palm fronds.

As we continued the noise and dust increased, and shapes emerged from the maelstrom like phantoms.

Yet how vivid it was, and how real! It seemed as if the hushed world from which I had come, where men and women glide by without a sound and commerce is conducted in whispers, was the true realm of ghosts, and this the place of the living.

A friend had told me of a shop that sold Chinese books about the science of yin-yang. It was located, he said, on a narrow street not far from the Eastern Marketplace. We stopped just short of the square, for it was too crowded to go further, and I had my escort take me to the entrance of the shop. I held my fan close to my face and gathered up my gowns as best I could, and tried not to notice the curious glances cast my way.

As we skirted the square I caught a glimpse of the stalls and the ancient cherry tree where convicts are whipped. I had read of it in books. It was less beautiful than I had thought, but perhaps that is fitting. There were no floggings that day, and it seemed as if the tree itself had been granted an amnesty, for its petals floated freely in the air and settled where they would.

The press of people frightened me. I saw women hawking nuts and sweets, and gamblers and wonder workers, and scores of beggars. A boy knelt on the ground by my feet, his palms open in supplication. As I walked past he lifted his face. His eyes were as white as boiled eggs, and his cheeks were pitted and shiny with scars.

I stepped inside the shop, carrying a parcel of cloth I had brought to do my trade. My escort, at my request, waited outside. The place was dim and quiet – and empty, as far as I could tell. The walls were ranged with books and scrolls, and there was an alcove at the back stocked with jars of teas and medicines. I tapped my fan on a shelf, thinking it unladylike to call out, and then I heard voices, and a man appeared through a curtained doorway to my left.

He wore an azure coat and a black silk cap. I couldn't fix his age, for his face was unlined and his hair was dark, but there was something in his manner that suggested a vast experience, as if the blinds that shutter the knowledge acquired in past lives had in his case remained unclosed. I thought that perhaps he was Chinese – for there was something about him that reminded me of the portraits of Chuang-tzu – though he might have been Korean. And there was something chimerical in his manner, as if he were the boy in Chuang-tzu's story, who could never tell if he was a man who dreamed he was a butterfly, or a butterfly who dreamed he was a man.

He bowed and showed no sign of surprise, as if he were visited by ladies-in-waiting every day, and I returned his courtesy.

'I'm sorry I couldn't attend to you earlier,' he said. 'I was speaking with a customer in the back, and I didn't hear you.'

I explained my errand, anxious to be gone as soon as I could, for I knew how far I was straying from propriety by appearing in such a place alone, and in such an open manner.

'The Book of Changes,' he said. 'Yes, we have several copies.' He led me to a little room in the back, and bade me sit on a cushion behind a standing screen. Then he brought several books and told me to take my time. He would leave me to read at my leisure, and I should clap if I needed him.

Then he left me and disappeared into the side room. From time to time I could hear him speaking in a low voice to another man.

My hands turned cold. What if they should approach me, as the thieves had Izumi? My escort was just outside, but perhaps he would not hear if I cried out . . . but it was absurd to be so fearful. I would simply choose my book and leave.

I picked up the volumes one at a time. They were written in Chinese, and some seemed very old. One caught my fancy. It was covered with indigo silk; the text was clear and written on thick yellowed paper, and there were commentaries at the back explaining the methods of divination.

I clapped my hands to summon the owner, and I heard the voices break off. In a moment he was there beside the screen. I handed him the book.

'This one, please,' I said from behind my fan.

He looked at me in his sagacious way. 'Yes. It is the oldest. It is from Chang-an.'

'Is it possible,' I asked, 'for someone to learn to read the hexagrams by studying the commentaries?'

'Yes and no,' he replied. 'The hexagrams speak for themselves. But it takes many years to learn to interpret them, and of course one's success depends on one's intentions.'

'So,' I said lightly, 'the book can divine one's intentions?' And I remembered that Masato had also said something to the same effect.

'Why, yes,' he said mildly. 'If a question is posed frivolously, the I Ching will answer in a frivolous manner.'

'And do women always pose frivolous questions?' I asked. 'Not that the book is for myself,' I added. 'It is for someone else.'

'I would not presume to know, though it is rare to find a woman who takes an interest in such things.'

'Perhaps that is because the I Ching instructs us to be taciturn.' Why was I so bold? Perhaps it was the strangeness of the setting that gave me licence.

'Taciturnity,' the bookseller said – and I could tell he was concealing a smile – 'is a virtue highly prized by the Superior Man. So you have studied the I Ching?'

'A little. I know someone who knows it well.' It occurred to me that perhaps Masato had been here, and had talked with this man himself.

I would never speak of him, would never say his real name. Yet it gave me pleasure to allude to him, and I imagined him holding the book in his hands.

'Then you must respect it as he does.'

'I do.'

'Please,' I said, handing him my parcel. 'I hope this is sufficient in trade.'

He unwrapped it, and I noticed the prominent veins in his hands, which were as sensitive as a musician's, and shook with a visible tremor. He examined my length of antique gossamer, the colour of carp swimming underwater, and flickering with the same iridescence.

'Yes,' he said, folding the cloth back in the paper. 'It is more than sufficient.' Then he took the book and wrapped it in heavy purple rice paper and tied it with green twine.

'You need nothing else?' he asked when he returned. 'No teas or other remedies?'

His question took me aback, though it was commonplace enough for a man reliant on custom. Did I look as if I needed them? 'No, thank you, nothing at all,' I said.

I heard a cough from the side room, and the man excused himself for a moment. I stood and waited, as if our business were not quite transacted. He returned after a short time and held out a folded sheet of paper.

'Forgive me,' he said. 'A message from the gentleman.' There was something disconcerting about his expression, a nervousness that seemed at odds with his imperturbable manner.

I hesitated, but my curiosity overcame my modesty, and I accepted the note along with the parcel, and left the shop. My escort was there on the step. I followed him down the street, looking neither right nor left. Only when I was safely installed in my coach and we were well along Suzaku Avenue did I find the courage to unfold the note.

It was written in *kana* script in a hand of great distinction, the strokes bold and well formed and the spacing wide and elegant. It was very brief. The author praised my looks, and asked if we might meet.

It was clearer than clear to me: he thought I was a courtesan. He had hoped I would read the note before I left the shop, so that we might leave together.

My cheeks flamed, though there was no one to notice my chagrin. How foolish I had been to enter the shop alone. I began to cry. So this was what I got for acting on my secret plan! The bookseller's client had not spoken to me; there had been no direct advance, yet I felt soiled and trodden upon.

We rattled past the gated mansions. This must be how Izumi felt, I thought – though her experience was far worse. How glad I was that no one knew of my shame, as others know of hers! I tore the note into pieces and threw them out of the window, and they floated to the ground and were dispersed amidst the crush of hooves and wheels.

Hail falls on the bamboo leaves. What a forlorn sound it makes! I walk alone along the galleries, wondering if it was just last night that I saw Masato. He came late and left before it was light, and I thought I had dreamed him.

Yet I know it was real, that time we spent together. I watch the hail turn the spring to a colder season, and I remember it.

I woke last night to a tapping on my screen. Then, before I knew what was happening, he was there. He took off his damp cloak and lay beside me in the darkness. The scent of his robes brought back the nights I had spent with him so vividly that I couldn't speak. For that scent revived not just his presence but his absence, to which I had forced myself to be inured. And I found as I rose to the surface of my consciousness that I had to give up not just my dreams but my self-protectiveness.

'It's all right,' he said, sensing my confusion. He put his hand over my face, and within that double darkness I felt the coolness of his palm.

'I'm sorry I couldn't come sooner.' He kissed me, as if in recompense for his lack of explanation. Then he stripped me of all that had sheltered me – clothes, fears, dreams – and said my name not once, but twice.

'Light the lamp,' I urged him when he had pulled his robes over us. 'I want to see your face.' He did so, but he kept the flame low so as not to attract notice. I saw in his eyes the same tenderness he had expressed with his body. Yet there was something in his look that reminded me of the bookseller I had met in the marketplace, and I was tempted to tell him what had happened. Had he been to that shop, I wondered, and leafed through the same books? Yet I knew I mustn't ask him, for I would have to explain the purpose of my errand, and I didn't want him to know that I had bought a book for Kanesuke. And the terrible affront of that note from the man I had never seen: how could I hide that sequel to my tale? Surely he would read the shame of it in my face.

'What is it?' he asked, but I turned my head away from him.

'Nothing.' I let him stroke my hair. 'How is your mother?'

'Better. She is going on retreat to Ishiyama as soon as she is strong enough.'

'And will you go with her?'

'No. My father will take her.' He pulled the robes more closely around us. 'Is your mother alive?' he asked.

'No. She died when I was twelve.'

He looked at me. His eyes were wide and calm. 'And your father?'

'He died four years ago this autumn. He had been ill for some time. He wasn't clear in his mind.'

'So you have no one, apart from your son.'

'I have a brother.'

'And do you love him?'

'Yes. Or I did once.' It occurred to me that he and Ryūen were almost the same age. I wondered if they would get on. Metaphysics would be their common ground. I pictured them arguing some point of Buddhist doctrine.

'And your son? Do you love him?' The same calm look, the same concern.

'Yes.'

146

'But he doesn't live with you.'

'How could he?' I asked bitterly. 'A woman of my position is not supposed to have encumbrances.'

'So that is the reason?'

'Not the only one.'

'And the other?'

'He would be tainted by me.'

Then for some reason I can't explain I found myself telling him the story of the dead fox in the garden. Yet I didn't tell him where I had seen the tree that had revived its memory, for I didn't want him to know about my clandestine visit to the house west of the city.

He listened, and drew me close under the layers of silk. I felt the smoothness of his chest against my back. He smelled of juniper and sweat. His arms encircled me, and I had no desire to be anywhere else.

'How can I be sure,' he teased me, 'that you're not a fox? A live one – a shape changer. A fox turned into a beautiful woman.'

His question threw me off balance, for it reminded me of something Kanesuke had once said, but I replied in the same playful way, 'If I were a shape changer, you would know me by my wounds.'

'What do you mean?'

'The wounds supernatural creatures have that show they are not human.'

'Ah, yes – those wounds. Come, I will search you, then.' And he did so, with his hands and with his mouth, pausing just long enough to say, 'No, I can't find a thing. I must have been mistaken.' If the moans I heard were mine – for they seemed to appear from nowhere, from some disembodied creature – they must have been caused by sorcery of another kind.

Some time later, as I lay with my head on his chest, I

asked him, 'Why do I never dream of you? If I did I would be less lonely.'

'We seldom dream of what we want. We dream of what we fear.'

So that is why I dream more of Izumi than Kanesuke. That is why I dream of standing in the courtyard by the ancient cherry tree, with everyone in the palace whispering and pointing their fingers at me.

'What are you afraid of?' he asked, as if he had read my mind.

'That people will see me for what I am, and hate me.'

He propped himself up on his elbow and looked at me. 'I see you as you are, and I don't hate you.' He brought the lamp close and searched my face. 'I see nothing here to hate.'

Yet he wouldn't say that he loved me. The words hung in the air, but he would never say them.

I kissed him despite his reticence and asked, 'And you? Do you have wounds?'

'Yes.' He smiled as he said it, but there was a distance in his look, though I knew him well enough not to expect an explanation.

'And have they healed?'

'I don't know. Tell me.' He lay beside me and guided my hands. And then – how could I have been so bold? I suppose because he had done the same – I explored him as he had me. Then he turned face down and bade me search again, and I did so. Seeing him that way, so pale and thin in the dim light of the lamp, I felt an impulse to shelter him, so I lay on his back as if I were the robes we had discarded.

'You must be cold,' I said, and kissed him on the cheek.

'Not now. Cover me with your hair.' I shook my head so that it spread all about him.

'It is like grass,' he said. 'Like uncut grass in summer.'

This remark made me so happy that I asked in spite of myself, 'Do you love me?'

I felt a change in his body – a change so subtle I was tempted to deny it had occurred, though his silence confirmed it. And though I didn't cry – for I was determined not to show how he had hurt me – he must have sensed a change in me as well, for he turned and held me in his arms.

'Don't,' he said, for he had seen my eyes fill with tears. He stroked my cheek. 'Some things are best unsaid.'

I made no reply.

'Come,' he said, brushing the wet strands of hair from my face. 'You mustn't think so much. Your thoughts will consume you, like the phoenix burnt in its nest of spicery.'

I had written of the phoenix once, when I was recalling that spring outside of time I had spent with Kanesuke. Could he read my thoughts?

'Will you tell my fortune?' I asked.

He smiled and stroked my cheek. 'I told you. I'm not a fortune teller.'

'You know what I mean.'

'So you want to ask a question of the I Ching?'

'Yes.'

'And you want me to interpret the answer.'

'Yes.'

His face changed. 'Perhaps. It is not a frivolous thing.'

I thought of the bookseller and his chimerical expression. We had had the same conversation. 'And I am not a frivolous woman.'

'I know,' he said, and kissed me.

'Smooth my hair again, and tell me it is like grass.'

He did so. 'Are you thinking of the poem in The Tales of Ise?'

'Of the boy who covets his sister, and regrets that someone else will tie up her hair?' I asked. 'Yes.'

'I like the sister's answer to him best – when she says,

"Have I not always loved you without reserve?"'

I laughed despite my hurt. 'So do you think she is placating her brother or encouraging him?'

'Encouraging him, of course,' he said. He drew my hair back from my face and held it in his slender hands.

'If I were to fall,' he asked in his lovely serious way, 'if I were to fall very far, would you stop me?'

'I would try.'

'You must,' he said. He pulled my hair back so hard as he kissed me that I cried out, and he put his hand over my mouth and I bit the flesh of his palm until it bled.

When I awoke the day was half gone, the air damp and the sky leaden. Ukon glanced at me distastefully as she brought my rice, and I wondered how much she had heard, and what she would repeat. I gathered up my gowns and saw a stain on the mat. Perhaps it was from the cut on his hand. When Ukon left the room I knelt and touched it with my tongue. It tasted of gallnut and iron. I bathed and dressed and walked up and down the galleries, reliving the hours that had come and gone so quickly. Then the hail came down and battered the leaves in the garden, and I returned to my rooms.

I wrote to Izumi and asked if I might see her. What reason did I give? I simply said I had a message regarding Kanesuke that I needed to discuss with her. I can't deny that I implied he had written to me. How useful the ambiguities of our language!

My true motive, of course (though I admit there are others) is to propose that she deliver my book to Kanesuke. I have no doubt that she will resist. Why should she be errand boy for her rival? Yet if I tell her that it is a book of magic, and that it has talismanic powers that exceed her wiles and my own, perhaps she will change her mind.

150

I will tell her that the book was sent to me by an elderly friend of Kanesuke's, a diviner and practitioner of Chinese medicine. She knows as well as I of Kanesuke's regard for men of learning. I will say that this man had a dream that Kanesuke was in danger, and that he thought that the book might reveal the means for his escape. He insisted that his gift be delivered by someone who knows Kanesuke well. As Kanesuke had spoken of our attachment, the diviner sent the book to me.

How will I explain my knowledge of Izumi's intent to go to Akashi? (Indeed I am not certain of her plans. Dainagon and I have surmised them, and they may have changed after her recent indignity.) My ruse is this: I will say that the diviner foretold her journey. In his dream he learned that a woman who loved Kanesuke was planning to visit him secretly. He assumed that the woman was I. Having no such plan, I realised that the dream referred to Izumi. I will tell her that I decided that for the sake of the man we both adore I had no choice but to appeal to her.

If she is as superstitious as I, and as concerned for her lover's welfare, she will have no choice but to comply. The irony, of course, is that she herself is the danger that my imaginary scholar has divined. For isn't she devious and cold? Isn't she cruel and manipulative? Doesn't she seek to possess Kanesuke as a ghost does a living person?

Perhaps the book will warn him of her guile. At the very least it may provide him with some insight into the nature of his misfortunes. For haven't I found, ignorant of its subtleties though I am, that when I open it the very page to which I turn reveals some secret relative to my troubles?

So I will give Izumi the book and the letter that accompanies it. Yes, I have contrived a letter, too. I obtained from the imperial stores some leaves of rare Chinese paper, and wrote a message from my fictitious scholar in a disguised hand. In trembling cursive script (five drafts before I mastered it!) I wrote:

'For Tachibana no Kanesuke, in the hopes that this will ease the solitude of your exile, and forewarn you of any dangers that may come your way. From your friend who once so reluctantly yielded his hand to you one rainy Night of the Monkey.'

I concluded with a signature so ornate as to be illegible, in the manner of educated men.

The dear friend, of course, is I; the game of *go* to which I refer was the match that Kanesuke and I had played the night when we first became lovers. Even if he doesn't recognise my disguised script, he will know by my allusion that the gift comes from me.

And if I find during the course of my interview that Izumi doesn't intend to go to Akashi? Then I will ask her to return the book, and I will resort to a more straightforward means of delivering it into Kanesuke's hands.

Even then my meeting will not have been in vain. I will have seen how she looks, with what tones she speaks, and the means by which she contrives her own fictions. And I will show that I do not fear her, and that I am someone to be reckoned with.

I was surprised to find, hours after the delivery of my letter, a white folded note containing Izumi's reply. It was handed to me by a page I had never seen, a tall boy of twelve or thirteen whose manner was as supercilious as his mistress's.

Dainagon was with me when I received the letter. I thought of saving it for later, dismissed this impulse as cowardice, and read it in her presence.

Like the message from my anonymous admirer in the Eastern Marketplace, it was brief and to the point. Yes, she would see me – tomorrow, in her rooms, at the Hour of the Horse.

She didn't sign her name, but I knew the writing well enough. She had taken pains to make it fine. Its beauty struck me with an almost physical force. She had written to me in this hand, not once but many times, in those early years when we were friends. And I wondered if, when she devised her malicious tale about me, she wrote it out in this very style. What a waste, when a skill so fine is made to serve a wicked purpose.

'So you will see her,' Dainagon said, putting down the gown she was embroidering. Her lilac dress was as pale as her face; her hands, poised over the filmy cloth, tensed with expectation.

'Yes.' I kept my tone as neutral as I could, not wanting to show my misgivings.

'You will find her much changed.' She told me that she had seen Izumi soon after our visit to Sadako, and that she had been shocked by the difference in her looks and manner. But when I pressed her to describe just how she had found her she refused to elaborate, and told me I must see for myself.

'Her writing is the same,' I said. 'As beautiful as ever.' The envy in my voice must have been apparent even to Ukon, who was busy airing my summer gowns. I asked her to fetch some tea, saying that Dainagon had a headache.

Dainagon lifted her brows as if to confirm my desire for privacy, and when Ukon left (sighing audibly in resentment of my ploy) she told me, 'Try to keep your head when you speak to her. Don't be spiteful.'

'Have I any reason to be?'

'You do, and you know it as well as I,' replied Dainagon, and I knew she was recalling my dismay on the day of the blossom viewing. 'Even so, you must try to restrain yourself.'

'I am the model of restraint.'

Dainagon smiled. 'Yes, I know all about your restraint,' she said. 'It is exceeded only by your capacity for self-deception.'

Our conversation continued in this vein until Ukon returned with a cup of magnolia-leaf tea, which Dainagon refused with a wave of her hand, saying her headache had gone completely.

I woke early and called the chambermaid to bring water for a bath. I washed and stained my teeth and dressed as carefully as if I were meeting a lover. Red trousers, a white shift, wisteria robes of glossed purple silk, a jacket of Chinese damask embroidered with violets, and a cypress-wood fan. I had burned into my robes a scent of my own invention, of amber, clove and tangerine.

Ukon helped me dress and combed my hair. Her amusement was all too clear. All this, she must have thought, just to impress a woman!

I was so preoccupied I barely took note of the morning gongs, and must have left my room well past the appointed time. I had wrapped Kanesuke's book in heavy green paper, the counterfeit note folded inside. Holding my fan to my face, I hurried down the halls, avoiding the glances cast my way.

Near the Shōkyōden I came upon a Captain of the Bodyguards of the Right who had once sent me a spate of amorous letters. He looked me up and down as if I had not a scrap of clothing on and inquired in an insouciant way after my health. His black eyes shone like his lacquered cap, and his red twill cloak gave him the look of a man just returned from a hunting party; I half-expected to see a string of quails and skylarks dangling over his shoulder. I told him I was well and darted past him to safer territory.

In Izumi's courtyard the leaves on the pear trees were just coming out, spreading like green satin tents over the last of the withered blossoms. How long it seemed since I had seen Izumi that windy autumn day when she cast her hateful look at me. A woman from the Office of the Grounds was sweeping, and I took comfort in that humble domestic sound. Would Izumi be like the broom tree, I wondered, that looks distinct from afar but loses its clarity when one approaches?

I rapped on the door to her rooms with my fan. I heard voices from within and recognised Izumi's. It was the same low voice that I remembered, but there was some change in its timbre that I couldn't place. Perhaps it was merely unfamiliarity that made me think it altered.

My heart raced. I held my parcel to my chest. The door slid open a crack, and Chūjō's round face appeared. She looked as unsurprised as if I came calling every day (for Izumi trains her servants well, polishing their manners to a high gloss of implacability) and she let me in. A lacquered screen had been set up in the corner of the anteroom, with hangings of lavender damask edged with green brocade, and tinted paper panels inscribed with poems whose texts, in my nervousness, escaped me.

So we were to be separated. I was not surprised. She would treat me as the Empress does the wife of a visiting provincial official, whose country ways and narrow sleeves preclude a greater intimacy. She would treat me as a woman does a man she doesn't trust.

I realised with a shock that she was there. I could hear her breathing.

In the gap between floor and screen I saw the hems of her robes and sleeves, piled fold upon fold like water flowing over a weir. White on white, green on green – the colours of deutzia in the first days of summer. They were scented – faintly, but perceptibly – with cedarwood and orange blossom. Why had she chosen that perfume? Because it is the scent of remembrance, and because Kanesuke favoured it.

So we were to be rivals even before we spoke. I sank onto my cushion and tried to calm myself as I arranged my robes.

Chūjō bowed, and closed the sliding door.

'So,' Izumi said, 'after all this time you wish to speak to me.'

'Yes.'

'I believe you said it was about a message from Kanesuke.' I had never heard her speak his name. She drew out the syllables, as if to prolong his presence.

So my ambiguous note had done its work. 'Not from him, but about him,' I said, and I explained my errand. I told her of the scholar and his ominous dream, and the book that might forewarn Kanesuke. I told her of the woman in that dream who was planning a visit to Akashi, and how I knew it must be she.

'If you love him,' I concluded, 'If you love him even half as much as I do, then you will take this to him.' I slid the book beneath the curtain.

'So this is the vaunted book of magic,' Izumi said. 'May I look at it?'

How could I refuse? 'You may. There is a note from his friend inside.'

I heard her unwrap the paper and pause to read the letter. Would she look at the tentative script and recognise it as mine? Would she discern in the dedication a devotion that was more than fraternal? My hands shook. How could I expect her to believe my story? Yet if she loved him she would set her doubts aside. If she thought that Kanesuke might come to harm, she would sacrifice her pride to try to help him.

She turned the pages. 'I have heard of the I Ching,' she

said, 'but I never took an interest in it. It is a book for soothsayers.'

'It is a powerful book,' I said.

'Is it?' she asked. 'Have you become so superstitious?'

'No more than you were once,' I replied, for I remembered how, when we were young, she would wear her robes inside out at night so she would dream of her lovers.

'Then let us see what wisdom it offers us. Here: "Hexagram Nine,"' she read.

' "Wind blowing across the sky ... The rains are falling and a time of rest has come. Virtue continues to increase. At this moment, persistence would bring serious trouble to women." So it is speaking to us,' she said in that ironic tone I remembered so well. 'But whose virtue? And whose persistence?'

Indeed. I wasn't sure myself. Was it warning me against my course of action? 'It is not to be taken lightly,' I replied.

'You speak as if it were a living person. But you always did prefer books to people.'

'And you,' I retorted, 'prefer lies to truth.'

'Lies?' she asked. 'Don't speak to me of lies. Who stole a letter from my room? Who spread false rumours about Sadako? Kanesuke told me they were untrue. That story I wrote about you – there is not a breath of falsehood in it. You are exactly as I said.'

So she knew the degree of my deceit. My ploys hadn't misled her. Even so I had to stand her to this test. Did she love him as I did?

'Say what you like,' I said, 'but take the book. If you love him, you will take it.'

'How do you presume to know my plans?' she asked. 'You have invented them, just as you have invented this scholarly friend. You make me laugh. Your lies are as transparent as a child's.'

So she would have none of it. Still I tried to introduce

some doubt. 'The danger to him is real,' I said. 'Believe what you will, but if you want to help him as I do you must take it.'

She was quiet for a moment. I heard the rustle of her gowns.

'Perhaps I shall,' she said. 'For I plan to see him very soon.'

I caught my breath. Why this frankness? I trusted her no more than she did me; she was only trying to make me jealous. I answered as evenly as I could, 'So it is true, the rumour of your departure.'

She laughed. 'So you admit to having heard the rumours!' she said. 'Yes, they are true. He has asked me to come, and I will go as soon as I am well.'

'As soon as I am well.' Dainagon was right; she had not recovered. I wondered how badly she had been injured.

'I heard about what happened. I'm very sorry.'

'Yes, I'm sure you heard about it in great detail. I can imagine the stories that are circulating – and no doubt you contributed to their embellishment.'

'I have no stake in increasing your hurt,' I said, remembering my own brush with shame in the marketplace.

She laughed again. 'No stake? I'm sure you would have been glad if I had been killed.'

I felt as if she had slapped me. Did she think my depravity as deep as that?

'I hope you wouldn't think me capable of so grave a fault. We were friends once.'

'Yes, we were friends.'

'And we love the same man.'

'And he has asked me to come and live with him, and I shall.'

Was she lying, or was it true? If he had asked her that, there was no hope for me at all. 'I'm sure that a quiet life in the country will suit you,' I said. 'At least for a little while.'

'I don't think I shall be bored,' she replied. 'And his exile will not last long. You know as well as I do what will happen when the Emperor steps down.'

So she understood that it was likely that Kanesuke would be pardoned once Reizei assumed the throne. Did she realise that, had it not been for my false tale about Sadako, this fortuitous course of events might not be set in motion?

'So you plan to return with him when he is pardoned.'

'Of course.'

'Then if you wish to do me just one kindness, take him the book when you go.'

'Why this urgency about a book of omens and superstitions?'

'It is not a book of superstitions. It has powers that exceed yours and mine.'

'Perhaps. If it is so powerful, then why not send it with a messenger? It will protect itself.'

'Because I want you to take it. Because I want Kanesuke to know that it came from your hands.'

'As the dream foretold it.'

'As the dream foretold it.'

'And shall I take your specious note?'

'Take it, and let Kanesuke decide if it is specious.'

She stood. 'As you wish. I shall take your book. But I have something for you to see in return.'

What could she mean? Had she intended this exchange from the beginning?

Then before I had time to take a breath she appeared from behind the screen, holding a letter in her hand.

She was as I remembered her – but changed. Her haughty face, her thick dark brows, her vivid mouth – all were as I recalled. Yet there was a flaw. From her right cheek to the collar of her Chinese jacket ran a thin red line. She looked like a doll sewn badly at the seam.

She noticed my look. No doubt she had anticipated it. 'It runs,' she said, 'from here' – she touched her cheek – 'to here' – and she traced a line to a place below her breast. 'And there are others.'

So her damage was indeed far greater than mine. The welts might disappear, but the memory of how she received them would remain. I found myself astonished by her courage. To think that she would go to Kanesuke in this state – and that he would accept her as she was. Unless, of course, she was inventing the story of their reunion.

She looked me up and down, as the Captain of the Guards had done, but whether her appraisal was favourable or not I couldn't tell from her expression.

She handed me the letter. It was written on blue-grey paper. I wondered if she had as many of that shade as I did.

'If it is from Kanesuke I will not read it,' I said.

'It is, and you shall. Otherwise I will not be your messenger, and your book of magic stays here.'

She was testing me as I had tested her. And she wanted to see my face when I read what he had written. That was why she had come out from behind the screen and risked humiliation. She wanted to make my pain worse than hers.

My hands shook so much I could barely unfold the paper.

It was his script. There was no signature or date. He was writing to her, he said, because he couldn't sleep. The letter had that vertiginous quality of those written late at night, when all is still except one's thoughts, which turn without ceasing.

He told her that he missed her. He said that at night the hours went by so slowly that he felt as if he were climbing a great tower until he stood alone at its rim. Then he would lean out as far as he could without falling, and he would see her. She was bright, like the moon, and she shone on him until he forgot whether it was day or night. She shone until he forgot his very name and where he lived and what it was he was going to do with his life. Then he quoted the poem that says:

From darkness I fear I shall enter the path of darkness
Light my way, moon on the mountain's rim.

He said that he loved her like no other. He had said the same to me.

'Here,' I said. 'Take back your trophy.'

I gave her the letter, and her eyes glinted as I handed it to her. So she was satisfied to see the change it had wrought in me.

'And here,' she said. 'Take back your book. Deliver it to him yourself – if he will have you.'

She had tricked me. She had never intended to take it to him. Even if he needed it – even if he were threatened in some way.

'You don't love him,' I said. 'You don't love him as I do.'

I left her then, the book in my hand, tears streaming down my face even as I tried to hold them back. She didn't love him as I did, but it didn't matter, because he loved her best.

Fourth Month

Four days since I saw Izumi.

As I sit before the mirror in the mornings, striving with my tints and powders to create the face that is expected of me, I see that livid line running from her cheek to her chest.

What would it be like to be marked in such a way? How would it feel to display one's wounds so visibly? How unjust, that a man should wear his scars like a badge of honour, while a woman wears them with shame.

Yet I fear the consequences of her excoriation. Should those scars worsen her temper, will she not inflict her asperity on me? How I dread her vengefulness! She has damaged me enough already.

Dainagon says I should have been more kind. I should have let her tell the story of her assault; I should have shown more sympathy. Yet it was Izumi who assaulted me! The first words that left her mouth were cruel.

Her selfish guile harms even those she says she loves. The book she refused to take sits on my shelf, its very presence proof of her negligence.

Yet why can I not send it to Akashi? Something stops me.

Is it because I know Kanesuke loves her best? Or have I given up the thought that those lines and hexagrams can ensure his happiness?

Still, I know that if I loved him as I profess I would send it. Perhaps I fear that it will warn him not against the dangers of loving Izumi, but of loving me.

I have become too superstitious. I am like the blind

women in the marketplace who beckon ghosts with their rosaries.

The eighth day of the Fourth Month. The Washing of the Buddha.

It is late. I spoke to Ryūen, I watched the priests wash the statue of a child, and I am sad.

I saw Ryūen in the morning, before the ceremony. He sat before my screen and I heard his voice drift past me like the memory of our childhood, when we loved each other and would not suffer to be separated.

He sounded tired. Perhaps it was the journey or the strain of his obligations. The Abbot calls on him night and day; he relies on Ryūen's fine hand to dispense both good news and bad. It appears that the Emperor's abdication is imminent. Ryūen knows more than he can tell me, but he said that by the time of the Great Purification we can expect that it will be Reizei who will lead the prayers to purge us from sin.

Less than two months' time, and all may be changed! An amnesty declared, and Kanesuke pardoned.

I had not thought that this cascade of events would be so precipitous. Dare I wish for it?

The Emperor is expected to retire to the Southern Palace. No doubt he will continue to live in lavish style. I wonder if he will speak to his daughters before he takes his vows. Perhaps he will enlist Ryūen's services, and will ask him to contrive some stylish means of conveying his hopes for their health and happiness.

And what of Reizei? Will he miss his father, and will the Emperor miss him? They stood side by side at the ceremony, the boy nearly as tall as his father, his long hair soon to be cut, just as his father will have his shorn when he takes his vows.

The elder renouncing the world, the younger entering

it. The father discarding his pride and cynicism, the son acquiring it.

They watched, father and son, as the priests poured coloured water over the statue of the infant Buddha. And the whole court watched the two of them, the fathers of our fates and protectors of the realm. What will happen to us during the course of Reizei's reign? Will his naïve beneficence restore some calm to our kingdom? Will fires, storms and earthquakes be kept in abeyance?

What expectations we place on the narrow shoulders of that boy! Yet he will not rule alone. He will be ruled by others.

One by one they came forward, the senior courtiers who will govern Reizei's reign. They lifted the silver ewer and washed the Buddha's gilded face. How graceful their flourishes! How sincere their obeisance! The Minister of the Left moved with such grand decorum that some of the women sighed and hid their faces behind their fans.

He will be regent soon, and we will make our obeisance to him.

The Buddha sat unmoved by these attentions. His face was as calm after his ablutions as it was before they began.

Something about the sound of the water as it trickled over him reminded me of my own son when he was a baby. How I worried that he would drown when the nurse lowered him into his bath! A single moment of negligence and it would be too late. Then she would hand him to me, the hair at his nape curled and damp, and I would stroke it smooth and feel the soft spots on his skull. How strange it was to touch those yielding places. I feared they would never disappear, and that he would be as vulnerable as the Leech Child.

Did anyone notice my tears? My cheeks were as wet as the infant Buddha's. I held my fan close to my face and hoped that my emotions would seem to have been stirred

164

by the splendour of the priest's surplices, and the sounds of the bells and cymbals, and the great white bouquets of deutzia and lilies.

How stifling it has been! It is as if midsummer had arrived already. The heat seems to wax with the moon, and at night the rain beats down so insistently that the sound intrudes upon one's dreams. Pools of water stand in the courtyards and gardens, and the frilled petals of the peonies lie on the muddy ground.

The women amuse themselves with their tinted pictures. They entice me not. My shift sticks to my back; my temples throb from sleeplessness. I turn away my cold rice; even the thought of it makes me nauseous. I will ask Ukon for a cup of iced water instead.

The rivers are high, they say. The Kamo has almost burst its banks. I am tempted to go and see it. When I was there the other day it was not as swift, and I could float in the eddies, my gown billowing around me, with no fear of the current. Or did I imagine it?

Last night I dreamed that three cuckoos sat on the branch of an orange tree and sang to me. The song had words – sharp admonitory ones – but when I awoke I forgot them.

Rain drips from the cypresses. The leaves of the Chinese hawthorns, ever conspicuous in their senescence, are already red. The wizened flowers of the maples cling to their branches like insects.

There is talk that people in the lowlands of Yamato are dying of smallpox. It is no wonder, given this heat. Let us hope that the outbreak does not spread.

A messenger came this afternoon, while I was chatting to Dainagon, with a letter from Masato. It was written on fine

Koma paper, and tied to a hawthorn branch whose leaves had already turned. So he had noticed them, those unseasonably red leaves. I was glad that the rains had not leached their colour.

I longed to read it, but forced myself to set the letter aside. Dainagon would see too much in my face if I opened it in front of her. Yet she, my heart's soothsayer, read my thoughts as clearly as Masato reads the covert clouds.

'So it is from your young suitor,' she said. 'I have heard of him.'

From whom? I was not pleased. Had people learned of our meetings at Hasedera and the Otowa Falls? Had they overheard our secret meetings in my rooms?

I fear for him. If I have little to gain from this talk, he has much less. What good can come from having his name connected with mine?

Yet I was not entirely displeased that Dainagon should have heard of him. It made me happy to speak of him obliquely, and sense his presence in the colours by my side.

'He is not my suitor,' I protested. 'You mustn't speak of him that way.'

'But you love him.'

'Yes.' What a pleasure it was to say it – that which I had disclosed only to myself.

'And because you love him, you must protect him.'

'From what?' I asked, though I knew the answer.

'From yourself.'

'Am I so very dangerous?' It was true, but it hurt to hear her say it.

'He is a young man at the start of his career.'

'He is not as ambitious as some men are.'

'I know,' she said. 'It is rare for a man of his rank to waste his time with fortune tellers.'

'He isn't a fortune teller. He is a scholar. He has studied in China.'

Dainagon laughed. 'Has he? Whatever for? Well, at some point he may seek an office that suits him. And you,' she added, rapping her fan on my arm, 'mustn't impede him.'

'Why would I?'

Her face grew serious. 'You may not, but the rumours about you will.'

'Which rumours?'

She lowered her voice. 'There is talk that you and he are meddling with some book of magic.'

Izumi had spread the story; I was sure of it. She must have heard of my meetings with Masato, and linked his name with the I Ching. How wrong I was to take that book to her! Did she think that Masato had encouraged my plan to deliver it to Kanesuke? And to what purpose?

'We are not meddling with anything or anyone,' I said. 'What we speak of is our concern.'

'But the rumours –'

I cut her off before she could finish. 'They don't concern me either,' I lied.

'They will, if they harm him.' She drew herself up and gave me an intent look. 'I warned you to try to show some sympathy for Izumi. Since you did not, you must bear the consequences. She will damage him as well as you now, if she can.'

Dainagon was right. I trembled to think of it. 'What shall I do?' I asked.

'Break with him,' she said. 'At least for a while. And deny Izumi the chance to hurt him.'

'She has already, if what you say is true.'

'That is why I am speaking to you now.' She took my hand. 'Break with him. If you love him, you will give him up.'

I dropped my hand and turned my face towards the wall. 'Leave me now,' I said, and I heard the retreat of her starched gowns.

I sat in my room until it grew so dark I could barely see the letter by my side.

Am I so defiled that I ruin everything I touch? Shall I adorn myself with willow tags to warn those too blind to perceive my faults? Shall I swathe my body in black crêpe, like the mourners on the road to Adashino? Shall I insist that people stand in my presence, for it is too dangerous to sit with me, too dangerous to lie with me, too dangerous to be with a woman whose very blood runs thick with jealousy and lies?

I renounced my son before he could stand so I wouldn't taint him. I gave him up before he could walk so that my imperfections wouldn't mar him.

I gave up his father, who knew as well as I did my capacity for injury. I have been advised to give up Kanesuke, though he is my soul's double, and my equal in all things.

And now I am told to break with this boy who is my only happiness – this boy who loves me in all his innocence, though he will not say so.

I lit the lamp and unfolded the letter. Perhaps it would make my choice easier. He would tell me he had changed his mind. I was too much for him. My moods were too unsettling. He had heard about Kanesuke, and my vicious rivalry with Izumi, and my duplicity. Nothing would come of our relation.

But the letter didn't deliver me. It made things harder still.

He tells me that he misses me. He says he stays awake and thinks of how my hair covered him like grass.

His mother is much better, he says. In a few days she will leave with his father and go to Ishiyama to give thanks for her recovery. He will be alone in his house in the Fourth Ward.

If I like, he offers, I might come in the evening in three days' time, and he will let me ask a question of the I Ching. He will take up his yarrow sticks and count them out, and he will draw the hexagrams. He will interpret them as best he can, but he promises nothing.

Think about your question, he says. It should be simple and clear, neither too narrow nor too broad. It should not be trivial.

I pondered my answer the whole night long. I will go to him, as discreetly as I can. I will tell him that I have been advised to break with someone. Must I do so?

That is the question I will put to his book of knowledge. He may think that the one I must renounce is someone else, but the book will know otherwise. If the hexagrams tell me to give up this boy I love then I shall – at least for a while. I am not strong enough yet to leave him altogether.

I wrote to Masato and told him I would come to him. Three days of waiting; three days in which to consider my question.

Was I right to ask my question as I did? When I think of all that happened that evening . . . could I have avoided that chasm that opened between us, leaving him on one sharp rim and me on the other?

Yet how glad I was that night when I set out for his house! Glad and afraid. I dressed in disguise, in borrowed clothes, though I didn't go so far as to cover my face. I hid my madder silks beneath a plain brown robe. No one saw me leave, as far as I know, for I had sent Ukon off the night before, and I glided as lightly as a moth through the halls and galleries.

It was nearly midnight when I left. The air was cool and damp, for it had rained in the afternoon, and my shoes were muddied even before I reached the Kenshun Gate. The guards loitering nearby either failed to notice me or found me so drab as to be beneath their acknowledgement.

I had no escort, despite the hour, and I thought once more of Izumi's livid scar as I walked through the gate into the quiet street. How desperate she must have been, to go alone into a precinct far more dangerous than this.

The black bulk against the earthen wall proved to be my coach. I climbed inside in the dark, having told the driver to keep the lamps unlit. We jolted through the Yōmei Gate, and when we turned south onto the Ōmiya I allowed myself a glimpse through the blinds.

Through a heavy veil of cloud the gibbous moon shone with marred perfection. How it frightens me! It is as if it had been deformed by the darkness that defines it, the shadows bruising and distending it so that its very light seems diseased.

The houses along the avenue were dark and quiet, though at times I could hear music drifting over the walls. Within the gated gardens black pines and cypresses waved their boughs.

As we approached the Fourth Ward my resolve weakened. Perhaps I should ask another question. Perhaps I should defer the reading altogether and tell Masato that all I wanted was for him to reassure me. For I remembered how skilfully he had comforted me after my injury, and how he had smoothed my hair the night when it hailed. And I tasted once again the bitterness of his blood as it lay pooled on the mat in my room.

We turned onto the narrow street of Nishi no Tōin and pulled up before a double gabled door. Inquiries were made, and we were admitted into a wide courtyard. I tried to calm myself as the ox was unhitched. Then when I parted the curtain to step down Masato was there, and I felt the pressure of his hand and smelled the sandalwood burned into his robes as I leaned against him.

His face looked drawn, his eyes dark with fatigue and wariness. Was he as worried about the reading as I was, or did he mistrust me? Perhaps he had heard of Izumi's rumours; perhaps he regretted having invited me. I felt a tremor pass through me, and I stumbled on the gravelled walk.

And there, before the wondering servants, he touched my sleeve and said, 'Are you so sleepy? It's not even midnight. Let's have some tea.'

So he would banter with me despite his uneasiness. 'Tea?' I asked. 'Do I look so very ill?'

'Hardly,' he said. 'We'll take some to refresh ourselves. It focuses the mind.'

'So you think me scatterbrained.'

'Very,' he said, and smiled at me.

I was so fixed on him that I barely noticed the room in which we were standing. He was taller than I remembered, and more slender; his indigo robes patterned with hail had an iridescent sheen; his skin was very white even in the lamplight, and there were shadows under his eyes. And there was something in his manner I couldn't quite define, a careful equipoise, as if he were trying to convey an ease that he did not feel.

'This way,' he said, and I followed him as obediently as a child. We walked through rooms and hallways; I had a vague impression of space and coolness; but my eyes returned always to the nape of his neck, and the blue-black hair that shone with the same iridescence as his clothes.

He led me to a room that overlooked the garden. The latticed windows were open, and a breeze lifted the blinds and rippled the green standing curtains. I heard the rustling of leaves outside, and smelled a faint chaste scent.

'It's a laurel tree,' he said. 'A very old one – much older than the house.'

'So it is a new house?' I asked, trying to ease the constraint I felt between us.

'Oh, this house has burned down many times. Twice since I have lived in it.'

'I hope you rescued all your books.'

'We rescued most things the first time, but the second time we weren't as lucky.' He spoke with a lightness that didn't convince me. I wanted to ask more, but he turned and led me to some cushions arranged on the floor. 'Come and sit down. You don't mind if I keep the curtains to one side?'

Did I mind? Did he really think I would prefer such formality, with him on one side of that green divide, and me on the other?

'Of course not,' I said, as offhandedly as I could, and I knelt on the cushion he provided.

He called to a woman standing in attendance by the doorway and ordered some tea. As they spoke I glanced about the room. Two lamps burned on stands near the platformed bed, which was enclosed with mauve curtains, the colour deeper near the hem. Papers cluttered the writing table, the brushes and inkstand laid out as if he were in the midst of some private task; and the dark polished cupboards were filled with books and scrolls. I could smell them. Their mustiness mingled with the scent of laurel leaves and rain.

So this was where he slept, within that curtained bed. This was where he read. He knelt at this lacquered desk and wrote his letters. He lived in this room when I was elsewhere, remembering him. When he woke in the morning he looked out at this garden, which he knew in all its sheltered intimacy. He had grown up with these trees. He saw their blossoming; he watched the increase of their fruit.

And now I sat in this room and imagined his life as it was when I was not with him. The hidden rondure of it. The stories and secrets.

The books and scrolls in their particoloured dress reminded me of my ignorance. They knew him as I never would. And amongst them there was one that would decide if I would ever know him better, or if his life would be closed to me.

He walked across the room and I felt that tremor again – that bottomless fear.

'What is it?' he asked, for he read it in my face, and I saw a shadow of the same mood reflected in his own.

'Nothing,' I replied, and I tried to smile at him. 'I must be more tired than I thought.' I hoped he might invite me to lie within that curtained bed. But he simply said, 'The tea will do you good,' and I nodded.

It came, steaming, in two wide-lipped cups of fine blue porcelain, and we drank it. It had a sharp ascetic scent, like wood smoke in the mountains. I sipped too fast and it burned my mouth. My hand shook as I put down the cup, and it clattered on the tray.

I met his eyes across that little distance of tea and formality. He looked at me steadily, with the same guardedness I had noticed before.

'So you want to ask a question,' he said. 'Have you decided on it? For we must speak about it before we can begin.'

'Must we? Would it be enough just to have it in my mind?'

'And not tell me?' His raised brows mirrored his incredulity. 'If you like, but that makes it more difficult.'

'I don't mind.'

He smiled. 'You like things to be difficult, don't you? And you like secrets.'

'I prefer secrets to lies.'

'But you would lie to me about your question.'

He smiled again as he said it, but there was an edge to his voice. So he had guessed. Why had I hinted? 'All right, then,' I said. 'I'll tell you. I've been advised to give something up.'

'One of your vices.'

'Not exactly.'

'Well, what is this something? Has it a shape or name?'

'Yes,' I said, 'but perhaps it would be best if we didn't speak of it.'

'So you would give me an unsolvable riddle, and I must

put it to the I Ching. But you should know that if your question is vague, the answer will be vague also.'

'I don't mind.'

'So you want nothing more than that? A vague response to a vague question? Do you really want this guidance?'

'Yes and no,' I said.

'Yes and no. Tell me – is this something you have decided to do yourself, or is someone compelling you? You said you had been advised.' For the first time I sensed in him a strain of jealousy – of this unnamed person who had urged me to my indeterminate query.

'No one has compelled me,' I lied, remembering Dainagon's advice.

'So,' he said. 'We shall leave it at this: you must renounce something.'

'In a manner of speaking.'

'And you wish to know how your life will change if you take this step.'

Did I wish to know? I had to, for his sake. 'Yes.'

'Well, then, we shall ask your question, which is clear to you but not to me.' Then the words rushed out: 'Is it a person you must give up?' he asked. 'Is it some man?'

His impulsiveness threw me off balance. 'Not a person,' I evaded. 'A kind of bond.'

'I see, a bond.' And again I heard the jealousy in his voice. 'So. How shall we frame your question? For it is not advisable to ask something that can be answered with a simple yes or no. You might ask instead, for instance, "What will be the state of my life if I maintain this bond?" or "What will it be like if I break it?"'

How could I choose? Either way I risked an answer I didn't want to accept.

'The first,' I said. I knew well enough how bleak my life would look if I chose the latter.

'All right,' he told me coolly. 'Then we can begin.'

So we were to start with even more distance between us than when I arrived. It was all wrong. But there was nothing to do but watch as he made his preparations.

He stood and brought a lamp close to where we sat. He moved his mat some distance from mine, and in the empty space between he placed an incense burner and a red lacquered tray. Then he walked to the recesses of the room and returned with a book wrapped in violet cloth.

He knelt and placed the book between us, and folded back the cloth. The binding was black; there was no writing on the cover.

'It faces south,' he said, 'as you do, and I face north.' And I remembered how we had lain in my room at Hasedera, with our arms entwined and our heads facing north, as the Shākyamuni Buddha's had when he passed into oblivion.

He stood again and walked to a cupboard and brought back a long lidded box. Then he knelt and removed the lid and took out a sheaf of sticks.

They were nearly as long as my forearm, and as fragile as broken reeds. He laid them on the tray, and then he took off his shoes and placed them beside his mat. His feet were narrow and white, the arches high and the toes splayed, as if he were a diver poised on a rock.

He faced the book and stretched himself out on the floor, pressing his forehead to the mat. He repeated his prostration twice more, and then he knelt and lit the incense in the burner.

We waited as the scent filled the room. The silence was as tangible as the smoke, and within it I heard his breathing.

Moonlight lay thick as hoarfrost on the floor. Shadows stood in the corners; the curtains shifted. The sharp odour of cloves spread through the air and mingled with the sweetness of the laurel.

I watched him as he knelt. His hands rested on his knees; his long fingers tensed and then relaxed. His indigo robes with their pattern of hail fell in heavy folds all around him. He was watchful, but what he searched for I couldn't see. He looked neither at me nor at the book, and beneath the calmness of his face there was a sweet avidity. Then he glanced at me, and in his eyes, still heavy with tiredness, I saw both a rebuke and a challenge.

He was rebuking me for my pretences. He was challenging me to be still. And so we faced each other in quiet expectancy, with the book between us.

He leaned and picked up the yarrow stalks and held them over the incense burner, and then he passed them three times through the blue tendrils of smoke. For a moment his long sleeves brushed against the burner, and I stifled a cry for fear they would catch fire.

From the sheaf of sticks in his hand he took one and put it back in the box. 'It is the watcher,' he told me. 'The witness.' Then he counted the rest, so swiftly I could barely keep track. Twenty. Forty. Forty-nine.

He placed the stalks on the tray, and with a sweep of his hand divided them into two heaps. Then – I have forgotten the sequence now – he counted off each pile of stalks by fours, and put those that remained between the fingers of his left hand so that they bristled like claws. He repeated this three times until he arrived at a number.

'Eight for the first place,' he said. 'A yin line.' He told me to fetch his inkstone and a piece of paper, and had me write down the first of the six lines that would determine our future.

Yin. One broken line. A yielding line, dark and feminine.

He set the sticks that he had held in his hand back in the tray and began the ritual again: the sweeping aside, the dividing, the counting. And all the while he looked not at me – for I had become as featureless as the shadows in the room – but at the patterns cast by the yarrow stalks.

'Seven for the second place,' he said. 'A yang line.' So I

drew upon the piece of paper a new line above the other – a long unbroken one. Yang, the masculine, as dazzling as the sun, as straight as time's arrow.

When the yarrow yielded its count again he had me draw a yin line above the yang.

'The first trigram,' he said.

'What does it mean?' I asked, for I thought I saw his hands tremble a little as he gathered the stalks.

'It is K'an, the Abyss,' he said. 'Can you see it? The broken lines are the cliffs, and the straight one in the centre is the river at the bottom of the chasm.'

I looked down at the three lines I had drawn. To me they meant nothing. Yet I knew he could see in them a vivid scene: the broken rocks, the vertiginous drop, the swift water running from nowhere to nowhere.

It was the name of the hexagram that frightened me – the name and the expression on his face. He must have sensed my fear, for he looked up and smiled at me. 'It's not as dire as it seems. It can mean many things. And we still must draw the second trigram.'

We were halfway through, he explained. We had to place the last three lines atop the others. It was like building a tower, he said: one line stacked upon the other. We had finished the first storey, and now we were making the second. Only when the two were combined would the meaning be clear.

I closed my eyes and listened to the dry shuffle of the stalks, and I thought of how I had lain on his back without a single layer of gauze between us.

The wicks burned low, and I heard an owl call in the garden. My throat was dry, but I dared not ask for some tea, for I didn't want to break the rhythm of his counting.

What would I do should the message be bleak? How could I live with the possibility that there was to be no happiness for us? Should I lie and say I had asked the wrong question?

How had I let myself become so superstitious? Why did I look to this mouldy black book, its pages riddled with silverfish, for the answer to my quandary?

I tried to calm myself and watch his hands as if they were a woman's busy with some simple task: sewing, passing a shuttle, plaiting a ribbon.

He winnowed his stalks twice more. First an eight and a broken line; then a seven and a straight one.

Before he fixed the final line he hesitated. 'I'm not sure I've counted correctly,' he said. 'I may need to start again.'

What had he seen that made him so uncertain? It wasn't like him. Did he fear something in the outcome? 'Perhaps you should stop and rest,' I suggested.

He shook his head. 'No, I must count them all at once. But you mustn't put too much faith in this. I may be in error.'

So I let him determine his line, and it was a broken one. 'Six for the last place,' he said. 'A yin line – a moving one. Draw it, and then I will explain.'

I drew the broken line above the others, and then I saw what he had feared: the second trigram was the same as the first. K'an, the Abyss. I picked up the paper and put it to one side, as if that could protect me from its message. Then I drew in a breath and asked him, 'Tell me. What does it mean?'

He looked at me and said, 'That depends upon your question. And since you alone know what you have asked, you are the only one who can interpret the hexagram. All I can do is read you the text. You must take from it what you can.'

He took up the book and turned the pages. '"Hexagram Twenty-nine,"' he read. '"K'an, the Abyss." This is the text for all six lines,' he told me gently. 'Listen to it, and then I will explain the case of the last line.'

I sat with my hands in my lap and closed my eyes. Through the obscurity of my fear I heard his voice. '"Abyss upon abyss – grave danger! All will be well if confidence is maintained and a sharp hold kept on the mind."'

'Look at me,' he said. 'Let me try to explain.' Then he told me how K'an is like the heart enclosed within the body, or like the soul locked within the confines of the self. It is like a stream high in the mountains, which in the course of its fall creates its own danger.

But what danger? I asked myself. Does it come from without or within?

'Now I must read you the commentary on the sixth line,' he said. 'For it is a moving line, and has superlative meaning.'

I looked at the broken line at the top of the hexagram. It was just like the rest. It did not waver. And yet to him it moved like the lion of Manjushrī, whose flanks rippled though they were made of bronze.

'When I read you these lines,' he told me, 'You mustn't worry. For behind them stands another hexagram that is less dire than this one.'

'Six for the top place,' he read. 'Bound with black ropes and imprisoned amidst thorns, for three years one fails to obtain what one seeks.'

What was I to make of that terrible pronouncement? Were he and I to endure some excess of pain for such a long time?

'Three years,' I said, and the tears rolled down my cheeks even as I spoke.

He put the book down and came and knelt beside me, and held my face in his hands. 'Look at me,' he said. 'Three years is metaphorical; it is not a fixed length of time.' He kissed my cheeks. 'Now pull yourself together and listen to the last part of the reading. I mustn't break the ritual any longer. When I am finished we can rest.'

Was he inviting me to lie down with him in his bed? How I wanted to rest right then, and stop up my ears from the words he was about to read me. I was done with words; they were as frightening as the lines drawn on the paper. But for his sake I composed myself.

He returned to his place and picked up the book again. 'The top line,' he explained, 'is a moving line. It is a yin line – a feminine one – that inclines to the yang. It has been yin for so very long that it is impelled to become its opposite. And when it changes, we obtain a second hexagram.'

As he spoke I remembered something I had written. Had I not described the same paradox myself: how I, a woman, had striven to be like a man?

'Pick up your brush,' he told me, 'and draw the second hexagram. Start with the bottom trigram: the Abyss. Then above it draw a broken line and two straight ones.'

I did so, though my hand trembled. And again he picked up his book. '"Hexagram Fifty-nine,"' he read. '"Huan: Dissolution. Wind blows over the abyss. The water is dispersed, becoming foam and mist. It is advantageous to cross a great river. Perseverance brings reward."'

I was more at a loss than before. I felt an unreasonable anger rising in me, that these words should have such sway over me, though I understood them no more than a peasant understands a Chinese poem.

'It means nothing to me,' I said bitterly. 'What advantage is there in dissolution? This hexagram is as black as the first.'

'There is hope in it,' he assured me, 'and there is no contradiction. The first hexagram guides you in the present, and the second in the future.'

'So my future will be as difficult as my present? Am I to be dispersed? Am I to cross a river?'

'They are images,' he said. 'You must decide what they

mean. It may become clear over time. But you mustn't expect the book to foretell your future. You must decide how to take its advice. If you like you may disregard it altogether. For I was very tired when I counted out the lines, and I might have been in error.'

He smiled at me again, but it was a melancholy smile, and I wondered if his excuse was genuine. Was he as intuitive as a woman? Had he realised that he was the object of my question?

'It is enough now,' he said. 'I'll put the things away, and we can rest.' Then he performed the opening ritual in reverse, as if time were running backwards. He made his three prostrations; he wrapped the book in its violet cloth and replaced it on its shelf; he returned the stalks to their box. Then he came and knelt beside me, and once again he held my face in his hands.

'I must ask you one thing,' he said. 'Please don't speak any more about your question. I am as frightened of it as you are.' Then he put his arms around me and kissed me, and we lay together on the floor. For a long time I was aware of nothing but our pleasure, and when I opened my eyes and saw the first light falling on his upturned face I was surprised.

And then, because it was dawn, we parted the mauve curtains and shut ourselves within a second twilight. And this time we shed every colour, one robe after another, and then we crushed them with our weight until they bore the imprint not just of our bodies but of our deepest selves.

Then we were thirsty, and he brought me some tea. It was cold, and so bitterly strong that it furred my tongue. Something about its smoky taste prompted my question: 'Tell me about the fire,' I said as I stroked his hair. 'The second one.'

He looked at me with an expression I couldn't read. 'Why?'

'I want to know what you lost.'

'I lost my sister.' He turned onto his back and pulled my robe over him and closed his eyes. Then it came back to me: we were in the garden by the house near the Otowa Falls, and he told me I reminded him of his sister, who had died when she was nine.

'Tell me,' I said.

He turned his head and looked at me. 'Why? So you can write about it in one of your stories?'

'No. I won't. And you mustn't tell me if you don't want to.'

I didn't know what he had lost when I asked the question. But I had sensed something in him when he had spoken once before of that fire – some deep and painful withholding. So I chose it, that one piece of his past, as if it could help me understand all the rest that would remain unknown to me.

He turned his head toward the ceiling and closed his eyes. 'It was the Eighth Month,' he said. 'There was a drought that year, and the leaves had already fallen. It was just a simple thing, really. It was night, and she and I were asleep in our rooms in the north wing. Her room was next to our mother's, and mine was a little way down the corridor. We think someone knocked over a lamp. The curtains in my mother's room caught fire, and because it was windy it spread quickly.'

I moved beside him and lay my head on his chest.

'The first thing I remember is hearing my father shouting, and then he ran into my room and picked me up and carried me out into the garden. I could see flames, and there were people running back and forth. Then my mother was there, with her hair loose all around her. She came running toward me – she never ran – and I remember being surprised because her feet were bare. I had never seen her feet before. She shouted at me, "Where is your sister?" and I began to cry because I had no idea.

'The roof was burning, and the servants were carrying water from the pond and throwing it onto the eaves. And I remember worrying that my backgammon board and my bows and arrows would be burned up. I wasn't thinking about my sister.

'Then we saw her. She came running onto the porch and her clothes and her hair were on fire. She was screaming and flapping her sleeves. My father went running after her, and he pushed her to the ground and grabbed her by the feet, and his sleeves caught fire. But he dragged her to the pond, and there was a hissing sound when the flames touched the water.

'And then she drowned – or she stopped breathing when he was dragging her. When they pulled her from the water she was dead.'

I lifted my head from his chest and looked at his face. His eyes were still closed, but I could see the tears slipping down his cheeks. 'Don't,' I said, and I kissed his face again and again. 'What a dreadful story. I shouldn't have asked you about it.'

'I can still remember that smell. That horrid smell of burnt wet hair. And her face was black where the flames had licked it.'

I smoothed his hair back from his forehead.

'Only the north wing burned down,' he said, 'and part of the east wing. And then the wind changed. They laid her in this room and waited for a sign that her soul might return to her. But by the end of the second day it was clear it wouldn't, so we took her to Adashino and set her on a pyre and burned her again.'

He was quiet for a while, and I held him as tightly as I could. Then he said, 'My mother didn't speak for months. And she never forgave my father for rescuing me first.'

He held my face in his hands. His eyes were full of tears. 'I told you that she looked like you. She had the most beautiful eyes, and the thickest smoothest hair. And now I shall lose you, too. I can feel it. I dreamed of it two nights ago.'

Then the fear we had both held back came rushing upon us, like a black wind from the northeast.

He pulled my hair back so fiercely I felt it would tear from the roots. 'I didn't want this,' he said. 'I didn't ask for it. Why did you make me love you so?'

So we leapt together, he from one steep bank and I from the other, and we held each other with all our strength, as if that alone could break our fall.

The Kamo Festival has come and gone, and I have spent the whole time in my rooms.

It began just after I saw Masato. Perhaps it was the strain of the reading. I have had fever and chills, and even the smell of rice makes me nauseous.

When the fever was at its worst I would close my eyes and watch the patterns of straight and broken lines flicker against my lids, one hexagram shifting into another.

Buzen came and tried to entice me with some chestnuts. Why is it that friends who have been distant for months become tenderly familiar when one is ill? Perhaps it was curiosity, for she seemed concerned about my complaint. I suppose she thought I had invented it.

My only consolation is that I have been spared the usual defilement. It is beginning to worry me, for it has been two months since I have endured it.

At night when everything was still I would see that fire. The girl waving her burning sleeves. Her quenched face as it lay on the bier. Then Masato would be there and I would taste the salt of his tears as he kissed me. That dream he had of losing me: I think of it all the time. There is a reason for it, just as there was a reason for those two hexagrams.

But what is the reason? My fear conceals me from it as the clouds hide the moon's deformities.

All around me I heard sounds of gaiety. Women arranging their hair, and garlanding their necks with hollyhocks, and shouting in peremptory tones for their maids: 'Where is my fan?' 'Fit the cords on my clogs!' 'This robe isn't starched properly!' Couriers delivering boxes of clothes for the festival: gowns of violet and yellow-green, figured jackets, beaded trains.

I wore clothes like that last year, when I was part of this pageant. But now my own plain mauve gowns – the penance decreed by the Empress – lie in their long lidded box like an unstuffed corpse. I didn't ride in a carriage adorned with laurels and hollyhocks, or fight for a place amongst the crowds on the Ichijō. The musicians didn't play for me; the dancers did not dance. I missed the purification at the river.

They say the river is still high. The viewing stands along its banks stood close to the floodline. The auspicious place fixed by the diviners (was it Masato himself who advised the geomancers?) was so treacherous that the ceremony had to be changed. The Virgin of Kamo couldn't bathe in the stream; the stream was brought to her in a silver basin. For what would happen if the Kamo Virgin were swept away? There would be no protectresses of the city. How ludicrous it would seem: the Vestal of Ise defiled, and the Kamo Virgin drowned during her own purification.

Dainagon told me everything. She cooled my cheeks with a piece of ice and described all I had missed, and the undercurrents of intrigue. Whispers about the Emperor's abdication. Tales of a rift between the Minister of the Left and his jealous counterpart. Arguments between the Emperor and his wife. Stories that Kanesuke may be given the post of Palace Minister should he be pardoned.

I can't be distracted by him now. I have tried hard to keep him from my thoughts, and now that he may return I must banish him further still. He cannot control me as he once did. When I think of all that anguish and vitriol – how can I face the prospect of enduring it again?

And yet I think of him. How he will look and act. His voice. The lines at the sides of his mouth. His walk. His moodiness.

I am sick of this vacillation. It is only an excuse for histrionics. I am done with it: the mirroring and doubling, the duplicity and mean-spiritedness.

Why, at the very time I should find another kind of love, must it, too, be taken from me? And by the same woman who stole Kanesuke. Izumi. Izumi. To think that I spoke that name once with trustfulness. Now the very taste of those three syllables is as bitter as gall to me.

I thought I could find it in myself to think of her with sympathy because of the shock she endured. But now I must fight the urge to despise her.

Did she see Masato at the festival? Has he been pointed out to her? 'Look – there is your rival's lover.' Would she say to herself, 'What a lovely boy. What a waste and a pity!' Then she would proceed with her vicious whispers, all in the interest of destroying me.

I cannot give her that power. Perhaps it is all in my mind. Perhaps she stayed in her rooms as I did, unable to meet the gaze of those anxious to see the evidence of her disgrace. For her damage is visible, whereas mine is hidden by pride.

I am not strong enough to be proud now. My very thoughts undermine me.

How painful it is when one's mind becomes one's worst enemy! Nothing is what it seems. It is like that feeling I have dreaded since I was a child: that terrible moment when the earth begins to quake, and even the ground is suspect. My thoughts are not a refuge now. My moods shift like the hexagrams, one emotion bleeding into the next: the desire transformed to fear, the fear to anger and spite and vengefulness.

I dreamed last night of Izumi.

It was not as I expected. We didn't tear each other apart as one tears a piece of cloth. That vicious sound when what was whole is rent in two: I didn't hear it.

It was quiet in my dream. The cloth was whole, and we wrapped ourselves in it. We were friends. She lent me her comb. We exchanged whispers.

We spoke of the man we love, and we made of him a precious shell that we held between us. Within it lived the ocean of our double experience.

We were changed by that experience, and we changed each other. My anguish greater because of hers. Her joy stronger because of mine. The colours of our mutual fidelity deepened and intensified.

She looked at me and her eyes were calm and full of light. And I thought: this is how she looks when they are together. This is what it would be like to be loved by her.

More false solicitude. The Empress wrote to me and inquired after my health. She had heard that I was ill. Is that why I had missed the Kamo Festival? A pity, she said; she was looking forward to seeing me in my mauve gowns. She was sure they would have suited me. Perhaps there would be another occasion on which I might wear them.

In fact, she said, she was planning a little gathering in two weeks' time, on the First Day of the Hare. Just a few women for a game of comparisons – of fans, perhaps, or flowers, or something else; she had not yet decided. Perhaps I could lead one team, and Izumi the other. I could wear my new gowns, and everyone would admire them.

187

She was sending me a basket of dried persimmons and some Chinese sweets. They would tempt me, she hoped; she was sure I wasn't eating enough. Everyone remarked on how thin I had grown. I must be plumped up; she would send me delicacies from her own stores.

'You must write me some more tales,' she told me. 'You must keep up with your work or you will lose your touch. And I do so miss,' she confessed, 'that fine high-minded tone of yours. It always makes me laugh.'

So we are to have a game of comparisons, Izumi and I. We are to choose from an array of fans (or paintings, perhaps, or wild carnations, or songbirds in wicker cages) and decide which is best. Which fan has the loveliest design. Which landscape surpasses the rest. Which single wild carnation embodies the ideal of all carnations. Which thrush sings like the birds in Amida's Paradise.

And the Empress will sit before us and judge us on our wit and discernment. Our very gestures will be judged, and the timbre of our voices. The grace of our hands as they pick up the specimens. The colours of our sleeves: Izumi's varied, subtle, rich; mine as drab as a broody bird's.

Why has she chosen to set Izumi against me, to lay us out to scrutiny like the objects we must judge? Why are we to be the prime exhibits at her gathering? She is cruel. She wants to find in me a flaw and a weakness, and display it for everyone to see. I am not done with my chastisement. She must punish me twice over.

And what of Izumi? Is the Empress championing her? Is the contest a means of bringing her out of the gloom of her own private shame? Yet even if that is so Izumi will dislike this spectacle as much as I. Even if she wins – and I have no doubt of her success – she will not relish her victory.

For the more devious Izumi becomes the more she hides

behind her modesty. She conceals the brilliant plumage of her lies with her demureness. She will not want her virtues paraded in contrast to my vices. Those who are guilty of falsity seldom relish praise, even if it is sincere.

Yet I wonder if Izumi will still be here in two weeks' time. Perhaps the prospect of this contest will speed her departure for Akashi. Even if the marks from her injury are healed, she will have reasons to avoid the Empress's little game. She will leave to join Kanesuke before the First Day of the Hare; I am sure of it. I will dispatch a friend to gather evidence of her preparations.

News has reached us that people in Yamato are dying of smallpox at an alarming rate. A messenger arrived yesterday from Nara and told the Emperor that the toll among the common people is already high, and there are fears that the disease will spread to the temples and aristocratic circles.

The messenger said that he had heard that the outbreak had spread to towns along the Yodo River less than a day's ride from here.

How I dread that disease. I remember the smell of it in my mother's sickroom in the garden. We were not allowed inside that room, Ryūen and I, but they couldn't hide the smells from us. The smell of coptis root and boiled rhubarb, of soiled clothes and burnt poppy seeds. They couldn't hide the sounds, either. The chants of the priests. My father's worried voice. My mother's screams when they changed her dressings, and her skin came away with the wads of floss.

Later, when Ryūen and I came down with the same fever, it was almost easier. For the delirium lifted us out of our fear and transported us to the same disembodied realm, where day is indistinguishable from night, and dreams are more real than life itself.

But my mother stayed in that realm, and Ryūen and I

returned. Why is it that this disease should take mothers in all their strength from their children? We came back, and when we did the funeral was over, and we sat with our father in the mourning chamber with its grey curtains and dirt floor that smelled of earthworms.

And soon Ryūen was strong enough to kick a ball, and the sickroom in the courtyard was dismantled. My mother's robes were put away in a cedarwood chest. Her combs and hairpins shut in a red lacquered box. Her papers burned. I can still see my father's face as he stirred the ashes, and I remember thinking even then, though I was just thirteen: don't forget this. This is the face of grief. Remember it in all its vividness.

Masato wrote to me. He had a dream that he couldn't understand. Perhaps I would have some insight, he said. 'Send me a letter soon and tell me.'

He dreamed that we were standing on a beach in half-drenched robes, our feet bare on the cool white sand. (Oh, the improbability of dreams: that a woman such as I would stand barefoot with her lover on a beach! I laugh to think of it.) We were throwing shells into the water to see how far out they would fall.

It was morning. Clouds billowed on the horizon. The sea was calm, the waves barely crested with foam. The sun beat upon our backs.

But things were not as they seemed. I was too young, no more than a girl, my hair falling just short of my ankles. Yet he loved me like no other, and felt he had known me since I was born. And he laughed as I did, at the sheer improbability of it, and we watched the glinting shells as they fell into the water.

He heard a noise (the call of a gull, perhaps; he wasn't sure) and turned his head. When he looked back I was gone.

What could have happened? The waves were not high. I did not cry out.

He stood on the sand and called my name but there was no answer. The clouds vanished; the sun dried his robes.

Far out upon the surface of the sea he thought he saw a flash of colour. Then it was gone. It might have been a trick of the eye. The sun was too bright, the strain of searching too difficult.

He saw the flash again and dived straight into the waves. Then he awoke. His robes were drenched with sweat, and there was a bitter taste in his mouth.

What did it mean? He tried to puzzle it out but his books were no help to him. The characters shimmered before his eyes; the meanings shifted and changed.

What did it mean? he asked again. 'Send me a letter soon and tell me.'

I pondered his dream all afternoon and into the evening. For several hours I fought against the meaning of it until I grew so tired from the effort that I lay down.

I lay within the shifting curtains and thought of the Leech Child, set in his boat and left to drift out on the sea. Why his mother had chosen this. How she had abandoned him. The enduring pain of it.

And now Masato had dreamed of the same thing. Had he sensed it somehow, the knowledge that I have concealed even from myself?

I can ignore it no longer. The signs are too clear. I remember them from the first time, during the months before my son was born. The nausea and exhaustion. Every sound and scent intensified. And the strange unfathomable desire, deeper than ever, strong beyond reason.

What am I to do with this new child? Will I mark it with my guilt and deceit, as I have marked my son? Will it bring no pleasure to Masato, who will only suffer from the slanderous talk of our liaison? (And he is too young to marry me; it would be unseemly; it hurts even to think of it.)

Only a little while now before I must decide. The evidence will soon become too clear. I know full well that by the time the child quickens I must leave. I cannot stay in the palace: it is against all custom. A pregnant woman is even more polluting than a bleeding one. And who knows what blame might be cast on me should my condition be revealed?

There is another means of escape. I can make a second trip to the Eastern Marketplace to procure the bitter herbs that will resolve my dilemma. I am sure to find them there . . . or in the shop by the marketplace. Is my memory playing tricks on me, or did the bookseller not ask me if I needed some of his remedies? Could he have sensed that which I did not know myself? Or did he assume, as his hidden client did, that I was the sort of woman who resorted to this method from time to time when circumstances demanded it?

I mustn't dwell on it. The prospect makes me ill. I cannot seal this body in a jar and bury it on the bank of the Kamo River as other women bury their guilty secrets.

A child who might have his hands, and his eyes flecked with brown. A child whose hair curls at the nape of her neck, as his does. A serious child, a tender child, a child who conceals her fears behind her incessant questions.

Why am I sure this child is a girl? Perhaps because Masato dreamed of it, though I sensed it even before he told me.

Shall I answer his letter? Yes, even now, when I am done with this page. But I won't interpret his dream for him. I will ask him to come to me as soon as he can, and I will comfort him without words.

A thunderstorm in the night, two hours of coolness, then the same oppressive heat.

Buzen came to me as I was searching for a fan. The disease has spread to the southern reaches of the city, she told me. I could see the fear in her eyes as she described what she had heard. People falling ill in the crowded streets by the Rashō Gate. Men with fever and rashes, and spots on their arms and faces; women who vomit and lie prostrate on their beds. There are rumours of deaths. A vagrant found face down in a muddy ditch by the Ōmiya. A silversmith stricken so fast there was no time to call a priest. A woman brought in a cart from a farm to the west, her eyes already glazed by the time her frantic husband found the exorcist who could rid her of her demons.

As Buzen spoke I thought of the boy I had seen in the marketplace, the one with eyes the colour of boiled egg. How many of us will be afflicted as he is? How many of us will be marked so deeply that no quantity of white lead paint, no poultice of silk cocoons or falcon feathers will heal us?

How many of those who have not suffered this sickness before will die? On this hot summer day, what vapour creeps through the heavy air and steals into our bodies?

Which mothers will be taken from their children? Which fathers will be parted from their sons? Which lovers, friends and neighbours who live side by side will be divided by a banner of black crêpe and a willow tag that says: 'Touch me not. I am polluted. Stay away.'

Buzen rushed off to tell her beads. I will not finger mine. I wait only for Masato, and an hour without words or fears.

Why doesn't he come? What has detained him? Another day and still no word. I sent off a second letter and told the messenger to report back what he could.

Only two days since Masato pleaded with me to interpret

his dream. Now I must plead for news of him. How I detest this waiting!

The mood at court reflects my state. News contends with rumour, and anger with unease. The Emperor, no doubt shaken by the vicious whispers that his ineptitude has brought on this malaise, has announced that in three days' time he will go into seclusion. If I do not hear from Masato before then I must wait until the Emperor completes his abstinence, and the palace gates are reopened.

Will this disease turn us into exiles from our own city? Are we to spend the summer barricaded behind the palace walls? Everyone knows it is likely that if the epidemic spreads the court itself will be sequestered. The inner gates closed and guarded. Every stranger questioned. All movements watched.

Must I be separated from Masato, or will he find some pretext to visit me? And how can I go to him? If the pestilence spreads, even the shortest journeys become difficult, and longer ones will be more hazardous still.

It occurs to me even as I write that Izumi may suffer as much as I do. How can she leave for Akashi if the court is on retreat? She cannot visit her exile if she is exiled herself.

Why she has not gone already is a mystery. I can find no evidence that she is making plans to flee. Perhaps she is too clever to betray her intentions. Or perhaps this sudden shift in our fortunes will force her to reconsider. Will she risk her own health to join Kanesuke? Her journey would take her through infected territory, and she hasn't fought this scourge and won, as I did when I was a girl.

What will we do, she and I, during these long summer months if we are trapped in this cage? I almost wish she had left already. Yet part of me would rejoice if her plans were thwarted by this plague.

★

194

The Emperor has dispatched messengers to the home provinces, warning the governors to take protective measures against the spread of the epidemic. Envoys rode out early this morning to the twenty-two shrines, and to the guardians of the imperial tombs.

It is everywhere, this fearful pressure. Courtiers running back and forth. Whispers in the galleries, and conclaves in the Great Hall of State. News of priests being called down from Mount Hiei, from Kasuga and Kōfukuji, from Sumiyoshi, Kitano and Gion. Tales of diviners meeting to fix auspicious dates for ceremonies to appease the wrathful gods and spirits.

I picture the messengers riding through the woods and fields, fighting the invisible tide of sickness that washes over them even as they carry their admonitions.

What good will their warnings do? What good the offerings and sprinklings of salt, the chants and supplications? With every new era these diseases worsen. We suffer from boils and bright red spots; from unnamed scourges that suck the moisture from our bodies, leaving us as dry and brittle as reeds.

Will we become like the thin men of Gion, who dance to ward off pestilence, only to find that their masks do not protect them? Shall we hurry here and there, our sleeves pressed to our faces, hoping that a few thin layers of silk will shield us from this illness?

I am not afraid of it, and I am done with waiting. Since my messenger could find out nothing (for there was no answer when he knocked at Masato's gate) I will go to his house myself. For in two days' time the Emperor will go into seclusion, and I will be locked up with my thoughts.

Dainagon came by as I was dressing to go to Masato. She told me that the Empress has postponed the game of comparisons. The general mood is too unsettled. With the Emperor going into seclusion and the court itself on the verge of sequestration it hardly seems the time for such frivolity.

'And you know as well as I,' Dainagon told me, 'that the Emperor may abdicate any day.'

So that is the reason for the Empress's preoccupation – though she will hardly regret the change. With her husband retired to the Southern Palace, and her brother installed as regent, she will be freer to act as she pleases. She can devote her time to her son, and nurture his ambitions. And perhaps her daughter and Sadako will be forgiven – though that depends on her husband's whim.

The princesses. In my worry over Masato I had almost forgotten them.

'Have you had news of Sadako?'

'Not recently. Why? Are you feeling guilty?'

I let that pass. 'I heard that people are falling ill not far from where she lives. And she is weak already.'

'Yes, she is.'

'Have you written to her?'

'I have. This morning.'

Her reticence said more than any remonstration. 'You won't forgive me for spreading the rumour about her, will you?'

'Not yet.'

'But you would lie for me,' I said, remembering how she had protected me from the Empress's insinuations.

She smiled as one does at a truant child. 'Once, at least. Perhaps not again.' She glanced at my green gowns. 'You are looking very lovely,' she said, 'though you are still too thin. Do you have a rendezvous?'

'No. An errand.' Something in my face must have betrayed me, for she said, 'You're not leaving the palace! Not with things as they are.'

I couldn't dissemble a second time. 'Just for a little while.'
I touched her sleeve. 'If anyone asks,' I said – and she knew
I meant the Empress – 'will you say I have gone to Shakuzen
for the evening prayers?'

'Surely you could think of something more plausible than
that.' Her face grew serious. 'You're going to see him. That
young man of yours.'

'No.' I lied in spite of myself, though I added truthfully, 'I
don't even know where he is.'

'Then why take such a risk?'

I took such a risk just for a book, I thought, and I remembered again the white-eyed boy in the marketplace, and the
bookseller's impertinent questions, and the note from his
hidden guest. I had done all that for Kanesuke, and now that
book sat on my shelf. I hadn't helped him. Would my second
errand fail as well?

My eyes filled with tears, and I looked down and arranged
my sleeves.

'How did you find a carriage to take you there?'

'You know how conniving I am. I have means.'

'I suppose it won't do any good to tell you not to go.'

I shook my head.

She came close and lifted my chin, and the tears ran down
and ruined the powder on my cheeks. 'You aren't strong
now,' she said. 'I don't want you to suffer more than you
have already.'

'I had this disease when I was young. I doubt I will suffer
twice over.'

'That's not what I meant.'

'He isn't like Kanesuke.'

'He is a man,' she replied, 'and no amount of pain from
the past will protect you from him.'

'I don't want to be protected,' I said.

She spread her fan. Above the curve of pleated silk her
eyes were sad. 'Come and see me when you get back. Come

197

any time; it doesn't matter how late.' Then she left me, and I turned trembling to my mirror and repaired my damaged face.

As I left I heard the temple bells at Shakuzen ring in derision of my lack of faith. The streets were half empty, the houses shuttered against the heat. There was no wind, not even a breeze. Dust rose from the carriage wheels and filtered through the blinds.

I clutched my fan and wished I had a talisman to ward off the news that might await me. An amulet, a wand, a precious stone to wave away the possibility that I couldn't see him. Perhaps he was gone on some errand he had not foreseen. Perhaps he was ill; perhaps he was angry. How else to explain the disparity between the pleas in his letter and his failure to visit me?

Unless he were seeing another woman – someone who demanded his attention to the exclusion of all else. And I recalled the knowing ease of the servants at his house in the city and in the eastern hills, and his reticence when I asked about his past.

My palms began to sweat, and I was half-inclined to tell the driver to turn back. What if I should surprise him in some tryst? No, it was absurd. Women don't go alone to a man's house; it is against convention. Yet if I could break the rules, why couldn't someone else?

I felt such a wave of jealousy that I had to shut my eyes. Why must I be plagued again with this insidious emotion? Why should I feel this anger and suspicion? I thought I could confine those doubts to Kanesuke and his lies.

I pushed back the curtain to get a breath of air. From somewhere over a wall came the scent of camphor. A dog ran across the street, saliva dripping from his panting tongue; and a man hurried past, his sleeve pressed against his face.

Perhaps it was merely the dust he was escaping. How tempting it is, when one is afraid, to take each passing thing as an omen.

We soon approached the gate. I held my breath as the driver announced me, and leaned back and fanned myself as we waited.

After what seemed a long time we were let in. Masato was there in the courtyard when I stepped down.

He looked surprised but not dishevelled; if I had interrupted him in some secret occupation he had put himself together with admirable speed. The possibility seemed unlikely, for there was no other carriage in the courtyard.

The realisation that my suspicions might have no ground made me almost as light-headed as if they had been confirmed, and I swayed as I climbed the steps to the house.

'You aren't well,' Masato said. 'You shouldn't have come here in this heat – and with all this illness. It was very unwise of you.'

Something in the sharpness of his voice revived my doubts, and I searched his face for signs of disingenuousness. But he looked just the same, though beneath his concern I felt the wariness I had noticed the last time I had seen him, when we stayed up all night and he interpreted those dire signs to me.

'I'm sorry,' I said. 'I shouldn't have come.'

'Don't be.' He touched my sleeve. 'Come and have some iced water. We'll sit here, by the veranda, where it's cooler.'

I felt a pang. So we would not go to his room. We would sit in this formal place, hung with Chinese scrolls and pale damasks, and we would speak with the reserve that the room required, of trivial things.

'My room is very cluttered,' he said, as if he had read my mind. 'I just returned this morning. I've been away for a few days.'

So he had been away – seeing someone else, perhaps.

That was why he hadn't come to visit me. But why the pleading letter about his dream, and then this sudden change of plan? This woman – for I couldn't quite dispel her from my mind – must have great influence over him, that he would accommodate her so willingly.

'I had to go to Otowa Falls,' he explained. And again I felt that pang. Had he taken someone there as he had taken me? He glanced at me keenly as if he felt my unease. 'I've been corresponding with my parents,' he said. 'You know they are at Ishiyama. When the news of this epidemic broke I persuaded them to stay. My mother is still not well. They are safer outside the city. I've persuaded them to move to the house at Otowa Falls through the summer, until the worst of this is over.'

'I see.' I sipped my iced water and strove to hide my feelings. Was this truly the reason for his absence?

'I went up to the house to supervise the arrangements and take them some things. I'm sorry I didn't have time to tell you.'

How many times had Kanesuke made the same excuse? He didn't have time; there had been a sudden change of plan; he wasn't aware of my expectations. Yet why should I assume that Masato would be guilty of the same deviousness? Had I found some cause to mistrust him as a means of imposing a distance between us?

'I was waiting for you,' I said, and then despised myself for my weakness. 'First your letter, and then this news. You know the Emperor is going into seclusion.'

'I heard just this morning.'

'Why is this happening?' I asked, as irrationally as a child. 'Did your book foretell this, too?'

'It is happening because it is summer, and that is when diseases spread. It has happened before, and it will happen again.'

'How can you be so calm? Do your books teach you that?'

He looked past me into the garden, where the paulownias bloomed in violet profusion, and sweet flag grew thick around the pond. 'They only teach me things I don't want to know.' He turned and looked at me, and I saw that his anxiety was as deep as mine. 'Come,' he said. 'You must rest awhile, if you can forgive the state of my room. You look very tired.'

Come rest awhile. They were the words I most wanted to hear. I followed him to his room, which was as disordered as he said it would be, though not in the way I had expected.

It was the same room I had held all these days in my mind, though I saw it now in the slanted light of a summer evening. The same spaciousness; the same latticed windows, open wide to let in the slightest breeze; the same lacquered desk and green standing curtain. And scattered everywhere were robes, papers, scrolls; a pair of riding boots in one corner; a wooden tray with a cast-iron pot and a single half-drunk cup of tea.

'I'm sorry,' he said. 'You see I wasn't expecting visitors.'

Indeed. He had no idea how relieved that made me.

He walked to the bed, parted the curtains and spread a robe for us to lie on.

'Come,' he said. He stood close and took off my robes and let them fall on the floor around us: the deep blue-green one, and then the pale green; the white, the dark rose and the light, until I stood in my thin gauze shift, so transparent that I blushed.

'How lovely you look in white,' he said and he touched my nipples with his slender hands, and then he bent and kissed them through the gauze until I could barely stand. Then he let go of all his soft brown robes until he stood as I did in a plain white gown. Then I touched him as he had me, his nipples just visible beneath the delicate cloth, and he trembled as I did so.

Why did he cry when I did not? Could he have felt when

he lifted my hips and pressed so deep inside me the child that we had made? I turned my head so as not to reveal it to him. Yet I was certain that he knew. And when I felt his tears as he lay with his head against my chest I forced myself not to cry as he did. I would later, when he wasn't there. I cry now as I write and remember it. His hands as they held my shoulders. The arch of his back. The bones of his hips.

Later he brushed the hair from my mouth and kissed me. I saw his face stained with tears, the lashes still wet, his eyes so full of sadness that I closed my own so as not to reflect it back to him.

'I'm going to lose you, aren't I?' he said again. 'All the signs foretell it.'

I turned my head. The beaten silk of the robe he had spread was smooth against my cheek. 'Perhaps you wish them to,' I said.

'Why do you say that?'

'You told me yourself that we must take from these signs what we will. Perhaps you want me to go away.'

'No, I don't. You mustn't say so.'

'That is why you didn't come to see me,' I said. 'You could have come before you went to Otowa Falls. You could have sent me some word, but you didn't.'

'That wasn't the reason. It was that dream. I didn't want to hear you tell me what it meant.'

What was I to say? 'How do you know I was the woman in your dream?' I evaded. 'It could have been someone else.'

'But she had your eyes, and your long thick hair . . .'

I kissed him on his forehead and told him as he had once told me, 'Perhaps it's best if we don't speak of it.'

For some time we did not. The room grew dark. Through the open windows came the scent of orange blossom and laurel. We heard crickets, and then a nightingale, the notes falling through the air clear as water.

I lay on my side, his arms folded around me, his breath against my neck. Then before I could stop them the words rushed out: 'I would ruin you. You know that, don't you?'

'What nonsense are you saying?'

'You told me so yourself, that first night at Otowa Falls. We were talking about Sadako, and how easy it is to ruin a life, and I asked you if you thought I would ruin yours, and you said, "I don't think so, but you might try."'

'I don't remember that.'

'I think you do.'

He turned my face toward his. 'Why must you think you are so dangerous?'

'But I am,' I told him. 'There are those who know it far better than you.'

He gripped me by the shoulders, and his eyes were full of anger; I could see it clearly even in the half-dark. 'What is this romance you have with your own capacity for destruction? You love that power of yours more than you love anything else.'

How could he think that? Did he know me better than I knew myself? 'I don't love that power,' I said, 'but I live with it, and I must warn you against it just as your books did.'

He stroked my hair, and his anger faded with the light, until it grew so dark that I had to read his emotion in his voice. 'Who did this to you?' he asked me quietly. 'Who hurt you so badly that all you want is to hurt yourself? Was it that man – the one who told you to give me up?'

So he had guessed half the truth that night of the reading. He knew he was the object of my question – but he thought it was Kanesuke who had forced me to ask it. I had told him that first night at Otowa Falls that I was in love with someone. Did he think I still loved Kanesuke as I did him?

'No one advised me to give you up,' I lied, remembering Dainagon's warning.

'Are you waiting for him?' Masato asked. 'Are you waiting for him – this man in exile?'

'No,' I said, keeping my reply as brief as I could so that the bitterness wouldn't bleed into my voice.

'Do you write to him? Does he write to you?'

'Not now. Not for quite some time.'

'You don't communicate with him in any way?'

I thought of the book sitting on my shelf, the one I had never sent him. What would Masato think if he knew that I had hoped that book might lead Kanesuke to break with Izumi? What a game it seemed to me now – a vain destructive game. Is that why I hadn't sent it?

'No,' I said. 'We don't communicate in any way.'

'But you still love him.'

I shut my eyes. Why couldn't I answer? A denial would make him suspicious; an affirmation would cut too deeply. I no longer loved Kanesuke as I did him, but he was there at the back of my mind all the time. His thoughts bound up with my thoughts. His past tied to mine. His future as uncertain as my own.

'It's not the same,' I said, as honestly as I could.

'I know.' He lay still by my side as I drifted away from him. 'But you mustn't let him have this sway over you, unless you want it.'

'I don't want it,' I said, fighting the current as much as I could. I held him fast even as I felt the sand fall away beneath my feet. 'I don't want it,' I said again, and I kissed him so hard that he trembled, and I tasted his fear as the tide swept in and carried me off until I was so far away that he couldn't see me.

Fifth Month

A messenger came this afternoon with a letter from Takumi. The cover was stained from the journey, and the pages smelled of must.

She tells me in her faulty script that my boy is changing. His head is level with her shoulders. He is thin. Every spare moment of his time he spends in the woods, and sometimes they cannot find him. Twice he stayed out all night, and gave them no reason when he returned.

He sleeps with his bow and quiver by his mat, in readiness for his enemies. He collects the bleached bones of birds and squirrels and keeps them in a leather bag. He has invented his own language. They find the characters etched on stones and trees.

He neglects his studies, though he lives for stories, and asks Takumi to tell him the same ones again and again. Tales of the bamboo cutter and the hollow tree; of Yamato and the adventures of Heichū. Legends of Izanagi and Susano-o the Destroyer.

Takumi says he does not ask of me. When a parcel arrives from the capital he ignores it. He will not read the scrolls I send him. I'm sorry, Takumi says, but I feel I must tell you.

He is no longer the boy who comes to me in my dreams. He is a stranger to me. I cannot even picture how he looks. Only his eyes – those pools of limpid black, dark as the ink I mix as I kneel at my desk – are clear to me.

If I saw him those eyes would be full of reproach. I wonder if anything I said or did could change that.

Yet he keeps in a box a smooth green stone he found long

ago in the garden. When Takumi asked him why he told her that it reminded him of the green sleeve of his mother's robe. How he remembers this I don't know. I wore that colour the winter I gave him up, but perhaps he is thinking of another. A robe he lost. A robe he dreamed.

Why this strange confluence of events?

The summer rains have yet to arrive. After the deluges of last month the sky is unnaturally clear. The heat gives no respite. The cicadas whir.

The Kamo has subsided, and the ravines are dry. Crows sit on the gates and ridgepoles, their predatory eyes bright as the midday glare.

The first priests have arrived for the services of intercession. I hear the click of their clogs and their unctuous voices. They gather like flies in the halls and courtyards, their shaven heads blue-black and gleaming in the heat.

Ryūen wrote to say he will be coming with the Abbot in two days.

There was talk of postponing the Iris Festival but the diviners pronounced this unwise. It will be held tomorrow, on a smaller scale. The banquet has been reduced to an evening supper, to which I have not been invited. The Emperor will preside before he goes into seclusion.

All the women are assembling their gowns. Robes of green, white, rose, lavender, plum; embroidered jackets and trains. Couriers arrive with boxes of sweet flag. The women of the Office of the Grounds braid the swags of calamus and artemisia to be hung from the eaves.

Will these bright colours conceal our malaise? Will these nosegays fend off this disease?

Already there is talk of people falling ill. The Middle Captain of the Bodyguard of the Left lies in bed with a fever. The Minamoto Major Counsellor and the wife of the Governor of Iyo are not well.

I lay out my gowns with shaking hands. I cannot bear to wash my white shift, the silk still creased at the front where Masato kissed my breasts.

He wrote to me this morning to say he will try to see me for a little while tomorrow at the close of the festival.

The letter was tied to a branch of laurel. I placed it by my pillow and tried to calm myself with its scent.

Three days since the festival. Masato didn't come. He sent word that evening that he had been called to Otowa Falls because of some difficulties with the house. No choice but to trust him – for I refuse to indulge in jealous thoughts – but I resent each moment that he is gone.

The Emperor has completed his abstinence and spends his days shut up with his counsellors. Priests in all their finery have descended from Mount Kōya. The Abbot arrived yesterday from Mount Hiei, presumably with Ryūen, though he has not come to visit me. Perhaps he finds my presence contaminating. I must say I am relieved.

Today the rites of purification were held in the forecourt of the Shishinden and at the Kenrei Gate. I didn't attend. My dizzy spells are worse, and I couldn't face the prospect of standing in this heat.

Dainagon called on me after the ceremony. I have never seen her so anxious. She said that the Minamoto Major Counsellor has broken out in spots. The exorcists labour by his side to no purpose. Two of the consorts have fallen ill, and so has the Mistress of the Wardrobe.

The Empress and Reizei have left for the Ichijō Mansion. There is no news of Sadako. Rumours are about that the Emperor will grant a general amnesty in the hope of appeasing the spiteful ghosts who may have provoked this plague.

An amnesty: it was once my greatest hope. And now I must face its prospect – and the possibility of Kanesuke's return – even before the Emperor steps down.

'You look feverish,' Dainagon said, glancing at the bowl of ice by my mat. 'I will have one of the doctors come to see you.'

'No,' I protested. 'I'm just a little light-headed. It must be the heat.'

'You shouldn't have left the palace. I knew it would make you ill.' Then, for the first time I can recall, her eyes filled with tears.

'You mustn't worry. It isn't what you think,' I said too vehemently, for she looked at me closely, and her expression changed.

It was tender and distant at the same time. 'So it is that,' she said. 'I thought it might be.' She picked up a piece of ice and glided it across my forehead.

The ice melted and sent false tears running down my face. I struggled not to dilute them with my real ones. Was it because she had never had a child that she took so long to guess the nature of my symptoms? Or had she tried to protect herself from this knowledge for her own reasons?

Then she answered my question, as if she felt it suspended in the air between us.

'I felt as you do once,' she said. 'It was in the spring, the second year I was married. Even now the scent of plum blossoms makes me nauseous.' She smiled a rueful smile, and then looked past me at the arabesques on the brocade curtains. 'I lost him,' she said, anticipating what I didn't want to ask. 'Some time in the Fourth Month. If he had lived I would never have sent him away.' She couldn't keep the reproach from her voice, though perhaps it was my guilt that made me sense it.

'Of course not,' I replied, and I imagined her hands as they folded away the clothes her child would never wear.

'You mustn't stay here,' she said with a different kind of vehemence, and I answered in the same tone, 'Please don't tell me what I should do. And you mustn't say anything to anyone.'

'Why, after all this time, must you feel you need to say that?' It was the closest thing to anger I had ever seen in her.

'I'm sorry.'

'You mustn't stay here,' she repeated. 'For your sake and the child's. Have you told this man of yours?'

'No.'

'It would be better not to.'

I closed my eyes and felt the room spin with my thoughts.

'You know you have no future with him.'

Why did she see so clearly that which I had tried so hard not to see myself? Why should she and that black book conspire against my happiness?

'You have other loyalties,' she said.

'To the Empress?' I asked bitterly, thinking of the thwarted game of comparisons and my penitential gowns.

'No. Not to her.' She dipped her fingertips in the bowl of melted ice and touched my cheeks. 'Rest now. I'll come by in the morning.'

I lay there in the dark until the water in the bowl was warm, thinking of the child she had been denied, and the advice I hadn't wished for.

Ryūen came to see me. I have seldom been as grateful for the silk that divided us. Even when I had little to hide I found his canniness unnerving. He has a second sense for lies and pretence – a skill that his celibate years have only sharpened.

Why should a man so cynical have such penetration when it comes to human behaviour? Perhaps for Ryūen this is no contradiction.

Yet I have seldom felt as close to him. What a paradox it

would be if this plague were the one thing that could bring us nearer.

I sensed a fear in him. He told me what he had seen when they came down to the city – and he infected me with the same feeling. Men hurrying by with willow tags fixed to their caps, their faces pressed to their sleeves. Shuttered houses and half-empty streets. The scent of burnt herbs. Bodies in the dry ravines and ditches. He saw a boy lying on his back by a heap of rubble, his face covered with pustules.

'Do you remember,' Ryūen said, 'kneeling on the bench in that room with the dirt floor?'

The mourning room in our house in Mino. The room that smelled of earthworms.

'Yes,' I said. 'It was hard to keep you still. You kept fidgeting.'

'I saw a spider crawl across the floor. I don't know why that should be the one thing I remember.'

'You were very young,' I said, and was surprised by the gentleness in my voice.

'I still dream of her.'

'So do I.'

'Are you well?' he asked with a suddenness that disconcerted me. 'You said you missed the Iris Festival.'

Once again I was glad of my curtain. 'I was tired. That was all.'

'Here,' he said, and pushed a small lidded jar under the screen. 'Put two drops in your nostrils when you wake in the morning. It will keep away the vapours. The Abbot swears by it.'

So he was protecting me. I thanked him for it, formally. His kindness so took me aback that I was afraid to show much feeling.

'I will say the sutras for you,' he said, and then he left before I found my voice to answer him.

*

Can a woman be a ghost, yet live and breathe? Can she, weary of her supernatural ways, die and become a ghost again – the spirit's double?

As I sit in my room, surrounded by the paper walls of my private prison, I remember the story of Rokujō.

How often I think of her, that jealous woman who killed her lover's lovers. Rokujō: the Haven of the Sixth Ward. The widow who fell in love with a prince and destroyed his life.

He was eight years younger than she, and their liaison was a secret. She didn't know why she felt so strongly for him. It was clear they had no future together, and though he was tender when he saw her she knew he lavished the same feeling on others.

When she heard he was to be married she sent a wedding present. She was not invited to the festivities, nor would she have wished to be. In the evenings when she lay on her mat she pictured his wife in her robes the colour of carnations and azaleas. He loved that body in all its carmine finery. He held it in his hands as if it were a peach ripe to the touch. When Rokujō walked in the garden she saw his wife's face reflected in the surface of the pool. The placid carp rose from the silt and devoured it.

How did Rokujō live with her lover's absence? She grew so used to it that his rare visits were a shock to her. She lay in his arms as quietly as a girl. At times she was tempted to detain him with some strong show of feeling. But she let him go and never asked when she would see him again.

She vowed she would never show her possessiveness. But her dreams revealed it. How she hated the women who had a claim on him!

I know that malevolence. I fight it daily.

The next spring, when her lover's son was born, she sent a poem. The thought that his wife had given him what she

211

could not made Rokujō so bitter that even her music gave her no pleasure, and the rice offered up by her servants swelled in her mouth so she couldn't swallow it.

Yet when she heard that his wife bled for four days after the birth was she pleased? No – she was afraid. When the priests began their five-altar rites she smelled the acrid scent of the poppy seeds that they threw on the fire. Her hair stank of it. Even when she washed it the odour persisted.

She dreamed that the mediums who laboured by the bedside had spoken in her voice.

After his wife's death Rokujō sent her lover a letter of condolence. He didn't reply. Perhaps he blamed her in some way. He must have sensed her ill will. For his sake she resolved to leave the city. She went to Ise, to a house near the shrines.

For six years she tried to forget him. She didn't write, fearing that even the imprint of her fingers on the paper would harm him.

Then one day she saw him at the shrine. It was luck that she glimpsed him. He was standing outside the brushwood fence. His back was toward her, but when the flutes were blown he turned and she saw his face in profile. He was holding a branch of *sakaki*. His full lips were as she remembered; the slant of his cheek the same.

Six years since she had seen him, and he hadn't changed. She felt a wild impulse to approach him and ask him to forgive her. Yet something restrained her. She couldn't face the possibility of his hatred.

So she stood and watched him walk through the gate of the shrine. That night she took from a red lacquered box a comb etched with phoenixes and paulownias. He had given it to her before he married. She held it to her chest as he had held the sacred branch of *sakaki*.

A few years later Rokujō died of a fever. The stories say that her ghost returned to the house of her lover. It sat every night by the mat where his second wife lay, and watched her. And when the new wife died, wasted by an illness that seemed to have no cause, Rokujō was there holding her hand as it turned cold. Then she led her rival across the River of Three Fords and waited with her on the slopes of the Mountain of Death until her soul was reborn.

Shall I do the same? I spend each day with my rival. I think her thoughts; I hear Kanesuke's endearments as he whispers in her ear. Her gestures are mine, her passions identical. I look down at the hands in my lap and I detest them, for they are just like hers. At night she caresses her body when she misses him, and my hands do the same. I breathe her breath; I am never rid of her. She picks up her brush as I do, and writes out my thoughts. She is watching as I finish this page.

I saw Masato, briefly, in the most frustrating circumstances. He came in the evening, and I sent Buzen off on a trivial errand, but we could hear people coming and going in the halls, and we suppressed our voices and our desires accordingly.

How little time I have with him! In the moments we spent together the dripping clock would not have filled the smallest leaf.

He was tired. How I wished he could have rested with me. He had just returned from Otowa Falls, and his robes were covered with dust and smelled of horses. He had seen the same dreadful sights that Ryūen had, and had returned though the same gate. And I saw in his expression the fear I had imagined in Ryūen's.

He held my face in his hands and I felt their tremor, and it sent a wave of feeling through me that grew greater and greater, like the circles spread by a stone cast in a pond.

The stone sank, and so did my expectations. He told me

that he had heard that the Council of State was meeting to decide if the court should be sequestered. The counsellors are issuing a warning about the spread of this disease, describing its symptoms, its treacherous course through our bodies, its relapses. Rations of rice, salt and medicine are to be distributed to the commoners in the capital. If they are fortified, perhaps the epidemic will not strike the highest ranks.

Yet it already has. The Minamoto Major Counsellor died just this morning, Masato said.

There is talk of omens. A snake on the veranda of the Kokiden. A strange noise late at night in the Burakuin. A rainbow. A flock of doves trapped inside the Bureau of Artisans.

'I will come when I can,' Masato told me, 'and if I can't I shall write.'

He kissed me with all the tenderness that our narrow confine would allow. And when he left I had a nasty shock, for I went to the door to catch a breath of air and saw Buzen on the veranda, whispering with Izumi's maid.

The gates are closed now. Palace Guards man the watches day and night. Yet our misfortunes continue both within and without, heedless of boundaries.

Reizei has fallen ill. For three days he has suffered from fever, and he has a rash on his mouth and throat. The Empress has marshalled her own priests, but their prayers do no good. In the Shishinden monks of both sects chant for his recovery, but their clamour goes unrewarded.

The Emperor is beside himself. He has gone into seclusion for a second time, and has increased his penances. The doors of the Seiryōden are closed, and the blinds lowered. Messengers arrive several times a day from the Ichijō Mansion; they stand on the veranda and whisper their reports.

I think of the Empress shut up in her house with her priests and exorcists. Will the Vestal comfort her, I wonder? Does she blame herself – or Kanesuke – for her brother's illness?

In the palace the women twist their rosaries and trade stories about those who have fallen ill. It is said that the Minister of War fought for a dispensation so that one of his attendants, a lowly girl from Kazusa, could be treated by the doctors from the Bureau of Medicine. And rumours are about that the first wife of the Head Chamberlain came down with the quakes because he insisted that she perform her conjugal duties before her boils had healed. Now he sits beside her, offering her water boiled with ginseng. His disregard for his own health is said to be touching indeed.

Traffic in amulets and potions is brisk. Faith is professed in prophylactics. A certain Naishi no Suke stuffs her nose with garlic; the wife of a Lesser Counsellor consumes great quantities of boiled scallions; a resident of the Fujitsubo recites the Nembutsu and fumigates her clothes with camphor.

Yet am I not just as superstitious? The only difference is that I have no faith in my remedies.

At night I study the hexagrams. I pick up the book and let the pages fall open where they will. Today there were two admonitions, the second so painful that the characters blurred even as I read them.

'Hexagram Twenty-eight. Ta Kuo: Excess. A forest submerged in a great body of water. The Superior Man, though standing alone, is free from fear; he feels no discontent in withdrawing from the world.'

Then came the lines that made me cry: 'Nine for the Fifth Place. The withered willow tree puts forth blossom. An old woman takes a young husband: no blame, no praise.' And the commentary said, though I knew it myself already: 'How can such blossom endure for long? Both of them should feel ashamed.'

A messenger arrived two hours ago with a letter from Masato. What a relief to know he is not ill.

He hadn't written earlier, he said, because the demands on him are so heavy that he has hardly slept for days. The signs and portents conflict, and the diviners are at odds. The astronomers see disaster in a shower of meteors; the astrologers take hope from an alignment of stars. Messengers arrive from the shrines each day with new oracles: the turtle shells point to one course of action, the deer bones to another.

How are the yin-yang masters to interpret these signs? Which are baleful, and which less dire? Which spirits have been offended, and which rites will subdue them? Which days are safe, which directions least perilous?

The politicians, he told me, use the signs for their own purpose. The Emperor's enemies see in them cause for his abdication; his friends find reason to retain him.

Masato promised he would try to find a way to see me. The diviners are called to the Seiryōden every day to advise the Emperor on the course of his abstinence. Perhaps Masato can go with them.

Yet he knows as well as I what a risk it would be. To be seen with me would cast doubt on his integrity. It may have done so already. How painful it is to realise the power I have to harm him!

The closing lines of his letter made my plight harder still. He hoped I was well. He told me to take utmost care not to come near any source of infection. Then, for the first time – I read the characters over and over, as if to assure myself they were not an illusion of my overwrought mind – he told me that he loved me.

In the midst of all this fear I dreamed of happiness.

I am not sure if I was asleep or awake. It was early morning. The air was still fresh. I thought I heard a thrush singing.

Then the bird's song changed into the anxious cry of a child. I turned on my side and picked her up – for she was still just a baby – and held her to my breast. I stroked her hair and felt the damp wisps at the back of her neck.

Then he spoke, so softly that at first I thought I had imagined it, for I was sure he was sleeping.

'Let me hold her,' he said. He moved closer and put his hand on my hip.

'Wait.' He lay there in his calm patient way until she was finished. Then I lifted her and settled her on the mat between us, and we watched as she waved her arms and reached for the billowing curtain.

'She has your eyes,' he said.

'No, she doesn't. They are just like yours.' I knew that I was right, for her eyes were the same colour as his, as deep as an abyss, and as wise as if she had lived a hundred lifetimes.

He picked her up and put her on his chest, and in a little while she fell asleep. Then for a long time we said nothing, content to watch the unfurling cloth and listen to her breathing.

Reizei is worse. Dainagon came by with the news this morning. The spots have spread from his face to his arms and chest. The doctors have applied poultices of red bean paste and have given him seaweed to suck, but it does no good. He refuses the gruel that they offer him and takes no more than a few sips of hot water.

The priests have begun their seven-altar rites. They make

their mudrās and pray to the Five Mystic Kings; they light tapers and offer flowers and rice wine – and all for nothing. All for nothing they strive for the honour of saving their illustrious victim, and they will be rewarded with silver and silk even if he dies.

I am becoming even more cynical than Ryūen.

Reports of conditions in the city are as bleak as those from the First Ward. There are stories that the ravines by the Kamo and the Shimada are full of corpses. The Imperial Police can no longer keep order. Thieves broke into the house of the Minister of Ceremonial and took several hundred *ryō* of gold; others raided a temple on the Rokudō no Tsuji and stole a fortune in scrolls and vestments.

There are rumours that crowds are gathering at the well on the Abura no Kōji, for its water is said to cleanse the body of infection. Hawkers walk the streets selling scent bags and amulets. Priests are charging exorbitant fees for rites for the dying.

The throngs of mourners are said to be so thick that it looks as if a host of crows had descended upon the city. Demand for sombre shades of cloth is so high that stocks are running short.

I think of the beech groves near the Katsura, where we went to pick spring herbs. How many of those trees will have to be cut to yield the dark dyes that will convey our losses?

Reizei died this morning, hours after his father declared a general amnesty. The Emperor's cry upon hearing the news could be heard as far away as the Kokiden.

Though it was hardly unexpected everyone is stunned with grief. I walked to the courtyard of the Shishinden to escape the women's wails and saw a young monk sitting on the floor of the veranda. He was rocking back and forth, his hands clasped to his knees, his face streaked with tears. A priest stopped to comfort him, and I heard the novice say bitterly what a shame it was that he could not give his worthless life for Reizei's.

Far away we hear the bells at Shakuzen. The Empress's sorrow can hardly be imagined. She has seen no one, apart from a few of her women. I hear that Izumi was among them.

All of us wait to hear the advice of the diviners as to when the body shall be coffined and where it will rest until the cremation. Everyone expects that the funeral will take place at Toribeno, though Dainagon thinks it might be held at Funaoka.

I saw her a few hours ago, soon after we had learned the news. Her face was drawn; her whitened cheeks marred with tears.

'Will you go?' she asked.

'To the funeral? Yes.' I had decided even before she came. Perhaps I will see Masato, just for a moment or two, even if we cannot speak.

Yet I realise now that I have a second reason. I want to see for myself how the people in the city are suffering, even if all I have is a glimpse through the carriage window.

And the prospect of fleeing the palace even for a day is all too tempting. That my pretext should be a funeral is an irony that has not escaped me.

'You have heard about the amnesty?'

'Yes.'

She searched my face for some sign of emotion. I strove for neutrality, but she hazarded a guess. 'You don't want him to come back, do you?'

'I don't know,' I said.

Even as I write I cannot make up my mind. I doubt that Izumi's feelings are as divided. Will I see her at Reizei's funeral? Will she give me the same triumphant look that she gave me months ago when she received a letter that was more tender than mine?

It makes me tremble to think that Kanesuke might be here in a few weeks – or even less, if his reasons are pressing. Yet who can say what the future holds for him, with the Emperor still in power, and his enemies unsilenced.

Will he risk returning from Akashi at such a time? Izumi risked everything for his sake on the night she was attacked – though she couldn't have foreseen her misfortune. I wonder if he, knowing full well the dangers that await him, will take such a chance.

If I had sent him that black book perhaps he could find some sign to guide him. How I regret that I changed my mind.

The coffining took place last night at the Ichijō Mansion. Dainagon was there at the request of the Empress. She woke me early this morning to give the news to me. She had not slept at all; her face was crumpled like a sheet of paper, and her red-rimmed eyes conveyed all the sorrow that her reserve contained.

I write in haste, for I must prepare for the funeral, which is to be held this evening.

Dainagon told me she had seen Masato. He was there with the diviners when they made their pronouncements. How was he? I asked. How did he look, and what did he say?

'He was very calm,' she said. 'Calm but tired.' He must have been awake for days, ever since Reizei fell ill: directing the rites, helping to fix auspicious places and dates, interpreting the ravings of the mediums. 'What a gentle voice he has,' she told me, and I knew she was saying in her circuitous way that she liked him.

Then she began to cry. The sight so unnerved me that I looked away.

'I am so glad now that I never had a child.' Her voice was so low I could hardly make out the words. 'If you had seen the Empress . . .'

'Tell me.'

She knelt on my cushion and described the scene. When the diviners said that Reizei should be taken to the Hōkōin that very night the Empress tried to detain them. He was sure to revive, the Empress said. She told them to mark the colour in his cheeks – though they were as pale as pale, Dainagon told me. They laid him out with his head facing north, just as Masato and I had lain in my room at Hasedera. He is only sleeping, the Empress pleaded; he mustn't be shut up in a box. But the Emperor persuaded her, and the lamps were brought, and the servants bathed Reizei's body and put on his scarlet robes.

The priests inscribed the corpse with their mudrās, and the mediums, deprived of their raucous voices, wept along with the others.

As they lifted Reizei to place him into the coffin the Empress leaped up and clasped his feet. They had to pry her fingers from him, Dainagon said. It was a terrible defilement. The Empress's brother sought to calm her as they laid Reizei's belongings beside him. The Emperor himself placed his son's flute on his chest.

When they sealed the coffin and carried it to the un-hitched carriage in the courtyard it was the Emperor who lost his composure. He commanded that they open the lid so he could see his son's face one more time. When the Abbot told him quietly that they could not the Emperor fell to the pavement and scraped his knuckles against the stones until they bled.

Dainagon said she didn't join the procession to the Hōkōin. She stood in the courtyard of the Ichijō Mansion and watched the Emperor walk behind the carriage, supported by the Abbot and the Minister of the Left.

I see them myself: their tear-streaked faces ruddy in the torchlight, their sumptuous robes muted by their black cloaks, their straw sandals shuffling on the paving stones.

I have seen so much in the course of a single night that I feel as if time had dilated in measure with my grief. I am great with it. It fills my body like a second child.

I hadn't known how much this death would affect me. I didn't love Reizei. I was fond of him – that was all.

Perhaps I was so moved last night because of the other deaths I saw. I have never seen death on such a scale. There was something magnificent about it. It unfolded before my eyes like a gorgeous scroll.

Why, in the midst of this common grief, should I have felt such exhilaration? Was it because I saw Izumi and wasn't afraid? Was it because I saw Masato and knew he was well? Yet now that I have returned to my rooms I find my mood as diminished as the view. How trivial it seems to be bound by my worries and imaginings.

I could never have imagined what I saw last night. My mind isn't capable of it.

Even as I dressed to leave for the funeral my hands trembled in anticipation. I would see for myself all that had been denied me during my weeks of confinement. I would be confronted by the same sights that shocked Masato and Ryūen.

At the Hour of the Bird Dainagon and I joined the throng by the Kenshun Gate. The sun had just set, and it was still very hot. Dust rose from the carriage wheels, and there was a clamour of oxen and men.

We shared a coach with two matrons from the Emperor's entourage. To their annoyance I insisted upon raising one of the blinds. They protested that this breach of privacy made them feel like goods on display in a public market. Judging from their looks they had little reason to be concerned.

The Imperial Police had worked throughout the day to clear our route, but the streets were still jammed with people and vehicles, and the forerunners had difficulty getting through. As our procession joined the mourners at the Hōkōin we caught sight of the yellow silk pennants borne by the vanguard. The litter bearing the coffin was screened from our view, but we caught sight now and then of the dignitaries who followed behind, dressed in grey and carrying their wooden staves.

The Emperor was not among them. We had heard that he was too exhausted by the vigil at the temple to make the journey to Toribeno on foot. Both he and the Empress followed in coaches. The chants of the monks enveloped them like the clouds of incense.

I searched for Ryūen but couldn't find him. I thought of the potion he had brought to protect me, and tears stung my eyes.

Where were they, those invisible vapours that infect people of every age and rank? As dusk fell I searched for evidence of their malignity.

The light of the torches revealed it to me. Their vermilion glow lent the scene a false theatricality. I must be careful that my brush does not do the same.

How can I describe those images so far removed from my experience? Shall I say: 'I saw a dry riverbed full of corpses' or 'I heard a man reciting the Nembutsu over the body of his son.' Or shall I lay one plain line beside the next, like a man lashing the palings of a fence: 'I saw crowds of beggars, and miracle workers hawking their cures. I saw a child whose face was so swollen that he couldn't open his eyes. I saw a dog gnawing on a severed arm. I saw roadside temples along the Rokudō no Tsuji so packed with mourners that they trod upon one another as they climbed the steps to lay their offerings to the Amida.'

The city itself was not as I remembered it. It was like a lover one has not seen for a long time who has aged unexpectedly. It sprawled on the hillsides and spread into the valleys; it meandered with the course of streams and ravines. The waxing moon shone on its shingled houses; a pall of mist spread over its fields.

Sometimes a breeze would lift the curtains, bringing with it the incongruous odour of orange blossom and carrion. I have no doubt that I will never again breathe in one scent without thinking of the other.

We reached the burning ground at Toribeno at the Hour of the Rat. The driver unhitched our coach on a rise over-looking the site, which was lit with torches. White sand had been sprinkled upon the ground, and two gates and a barricade of silk screens had been erected around the place where Reizei's bier would lie.

We peered through the blinds and watched the prep-arations. White-robed priests hurried back and forth, carry-ing water and firewood.

The hill where we kept our vigil was soon crowded with carriages. It seemed that every woman of consequence had chosen the same vantage.

Below us the litter bearing the coffin was carried through the western gate. Between the panels of rippling silk I saw the Emperor and the Empress. The Vestal stood nearby, as demure as a nun in her mourning clothes, her billowing hair shielding her from view like a second curtain.

But where was Sadako? Was she ill, or had the suddenness of her brother's death caught her unawares? Perhaps her father hadn't wanted her to come to the cremation. For the first time in days I felt a wave of nausea, and I leaned against the window frame and closed my eyes.

I heard Dainagon's voice. It seemed to come from far away, though I knew it was muted only by my guilt. 'I expect that the journey was too long for Sadako. She would never have been able to come so quickly.'

So she had read my mind. I wondered if she thought her explanation plausible, or if she had offered it merely to reassure me.

'Have some water,' she said. 'You look pale.'

I wanted to ask her if she had seen Izumi's carriage, but I glanced at our inquisitive companions and changed my mind.

We sat in silence and scanned the crowd below us. 'Ah – so he is here,' murmured Dainagon, and I searched to discover whom she meant. My pulse told me before my mind did. It was Masato. He was dressed in grey like the others, though now and then I saw a flash of red at the hem of his sleeves.

He was conferring with the Archbishop. I could sense his deference even at a distance. He seemed entirely absorbed in his role. I wondered if he had any awareness of my presence, and found myself hoping that he didn't. It was better that he not think of me. I didn't wish him to be divided.

So I watched him as he was when I possessed no part of him, with neither demands nor constraints. This is how he would be when I could no longer see him. He would stand as he did now; he would speak with the quiet avidity that I loved. His hands would move with the same gestures.

I closed my eyes and saw his hands as they divided the yarrow stalks. That slow sweep of his wrists: I remembered the ease of it.

I looked down again and watched him as the priests removed the lid of the coffin. I saw how he turned towards the Empress as the kindling was laid inside. When she swayed as the wood was lit I saw him stiffen. Later, when the priests recited the verse in which Siddhartha carries his father's silver coffin on his shoulder, I saw his look of pity as the Emperor cried.

The burning lasted until dawn. We watched the priests sprinkle wine on the pyre and seal Reizei's bones in an urn.

Dainagon leaned her head on my shoulder. Our two companions had fallen asleep. Masato had disappeared with his monks and diviners.

The sky lightened like indigo silk left out in the sun. Two cranes started from the reeds and wheeled over the plain.

As the driver turned the ox onto the rocky track we passed by a palm-leaf coach with gilded finials. I looked in the open window and saw Izumi's face.

She didn't shrink back but stared, as I did. Her eyes widened and her lips parted in surprise. She didn't incline her head or recognise me in any formal way. But I saw – or rather felt – her features harden, like porcelain left in the heat to dry.

Yet I wasn't afraid of that look. Her aversion to me had made her brittle; she was not as invulnerable as she seemed.

Our coach pulled ahead, and I was left with an impression that worked on my imagination throughout the hours of our return. Every scene I took in was coloured by Izumi's presence. In the gaunt faces of the women who held out their hands as we passed by I sensed her need. How heavily time must weigh on her, as it does on me. In the feverish barters on the street corners I felt her urgency. How she must long to claim her destiny, as I do.

Yet she must wait. She waits while the bells ring at Shaku-zen and Hōkōin; she waits while the bodies pile up in the streets. She waits just as the boy I saw on the Ōmiya waited to sell the single red pomegranate he held in his hands. It was sliced like a wound. He proffered the double portion to every stranger who hurried by.

It was when I saw him that I realised that Izumi's face had

changed. The welt was gone. It was as if she had never been injured.

Had her other scars disappeared? Would Kanesuke find her unblemished when he returned?

'What is it?' Dainagon asked as we drove toward the Kenshun Gate. 'You look as if you had seen a ghost.'

Even now he might be riding towards the city. He might be writing a letter to Izumi, telling her he would be here in a few days.

'It's nothing,' I lied. 'I was thinking of Reizei.'

'Do you remember how afraid he was of the dark? His nurse had to keep a lamp burning all night – and she was terrified of fire.'

I thought of Reizei's face the morning he came running up to me in the garden of the Ichijō Mansion. His face was flushed and his eyes were bright. When he smiled I could see his dark stained teeth. How vulnerable he had looked. We had talked about the cherry tree. Hadn't I noticed, he asked, that the blossoms were artificial?

Less than four months since we had had that conversation. The hut they had built him when he fell ill was in that very garden. He had died there, his body ravaged by the plague.

All the exhilaration I had felt, all the thrill of being part of a pageant in its doleful excess, had vanished. I felt as brittle as Izumi, and as flat as the shadows of the cypresses on the palace walk.

Only my grief filled me. I had suppressed it as much as I could. Grief for that boy with the darkened teeth who would never be Emperor. Grief for his father, who wished he had carried the coffin lightly, on one shoulder, as Siddhartha had done. Grief for Masato, who would not know the child within me, who would carry on without me, casting his yarrow stalks to determine other fortunes.

*

I dreamed last night that Kanesuke was dead. His ghost came to me and told me to comfort Izumi.

I did as he asked, without questions or misgivings. He didn't frighten me. His voice was the same as always; his breath warmed my cheek.

As I walked down the corridor in the dark I couldn't tell if I was awake. I had wandered there before, on other nights, hoping to catch a glimpse of the woman who has deprived me of my happiness.

I felt a strange exultation. I would see her in the extremity of her grief. Why had he chosen me to deliver the news to her? Perhaps because he thought I was strongest – or because he loved me best.

I heard the murmur of silk and saw a woman walking towards me down the hall.

Everything unfolded with the slow inevitability one feels in dreams. I recognised Izumi long before I could see her. Perhaps it was her scent, that heavy distillate of roses. Perhaps it was her walk. She was wearing straw sandals and a dark grey robe.

By the time she reached me I was angry. Her brows lifted as she tried to read my expression.

'Why are you dressed like that?' I asked. 'He was not your husband.'

'He asked me to wear mourning,' she replied. 'Didn't he ask you?' From my silence she extracted every dreg of her revenge. 'You have forgotten your letters,' she said. I saw that she held in her hands a blue damask bag.

'My letters?'

'He told us to burn them.'

'He didn't tell me.'

'That is why I have come. He told me to tell you that we mustn't keep them.'

'I will keep them if I like.'

'You may regret it.'

'Why? Because you might steal them?'

She smiled. 'Why would I do that?' Then she turned and walked into the courtyard. The red plums bloomed improbably in the clear midsummer night. 'Come. Watch me burn them.'

She brought a brazier from the porch and knelt and breathed on the coals. Her face was calm, but when she drew the letters from the bag her hands shook.

'Help me,' she said, handing me the scented packets.

I knew that scent. It was his incense, the one he invented for our competition. The scent of cypress and clove. The scent of dissolution.

I threw the letters on the coals and watched them burn. As the flames leaped up I saw her eyes glisten.

She looked at me through the glaze of her unhappiness and said, 'When you are ready to burn yours you must tell me.' Then she turned and walked back to her rooms.

I sat on the floor facing north and set the book in front of me. Masato's letters to my left, Kanesuke's to my right. I lit the incense and the fronds of smoke unfurled and spread, each tendril drifting where it would, unpredictable.

I didn't bow. That reverence belongs to Masato. I merely closed my eyes and asked my question. The pages parted of their own accord but I didn't look at them. I touched them with my fingertips, as a blind man reads a face.

In the dark of my apprehension I imagined the characters. I felt the ink thick upon the page, laid down long before I was born by a man in a foreign country.

I opened my eyes and read the name of the hexagram. Innocence: The Unexpected.

'Innocence,' the judgement read. 'Supreme success. Perseverance brings reward. If someone is not as he should be,

229

he will meet with misfortune, and it will not help him to undertake anything.'

I shut the book in frustration. It was mocking me. I heard the words again in all their irony, and I recalled what the bookseller had said. A frivolous question begs a frivolous answer.

Had my question been so trifling? I hadn't intended it to be. How I wished I had Masato's subtlety. He would have helped me understand the commentaries. He would have resolved the contradictions within each line.

Why should I have thought that my childish method had any purpose? Why should a book opened at random offer any guidance?

There were still the letters.

I chose Masato's first. He had sent me only nine. I closed my eyes and picked one from the stack on my left.

Why of those nine did I choose that one? It was the letter about his dream. He had thought it was I who had disappeared, but I knew it was our daughter. The waves swept over her and all that he could see was a single flash of colour.

I placed the letter beside the book and turned to the heap on my right. I knew how many there were: eighty-seven. Kanesuke had written me others, but some I had destroyed in anger and others I had returned. I wonder where they are now, and if I shall ever reread them.

I closed my eyes and reached for a letter. As soon as I looked at the creased yellow paper I remembered what it said.

It was a letter Kanesuke wrote me two years ago this autumn. We had just come back from Hasedera. On our return we stopped at an inn east of Uji, on the north bank of the river upstream from the bridge.

I remember the day clearly. It was a cold autumn, and the leaves of the oaks and maples had already begun to turn.

They floated downstream and drifted in the eddies, and my thoughts drifted with them. Kanesuke sat beside me, braiding my hair.

He twined the strands over and under, and we watched the fishermen cast their nets. The water ran over the weir. I could hear his voice weaving in and out of my reverie. He was telling me how the Emperor had held a service of Eight Expositions at the Uji Mansion, to atone for the sin of catching fish.

'Shall we hold our own expiation?' I asked.

'Yes, a very long one, with supplications in Sanskrit and offerings of lotuses and gold and silver branches. I will be the questioner for the Devadatta Chapter, and you can be the judge.'

'And will you dispute the claim that women can reach salvation?'

'That depends on their sins.'

'And if they are sincere in their confessions?'

He laughed. 'Then there may be hope for them. But they must first make copies of the Lotus and the Four-Scroll sutras, and draw a thousand Amitābha mandalas. Here – I'll draw the first one for you.' He picked up a stick and traced the design in the dust.

Later in the evening he told me he had to leave me for a little while to write a letter. I combed my hair and wondered who the recipient might be. At the time I didn't know about his liaison with Izumi, though I think I must have sensed there was something between them.

Why, on that calm autumn day, when there was no one nearby to divert his attention, should I have felt such jealousy?

An hour later a boy rapped on my screen and placed a twisted note into my hands. The paper was yellow, the script rapid but clear.

'I have been thinking of the Devadatta Chapter,' he told

231

me. 'There is one thing I can't remember. Do you recall the story of the Dragon's King's youngest daughter? The jewel she gave to the Buddha – I can't remember its colour. Write and tell me what it was.' And then he praised me in all his fine metaphorical ways and told me that he loved me.

As I was reading those lines that evening at the inn east of Uji I heard Kanesuke call one of our men into the court-yard. He gave him a twisted letter written on yellow paper and told him to ride to the capital as quickly as he could. 'You know where to find her,' I thought I heard Kanesuke say – but I might have been mistaken.

The next month I discovered that he and Izumi were lovers, and I remembered the letter he had sent that day. Was hers as passionate as the one he wrote to me? Perhaps he had simply copied out the same words twice.

Last night I sat in my room until it grew so dark I could barely see the book in front of me. Outside the cicadas spun their song with the same insistence as the word revolving in my mind: Innocence. Innocence. Innocence.

I took the letters from my two lovers and folded them together. Then, to prove I was as strong as Izumi, I burned them in the fire.

I heard a rumour that Kanesuke has left Akashi for the capital. Buzen told me this morning. We sat in my room as the rain pelted down and fell in sheets from the eaves. She had to raise her voice against the noise, and looked around her as if my curtains hid a hundred spies.

It was clear she was nervous. Her plump hands lay like carp in the blue lake of her lap, but when she spoke they would flop back and forth, and I could see the moistness in the creases of her palms.

At times I felt that she was the spy. She seemed to want to extract gossip rather than impart it. How had I been feeling? she inquired. Had my nausea gone away? (Ukon must have told her. How furious it made me.) Was I sleeping well? As well as anyone could be expected to, I replied, given the general state of things.

'You know there is talk,' she confided, 'that you were wandering the corridors two nights ago, near the Nashitsubo.'

So Dainagon was right; someone had noticed me. I hid my apprehension behind a blind of sarcasm. 'I am sure there are plenty of women who have reason to go traipsing about in the middle of the night,' I said. 'I'm afraid that my life is far less interesting.'

'That is not what I've heard.' The corners of her mouth curved upward. 'He is very good looking, your young man. It seems you have taken all sorts of risks to visit him.'

'I don't know what you mean.' So I had been seen the night I went to Masato's house. And I could well imagine the salacities that Ukon and her friends must have spread about his visits to me.

'He had us quite in his thrall at Toribeno,' she said. 'Even Izumi, who only thinks of that exile of hers, told me how well he looked in his mourning clothes.'

So he had been subject to vulgar gossip even then. The thought was sickening.

The rain voiced its insistent complaint. We sat in silence, my anger no less evident than Buzen's unease. Despite the storm the air was close. My gown stuck to my chest, and my hair hung dank as mildewed grass down the length of my back.

'If you will excuse me,' I said, 'I have letters to write.'

The fish flopped in her lap as if they had been pierced by a hook.

'You know that Izumi has heard from Kanesuke. Dainagon told me a messenger came from Akashi yesterday.'

Why had Dainagon not told me? Perhaps she had seen

me conferring with my oracles and had decided not to disturb me. Or perhaps she thought it best to spare me the news.

'Imagine him riding back amidst all this illness. But it is so like him, don't you think, to go to such extremes.'

'Yes, very.' I pictured him confronting the sights I had seen on the way to Reizei's cremation. Perhaps he would be so moved as to write poems about them. He would show them to Izumi to confirm his depth of feeling.

Yet hadn't I done exactly the same? Hadn't I used the extremity of that scene to deepen my emotion?

I am tired of living off the lives of others. I am no better than the crows that feed on the succulence of corpses.

Sixth Month

When truth is scant it must be sought. I hurried to Dainagon, my sole repository of that rare quality, to purchase what I could.

I wanted to hear if it was true that Kanesuke had left for the capital. I wanted to know if the gossip about Masato was as pervasive as I feared. And I hoped – though it is painful to confess it – that she would confirm my lucidity. Buzen's story about my nocturnal wanderings had unsettled me more than I wished to admit. Had I gone to Izumi's rooms, or did I dream it?

Yet even Dainagon wasn't candid. I felt her guardedness as soon as I saw her face. She was tuning her *koto*; her dress the colour of flax as subdued as the mode she had chosen.

When she heard the sweep of my robes she glanced up and smiled at me. But her eyes were wary, as if in the few days since I had seen her she had changed.

'I came to you yesterday,' she told me, 'but you were busy with your rites.'

So she had seen me amidst my piles of letters, trying to make sense of the rebuke my book had sent me.

'You were burning something,' she said.

Her words turned me cold. Was I so contrary that the suggestion of heat made me feel its opposite? 'They were only letters.'

'I hear you put great faith in that book of yours.'

From whom had she learned this? Had Izumi told her how I had hoped to protect Kanesuke with its prophecy? 'It is a book like any other,' I replied. 'It's a diversion – nothing more.'

'Why must you think that you can meddle in the lives of others? You should confine your plotting to your stories.'

I had never seen her so angry. She lay down her instrument and walked to the double doors that give onto the courtyard. Water lay pooled on the gravelled ground, holding the sky in all its blue imperturbability.

'Kanesuke is coming back,' she said. 'You will have heard, I expect.'

I let her interpret my silence as she would.

'You mustn't interfere with him or Izumi. They have their own history. You can't presume to change it.'

'I have no intention of interfering.'

'Then why were you seen two nights ago hovering near Izumi's rooms?'

So I had indeed gone – though what transpired between us later was surely a dream. Yet I would gain nothing by admitting to my wanderings. 'I don't know what you mean.'

'You were seen. It doesn't matter by whom. And it doesn't matter what you give as a reason. People will draw their own conclusions.'

I felt so dizzy I could hardly stand. When she saw my precarious state her expression changed.

'Sit down,' she said gently, offering me a cushion. 'I will fetch you something to drink.'

We sat for a while and watched the clouds float in the blue pools on the ground. From somewhere in another quarter came the sound of chanting. Someone else must have fallen ill, and the priests were trying to appease the unseen spirits.

I thought of Reizei lying on his pallet in the house in the First Ward, and his mother's grief at the funeral. 'How is the Empress?' I asked.

'Distraught. She sleeps with Reizei's robes.'

'And the Emperor?'

'In seclusion.'

'And the succession, if he abdicates?'

'Still in doubt. All that is clear is that as long as he is in power he will be blamed for all our misfortune.'

'And Sadako? Why didn't she go to Toribeno?'

'Because the Emperor didn't want her there.'

'So he isn't likely to forgive her – or the Vestal either.'

'It appears he will not. But he may have a change of heart. Sometimes it happens.'

She turned and gave me a searching look. 'You didn't go to the Ichijō Mansion when Reizei was ill.'

'No. The Empress never asked me.'

'I didn't think so. But there are those who say you did.'

'Whatever for? Why can't you speak to me plainly?'

'You mustn't listen to the rumours,' she said. 'They are bound to reach you.'

'What rumours?' I felt like crying in vexation.

In her face I saw not reproach but distress. 'You mustn't stay here,' she said. 'I warned you before, but now the reasons are doubly strong.'

'What has changed?' I persisted. 'Why are you so bent on my leaving?'

'I told you earlier I thought it was best.'

'But not with this urgency.'

She wouldn't look at me. We sat in silence and watched the clouds drown in the pools of rainwater. When I stood she caught my sleeve and said, 'Just one more thing.'

'Yes?'

'It would be best if you weren't seen with this man of yours. Best for you and for him. I know better than to ask you again to break with him. But be discreet.'

As I was walking back to the Umetsubo I passed three men in the corridor. Two were priests, the splendour of their robes mocking the drabness of their expressions. The third was an ascetic from the mountains. His feet were bare and his robes were made of deerskin. In his right hand he carried a staff tipped with horn.

For an instant his eyes held mine. They didn't judge or appraise; they simply took me in. I felt monstrous in my own inconsequence, my every ruse and guise as transparent as my gowns.

My dreams are false; my apparitions hard as ice.

I think of Siddhartha, who wasn't frightened by his phantoms. He found them instructive. Perhaps his story shall instruct me.

The night Siddhartha was conceived his mother had a dream that the diviners took as a sign of his singular destiny. When the boy was born his father, determined to thwart his son's fate, shut him in a palace. For twenty-nine years he lived there happily, unaware of the corruptions of time and human nature.

But one day when Siddhartha was riding in his carriage he saw a man walking with a stick, his back bent in pain. When the boy asked what was wrong with the man his driver said that he had grown old, as everyone did.

Another time the boy glimpsed through the carriage blinds a man covered with sores. Again he was told that there was nothing unusual about this condition. Even so the man appeared each night in Siddhartha's dreams.

On a third occasion they passed a funeral procession, and Siddhartha marvelled at the stillness of the man laid on the bier. He was as motionless as the lions carved on the sandstone friezes of the palace; he didn't even seem to breathe.

When the driver explained that this was the common end of man Siddhartha was disconcerted. It wasn't until he saw the face of a priest, so like the dead man's in its vast indifference, that Siddhartha understood the meaning of the four encounters.

He left the palace that same day, dressed in the saffron robes of an ascetic.

So the story ends – yet I wonder if it is all a fiction. How else are we to explain Siddhartha's twenty-nine years of obliviousness? Clearly they are a lie. Even in the palace he must have noticed signs of decay. The roses in the gardens must have withered. His nurse's hands, which massaged his limbs with such gentleness, must have changed: the veins growing more prominent, the creases at the wrists deeper.

And the men Siddhartha glimpsed from the window of his carriage? Perhaps all four – cripple, leper, corpse, priest – were ghosts made by the gods for his instruction. Or perhaps Siddhartha himself created them, just as we invent words to be beguiled by their ambiguities.

It is clear to me now. The world within Siddhartha's palace walls was no less false than the one he saw when he escaped his prison. The flowers in his garden as scentless as the mandāravas that fell from the sky when he preached the sutras. The terraces, where he ran in his bare feet, paved with crystal and lapis lazuli. The turrets where he climbed as tall as the bannered towers of the Phantom City.

It was a world of metaphor, of superlatives and infinite number. A world where truth was as illusory as deceit, where love was as dangerously binding as its opposite. A world of dragons, nuns and ghosts; of petty kings and wheel-turning sages. A world that Siddhartha could not quit until his soul burned like flame, and he passed into the realm of no remainder.

I have been accused of such treachery that I can scarcely take it in. How could I profit from such a thing? It makes no sense – yet the damage has been done. I feel it when I walk down the halls and I am met with stares. I hear it in the vicious whispers. They are everywhere, those whispers; I hear them even when I am shut up in my room. They are in my dreams, and when the light strengthens in the morning they grow louder still, and it is all that I can do not to run away from them.

But I must be calm. If I am not it will be seen as evidence of my guilt. I must bow and smile and modulate my voice; I must be discreet and decorous; I must defer to those who would harm me. How many of them there are, those people who wish me ill; I can feel their malice.

How I long to go to Masato and have him comfort me. But I mustn't risk it, and I am afraid that if I did I would find him as mistrustful as the others. Even Dainagon is turning against me, and he is bound to hear the same talk that poisoned her.

And Ryūen – that it should be he who accused me! I suppose I should have expected nothing less of him. He has always had nothing but contempt for me, and those gestures that I took as kindness – the gift of the medicine, his offer to recite the sutras – were, I see now, nothing but false pity.

I thought he had come just to say goodbye to me. It must have been two days ago. He stopped by my rooms in the morning, before he left for Enryakuji. I was still asleep. He laughed at my indolence. I heard his voice, mocking as always, behind the standing curtain.

'I hope I'm not disturbing you.' As if I were lying there with a man – that is what he meant.

'No. I suppose brothers should be exempt from the rule that one must never call on a lady before noon.'

'I'm sorry.' He hesitated. 'Are you well? I trust you are looking after yourself.'

Again, that insinuating tone. 'I have no fever or boils, if that is what you mean, and if I did they are in remission, and you are in no danger.'

'You are very sharp today.' No more than he. 'I didn't see you at Toribeno. I looked for your carriage.'

'I was there.'

'Were you? I thought perhaps you had decided not to go.'

'I was very fond of Reizei.'

Another pause. 'I have heard he had enemies.'

'Enemies? An eleven-year-old boy?'

'It seems there were some who wished him harm.'

'How do you know? Where did you hear such a story?'

'It is about.'

Why was he so vague? 'Since you brought it up, perhaps you can enlighten me.'

He cleared his throat. 'Is there anyone nearby?'

'No. I don't think so. Ukon is away.'

'Draw close,' he said, and I heard him shift toward the curtain. 'Before Reizei died,' he told me, 'there were things found in the chest beside his bed. Instruments of magic.'

'Instruments of magic?'

'Toothpicks, and a vial of some kind.'

I laughed. 'Surely someone could leave things such as that by accident.'

'That is not what people think.'

'And what people think is more important than what did or didn't happen.'

'You don't need me to answer that.'

'And just who would have cause to hurt Reizei?'

'I don't know. Perhaps someone who bore a grudge against the Empress.'

'Is that what she thinks? So she has been told about this?'

'That is what she thinks.'

'But surely her judgement can't be trusted now. Dainagon says she is beside herself with grief.'

'Nevertheless she has her opinions.'

'And who does she think might be responsible for this treachery?'

'Certain names have been suggested to her.' From his tone I guessed what he would say next. I felt as if I had been thrown into a lake. 'Yours is one of them.'

I struggled for breath, as if my lungs had filled with water.

So it was Izumi who had hinted that I was to blame, knowing full well that even if I were not the rumour would damage me as much as any real incrimination. She must have gone back to the house in the First Ward after the funeral and spread her insinuations.

In my anger I forgot our need for discretion. 'How could anyone suspect me of such cruelty?' I fairly shouted at him. 'To wish to harm a child – it's inconceivable.'

'It seems you are thought to be capable of all manner of cruelty.'

So he had heard of my lies about Sadako. 'And you find those stories plausible.'

'All I know,' he said, 'is that you are not yourself.'

'Not myself? Who are you to know if I am not myself? You come here with your sarcasm and your high-minded talk and draw your conclusions. What do you know about me?'

'Very little.'

'So you know little, and suspect much.'

'I didn't say that.'

'You implied it.'

'I had hoped to speak to you reasonably, if only to warn you ...'

'Of what? The evil inherent in my nature?'

'Of the danger you pose to yourself and others.'

Something in his voice betrayed his intention. 'You said certain names were suggested,' I said.

'If there were others I didn't recognise them.'

'But you heard their names.'

'They were mentioned, yes.'

'But you don't know this person – or persons.'

242

'No.'

I had nothing to go on but his tone and my intuition. But I was sure of it: he meant Masato. Yet I could hardly ask him to confirm my suspicion; it would only substantiate our collusion.

'And how does the Empress intend to deal with these meddlers in black magic?'

'She knows she can do nothing. She has no proof. But the rumours will be damaging enough.'

I recalled her look of warning as she imposed my penance. It was true: if there were rumours she would have no cause to suppress them. Yet how could she fail to see that Izumi might have cause to malign me? Wasn't it convenient for Izumi to have her rival subject to vicious gossip on the very eve of Kanesuke's return? And to have drawn Masato into her slander – it was appalling. She would blacken his reputation as she had mine. And all because of that book, which she assumed had no less base a purpose than the instruments of magic she had accused the two of us of wielding.

Ryūen's voice interrupted my thoughts. 'You must go away,' he said. 'Soon – before the damage is too great.'

'But that will only seem to confirm my guilt.'

'Those who suspect you will do so whether you leave or not. But you will suffer more if you stay here.'

'But I have nowhere to go.' I nearly wept in frustration.

'You can go back to the house in Mino.'

The house where my mother died. The house where I abandoned my childhood. The house where my father grieved for so long that he lost his reason. Someone else drank the wine in his cup. Someone else snapped the stems of the irises in the garden, leaving only the juicy stumps. Someone else read his scrolls and spoke when he spoke, drowning out his voice.

All those letters that Ryūen wrote to me when our father was dying; I have them still. But I never read them.

'Sister,' he said – it was a word I had not hear him speak for fourteen years – 'there is no taint of death there. It is quiet and clean. The garden is changed. They have planted honeysuckle all along the south wall by the orchard.'

So he remembered that I loved that scent. 'But what would I do there?' I asked him. 'It would be a living death for me.'

'You could write.'

'I can't. I haven't written for months.'

'Consider it. Send me a letter if you change your mind.'

'I'll write to you, but not about that.'

'Write to me, then, but remember what I told you. You have no one to protect you now. Your enemies are stronger than your friends.'

'And do you believe them?'

'Who?'

'My enemies.'

'I never trust purveyors of rumour.'

'And do you trust me?'

His hesitation conveyed as much as his face would have done. 'Sometimes. But you are influenced now by things I cannot understand.'

'If I am swayed, as you describe it, it is only by love.'

'It is a strange kind of love that desires the unhappiness of others.'

'I wish for no one's unhappiness.'

'Do you not? I wish I could believe that.' He gathered the folds of his robe and stood. 'Write to me, and look after yourself.'

'Tadahira,' I said. It was strange on my tongue, that name that had come so easily when we were young and loved each other. 'The tangerine tree in the garden – is it still there?'

'I don't know.'

'Don't let them cut it down.'

'You are more sentimental than I thought.'

244

'Not sentimental. Just superstitious.'

'I feared as much. Remember not to travel west now; we have been told it is unlucky.' Then he left me, and I sat for a long time behind my curtain, waiting for his words to dissipate in the humid air.

I contrived a means of escaping my enemies but they found me. Perhaps it was by chance that we met, but I think not. They were waiting for me, I am sure of it. They were listening for my step. When I looked up and saw Izumi with the others I knew that they had planned it. I fixed her with such a stare that I was sure she would turn away. But she returned my look with doubled fury, and her companions drew close as if to shield her from my vindictiveness.

I saw them on my return from the Shinsen-en. I had not been to the garden since the moon viewing, though I have often dreamed of it.

Why did I choose to go alone on a hot afternoon, knowing that such rashness would only enhance my reputation for eccentricity? I confess I wasn't thinking clearly; I only knew I had to escape. I had to get away from Ukon's prying looks and the women's general secretiveness, and my worries about Masato. Two days and he hasn't replied to my letter. Perhaps he has heard the rumour about the plot against Reizei and has decided to stay away from me. I didn't mention it when I wrote; it is too risky. So I must wait and tell him myself.

But how can I manage it? I thought about it all the way to the Shinsen-en. The heat was as oppressive as my mood; the air thick with presentiment. Outside the Suzaku Gate a throng of commoners waited to receive their shares of rice and salt. A boy in a torn brown robe hit the wheel of my coach with a stick. I saw his face flash past, his eyes dark with anger. His look changed everything I saw. The walls of the Prison of the Left grew taller still; the shade beneath the willows deepened.

We stopped near the Pavilion of Celestial Presidence. I climbed down and told the driver to wait. Evidently he was shocked by my lack of escorts. I didn't care. I would have an hour of peace without surveillance.

I moved through the yellow orb cast by my parasol. The thin silk did little to deflect the sun's heat, so I kept to the shade as much as I could. For a while I stood beneath the oaks where we had gathered for the moon viewing. The leaves, aged prematurely by the drought, hung limp from their stems.

This year those leaves will not turn red. But even if they did I knew I wouldn't see their scarlet canopy. I wouldn't watch the moon climb, white and replete, above those arching boughs. I would be absent, like Sadako and Reizei. I would see those trees only in my memory, as they were that night in the Eighth Month, when I envied the beauty of two unbanished sisters, and wished for the return of a man who has caused me so much pain that I no longer care to see his face.

And what of this new man, whose face is dearer to me than my own? I didn't know him then. He came from nothing, like the acorns that ripened the whole year long and now lie scattered on the ground – like the child who grows within me and will not receive his name. And if he stands there in two months' time when the crowd gathers again to watch the moon rising he will not see those trees as I did. They will be new to him. If their colour lacks the intensity that I recall he will not miss it. Their boughs will shelter him as they did me.

I felt his absence then, in the stillness of that hot afternoon, as if I held the future in my hands like some rare fruit on the verge of ripeness.

The ground smelled of fungus and must. The uncracked

acorns bruised my slippered feet. A peacock fanned his plumes and stepped away from me.

I went a little further, past the fishing pavilion wrecked in the typhoon and down to the Dragon Pond. I saw the doused fires left by the priests who had come to pray for rain and the end of the epidemic. But I thought not of them but of the Dragon King's daughter, the one who gave the Buddha the jewel of indeterminate colour.

I recalled the letter Kanesuke had given me that autumn afternoon at the inn east of Uji. 'That jewel,' he wrote. 'Tell me what colour it was. I can't remember.' But I was too angry to send him a reply.

I saw the island in the pond and the red arch of the bridge, and I was tempted to cross it. What would I find in the tall grass by the maple trees? Two lovers could lie there. And I remembered what Masato had told me that night when the hail fell on the bamboo leaves, and he asked me to cover him with my hair. 'It is like grass,' he said. 'Like uncut grass in summer.'

I had told myself that I wouldn't cry, but I could scarcely see my way. I thought of the instruments of magic found in the chest by Reizei's bed. Who had put them there? Was it an accident – a simple act of carelessness – or was someone else guilty of the treachery of which Masato and I had been accused? Or had they been left as a sign of our complicity by those who conspired against us?

When I tell Masato about that plot what will he say? I never told him the whole story of my rivalry with Izumi. Will he think her capable of spreading such deceit, or will he say I invented her lies out of my own fear and suspicion?

The heat from the sun bore down so harshly that I retreated once more to the shade. I brushed away my tears with the back of my hand and found it streaked with powder. The quiet of the park, which I had sought so eagerly, grew sullen. The calls of the birds marked my solitude; the sound of falling water increased my restiveness.

I watched the swallows rise above their shadows and wished for their remoteness. From their vantage the view grew wide even as I diminished. My parasol a fleck of yellow, my movements barely discernible, my thoughts of no consequence. Everything reduced to form and pattern: the scattered trees, the walls and streams, the roofs and towers.

From that height all that was unknowable did not matter. The colour of the jewel beneath the water, the thoughts of the lovers entangled in the grass, the schemes and contrivances of those compelled by spite and jealousy.

As I walked back to my coach I felt as if my body had lost its substance, as if I were made of the same fugitive hue as the dyes that fade when the sunlight is too strong. I was becoming invisible. All the sights that had impressed themselves so vividly when I first arrived – the rough bark of the oaks, the sheen of the peacock feathers, the green freshness of the water oats that skirted the pond – receded from my mind, as I receded from them. I would not come back to the Shinsen-en. It belonged to my past, even as I beheld it.

When we drove through the Suzaku Gate my sense of dislocation accompanied me. I felt like a traveller who returns from a long journey and finds all he has left behind altered, though he cannot say how. Nothing seemed as it should. The crowds of courtiers and retainers, the familiar exchanges and obsequies only increased my isolation.

And they were waiting for me, those women who wished me ill. I saw them as soon as I crossed the hall by the Chamberlain's dormitory. They were standing by a pillar, whispering. Izumi turned as she heard my step and met my stare. I heard her say to her friends as I passed by, 'It's Lady Han. She's been wandering again.' Their laughter followed me down the corridor and into my rooms.

*

She came without warning, in the evening, as I was writing to Masato. When I heard her speaking to Ukon I turned so abruptly that I upset the jar where I dip my brush, and the water pooled on the paper and dripped off the edge of the desk. I snatched the ruined letter and crumpled it in my hand, and the ink stained my fingers and the hems of my sleeves.

It was Izumi, Ukon said, her gibbous face half-concealed by the standing curtain. Would I allow her in?

Before I could answer she was there, her look as dark as her figured dress, her lips trembling.

'You will be glad to hear that he is ill.'

I dismissed Ukon, who was listening behind the curtain. 'Who?'

'You know very well. I just got his letter. He is staying near Otoko until he is better. He has a fever.' She gave me an accusing look. 'You wished it on him, didn't you?'

'I did no such thing.'

'You did it just to spite me. You want to make me as unhappy as he made you.'

'You are the spiteful one!' The words came rushing out before I could stop them. 'You stole him from me, and you lied when I asked you about him. All that time when you were lovers, all that time when you pretended to be my friend – how you must have savoured it. And now you come to me with your accusations. Leave my room. You make me ill.'

'Not before you hear what I have to say. I didn't steal him from you. He left you. He would have left you even if I hadn't met him.'

I tried not to show my hurt, knowing the pleasure she would take in it. 'And I suppose you think I should trust your opinion.'

'It's not my opinion. He told me. We tell each other everything. Don't worry,' she said, reading my expression. 'He did love you a little once.'

How she relished it: that last twist of the blade. 'Leave me,' I said.

'One more thing. Tell this man of yours to quit his magic.'

'What man? What magic?'

'You know exactly who I mean.' Her voice was as cold as my hands. 'If you had wanted to protect him you should have been more discreet.' She gave me a hateful look. 'He gave it to you, didn't he?'

'Gave me what?'

'Your precious book. You planned it together, didn't you? That scheme to give it to Kanesuke. Tell me: why did you want me to take that book to him? Did it please you to know I would be the agent of your plan?'

'There was no plan,' I said.

'He taught you those rites, didn't he – those spells and incantations. He gave you that potion you keep by your bed. Did you think I hadn't heard? Your secret visits to his house, your wanderings in the streets and parks – don't you know what people think of them? What sort of woman goes out in the midst of pestilence? What sort of woman shuts herself up all day with her books and her instruments of magic? You are mad, just as they say.'

'Who says I am mad?'

She looked at me incredulously. 'Who does not? I never thought,' she said, 'despite all you have done in the past, that you would injure a child.'

So she would condemn me for Reizei's suffering. How furious it made me. 'It was you who invented the whole plot – you who told the Empress. You were the one who said I was to blame.'

She laughed, her black teeth glistening. 'Why would I do that? Given what you have become, who needs convincing?'

'And if I am mad as you say, why try to dissuade me?'

'Because I love Kanesuke, and I won't let you harm him as you have others.'

'I have no reason to wish him ill. I loved him more than you did once.'

'But you don't love him now. Listen to me.' She came so close I could smell her sweat and that florid scent of roses. Her lips were parted in anger, as they would have been in love. How often he must have kissed them. 'If this illness of his proves serious – if he gets worse, if he suffers – you will answer for it. And stop loitering around my rooms. I will not be the object of your superstition.'

All night as I lay on the floor I saw that face: the thick dark brows, the spiteful eyes, the lips swollen as if they had been bitten by a lover. It doesn't matter who spread the rumour about Reizei. It doesn't matter whether I am mad or sane. My part has been given to me and I must play it. I have no freedom; even my escape is part of her plan.

I must be brief or she will see me at my desk. Too much risk to be direct. All must be occluded.

He is worse, and her hatred has begun. I feel it even as I sleep. It presses on me, greater than the weight of water. Drowning would be easier.

She has told her friends, and they have told theirs. I am borne along by the current of their hatred. The cliffs rise up on either side, the sky a thin white line above my head, and I am carried endlessly.

How far must I fall? The abyss has no limit. Last night even the chasm disappeared and I had only the sensation. I fell and fell; the stars behind my eyes gave no guidance.

I must finish before she comes. I saw her only yesterday. I opened one eye – for she thought I was sleeping – and saw a hand draw back my curtain. How quickly she turned when she saw I was awake! Her robes rasped on the floor like the wings of an insect; her perfume betrayed her.

I must warn him of her intent – soon, before he falls as I have. I see him poised upon the rim. We fell together once, for love – that black delirium – but I will not let him fall again for her hatred.

Is it far, this place I seek? Has it hills or valleys? I was a valley once, my white skin mottled by the flickering leaves, my body lost in a profusion of azaleas.

Will I lose myself again? The long-limbed beeches will give me welcome. Chestnuts will spread their drapery. The vestal pears will arch their sprays above my head.

All that was unknown will open to me. The ginkgos will unfold their pale green fans. Shells will disclose their treasure. The finch's song will become intelligible; words etched on stones and trees will reveal their meaning.

I will be nowhere then. There will be no sign of my passing. The circling crows will move on; couriers will ride past; carriage wheels will impress their track on my footprints.

The valley spreads into a broad green field; the rice glistens. My slippered feet sink into the silt. A breeze parts the stalks and I see their faces. Two children, one on the verge of speech and the other past it, one new to my trust and the other beyond it.

Will they retrieve me then, those two children whom I seek? Their eyes reflect their absent fathers. I lie and listen to their speech. The grass waves above us, rustling with its own language.

It was there by my pillow when I returned to my rooms in

the evening. I had gone out for less than an hour, to walk in the gardens of the Shishinden.

It was a threat, like the last one. There was no hand-writing to betray the identity of the sender, though I needed none. Her name is plain. My treacherous friend, my deceitful double.

She tore a verse from the sutras and pasted it onto a sheet of yellow paper. No need to explain its origin:

Suppose with curses and poisonous herbs
Someone should injure you.
Think on the power of the Perceiver of the World's Sounds
And the injury will rebound on the perpetrator.

She is listening now. I will not gratify her with my profanities.

I write with his scent on my hands. My hair dishevelled. My body marked. That fury that left its signs upon my body, as priests trace their mudrās on a corpse: what words did it leave there? I try to read them, but the light is too dim. There – on my wrist, a faint red line. On the hollow of my thigh two marks made by the same vehement gesture: what do they say? How long will they last? As long as his scent or longer? As long as the look in his eyes when he made his entreaties?

'Tell me,' he said. 'Why are you crying?'

I lay on his bed and looked through the open lattices into the garden. A twilit green. Swallows descending. The scent of laurel. All fading and receding, gone even as I perceived them. The damp air thick in my chest, my sobs rising, his hand gentle on my face, stroking away my tears.

'You mustn't cry like this. Tell me.'

So I told him what I could, about the plot against Reizei, and Izumi's threats.

'Why would she accuse you of such a thing?'

'Because she hates me.'

'If she hates you she must have a reason.'

'She has plenty of reasons to hate me, as I have to hate her.'

'I didn't think you were capable of hatred.'

'Oh, yes,' I said. 'One doesn't have to be mad to hate.'

'Who says you are mad?'

'Haven't you heard?' His ingenuousness surprised me; I couldn't bear to think it wasn't genuine.

'Heard you are mad? No,' he said.

'And you don't think so yourself?'

'Hate makes even those who are not do mad things.'

I trembled. 'So you think I could have harmed Reizei?'

'No. You don't despise the Empress. You would never retaliate in that way.'

'But I could harm Izumi.'

'You must answer that yourself.'

'And would you hate me if I did?'

'No,' he said. 'But I detest your self-destructiveness. It does no good to anyone.'

'I would do anything I could not to harm you,' I told him. I saw his eyes fill with tears, and I brushed them away as he had mine.

'Don't,' I said, and I kissed the hollow of his cheek, his forehead, his lips.

'You can't hurt me,' he said.

'Yes, I can.'

Something flashed across his face. He pulled me up by the shoulders. 'Stop it. You mustn't say things like that. If you want them badly enough they will happen.'

'Does your book foretell it?'

He shook me. 'I don't need my books to foretell it. I can see it myself.'

'I don't want to hurt you,' I said, 'but I will. I have already. You know it as well as I do.'

'Why must you do this to me?' He held my face tight between his hands. 'I'm sick of your selfishness. All you want is to shut me out.'

'That's not true,' I said.

'Sometimes,' he replied, 'I think all you want is to be like Izumi. You crave her. You thrive on her dislike.'

'I don't thrive on it. She has turned me into a ghost.'

'You are not a ghost,' he said quietly. He kissed my hands. 'Are these the hands of a ghost?' He closed my eyelids and kissed them. 'Are these the eyes of a ghost?' He tilted my chin. 'Look at me. These are living eyes.' He kissed me again, and I closed my eyes and saw Izumi, her bitten lips swollen like mine, her eyes full of hatred. 'This body is living,' he said. His hands circled my waist.

'Don't,' I said. His hands tightened and I struggled against them. 'She has made me into a ghost, and she will do the same to you. She always wins – always. She won before, and she will win this time, with you.'

He shook me. 'Don't talk like that. I'm not like that man – Kanesuke.'

I felt as if he had slapped me. I had never heard him say his name.

He shook me again. 'You love him still, don't you?'

'No.'

'I don't believe you.'

'Ask Izumi then. She knows it as well as I do.'

'Izumi. Kanesuke. I despise their very names. Leave them out of this. You are possessed – '

He stopped himself and released my wrists. I told him calmly, 'So you do think I am mad.'

'That's not what I said.'

'Like Lady Han. That's what they call me, you know. Kanesuke used to call me that. "My dear Lady Han," he would say. Did I tell you how he ruined my mirror? He cut two characters into it, the ones for beauty – so that when I looked in the mirror I would see what I was not. Do you understand that? Can you comprehend that kind of cruelty?'

'You make me hate him, if that's what you mean.'

I looked in his eyes and saw the same intensity I had seen in Izumi's. 'So I have made you capable of hate.'

He shook his head. 'You forget that I saw my sister burned alive – there, in that very garden. Do you think that someone who has seen a child scorched to death wouldn't be capable of hate?'

I spoke as gently as I could, as if my tone could soothe him. 'So you look to your books to make sense of it.'

'There is no sense in the death of a child.'

'Yet you and I are accused of just that by the woman I detest. Isn't that reason enough to despise her?'

'You don't know that,' he said. 'You're assuming it. You told me that Izumi denied spreading those rumours.'

'You and your assumptions. I know it. I can feel it as surely as I breathe.'

'You will destroy yourself with these suspicions.'

I pointed to my chest. '*I* am the object of suspicion. I am the court's plaything, its favourite miscreant. It is my role, don't you see? I am Lady Han, who wanders the corridors for no reason, who talks to the trees in the Shinsen-en, who drives to her lover's house in the midst of an epidemic: that is how they see me. And you are Lady Han's colluding lover. And what we say is what they wish us to say, and we act as they want us to act. All your protestations, all your pretty pleas and entreaties are part of their plan. They will mock your innocence. They will ruin you as I do.'

'I'm not innocent. You think me so for your own reasons.'

'I do not. I make you the opposite. I stain you with my own dye.'

'How you savour this bitterness.'

'I do not.'

'Look.' He turned my face towards the garden. 'Do those trees thrive on bitterness? Does that fruit ripen out of spite? You must tear it out, this bitterness. Where is it? Is it here?' He wrenched my robes. 'Is it here? I will find it for you.'

I twisted from his grip, and as I struggled I saw Izumi's face as she confronted her attackers. I would be brave, as she was. I would wear my marks. He scratched my wrist; he grazed my thigh, twice, with his nails; and I fought him as Izumi fought her intruders.

I scratched his cheek. He drew a breath, and in that pause we lay suspended. He put a finger to the cut – his blood as bright as mine – and sealed my lips with it.

Postscript

As far as I can ascertain – for it is possible that some pages are missing – the manuscript ends here. But there is one more thing. When Izumi gave these pages to me she entrusted me with something else. It is a book of divination, of Chinese origin, bound in black silk. Between its yellowed leaves – for it seems to be of some antiquity, and resembles in every detail the one described in this account – I found this note. The handwriting is identical to the narrator's. I have included it as a postscript, for it seems to throw some light on her mental state near the time of her departure. The first passage seems to be taken from the book in which it was found; the rest must be her own.

Hexagram Forty-one: Loss

Loss accompanied by confidence – sublime good fortune! It is favourable to have in view some destination.

> At the foot of the mountain, the lake:
> The image of loss.
> The Superior Man controls his anger
> And restrains his passions.

9 at the beginning:
  To hurry away when work is done is not wrong, but one must consider whether a hasty departure will harm others.

6 for the third place:

If three set forth together now, one will be lost on the way, but one going forth alone will find company.

6 for the fourth place:

The Superior Man decreases his faults and thus hastens the arrival of happiness – no error! There is no gain without loss; the lake diminishes to increase the height of the mountain.

Lies, lies and love: I am twice defiled.

How shall I find the way? It is too far, and I am not ready. They will mock me and throw stones in my path. I will hold up my fan and walk past them.

And at night, when the swallows descend in the darkness, what will I become? A ghost within ghosts: two sisters lamenting their lost lover; Rokujō at the shrine of Ise.

What did Rokujō do that was so brave? She left him, the man she loved as she had no other. She watched him wash his hands outside the shrine. How she had loved those hands. Now they would not touch her. He would not reach for the red cord at her waist; he would not caress her. She had become invisible; he would not look her way. She had given him the only gift that she had left: her absence, her enduring absence, still and perpetual. He walked past, and she was left with her loss.

Glossary

ABSTINENCE. This Shintō concept pervaded Heian life. The average nobleman could expect to spend several weeks each year in ritual seclusion, either to avoid danger (due to inauspicious dates, unlucky omens and the like) or to purge himself. As protector of the realm, an Emperor was obliged to endure even longer bouts of abstinence. During his seclusion he wore purified robes, fasted and refrained from various activities, including reading and sex. (See Shintō.)

AINU. Maligned by the narrator as blue-eyed barbarians, the Ainu were an ancient people believed to have come to Japan from Siberia. During Heian times they were forced further and further north by government troops. Some of their descendants still live on the island of Hokkaidō.

AMIDA. The Buddha of Infinite Light. The Amidist cult, introduced from China in the mid-ninth century and supported by the powerful abbots of Mount Hiei, appealed to the poor and the aristocracy alike. Its followers believed that in order to be reborn in the Pure Land they had only to call on the Amida using a seven-syllable formula known as the Nembutsu. In the unsettled times of the late Heian Period, the promise of personal salvation through faith alone proved enticing for many, including various emperors and empresses. (See Buddhism, Nembutsu.)

ANISE. Branches of star anise (*Illicium religiosum*) were often placed as offerings on Buddhist altars.

ARIWARA NO YUKIHIRA. A ninth-century poet and statesman who was exiled to Suma, a stretch of coast southwest of the capital. His younger brother, Ariwara no Narihira, was banished for having an affair with a wealthy Fujiwara girl. (See Tales of Ise.)

ASSIGNATIONS. Noblemen often went to their rendezvous in disguise. The eponymous hero of The Tale of Genji often travelled in an inconspicuous coach, and would hide his brocade robes beneath an ordinary cloak. At times men went so far as to conceal their faces with a band of silk during their amorous encounters. It was entirely possible, therefore, that a woman might not know the identity of her lover.

BEAUTY, FEMALE. Diminutive, wan, swathed in up to fifteen layers of clothing, the ideal Heian woman barely seemed to possess a body at all. Only her face – whitened with lead paint, the eyebrows plucked and redrawn high on the forehead, the teeth blackened and the mouth red with carmine – had any tangibility, and even that was half-hidden by her fan. Her greatest asset was her hair, which was worn so that it flowed over her shoulders and trailed along the floor. Heian men, who were susceptible to *coups de foudre*, were often overcome by a single glimpse of a woman's tresses. (See Teeth.)

BEAUTY, MALE. Kanesuke and Masato hardly conform to the ideal of the Heian man. The latter was portly, round-faced and narrow-eyed, and sported a wispy beard and (occasionally) a moustache. Susceptible to drink and more fond of poetry than exercise, he often died of diabetes at an early age. Prone to tears – which evinced his delicacy of feeling – he was as accomplished in calligraphy and music as he was in lovemaking. The trait he most conspicuously lacked, in contrast to the men of the Kamakura Period who succeeded him, was bravery.

BEAUTY, THE NATURAL WORLD. Heian artists were acutely aware of the link between beauty and transience. The notion, embodied in the term *mono no aware* ('the pathos of things'), pervades the literature of the time and had a lasting influence on Japanese aesthetics. Falling autumn leaves, melting snows, fading blossoms: all evoked the feeling that what was lovely in the world did not last. It is impossible to know where such an idea originated, but it was clearly influenced by Buddhism (with its admonitions against attachment to fleeting worldly passions) and Taoism (which stressed the mutability of earthly things).

BIRTHS. As girls were generally less desirable than boys, their birth was often met with pointed silence. If they were fortunate enough to be born into one of the powerful clans such as the Fujiwara, however, they were greeted with more enthusiasm, as they had the chance to marry into the imperial line.

BIWA. A pear-shaped lute with four strings and four frets.

BLUE HORSES. According to the Chinese principles of yin-yang, green was the colour of spring, and it was thought to be auspicious to behold green (or blue) horses during the festivities of the New Year. The twenty-one horses paraded in the festival were originally blue roans, but as these were rare in Japan, they were in time replaced by white ones.

BROOM TREE. The *hahakigi*, a tree from which brooms were made, was said to be clearly visible from a distance but indistinct when one approached.

BUDDHISM. Introduced from Korea in the sixth century, Buddhism was divided into two major sects in the narrator's time: Tendai (based on Mount Hiei) and Shingōn (based on Mount Kōya near Nara). Many of the poor, and more than a few of the elite, were also drawn to a new cult known as Amidism (supported by the Tendai sect, and led by the charismatic monk Genshin). Nobles with sufficient means hired priests of various persuasions to conduct services in their private chapels. In times of extremity, ritualists from many sects converged on the Imperial Palace, along with Shintō priests, yin-yang diviners and mountain ascetics. (See Amida, Shingōn and Tendai.)

BUREAU OF DIVINATION. The art of divination was taken seriously in Heian times; the more unstable the political situation, the more the government relied on it. The bureau (staffed by a director, four aides, six yin-yang masters and a host of scholars and students) supervised investigations into astronomy, the calendar, divination and geomancy. The monarchy and the nobility made constant demands on its services: to fix auspicious dates, to interpret baleful signs and to perform rituals of purification.

BUREAU OF MEDICINE. Located in the Ninefold Enclosure south of the Banquet Pine Grove, this bureau ministered to ailments suffered by the nobility. (The doctors treated only those of the fifth rank and above.) Their methods were based on yin-yang principles derived from Chinese medicine.

CALLIGRAPHY. It is no exaggeration to say that the Heian nobility were obsessed by handwriting. Fine calligraphy was prized not only for its beauty, but for what it said about the taste and the character of the writer. A subtle hand implied a subtle mind. There were many calligraphic styles in use at the time, some imported from T'ang China. While women could avail themselves of a variety of styles, it was generally true that a female hand was expected to be graceful and lacking in boldness and ostentation.

CARRIAGES. Coaches were a status symbol in Heian Japan. Imperial edicts decreed the type to which each rank was entitled, and the number of escorts it might have. Carriages did not have seats; passengers sat on mats spread on the floor. People entered from the rear and descended from the front, after the ox (or oxen) had been unhitched.

Women travelling by coach indulged their vanity by hanging their multicoloured sleeves outside the carriage windows. Some travel ensembles were especially designed with sleeves that were wider on the side to be displayed. Even the flamboyant Sei Shōnagon condemned this lopsided fashion as pretentious.

CH'ANG-AN. The capital of China during the T'ang Dynasty (618–907). Both Heian-Kyō and Nara were modelled after it. (See Heian-Kyō, Nara.)

CHERRY OF THE LEFT. This tree, along with the Orange of the Right, flanked the southern steps of the Shishinden, the Great Hall of the Inner Palace. Parties were held in honour of the cherry tree around the twentieth of the Second Month. Noblemen recited spontaneous poems in Chinese and performed *bugaku* dances such as 'The Song of the Spring Warbler' and 'Garden of Flowers and Willows.' (See Shishinden.)

CHRYSANTHEMUM FESTIVAL. One of five great palace festivals held during the year, it took place in autumn, in the Ninth Month. Chrysanthemums were a symbol of longevity, and it was thought that the dew that collected on the flowers and leaves would rejuvenate the skin.

CHUANG-TZU. A Taoist philosopher who lived in the fourth century BC. The philosophy of Taoism pervades the I Ching. (See I Ching, Tao te Ching.)

CLASSICS. These works – including Chinese literature, philosophy, history and the like – were the backbone of an aristocratic education. Women, however, were discouraged from pursuing such serious studies, and were barred from the Imperial University. A rare few, including Sei Shōnagon and Murasaki Shikibu, were educated privately. Murasaki, by some accounts, learned Chinese so well that her father regretted she had not been born a boy. (See Murasaki Shikibu, Sei Shōnagon.)

CLOTHES. The image of the Japanese woman wearing a slender kimono bound with a broad sash, her hair piled high upon her head and skewered with lacquered pins, belongs to a later era. The style of dress for Heian women was quite different. Over their wide trousers and silken shifts they wore a series of flowing robes, diaphanous in summer and padded in winter. (Chinese jackets and trains were added on formal occasions.) The robes were coloured with extraordinary subtlety, in accordance with the wearer's rank, her taste and the season. The various hues were best admired in a woman's sleeves, which were of graduated length, the innermost being the longest.

COLOURS. The colours worn by both men and women had aesthetic and symbolic connotations. Many of the women's ensembles echoed the colours of the natural world: of azaleas and chrysanthemums, rue and maple, wisteria and cherry. Some gowns had linings of a different colour (willow robes, for instance, were white lined with green). Robes were also worn in complex layerings of colour known as *kasane*. (To wear even a single gown of the wrong hue was a dreadful solecism.) Here are a few of the colours alluded to by the narrator:

The Forbidden Colours (*kinjiki*) were shades of deep scarlet and purple that were barred to all but those of the highest ranks, with rare exceptions. (Head Chamberlains, for instance, were permitted to wear the colours as one of the perks of their office.)

Futaai was a twice-dyed colour made from scarlet (obtained from safflower, a rare and expensive vegetable dye) and indigo. It was worn in late spring and summer, and ranged in shades from deep violet (suitable for younger men) to pale blue with just a trace of red (for older men).

Grey-violet (*usu-iro*) was a colour associated with light mourning. Those in deep mourning wore grey or black.

Plum red (*imayō*) was associated with spring, and was worn around the time of the New Year.

Purple (*murasaki*) was a shade that connoted fidelity and lasting passion.

Sanctioned rose (*yurushi-iro*) was a light shade of scarlet. Men and women of the lower ranks – including the narrator – were permitted to wear it.

Scarlet, or rouge red (*beni-iro*), was made from the dye of safflowers. During various times in the tenth century, when sumptuary laws governing dress and other luxuries were in effect, imports of the dye were strictly controlled, though the regulations were often ignored.

CONCH SHELLS. Conches were blown at Buddhist temples to announce the hour. (See Time.)

CONVENTS. Buddhist convents were a convenient refuge for women fleeing social scandal. Less drastic measures were also available. Fallen women could also pursue a religious life within their own mansions, in sombre rooms fitted to the purpose. Cloisters were also a haven, of course, for those with sincere vocations, including the writer of the Prologue.

COURTESANS. The narrator was right to fear that she might be taken for such a woman. At the time she was writing, courtesans (*asobi-onna*) were indeed available to noblemen in the capital who could afford them, though such women did not play a prominent role in Heian society until the twelfth century.

COURTYARDS. The women's apartments in the Imperial Palace were centred on courtyards, many of them named after the flowering plants or trees within them: Umetsubo (Plum), Nashitsubo (Pear), Fujitsubo (Wisteria), Kiritsubo (Paulownia), and so on.

Consorts and concubines lived in spacious apartments; ladies-in-waiting such as the narrator and Izumi lived in smaller rooms under the eaves. The rooms were enclosed by a complex arrangement of partitions, shutters, blinds and screens. These flimsy constructions afforded little privacy, and the women were well aware of the conduct of their neighbours. (See Imperial Palace.)

CUCKOOS. While the cuckoo's song was pleasantly associated with summer, it also had melancholy connotations, for the bird was thought to flit between the land of the living and the realm of the dead. Flocks of cuckoos were a sign of bad luck.

DAGGERS. High-born girls (and boys) were given a dagger as a protective talisman when they were born.

DANGEROUS YEARS. In The Tale of Genji, thirty-seven is described as a treacherous age for women; it was known as *yakudoshi*, or 'year of danger'. (A few centuries after the narrator wrote her story this dangerous year shifted to the age of thirty-three; even today some Japanese women approach that age with trepidation.) Similarly, forty-two was believed to be a perilous year for a man, perhaps because the Japanese word for forty-two (*shini*) is homophonous with the word for death.

DARKNESS. When the narrator expresses her distaste for the colour white, she is reflecting the Japanese reverence for darkness. As the twentieth-century novelist Tanizaki Junichirō wrote, 'Our ancestors, forced to live in dark rooms, presently came to discover beauty in shadows, ultimately to guide shadows towards beauty's ends.' This regard for darkness, Tanizaki says, is linked to the Japanese affinity for art that is subdued, quiet, reticent and suggestive rather than direct.

DAYS. According to the sexagenary cycle, in any given month there were at the most three days that could be named after one of the twelve signs of the Zodiac. In the First Month, for instance, there could be three Days of the Rat. The imperial progress to pick spring herbs fell on the first of those three days.

DEATH. When a person died, the body was left to lie for up to seven days to see if the soul would return. Only when the signs of decay became obvious was the corpse cremated or buried. Corpses were thought to be polluting, and even the sight of a dead animal was thought to defile the beholder.

The wealthy buried their dead in one of the great cemeteries near the capital, such as Funaoka, Toribeno or Adashino. In times of pestilence or famine families too poor to afford proper burials dumped the bodies of their loved ones in ditches by the roadsides and in the ravines by the Kamo and Katsura rivers. When the piles of corpses grew high they were burned and buried by workers from the Hiden-in, the municipal refuges for the orphaned and destitute. (See Defilement.)

DEFILEMENT. Death, illness, pregnancy and menstruation were all thought to be contaminating. For this reason the Empress quits the palace when she is ill, and the narrator vacates her rooms when she suffers from 'the usual defilement.' The wives and consorts of the Emperor left the palace when they were between three and five months' pregnant, and the narrator herself feels great pressure to absent herself before the signs of her condition become clear.

It was thought that people could avoid being polluted by a defiled person by standing in their presence. Someone who visited a person in mourning, for instance, would stand rather than sit.

DEVIL CHASER. The main actor in the *tsuina*, an ancient Chinese ritual adapted by the Japanese. On the last night of the year, an attendant dressed in vermilion trousers, black robes and a four-eyed golden mask made his way through the palace, accompanied by boys beating drums and courtiers armed with bows and reed arrows. The ritual began as a means of warding off pestilence; over time the Devil Chaser was transmuted into the Devil himself.

DIARIES (*NIKKI*). When the *kana* syllabary – a phonetic form of writing – was developed in Japan around 900, women were among the first to experiment with it. Discouraged from writing in Chinese (which was considered too scholarly), they set down their thoughts in their own tongue. Some recorded their travels and observations of daily life; others their travails with wayward husbands.

These diaries were not published in the modern sense. They were copied out by hand and distributed to a coterie of sympathetic readers – or in some cases, to a single friend. As Fujiwara no Nagako, a lady-in-waiting to Emperor Horikawa, wrote in the epilogue to her diary, published around 1107, 'If I were to show this to someone who did not think well of me, the contents might create a furore if noised abroad, and that would be unfortunate. Then again, it would be a shame to show it to someone who was well disposed towards me, but had neither friends nor influence. I ... concluded that Lady Hitachi alone was the one who could fulfil these three conditions.' Clearly the authors of some diaries (including the calculating Nagako) hoped that their private musings would win them admiration.

DRAGON KING'S DAUGHTER. This story, found in the Devadatta Chapter of the Lotus Sutra, describes how the youngest daughter of the Dragon King, who lived in a palace below the sea, acquired instant Buddhahood through her faith in Shākyamuni. When she appeared before the Buddha, she presented him with a precious jewel that she had brought up from the deep. Earlier Buddhist scriptures had maintained that women were incapable of spiritual advancement due to 'five obstacles' inherent in their nature. The Lotus Sutra, then, can be seen as a radical Buddhist text, for it was the first to depict women as worthy of salvation. (See Siddhartha.)

EASTERN MARKETPLACE. The two main areas of commerce in the city, the Eastern and Western marketplaces, were located in the Seventh Ward, south of the Imperial Palace. Both were constructed around a courtyard with an ancient cherry tree. Public floggings were once conducted beneath those trees, though by the end of the tenth century such spectacles were rare.

EMPERORS. With a few exceptions, Heian emperors had less freedom and power than the aristocrats who served them. Forced into long bouts of abstinence, constrained in their daily activities by their exalted office, they spent more time presiding over festivals and banquets and upholding standards of taste than they did governing. Many retired at an early age, often to private palaces or retreats, where they continued to live privileged and highly secular lives. By the late eleventh century, cloistered emperors often exercised more power after they abdicated than they did when they were enthroned.

ENVOYS. Ambassadors were not sent to China in late Heian times, though cultural links with the mainland remained strong. Imperial envoys still had considerable prestige, however, though their role was largely ceremonial. While I have invented the details of Kanesuke's chequered career, some of his escapades (notably his affair with the Vestal of Ise) are loosely based on the life of Ariwara no Narihira, a ninth-century courtier who was sent to Ise as an Imperial Huntsman and met there in secret with the Vestal. (See Tales of Ise.)

ERAS. Borrowing from Chinese tradition, years were given auspicious titles, such as the First Year of Tengyō ('Heavenly Felicitation'). In practice, eras seldom lasted more than a decade, and sometimes no more than a year or two. In unsettled times of pestilence or famine, Heian emperors tried to appease the wrathful gods by changing the era name. For early historians, this constant shift of dates was a nightmare.

EXILES. It was rare for traitors of the state to be executed in Heian times; banishment was the preferred form of punishment. The notion of exile had romantic connotations, for many men of letters had suffered the same fate, including the T'ang poet Po Chü-i and the statesman Sugawara no Michizane. Exiles were legally permitted to take their wives (but not their lovers) with them, though literary sources seem to imply that they rarely did. (See Sugawara no Michizane.)

FALCONS. Some of these prized birds were imported from China. While Buddhist law prohibited the slaughter of animals, an exception was made for falconry, perhaps because Heian emperors were so fond of it.

FIRES. Residents of the Imperial Palace lived in constant fear of fire, and the chronicles of the time are filled with stories of the nobility decamping to private mansions while their quarters were rebuilt. In 960, for instance, the entire Inner Palace was razed by a conflagration. Some of the fires were blamed on angry ghosts; many were undoubtedly the work of arsonists.

FOXES. Mythical foxes (*kitsune*) were thought to assume various guises, particularly those of beautiful young women.

FUJIWARA CLAN. At the time the narrator was serving at court, the men of the Fujiwara clan were the most influential in the land. The powerful post of Minister of the Left almost invariably fell to them; they were frequently appointed regents or imperial advisors. Their daughters married emperors and bore sons who often assumed the throne. By the late tenth century the power of Fujiwara statesmen was so great that they could dictate the timing and terms of an emperor's abdication.

GAMES OF COMPARISONS (*MONOAWASE*). One of the

elegant diversions of courtly life. Contestants were divided into teams (of the left and right, mirroring the structure of government) and were called on to judge the aesthetic merits of various beautiful objects: flowers, iris roots, fans, paintings, songbirds, crickets, and so on. The contestants themselves were judged not just on their eloquence and sense of taste but on their manner and appearance. Similar contests involved the exchange of poems and riddles.

GO. A highly sophisticated board game introduced to Japan from China in the eighth century, *go* was popular with aristocrats of both sexes. It is played with smooth black and white stones on a board with 361 intersections. Once the stones have been placed on the board they cannot be moved again; stones that have been encircled by the enemy are usually forfeited. The game's erotic possibilities were exploited by Sei Shōnagon in The Pillow Book, where she describes how she and her friend Tadanobu used the language of *go* to discuss the sexual exploits of their acquaintances.

GOD OF SUMIYOSHI. This patron of seafarers and poets was worshipped at a shrine near the port of Naniwa, now part of the city of Osaka.

GOSECHI DANCES. Held during the Eleventh Month, these dances were one of the great spectacles of the winter season. Five young ladies of good family, arrayed in dazzling costumes, performed the Dance of the Heavenly Maidens before the Emperor, who bestowed his favour on the most accomplished by accepting her proffered hair comb.

HASEDERA. This Buddhist temple, located south of Heian-Kyō, was much favoured by aristocratic ladies. It was dedicated to the Eleven-Headed Kannon, one of the forms of the Goddess of Compassion, and is still a popular destination for pilgrims. (See Kannon.)

HAVEN (*MIYASUDOKORO*). An honorary title granted to a consort or concubine who bore the Emperor or Heir Apparent a child. The name means, poetically speaking, 'place in whom the august affection found rest'.

HEIAN PERIOD (794-1185). This span of Japanese history began when the capital was moved from Nara to Heian-kyō, the City of Peace and Tranquillity. The period was in fact a time of relative calm and political stability, during which the native arts, freed from overwhelming Chinese influence, flourished to an unprecedented degree. By the eleventh century, however, civil unrest was widespread, and the rule of the central government had been effectively usurped by the rising class of military provincials. Conflicts between two militant clans, the Taira and the Minamoto (or Genji), culminated in the thirty-year war that ushered in the Kamakura Period.

HEIAN-KYŌ (KYOTO). The city became the capital of Japan in the late eighth century and remained so until 1868, when the centre of government moved to Edo (now known as Tokyo). Modelled on the T'ang capital of Ch'ang-an, Heian-kyō was divided into wards, or districts. Those in the northeast quarter of the city, between First and Sixth avenues, approximately, were the most prestigious. The great mansions of the wealthy lined the avenues; the less fortunate lived on the streets and alleyways between them.

HEICHŪ: This inept lover, described in a tenth-century tale of the same name, was a familiar comic figure from Japanese folklore.

I CHING. The Book of Changes, or I Ching, originated in China as a book of oracles based on eight trigrams of straight and broken lines. Over time the trigrams evolved into a complex system of sixty-four hexagrams, each with its own images, judgements and commentaries. Each hexagram has a name – Grace, Deliverance, Elegance,

Oppression, Adversity, Restraint, Flaming Beauty, for instance – and its own gloss.

In Heian times the book was used in calendrical divination to fix auspicious dates. Some scholars such as Masato, however, regarded it in a more profound sense: as a guide to individual conduct.

The I Ching contains many references to the Superior Man, an ideal person of virtue inspired by Confucian values who possesses the qualities of the Tao. Chief amongst these is the quality of restraint or yielding, which derives from the female yin principle.

The traditional method of determining the hexagrams with forty-nine yarrow sticks has changed little over the course of 2,000 years. Masato prefers this to the quicker method of throwing three hollow coins, the customary practice of many professional fortune tellers in modern Asia. The sticks are divided and counted to determine each line of the hexagram. The first line is at the bottom; the sixth at the top.

The concept of moving lines is essential to the I Ching. Underlying it is the notion that no single state in the natural world is permanent. For this reason certain lines of each hexagram are inclined at times toward their opposite. Thus an 'old yin' line is inclined to the yang, and an 'old yang' line to the yin. In this way one hexagram can be transformed into another. (See Tao te Ching.)

IMPERIAL GARDENS. (See Shinsen-en.)

IMPERIAL PALACE. Also known as the Ninefold Enclosure, it was located in the north of the imperial capital and encompassed more than a hundred hectares. Surrounded by a moat and an earthen wall pierced by fourteen gates, it contained parks, gardens, government halls and bureaus, workshops, military barracks and storehouses. The Inner Palace, where the imperial family and members of its retinue resided, was situated within its boundaries. (See Courtyards.)

IMPERIAL REGALIA. The three emblems of royal authority. The Sacred Mirror was housed at the shrine of Ise; the Imperial Jewel and a replica of the Imperial Sword were kept in the Emperor's apartments in the Inner Palace. (According to some sources, the Emperor took the sword with him – or had it carried by a courtier – when he visited his concubines and consorts.) The colour of the jewel (or jewels, for it may have been a necklace) was a closely guarded secret.

INCENSE. Scent played as great a role as colour in Heian aesthetics. There were dozens of classic blends, each evocative of a particular mood, weather or season. Made from ingredients imported from as far away as Persia, incense took the place of perfume; its fumes scented everything from clothes to letter paper. The vocabulary used to describe its qualities was equally refined: the word *namamekashi*, for instance, denoted 'a warm, deep, damp kind of elegance.' Recipes were handed down in families, and were jealously guarded.

IRIS FESTIVAL. This festival was celebrated on the Fifth Day of the Fifth Month, a date that was considered inauspicious, for it coincided with the anniversary of the drowning of the Chinese poet Ch'ü Yüan. The purpose of the festival was twofold: to placate evil spirits and to ward off the diseases that ran rampant during the summer months. Medicinal plants such as calamus and artemisia were draped from buildings, carriages and bed hangings, and sweet flag flowers were twined in the hair.

ISHIYAMA. A Buddhist temple on the southern shore of Lake Biwa. According to legend, Murasaki Shikibu wrote the first chapters of The Tale of Genji there.

IZUMI SHIKIBU. A poet who served at court in the late tenth and early eleventh century, around the same time

275

as Lady Murasaki. She was notorious for her affairs with two princes. Less than a year after the first prince died in his mid-twenties of a sudden illness she took up with his younger brother, and he died too only five years later. She described this double tragedy in her diary, which reveals, in its poetry and prose, an extraordinary sensibility. Several of her poems are alluded to by Masato and the narrator.

KAIFŪSŌ. An eighth-century anthology of poems written in Chinese by Japanese authors.

KAMO FESTIVAL. Held in the middle of the Fourth Month, this was the great Shintō celebration of the year. It began with the ritual purification of the Virgin of Kamo, and ended with a magnificent procession down the Ichijō Avenue. Men and women alike arrayed themselves in sumptuous costumes and adorned themselves with laurel and hollyhock (*aoi*), an ivy-like plant with heart-shaped leaves and purple flowers. The festival was the occasion of intense aesthetic rivalry amongst women, who strove for the most subtle and striking combinations of colour, pattern and texture in their dress. Against this backdrop, the penance imposed on the narrator by the Empress would have been heavy indeed. (See Virgin of Kamo.)

KAMO SHRINES. Situated just north of Heian-kyō, these two shrines were sacred to Shintō. They were presided over by a virgin who was the protectress of the capital. A young girl of imperial birth, she lived in ritual purity in the Palace of the Fields. (See Virgin of Kamo.)

KANA SCRIPT. (See Diaries.)

KANNON. The goddess of compassion in Japanese Buddhism. She evolved from the Indian bodhisattva Perceiver of the World's Sounds, who was believed to assume thirty-three guises, both male and female.

KARMA. The Buddhist notions of karma or destiny (*sukuse*) and cause-and-effect (*inga*) pervaded Heian life and literature. The latter, according to cynics such as Kanesuke, did not imply blame or fault, and was thus a convenient excuse for liars and philanderers.

KICKBALL (*KEMARI*). A popular Heian pastime. Teams of boys (or grown men) repeatedly kicked a small deerskin ball without letting it touch the ground.

KIN. A seven-stringed instrument that originated in China. It was antique by the narrator's time, and was associated with the gentilities of a bygone era. (See *Koto*.)

KOKINSHŪ. A tenth-century imperial anthology of verse in Japanese. (See Poetry.)

KOREANS. By the sixth century, Korean immigrants, some of aristocratic Chinese descent, played an important cultural and economic role in Japanese life. Some of their clans specialised in certain trades (many physiognomists, for instance, were Korean). The man from whom the narrator buys her book may belong to such a family.

KOTO. A slender stringed instrument resembling a zither; there were several types, including the *wagon* and the *kin*.

LADY HAN. According to Chinese legend, Lady Han was a consort driven to madness by her love for an Emperor who deserted her. Her story appeared in Japanese folk ballads, stories, poems and plays.

LEECH CHILD. The ill-fated offspring of the goddess Izanami and her brother Izanagi who, through their coupling, created the islands of Japan. The story of Izanami's death and Izanagi's pursuit of her in the afterworld echoes the myth of Orpheus and Eurydice. According to the story, Izanami was thought to have brought about her first-born's deformities by making amorous advances on her spouse. Having learned her lesson, she waited for her husband to propose their lovemaking, and the children she bore him from that time on were without defect.

LETTERS. It is often said that Heian society was governed by rules of taste. Nowhere was this more evident than in the art of letter writing. Letters were not just clever or erudite, as circumstances required; they were objects of exquisite beauty. The handwriting of the sender, the colour and texture of the paper, the scent that was imparted to it, the sprays of leaves or flowers attached to it, even the looks and demeanour of the messenger who delivered it – all were scrutinised by the recipient as carefully as the message itself. Love letters (generally written on thin paper, folded tightly, and twisted at the ends or knotted in the middle) were subject to specific rules and regimens. If a man slept with a woman and was pleased with her, he would send her a letter the next morning conveying his sentiments. If she had no response, she could only assume that the liaison was over.

LIVING GHOSTS (*IKISUDAMA*). Thought to possess the bodies of living people, these malevolent spirits often seemed to act without the conscious approval of the person they inhabited. In The Tale of Genji, one of the prince's lovers, a proud and jealous woman named Rokujō, is suspected of being controlled by such a spirit.

LOTUS SUTRA. This poetic text, the pillar of Tendai Buddhism, pervaded Heian thought. Aristocrats as well as priests learned it by heart, and its images appear time and again in the literature of the day. The chapter on expedient means, of which the devious Kanesuke was so fond, describes how the Buddha told impartial truths in order to awaken his disciples to the deeper meaning of the Buddhist law. (See Buddhism, Tendai.)

MAGICAL GREEN STONE. This image comes from the Dream of the Red Chamber, a Chinese novel written in the eighteenth century that describes the fate of a stone endowed with supernatural powers. The stone acquires the power of speech, and begs a passing Buddhist monk and Taoist priest to allow it to 'take a turn in the Red Dust' – that is, to enter the world of men. The monk transforms the stone into a piece of jade, and inscribes upon it four characters. Eons later the priest rediscovers the stone in its original form. Engraved upon it is a story. 'The story was that of the Stone itself. The land of its descent, the place of its incarnation, the rise and fall of fortunes, the joys and sorrows of reunion and separation – all these were recorded in detail . . .'

MANDĀRAVA. A fragrant red flower, described in the Lotus Sutra, that was believed to bloom in heaven.

MANJUSHRĪ. This bodhisattva, who symbolised the perfection of wisdom, was often depicted riding a lion. Masato's description of the statue of Manjushrī in Wu-t'ai is taken from the diary of the Buddhist monk Ennin, who visited China in the mid-ninth century.

MANSIONS. Noblemen owned at least one mansion in the capital; emperors often had two or three. Built in the traditional style, with wide verandas, deep eaves, cypresswood floors, and cedar-shingled roofs, they were large enough to accommodate various wives, consorts, attendants, relatives and children. The three main wings faced onto a garden, with its ponds, streams, artificial hills, groves of trees, and private chapels. The principal wife lived in the prestigious north quarter, and was commonly referred to as 'the northern person'.

MANYŌSHŪ. Dating from the mid-eighth century, the Manyōshū is the oldest anthology of Japanese verse. Many of its poems are far more direct in their passions and preoccupations than the more stylised poems in later collections. (See Poetry.)

MICHINOKUNI PAPER. A thick white paper made from the bark of the spindle tree, and generally used for formal correspondence. To receive a letter from a lover on paper of this sort was disheartening.

MIRRORS. Japanese mirrors of the period were made of cast bronze. The face was highly polished, and the back had a knob in the centre through which a silk cord was strung. Some were imported; others were replicas of Chinese or Korean designs.

MODES. Musical instruments were tuned to various scales or modes, each evocative of a certain mood or season. The *banshiki* mode recalled the austerities of winter; the *richi*, the melancholy of autumn. The *sō* mode, alluded to by the narrator in her poem to Masato, was associated with spring. *Ōshiki*, a mode thought to be close to the key of A, was linked to the idea of transience. (It was in this mode that the bells at Gion Temple in India, where the Shākyamuni Buddha preached, were said to have rung.) The Tale of the Heike, the great epic of the civil war at the close of the Heian Period, begins with the sentence: 'The sound of the bell of Gion Temple echoes the impermanence of all things.'

MONEY. Coins were not minted in Japan after 960, and currency was barely in circulation after that time, though the wealthy hoarded gold dust (weighed in *ryō*) and silver ingots. Virtually all transactions were material, with rice being the main medium of exchange, though textiles, clothing, musical instruments and art objects were also used.

MONTHS. The Japanese year was divided into twelve lunar months. Each had at least one descriptive name: the ninth was Long Nights Month, for instance. The Tenth Month was called the Godless Month, for it was thought to be inauspicious. According to Shintō belief, the spirits (*kami*), having ensured the safety of the rice harvest in the Ninth Month, were thought to go off on their annual holiday to a shrine in the province of Izumo, leaving the rest of the country in peril.

MOUNT HIEI. A complex of Buddhist temples northeast of the capital built on a mountain of the same name. Founded in the early ninth century, it was the repository of vast wealth as well as learning. Today nothing remains of the 3,000 buildings that once crowded the slopes of Mount Hiei, including the great temple of Enryakuji. They were razed, and their 20,000 inhabitants captured or beheaded, by troops led by the ruthless general Oda Nobunaga in 1571. The temples visited on the site by modern tourists are reconstructions. (See Buddhism, Tendai.)

MOUNTAIN OF DEATH. According to popular belief, a woman's first lover carried her to the Mountain of Death, where souls repose for up to forty-nine days until they are reborn.

MOURNING. The dead were mourned in austere chambers from which the floorboards had been removed. Wives lamented the loss of their husbands for a year; the grieving period for widowers was three months.

MUDRĀS. These magical hand gestures were used by Shingōn priests in esoteric rites; their origins can be traced to Tantric Buddhism. (See Shingōn.)

MURASAKI SHIKIBU. Diarist and author of The Tale of Genji (begun around 1002). Bookish, shy and haughty, Murasaki was widely admired for her literary talent, but was never as popular as her competitor, Sei Shōnagon. While the two women may never have been rivals in love, they shared a mutual antipathy. Here is Murasaki lacerating her enemy in her diary: 'Sei Shōnagon, for instance, was dreadfully conceited. She thought herself so clever and littered her writings with Chinese characters, but if you examined them closely they left a great deal to be desired. Those who think of themselves as being superior to everyone else in this way will inevitably suffer and come to a bad end.' (See Romances.)

MUTE PRINCE. A figure from a popular Buddhist tale who refused to talk throughout his youth because he feared the karmic dangers of speech.

NAMES. In Japanese, the family or clan name precedes the given name, and the particle 'no' sometimes separates the two. Heian women were generally referred to by the rank or office held by one of their male relatives, or by the name of a place connected to their family. (Dainagon, for instance, means Major Counsellor; Izumi refers to the eponymous province.) Personal names were rarely used in direct address, a taboo that persisted well into the twentieth century.

Heian Emperors and high-ranking aristocrats were sometimes referred to by the name of the street or ward where their principal residence was located. Prince Genji's lover Rokujō, for instance, was named after the Sixth Ward, where her mansion was built.

When monks – such as the narrator's brother, Tadahira – took their vows they were given a Buddhist name.

NAMING OF THE BUDDHAS. This ceremony was held for three nights near the end of the Twelfth Month. Priests chanted the Sanskrit names of 3,000 Buddhas to atone for sins committed throughout the year, and seven screens depicting the sufferings of sinners in Hell were set up near the Emperor's apartments in the Seiryōden.

NARA. Located south of Heian-kyō in the Yamato plain, Nara was the capital of imperial Japan from 710 to 774, prior to the Heian Period. (See Yamato.)

NASHITSUBO. (See Courtyards.)

NEMBUTSU. This seven-syllable prayer was recited to invoke the mercy of the Amida Buddha. (See Amida.)

NEW YEAR. Falling on approximately February 15 by the western calendar, the New Year was the first day of spring. It was also the day on which people celebrated their birthdays. The New Year festivities, many of Chinese origin, went on for several days. They included the custom of viewing auspicious blue horses, picking seven healthful spring herbs (including parsley, shepherd's purse, borage and bracken) and making full-moon gruel. (See Blue Horses.)

NIGHT OF THE MONKEY. Custom dictated that once every sixty days (on a Day of the Monkey) people were required to stay up all night to prevent malevolent worms from betraying them as they slept. (The worms were thought to leave the body they inhabited and report to heaven on the sins their host had committed.) These nights provided an excuse for nocturnal revels, during which participants would play games and hold contests to keep themselves awake.

OMENS. In Heian times portents – particularly dire ones – were scrutinised with care. In the year 986, wrote the author of the chronicle Eiga Monogatari, 'From the First Month on, a sense of alarm and apprehension pervaded the capital. Strange portents multiplied, causing the Emperor to observe one period of ritual seclusion after another.' These omens, according to the scholar Helen Craig McCullough, were 'a rainbow, a snake on the veranda of one of the Daijōkan buildings, a ghost, the invasion of a room by doves, and a strange noise in the Giyōden.'

ONO NO KOMACHI. Born in the early ninth century, she was one of the most celebrated poets of her day. Renowned for her beauty, she also had a reputation for wantonness and cruelty, and was the subject of numerous stories and plays.

ORACLES. Heian emperors consulted a wide range of oracles. Some seers were women; others were Buddhist monks. Sea turtle shells and the shoulder blades of deer were also inspected for ominous and auspicious signs. Their interpretation was overseen by two sacerdotal lineages: the Urabe and the Nakatomi.

PHOENIX. According to Chinese mythology, the appearance of this five-coloured bird foretold the ascendancy of a virtuous ruler.

PLAGUE. The Japanese suffered regularly from epidemics of smallpox and measles introduced from the mainland and, possibly, from cholera and influenza as well. (Bubonic plague, however, never reached Japan.) In 994-995, an outbreak of smallpox devastated the capital and the surrounding provinces. More than half the residents of the capital, including sixty-seven people of the fifth rank and above, died in the summer of 994 alone. According to the scholar Helen Craig McCullough, 'Prayers and offerings failed to moderate the virulence of the disease; emergency facilities were overwhelmed by the numbers of the dead and dying; and the streets degenerated into a nightmare of stinking corpses, preyed on by dogs and crows.' The disease was thought to have been spread by foul vapours (similar to the western notion of miasma) and struck adults with greatest force, for smallpox was not endemic in Japan until the twelfth century.

POETRY. Verse was woven into the fabric of aristocratic life. A man who couldn't write a decent morning-after poem had little chance with his lover – and she was expected to meet his mettle in her reply. Poems were written on fans and screens and were brushed on to clothing; paper strips bearing verses were hung from blossoming cherry trees. Bureaucrats exchanged poetic messages, courtiers extemporised in Chinese at ceremonies and festivals, and ladies-in-waiting diverted their mistresses with clever allusions. Men and women alike were expected to be able to quote at length from weighty imperial anthologies such as the Manyōshū and the Kokinshū. Those who could muster sufficient strength on their deathbeds bade farewell to the world in verse. (See Kaifūsō, Kokinshū and Manyōshū.)

PRINCESSES. Of all the members of the imperial family,

princesses were the most vulnerable. Not all were officially recognised. (The same was true for princes.) Even those granted an imperial title – such as the Vestal – could find themselves disowned. And even princesses who behaved themselves were often doomed to spinsterhood, for marrying a commoner – the only option open to them – meant stepping down on the social ladder, thus tarnishing the reputation of their family.

RANKS. As early as the third century Chinese envoys were impressed by the Japanese fondness for rank. By the narrator's time there were nine major class divisions for commoners (royalty had their own strata). While social divisions in China were modified by Confucian meritocracy, the Japanese notion of class was far more rigid. Rank determined the offices a man could hold, the emoluments and tax exemptions he received, the marriages he made and the respect he commanded. Even trivial distinctions – the type of carriage a man owned, the colours he wore, the number of folds in his fan, the size of his burial mound – were fixed by rank. Women, of course, were subject to the same system. Even royal cats, angry ghosts and ships were given ranks. (See Sugawara no Michizane.)

RETREATS. Outings to Buddhist temples provided Heian women with a rare opportunity to escape their claustrophobic lives. Some women visited temples to offer prayers and petitions, or to have a pleasant outing with their female friends. A few, like the author of the Kagerō Diary, fled there to escape an unfaithful husband, in the hope that this dramatic gesture might win him back. Although women had little privacy while on retreat (for they slept within screened enclosures in the temple itself, or in a cell borrowed from a monk) there were ample opportunities for trysts.

RIVER OF THREE FORDS. To reach the Buddhist afterworld, the dead had to ford a great river. There were three fords of varying depth; those who had sinned the most in their previous lives had to cross the deepest.

ROMANCES (*MONOGATARI*). These tales were a popular diversion for Heian aristocrats. Written in prose in Japanese (and hence looked down upon by men of learning), they were widely circulated at court. One person would read the text aloud while the others admired the accompanying illustrations, which were painted on hand scrolls.

SAKAKI. An evergreen shrub related to the camellia. Sacred to Shintō, it was often planted on the grounds of native shrines.

SACRED FIRE (*GOMA*). Kindled from sumac and other woods as part of an esoteric Buddhist ritual, the *goma* symbolised wisdom, and was thought to consume earthly passions and illusions. Poppy seeds and other offerings were thrown onto the flames.

SCREENS. Noblewomen spent much of their time hidden behind screens and curtains. There were several kinds, including the curtain of state (*kichō*), a moveable frame three or four feet high hung with heavy draperies. Rules regarding the separation of the sexes were so strict that women were hidden from their fathers and brothers – as well as from their suitors – by standing curtains. It was a bold man indeed who reached behind a screen to touch the hem of a woman's dress. Women in the imperial family were even more closely guarded. Empresses, consorts – and, occasionally, princes – were enclosed within screens even when they ventured outdoors for festivals and moon viewings.

SEI SHŌNAGON. The daughter of a provincial governor, she came to court around 990 to serve in the retinue of the Empress Sadako. An accomplished writer, her acid wit earned her a wide circle of admirers. She won fame (and considerable notoriety) as the author of The Pillow

Book, a collection of prose pieces written in the artfully casual manner known as *zuihitsu*. Her writing is still held up to Japanese schoolchildren as a model of style and clarity.

SEIRYŌDEN. 'The Hall of Cool and Refreshing Breezes' was the Emperor's private residence. Located within the Inner Enclosure of the palace, it was constructed in the traditional style, with wattled roofs, broad verandas, and cypress-wood floors. According to some historians, it was more romantic in name than in reality, for it was small, cramped and crowded both day and night with courtiers, wives, consorts and attendants.

SHINGŌN. Introduced from China by the aesthete and master calligrapher Kūkai in the early ninth century, Shingōn was one of the two main Buddhist sects. Influenced by Tantric practices, its priests specialised in sacred formulas and chants (mantras), magical hand gestures (mudrās), and spells (darani). Its secret teachings were transmitted directly from master to pupil. (Zen relied on the same tutelary tradition.) Based on Mount Kōya near the old capital of Nara, Shingōn was favoured by the aristocracy for its resplendent ceremonies. (See Buddhism, mudrās, Tendai.)

SHINSEN-EN. The Imperial Gardens, located south of the Ninefold Enclosure and replete with hills, streams, waterfalls, a sacred spring, a pond with an island, a fishing pavilion and groves of venerable trees. By the narrator's time it had been largely transformed from a pleasure garden to a sacred site where priests prayed for the surcease of droughts and epidemics.

SHINTŌ. The native religious cults of Japan, syncretised in Heian times with Buddhism. Shintō is based in part on the notion of *kami*, a divine presence found in certain heroes and ancestors and in particular rocks, trees, springs, boundary lines, and weapons. Shintō shrines, simple constructions of pine and reed thatch, are traditionally torn down and rebuilt every twenty years. They are entered through a *torii*, a wooden gate that is usually painted red. (See Abstinence, Defilement, Vestal of Ise, Virgin of Kamo.)

SHISHINDEN. The ceremonial hall of the Inner Palace. The courtyard to the south of it was used for official celebrations. (See Cherry of the Left.)

SIDDHARTHA (SIDDHARTHA GAUTAMA). The historic founder of Buddhism, born in northern India in the sixth century BC. He was also known as the Shākyamuni Buddha, or 'Sage of the Shākyas', after the name of the tribe into which he was born.

SORCERY. The narrator and Masato were not the only ones of their time to be accused of dabbling in black magic. In 1023, the wife of the courtier Norimichi died mysteriously soon after giving birth. The mediums at her bedside detected the presence of malignant spirits, including that of the deceased Bishop Ryūen. A few days after the wife's death a former governor came to the house where she lay and told the family that he had dreamed about her. He instructed them to look under the seat of her curtain dais, where they would find an object made of toothpicks, a common instrument of magic. The toothpicks were found, and amongst those blamed for the wife's unfortunate end was a former mistress of Norimichi, the widow of a prominent Fujiwara, who was thought to be bent on revenge.

SUGAWARA NO MICHIZANE. A ninth-century statesman renowned for his verse and stylish calligraphy, he wielded more power in death than he did in life. Exiled in 901 to the island of Kyūshū, he died two years later. A series of catastrophes – fires, floods, deaths of prominent men of the Fujiwara clan who had been his enemies – plagued the capital soon afterwards, and were attributed to

Sugawara's vengeful spirit. In an effort to appease it, his rank and office were posthumously restored. But the calamities continued, and it was not until eighty years after his death, when Sugawara was deified and a shrine built in his honour, that the disasters subsided.

TABOO TAGS. When a household was observing a day of abstinence or was defiled by death or illness, willow-wood tags were hung on the shutters to fend off prospective visitors, and even messengers with letters were turned away. Willow tags were also worn by those defiled by contact with illness or death. Men wore them on their caps; women on their sleeves.

TALE OF THE HOLLOW TREE. This lengthy tenth-century romance received its name from an episode about a young man who shelters his mother in an ancient cedar tree that had been abandoned by bears.

TALES OF ISE. A collection of delicate and elliptical poetry and prose. It centres on the life of Ariwara no Narihira, a ninth-century courtier who according to legend was exiled after his scandalous elopement with a Fujiwara girl who later became a royal consort. Various poems allude to that affair – and to Ariwara's romantic entanglement with two young sisters. The expression 'as unreliable as the Tales of Ise', used to describe anything that was less than credible, may be an unflattering allusion to the people of Ise rather than to the tales themselves. (See Ariwara no Yukihira, Envoys.)

TAO TE CHING. A philosophical work written (apocryphally) by Lao-tzu some time before the third century BC. The concept of yielding, as ice does when it melts, is central to Taoism. (See Chuang-tzu, I Ching.)

TEA. A medicinal beverage in Heian times. (Magnolia-leaf tea, for instance, was a common remedy for nervous complaints.) Imported from China from the ninth century onwards, tea did not become a recreational drink – and the centrepiece of the Zen tea ceremony – until the twelfth century.

TEETH. Aristocratic women of the time blackened their teeth with iron shavings and powdered gallnut dissolved in vinegar or tea. The practice may have originated with the Polynesian peoples who settled in southern Japan. It later spread to the lower classes, and could still be seen quite recently among women in remote rural areas.

TENDAI. In Heian times this Buddhist sect was virtually the state religion. Supported by the Fujiwara clan, it had close ties to the throne. Many emperors relied on the abbots of Mount Hiei for succour and counsel. Introduced from China by the monk Saichō in the early ninth century, Tendai was based on the teachings of the Lotus Sutra. Austere in the extreme – its monks endured twelve years of seclusion before taking their final vows – it became in time nearly as esoteric and extravagant in its ritual as Shingōn. (See Buddhism, Lotus Sutra, Mount Hiei, Shingōn.)

THIN MEN OF GION. Every year during the middle of the Sixth Month a Sacred Spirit Service was held at the Gion Shrine east of Heian-kyō to fend off pestilence and ill fortune. The service included a dance by 'thin men' wearing cloth masks.

TIME. At the Imperial Palace, time was observed and recorded by officials from the Bureau of Divination with a clepsydra, or water clock. The day was divided into twelve two-hour periods, each governed by a sign of the Chinese zodiac. (The Hour of the Rat, for instance, was from midnight to 2 am; the Hour of the Tiger from 4 am to 6 am.) Every two hours during the day a fixed number of strokes were sounded on a gong that could be heard throughout the palace. Each night at the Hour of the Boar (which commenced at 10 pm), Palace Guards twanged their bowstrings to scare away evil spirits.

TORIBENO. A burning ground east of the capital. (See Death.)

UDUMBARA. A mythical plant described in the Lotus Sutra that was said to bloom only once every 3,000 years.

UMETSUBO. (See Courtyards.)

UNLUCKY DIRECTIONS. This notion dominated medieval Japanese life. Some directions, such as the northeast (thought to be the abode of demons) were considered perpetually dangerous. Others were thought to be temporarily perilous due to the movements of various deities. By examining the calendar, for instance, the Emperor's diviners might determine that a journey to the west was fraught with danger on a particular date. The Emperor would then be forced to postpone his trip or travel by a circuitous route to avoid the unlucky direction.

VESTAL OF ISE. An unwed girl – presumably a virgin – of noble birth who was sent to preside over the great Shintō shrines in the province of Ise dedicated to the sun goddess Amaterasu. The daughter of an Emperor or a prince, she was chosen at the beginning of an imperial reign, and presided over the shrines in strict ritual purity until the Emperor abdicated or died. Because the shrine housed the Great Mirror, one of the three emblems of the imperial throne, its sanctity – and that of the Vestal – was believed to have a direct bearing on the fortunes of the Emperor and his realm.

A Vestal could be recalled because of illness or a death in the family, but there is no mention in the chronicles of a Vestal being removed from her office due to a scandalous romance. In the late ninth century, the courtier Ariwara no Narihira was rumoured to have had an affair with the Vestal of Ise, but as she was not recalled, either the liaison was conducted with the highest secrecy or it did not occur. (See Imperial Regalia, Tales of Ise.)

VIRGIN OF KAMO. A young lady of good family, the Virgin

was the protectress of the capital. She lived in ritual purity at the Palace in the Fields north of Heian-kyō and presided over the two Kamo shrines and the rituals of the Kamo Festival. In practice, some Kamo virgins lived opulent and wordly lives – though there is no proof that any were bold enough to have affairs. (See Kamo Festival.)

WASHING OF THE BUDDHA. In this ceremony, held on the eighth day of the Fourth Month on the anniversary of Siddhartha's birth, a gilded statue of the Buddha as an infant was presented to the Emperor, and coloured water was poured over its head. Variations of the lustration rite were also held in private mansions and Buddhist temples. (See Siddhartha.)

WESTERN HINTERLANDS. By the late ninth century, the marshy western districts of Heian-kyō were sparsely populated and frequented by thieves even during the day. Wild and overgrown, filled with the ruins of abandoned houses, the 'City of the Right' was an undesirable address indeed.

YANG KUEI-FEI. A concubine of the T'ang Emperor Hsüan-tsung, who was said to have been so devoted to her that he neglected his affairs of state. When an insurrection threatened to end his reign, he was forced by his own army to execute her. Their story was told in the long narrative poem 'The Song of Everlasting Sorrow', by Po Chü-i. The poem was hugely popular in Heian times, and cultured people could quote at length from it.

YAMATO. A broad alluvial plain south of Heian-kyō and the most fertile rice-growing region of Japan. The former capital of Nara stands within it. Yamato was settled from earliest times, and eventually its name became synonymous with Japanese culture and the country itself. In the narrator's time, for instance, the phrase 'Yamato speech' signified pure, uncorrupted Japanese.

Acknowledgements

I am indebted to the work of several scholars for making vivid to me a world that existed more than a thousand years ago. They include Royall Tyler (whose elegant new translation of *The Tale of Genji* I recommend to all my readers), the late Ivan Morris (author of *The World of the Shining Prince*, a description of courtly life in Heian Japan, and translator of Sei Shōnagon's ever-modern *Pillow Book*), Barbara Ambros, Sonja Arntzen, Brian Bocking, Richard Bowring, Edwin Cranston, Shirane Haruo, Donald Keene, Helen Craig McCullough and Edward Seidensticker.

I also owe a debt to two scholars of the I Ching. All the direct quotes from the Book of Changes are taken from John Blofeld's translation of the I Ching (New York: Dutton, 1968), with the exception of those that appear on page 229 and page 258, lines 18–21 and page 259, lines 6–8, which are from the translation by Richard Wilhelm and Cary F. Baynes (Princeton: Princeton University Press, 1967). Three practitioners of the I Ching, Brian Donohue, Lucas Mellinger and Ting-Foon Chik, offered me guidance in understanding the method of counting the yarrow sticks and the meanings of various hexagrams.

With regard to the Tao te Ching, all quotations are taken from Arthur Waley's *The Way and Its Power* (New York: Grove Press, 1958). The translation of the poem from the Manyōshū is from George Sansom's *A History of Japan to 1334* (Stanford: Stanford University Press, 1958). The two-line verse from the Lotus Sutra quoted by Izumi in her threat to the narrator is taken from Burton Watson's rendering of this work (New York: Columbia University Press, 1993).

In the Glossary, all quotes by Helen Craig McCullough are taken from her superlative translation, with William H. McCullough, of the mid-Heian chronicle Eiga monogatari (Stanford: Stanford University Press, 1980). Murasaki Shikibu's laceration of Sei Shōnagon is from Richard Bowring's translation of Murasaki's diary (Princeton: Princeton University Press, 1982). The quotation from Fujiwara no Nagako's diary is taken from Jennifer Brewster's translation of this work (Honolulu: University Press of Hawaii, 1977). The description of darkness appears in Tanizaki Junichirō's essay on Japanese aesthetics, *In Praise of Shadows* (London: Jonathan Cape, 1991), and the quotation from Tsao Hsuehchin's *Dream of the Red Chamber* is from the translation of this eighteenth-century classic by Chi-Chen Wang (New York: Random House, 1958).

Like the romances admired by my narrator, this is an allusive book. Readers will no doubt detect much of my thievery, but I should make clear that I am obliged to William Blake (for the phrase 'the long-limbed beeches,' and for the images of the abyss described by the prophet Los), Jorge Luis Borges (whose short story 'Forms of a Legend' informs the narrator's tale of Siddhartha), Alain de Botton (for his observations on travel), Guy de Maupassant (for his depiction of madness in 'The Horla'), and Rainer Maria Rilke (for his description of the tower in 'The Solitary Man').

I am grateful to many people who offered me encouragement and criticism: Cherry Boa, Edith Frampton, Kate Killeen, S.K. Levin, Karina Mellinger, Stryker McGuire, William McGuire, F.S. Naiden, Silvia Urrutia, Usami Hirokuni, and my editor, Alan Samson, who believed in the book from the beginning. I also owe thanks to the courteous staff at the British Library, the Richmond Library, and the Library of the School of Oriental and African Studies at the University of London.

One last thing. I was told by various academics that the Heian Japanese were not partial to kissing – or at least that this act is rarely described in the literature of the time. I hope that my readers will forgive me if some of my characters are fond of it. For this, and any other errors of fact or interpretation, I accept complete responsibility.